That had been close. Too close.

No suspect was worth what had almost happened. Kendall had to be more careful, less reckless. Skylar Dawn needed her parents to come home.

"You okay?" Heath asked, back at the passenger door. She nodded, still a little stunned by it all.

"I can't say I'm bummed about them getting away." The corner of his mouth barely rose as he leaned on the car.

"What? Why's that?"

"Where's the fun in catching them the first day I get to work with you again?" He said it with such a straight face that if she hadn't known him she never would've seen that playful gleam in his eye.

She couldn't argue with that logic either. She would've been bummed, too.

HER HOT PURSUIT

USA TODAY BESTSELLING AUTHOR

Angi Morgan &
Danica Winters

Previously published as *Ranger Guardian* and
Hidden Truth

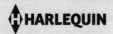

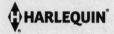

ISBN-13: 978-1-335-42473-0
Her Hot Pursuit
Copyright © 2021 by Harlequin Books S.A.

Recycling programs
for this product may
not exist in your area.

Ranger Guardian
First published in 2018. This edition published in 2021.
Copyright © 2018 by Angela Platt

Hidden Truth
First published in 2019. This edition published in 2021.
Copyright © 2019 by Danica Winters

This edition published by arrangement with Harlequin Books S.A.

For questions and comments about the quality of this book, please contact us at CustomerService@Harlequin.com.

Harlequin Enterprises ULC
22 Adelaide St. West, 40th Floor
Toronto, Ontario M5H 4E3, Canada
www.Harlequin.com

Printed in U.S.A.

CONTENTS

Angi Morgan writes about Texans in Texas. A
USA TODAY and Publishers Weekly bestselling
author, her books have been finalists for several
awards, including the Booksellers' Best Award,
RT Book Reviews Best Intrigue Series and the Daphne
du Maurier. Angi and her husband live in North Texas.
They foster Labradors and love to travel, snap pics
and fix up their house. Hang out with her on Facebook
at Angi Morgan Books. She loves to hear from fans at
angimorganauthor.com.

Books by Angi Morgan

Harlequin Intrigue

Texas Brothers of Company B

Texas Rangers: Elite Troop

Texas Family Reckoning

Visit the Author Profile page
at Harlequin.com for more titles.

RANGER GUARDIAN

Angi Morgan

Thank you, Amanda!
Thanks for the encouragement and the
major kick in the behind—just the right amount
of both. And a special thanks for being
such a great person to model a character after!

Prologue

Eight Months Ago

Heath Murray rushed through the emergency room doors. Yes, he'd used the entrance for the ambulances. Yes, he'd parked his truck next to the building, practically on the sidewalk. And yes, he'd taken advantage of having the Texas Ranger badge he carried.

What did anyone expect? His three-year-old daughter was there. It was the only thing he knew for sure. The message from his wife had stated only what hospital they were heading to.

Life was good. Life was perfect. He couldn't imagine life without his baby girl, Skylar Dawn, in it. He couldn't imagine life without his wife, Kendall. Six years ago, if you'd asked him if his life would be full of anything except law enforcement, he would have answered no.

Now?

Life was full of pink frills and satin sun dresses. Along with brand new ponies—plastic and real. And all the disagreements about whether Skylar Dawn was old enough to own a pony. Yep, life was full, and he was blessed several times over.

He rushed to his mother-in-law, who stood up from a waiting room chair. Her eyes were red but not swollen. Her old-fashioned handkerchief was twisted and streaked from her mascara. She looked like she'd been pulled straight out of a church service, but Naomi Barlow looked like that every day. And she didn't go to church.

"Where is she?"

"Kendall is with her. She's going to be fine. It's not a break that will require surgery."

"What kind of an accident were they in?"

"Accident? Did you think they were in a car accident?" Kendall's mom asked, then laughed.

What the hell? Why was she laughing?

"Where are they?"

"Oh, honey, you poor thing. Skylar Dawn just fell on the playground at day care. That's all. She'll be fine." Naomi's eyes darted toward a set of double doors. "Only one person can be in the room with her."

He didn't need her response. What he did need was for the attendant to open the doors from the other side.

"Excuse me." He headed straight to the front desk and flipped his badge so the person at the window could see it. "I need to get through."

"May I see your credentials?"

Heath shot his ID through the slot and managed to keep his toes from tapping the linoleum while he waited. "Thanks," he added politely to the man whose turn he'd interrupted, then paced back to his mother-in-law and handed her his keys. "Give these to the green-faced Texas Ranger who comes inside in a minute. My partner, Slate Thompson will take my truck home."

"Here you go, sir. I can buzz you through now."

He heard the door lock open and hurried to pull on the handle, but it opened at a snail's pace on its own. He rushed down the hall, glancing through the small windows. Then he heard her.

A quiet, polite cry for a child of three.

He rounded a corner and took a deep breath. *Okay, they really are all right.* He hadn't processed that information when Naomi had told him. He couldn't believe it until he'd seen with his own eyes.

So he took a second. They'd be upset as it was. He didn't need to add to the situation by not appearing calm. He shook his shoulders, slowed his racing pulse, became the dad instead of the Ranger who'd driven ninety across Dallas to get here.

"There they are." He thought his voice sounded excited to see them, instead of like the frightened-to-death man who'd just had his heart ripped from his chest.

"See, I told you Daddy was on his way."

"Daddy!" Skylar Dawn tried to lift her free arm to him. "I want Daddy."

"It's better if you stay where you are, baby. Mommy's got you." He honestly didn't think his shaking arms could hold her steadily.

Kendall tilted her cheek up for a kiss. He rubbed

Skylar Dawn's strawberry blond hair. One day it would be as thick as her mother's and out of the small pigtails.

"How 'bout I sit down here so you can see me?" He sat on the floor, pulling himself close to his wife and daughter, just about ready to cry from the gratitude he felt at them both being alive and safe.

There was no tension in Kendall. She seemed far calmer than her message had implied. She mouthed, "Sorry."

His wife could probably tell how frantic he was. She'd always been good at picking up on the nuances that gave away his emotions. In fact, she was practically the only person who had ever been able to see through the wall he'd built.

A wall that had been breached several times over by Skylar Dawn.

"Let me see." He leaned closer and puckered his lips for a loud smack without ever touching the skin of her arm. "Does that feel better?"

Skylar Dawn shook her head. "I broke it, Daddy. Does that mean we have to throw it away?"

He refrained from chuckling. "No, baby girl. The doctors can fix this all up. And you'll be as good as new."

"Oh, that's a relief." She perfectly imitated her mother.

"I've been explaining that her arm isn't a toy." Kendall smiled.

"No throwaway arms," he said.

Skylar Dawn dropped her head to Kendall's chest. "Just close your eyes for a minute, sweetheart," said Kendall. "I'll wake you up when the doctor comes back."

He placed a hand on Skylar Dawn's back and could feel when her body relaxed into sleep. *Nice to be a kid.*

"What took you so long?" Kendall whispered.

He followed suit, whispering back his answer. "We were in west Fort Worth. I did ninety most of the way. Slate thought he was going to puke."

"I just… I'm sorry about the wild message. The day care called without a lot of details. Then they told me I couldn't use my cell phone back here. I should have had Mother call with an update. I know it scared you."

"I'm good. All's good."

He listened to the details of Skylar Dawn climbing the section of the playground her age group wasn't allowed on. One of the older girls—probably about five—had helped her. Skylar Dawn had fallen.

They whispered about the X-ray and doctor's analysis. Just a hairline fracture, but they could go to the pediatrician for a cast in a couple of days.

The love Kendall had for their daughter radiated like sunshine. How awesome would it be to have another little girl as precious as this one?

The doctor came and went. Heath took Skylar Dawn from Kendall's arms and cuddled her against his chest. Her head had a special baby smell that he especially noticed when she first fell asleep. It was something he already knew he'd miss whenever she got too big to be rocked.

"Hey, for a couple who never wanted children, I think we're handling this pretty well." Kendall smoothed Skylar Dawn's hair while they waited on their release paperwork.

"Want to have a couple more?" he said, then gulped.

"What?" Kendall's eyes grew big. "Where does this come from?"

"It was just a thought. I mean… I love you guys. I love our family. And you're right. I think we're pretty good at this."

"I do, too."

Were those tears?

"Honey, what's wrong?" He opened his free arm and pulled her in for a hug.

Special Agent Kendall Barlow was full-blown crying, silent tears running down her face. And it took a lot—like the birth of their daughter—to bring them on. Heath never expected his spontaneous suggestion to affect her this way.

"I was… I was…" she tried.

"It's okay, babe. Everything's perfect the way it is. Nothing's wrong with our family."

"But I was just thinking the same thing, Heath. I'd love another baby."

He kissed her. As much as he was able to with his arms full of their daughter.

"I am definitely looking forward to getting you home and getting this one in bed." He waggled his eyebrows at her.

Kendall dabbed at her eyes. "We can't start this afternoon, silly. I'm helping Jerry with his cyber-fraud case. It's going to take weeks. Maybe months."

"You want to wait?" He was surprised. Seriously surprised. And then an ugly voice shouted in his ear, *How many cases will be more important?*

"Whisper, please?"

"Sure." He lowered his voice to match hers. "Why

would finishing cases be more important? It's not like you'll still be trying to move up the FBI ladder."

"I beg your pardon?"

"Well, if you have another baby, aren't you quitting?"

The words were there before he could mentally slap himself and stop them from forming. Mistake. It was the wrong thought to let out of his mouth.

"You want me to quit my job and stay home? What? Do you want me barefoot and pregnant in the kitchen, too?"

He tucked his bottom lip between his teeth. He wasn't going to say a word. Not a dad-blasted word. It wasn't the time. It wasn't the place.

Then she stiffened and pulled away from his arm.

Dammit.

"Kendall, we thought having any kids in day care whose parents are both in the line of fire wasn't a good idea. It's still not a good idea. But two? If you're pregnant, they'll call you out of the field anyway. Right?"

"For a few months. Just like last time. But I'm not going to give up my career. You stay home with the kids."

"I worked hard to be a Texas Ranger."

"And I worked hard to become an FBI agent."

It was the loudest whispered arguing they'd ever done. It gave him a bad feeling, like something ominous was about to happen.

"Maybe we should talk about this at home." He kissed his daughter's forehead. "When the munchkin is in bed, we can list the pros and cons."

"Or we could be honest with each other."

"I think I've been honest enough."

"Oh, that's a relief." She crossed her arms in typical Barlow fashion, after her sarcasm had a chance to sink in.

"It's going to be a long night, isn't it," he said. Fact, not a question. Just like he knew they were stepping outside into the backyard to have an extended argument once they got home.

"We both need to really think about your expectations for me. This is serious, Heath. I… It's not something I can take lightly and just forget that it happened."

"I'm sorry for jumping the gun." Apologizing was the easy part. Understanding what he did wrong would take a little longer.

Six weeks of continuous arguing began to take its toll on her family. Kendall sat at her office desk staring at the picture of Heath carrying Skylar Dawn on his shoulders. She missed him. Ached for him. Longed for someone to invent a time machine so she could take back the words she didn't even know if she meant any more. Just when Kendall thought things were getting better, her mother overheard Heath say he didn't understand why her work was more important than a family.

She didn't know which hurt worse—what he'd said or the fact he had talked to someone else and not her. He'd always been the strong silent type. Definitely a man of action and few words.

When Skylar Dawn complained of tummy aches, Kendall suggested counseling. If they couldn't communicate on their own, maybe a third party could help.

She'd never forget the stabbing pain she'd experienced when he said, "My world has pretty much crashed down around my ears by not keeping my mouth shut."

To keep from hurting their daughter, Heath packed a bag. He made a drastic, solitary decision.

If he was gone…they couldn't argue. So to solve the problem he moved into the spare room of Slate Thompson's house on a small ranch just east of Dallas. He worked in the barn and helped with riding lessons to pay his rent.

Or at least that's what she thought. They hadn't really spoken since.

They seemed to avoid each other by staying busy with their jobs. But he never failed to call Skylar Dawn at six each evening. When her caseload picked up, he stayed at the house two nights a week.

Her mother had objected to her marriage from the beginning. For some reason, her encouragement had always been for a career. Not necessarily the FBI, just something with a title and advancement.

"How did we get this far down the rabbit hole? Yeah… Where's that time machine when you need it?"

Chapter 1

Heath Murray was feeling just how crowded the small house he lived in had become. He slipped away to the rodeo every weekend, attempting to give Slate some privacy. But, man, come Sunday nights he needed to rest his weary old bones on a soft couch.

He needed to pop the top on a bottle of beer, prop his feet up on the coffee table and listen to sports while he drifted off into blissful slumber.

That never happened.

He didn't mind having his partner's mom cook. Saved him the trouble of constantly eating out. He didn't mind having Slate's new girlfriend sneak back up to the main house after not catching the front door before it slammed shut at four in the morning. Neither of them knew he hadn't really slept in months.

He didn't mind returning to his real bed twice a week

to spend time with his baby girl. Skylar Dawn loved it. Kendall tolerated it. They both agreed it was better than the nights he didn't see their daughter at all.

He could deal with all that. He'd been dealing with it for almost six months. But this...

"Dammit, guys. Do you always have to be making out when I open the door?"

"Oh, man. Is it already five? I'm supposed to go see my brother tonight. I should go get ready." Vivian Watts, his roommate's girlfriend, tugged her T-shirt to her waist, making sure it was in place. She gave Slate a quick kiss and ran past Heath.

"Thanks for making her feel bad," Slate said.

"Don't mention it." Yeah, he was being sarcastic. Yeah, he didn't mean to be. Hell, maybe he did. His attitude sucked, and his side hurt. The bronc he'd been thrown from had kicked his ribs. The skin had begun turning colors before he'd started for home.

"Well, I sort of am." Slate took his hands from his back pockets and crossed his arms in a move of determination. "You know she's had a really hard time lately. They told her it's going to be at least another six weeks before they'll think about clearing her brother to leave the center."

"Sorry. I didn't mean it and I'll apologize." He would. He'd probably screw up again, though. "Maybe it's time for me to find my own place?"

"That's not what you need to do," Slate said with a certain look on his face.

The same frustrated look his friends and fellow Rangers had at least once a week. Maybe even a little more often. Like each time they tried to get him to open up about his situation with his wife. Yet if he couldn't talk about it with her, he shouldn't talk about it with his friends. Their separation was a private matter.

"You, me, Wade and Jack are tight. We're more than just Rangers, and we're more than friends. We're brothers. We've got each other's backs. I'm telling you the truth. You should call her," Slate urged.

"I will. Tuesday."

"You are such a stubborn son of a...cowboy."

At that, Heath tipped his hat off his head and let the Stetson flip into his hand. A trick his little girl loved.

"You better head on out if you're going to catch Vivian and drive her to her brother's."

"Call your wife, man. Make up. It's been six months, for crying out loud. Tell her you don't think your job is more important than hers."

"You don't think I've told her? I haven't ever lied to her. I thought she knew that. But for some reason she still can't believe me." He pulled a beer from the refrigerator, glancing at the plastic containers full of home-cooked meals. He was too sore to eat.

"Dammit, Heath." Slate stuck a ball cap on his head. "Think hard about what you're willing to give up." He stomped to the door and slammed it shut behind him.

Alone.

It was how he liked it. Right?

"Right," he spoke out loud and tipped the beer he'd wanted for the past hour between his lips and swallowed.

Another couple of minutes, and he could call Skylar Dawn before Kendall put her in the bathtub. She was almost four years old, and it had been six months since he'd destroyed any chance at a normal father-daughter relationship.

He went through the motions, just like he did every night. Nothing there comforted him like it had when he was married. There was no one to talk to about the bronc ramming him in half.

No one to joke with about the young women hanging around the edge of the stalls. Or how he'd felt too old to notice. But they'd had fun with their wolf calls when he'd bent over and showed his backside. Kendall had gotten a kick out of coming up and laying a big, luscious kiss on him when that had happened before.

That had been before she'd gotten pregnant and the barn smell had made her nauseous.

Another sip of beer. It was almost gone, and he wanted another.

Was this what life was going to be like? Waiting around while Kendall—and her mother—made all the decisions about their life? He'd been ready for months to talk with her and apologize again. He just wanted their old life back.

Was that even possible?

Completely aware that pressure against his side would be painful, he went back into the kitchen, filled a couple of sandwich bags with ice, wrapped them in a towel and shoved it against his ribs.

The stinging cold brought him to his senses. He was getting too old for this routine. Too old to be afraid to talk with his wife. Too old to insult Vivian and Slate or any of his other friends because he was miserable with his own life.

It was time to make some changes.

Good or bad…he needed to talk with Kendall face-to-face. Soon. Maybe it would turn out better than he feared. Maybe it wouldn't. All he knew was that it was time to move forward.

Good thing he had a light load at work. He was mostly focused on court and testifying and paperwork right now. He set the ice on the table, then slid his shirt free from his belt. He tucked it up close to his armpit before looking closer at the bruise.

That was going to be a big boo-boo, as baby girl would say.

Yeah, it was time. Slate was right about that. Time to apologize and move on. How long could a woman stay mad?

Something in the back of his mind warned that *his* woman could stay that way a very, very long time. Especially with a mother whispering in her ear who hated him. Hell, his mother-in-law had shouted to the world that he'd never be good enough for her daughter.

He clicked on his phone, stared at the picture of Kendall holding a super pink baby girl and swiped to dial. He would talk to his wife face-to-face. Tonight, he'd read to his daughter.

"Hey there. How's my favorite munchkin?" He reached for the children's version of *The Wizard of Oz*.

"Daddy!"

"Jerry, I know it's Sunday night. That's why I'm calling. I need more people. I know I'm close to a breakthrough." Kendall Barlow didn't back down. Her supervisory special agent should know that. She heard the house phone ring in the background, as it did every night like clockwork.

In six months' time, Heath hadn't missed calling his daughter once. And not one time had he made a serious effort to reconcile. He was a man of few words—for everyone except Skylar Dawn.

"Kendall. It's been months and you've got nothing to show for it. You know we're shorthanded. Dallas Police Department is worse off than we are. You aren't going to get more qualified personnel for the joint task force than the people already assigned to it."

"If I had another competent person who knew their way around computers, I know I could prove that Public Exposure is fraudulent. We're close. Very close."

"Oh furgle. Our resources have been tapped out. Run with what you've got, and get me something to show for your time. Of course, there is one person already on your task force you haven't tried."

"Special Agent Fisher, I've asked you not to use that word. I've looked it up and it's inappropriate. It was fine in *Catch-22*, but come on. You know it doesn't mean what you think." She was tired of this conversation. Or was he trying to distract her? Did he really think that she needed something to justify the investigation? Couldn't he think of one more possible agency to check? "Jerry?"

"Yes? I promise I'll behave. I just love that word."

"Please don't—"

"You should talk to your ex. Ask him if he's heard anything about your case."

"That's a clear conflict of interest. No one would allow him on the team."

"Seems like that's my decision now. I'll allow him to help out until the Rangers can find a replacement. Use the taxpayers' money wisely. See you in the office."

The line disconnected, and she could once again hear the exclamations of surprise from her daughter as her father read about flying monkeys and sparkly red shoes. Had she mentioned to Heath that their daughter had outgrown two pairs of those red slippers while he'd been gone?

Skylar Dawn was sitting on the couch holding the main phone extension. Her grandmother listened on an additional handset just outside the door. Heath knew about the eavesdropping even if her mother thought it was a secret. He accepted it as part of his "punishment for whatever he blamed himself."

As if living away from their precious little girl wasn't punishment enough. Why he thought he needed to be punished, she didn't understand. And no matter how she tried, her mother wouldn't stop.

Constant jabs at Heath kept an undercurrent of tension in the air. Kendall wanted to avoid the subject and leaned toward avoiding her mother in the evenings when she helped out with Skylar Dawn.

Heath wasn't her ex, and finalizing their separation wasn't high on her priority list. So far there hadn't been any squabbles about how to do anything. He'd taken only a few of his things and the horses.

Other than a picture or two of Skylar Dawn, he'd managed to leave everything looking exactly like it had been when he'd walked away. Or when she'd driven him away. She could remember exactly when things had come to a pivotal breaking point. Most of that argument had to do with her mother.

Her mother's standards had been high her entire life. Heath had a father exactly the same way. But what had turned Heath into a strong man who held his opinions to himself—or himself and his horse—seemed to be turning her soul bitter.

I can't be my mother. I can't do that to Skylar Dawn.

"Do you have to say goodbye, Daddy?"

Kendall waited for the familiar "Good night" and "I love you." Her daughter clicked the red button on the phone and her mother followed a second afterward. She crossed her arms, enveloping the phone between a breast and a well-toned limb.

Her mother, a woman of sixty, made good use of the money she'd gathered over the years. Three stepfathers and three settlements later, Kendall had a college education and two letters of recommendation for her Bureau interview.

Getting along with the men in her mother's life had never been the problem. More and more recently, she'd been realizing how sad her mother had become. And how demanding.

Her mother didn't allow Skylar Dawn two seconds to linger or even to put the phone back on its charging station. She immediately clapped her hands, and her granddaughter jumped to her feet.

Oh my God! She's reacting like a trained puppy.

Kendall swooped in and picked up her little girl, who should need a bath from playing in the dirt. But she was perfectly clean.

"Wow. Let's go for a ride. What do you think, sweet girl?"

"Kendall, I was just getting ready to run her bath. Isn't it late to go out?"

"Actually, Mother, you might be right. But we're going anyway." Kendall smiled and steadied her daughter back down on her feet. "Let's go see if we can find some flying monkeys."

Skylar Dawn giggled as they skipped down the hall and out the front door.

It was clear that changes needed to be made for her and her daughter. She'd set paperwork in motion the next day. She'd find out the possibilities before she approached Heath.

Six months of living with her mother instead of her husband was long enough. Five minutes down the road, she realized she'd pointed the car east toward Heath. She slowed and turned into a drive-through. Then they got ice cream and played at the park until they both really needed a bath.

It was fun. Spontaneous. She used to be those things. It was the whole reason Skylar Dawn had come to be.

It was time to find that person again.

Chapter 2

Wade Hamilton shoved the last file into the back of the box. It represented months of work and the official end of his desk duty. It had taken him almost as long to heal from the beating he'd received six months ago. But everything worked again. Both with his body and his status as a Texas Ranger Company B lieutenant.

Ready to take his place at his partner's side. Ready to get out from behind his desk. Back to handling things by the seat of his pants instead of the rule book. Doing so had landed him in this desk chair. He'd learned his lesson to slow down and think a little. He liked field-work…not paperwork.

Unfortunately, Major Clements had discovered Wade was good at paper shuffling. He'd been allowed to assist with a few cases as backup for Company B brothers. But the paperwork grew while he was gone.

It seemed like the rest of the office had grown accustomed to him shuffling their requests, too. Coming in early and staying late was second nature now. Why not, since he had no life?

That's where he was bright and early on a Monday morning. At work before the rest of the staff or other Rangers finished their first cup of coffee, he was shuffling papers. Almost done, the latest request for his company's support caught his eye. He knew the name of the FBI agent heading the task force. He'd attended her wedding just over five years ago.

Kendall Barlow was the new team leader of a cybercrime task force and asking for computer and field support on the joint task force. Heath—her husband and the logical choice—had already been assigned to cybercrime. Now their relationship would need to be reviewed and disclosed. He'd been on the task force since it was headed by Jerry Fisher. But still, Murray was the best geek Company B had.

It was up to Wade to recommend someone else or okay Heath for a couple of days in the field with Special Agent Barlow.

It was also an opportunity to resolve his friend's problem. He'd been listening to Slate talk about his temporary roommate for six months. How he worked the horses, cleaned the stalls, never missed a phone call with his daughter and never—ever—spoke to his wife. Heath, on the other hand, never said a word. Wade held on to the paperwork and grabbed a second cup of coffee.

Who was he to jump in to the middle of a man's business? Especially marriage problems? But the more he tried to talk himself out of it, the more his gut told him to assign Heath to work with his wife.

Slate and Jack were both standing at his desk when he returned from the break room. Before he asked their advice, Jack pointed to the request.

"What's this?"

"You're sending him, right?" Slate asked. "It's exactly what they both need to force them to figure out what's going on."

"You think so?"

"Damn straight," they answered together.

"The man's turning into a bear," Slate said. "I might take his head off if he snarls at Vivian again."

"If the FBI put in the request, you should accommodate it," Jack stated, hanging his jacket on the rack.

"What if *she* doesn't want it?" Wade asked, already knowing that he would recommend Heath.

"Then she has a friend who is thinking along the same lines we are." Slate took his seat opposite Wade. "Maybe she's as cranky as he is."

"Who's cranky?" Heath asked as he walked through the door.

"The old man, Major Clements," Jack said, jumping in. "We're coming up with reasons he might be out of sorts. I say he's getting ready to retire. Wade says his wife might be cranky."

"My bet's on the wife." Heath winced as he took off his jacket, holding his side. "The old man's never going to retire."

The guys nodded in agreement. Slate mouthed "Bear," while pointing to Heath behind his hand.

Wade recognized Heath's movement. When his own ribs had been cracked, he'd held his side the same way. Heath had probably injured himself at the rodeo this weekend. But he'd never admit it.

Wade agreed with hiding it from the boss. If he hadn't been unconscious with an eye swollen twice its size, he probably would have taken a couple of days off and never admitted anything about the beating. Or about the woman who'd saved his life by alerting Jack to his whereabouts.

Time to put his own fantasies to rest and find the woman who haunted his dreams... Therese. If he couldn't work on that, the least he could do was help get Heath and Kendall back together.

He reached for the request, ready to recommend his friend and submit it to Major Clements. The old man would make the final decision if Company B would waive the conflict of interest. Maybe Heath and Kendall could find mutual ground and resolve their differences.

If not, then this assignment would at least help them reach that decision, too.

He completed the paperwork and sent it on its way. Assignment made.

Chapter 3

Heath held his side as he carefully lifted his arm into his suit jacket and then set his white Stetson on top of his head. The required Texas Ranger uniform wasn't what people expected when they saw the star on his pocket. Traditionally they all wore white Stetsons, but with suits rather than jeans. He even wore a white shirt and black tie today.

Good thing, since he'd been assigned to work with an FBI task force regarding potential cybercrime. The agent in charge thought a research company had some type of ulterior motive for collecting the data.

Cybercrime had a broad definition—it referred to any crime committed with a computer or through a computing device. The slim file he'd received held just the basics and an address where to meet the agent. He was curious to learn what had tipped the FBI off and what the specifics of the case were.

Why meet here in the field? It wasn't the norm. Neither was getting a last-minute request for field backup on a task force he hadn't been active with for a while. Jerry Fisher—his wife's old partner—had been promoted to group leader overseeing several teams in cybercrime. What was different now?

He waited for this mysterious agent at his truck. The older neighborhood was nicely kept up. The homes were on the smaller side for this section of Dallas. They'd eventually be sold and torn down to make way for larger lots.

It was a shame. Some of them looked really nice and were perfect starter places for couples. *Or to house mothers-in-law.* He'd been thinking about his wife the entire trip across town.

Only natural that he'd start thinking of her mother, since he half blamed her for egging on their arguments. He'd gone back and forth long into the night about calling Kendall. Even picked up his phone a couple of times. But the chicken part of himself won.

What if that phone call ended everything?

This morning he watched the sun rise while riding his mare and resolved to call Kendall today to make a date to talk. Not over the phone. Not around Skylar Dawn. Certainly not around his mother-in-law. The promise gave him peace of mind. Six months was enough time apart. He needed to try again. Speaking face-to-face would allow him to gauge her reaction. And if she called it quits?

Well, he wanted her to look him in the eye if she did.

There were several cars on the street of the address

he'd been given. None of them were a government-issued sedan. He glanced at his watch—only a couple of
minutes early.

If he was working with the FBI, he'd eventually have
to visit their Dallas field office. He wasn't excited about
running into Kendall accidentally. Or her supervisor,
Jerry Fisher.

Whoever his partner from the FBI was, they were
late. Unless he was supposed to meet them inside. He
walked around the truck, calling Wade to see if there'd
been a time adjustment to the appointment. When a
black sedan pulled up behind his truck, he disconnected. He leaned on the tailgate while putting his
phone away, waiting.

"Heath?" A familiar voice rang from the far side of
the government car.

The car door shut, and he stood at attention for
some reason. The face came into focus while his body
charged out of control.

Kendall?

Dammit. He'd almost dove into the truck bed. Hard
to do with his heart galloping up his windpipe like a
stampeding mustang. He wanted to leap on its back and
get the hell out of there.

His hands itched to wrap themselves in her wild
strawberry blond mane. But no wild mane flowed down
the back of FBI Special Agent Kendall Barlow. It was
pulled smoothly against her head into a ponytail. A few
short tendrils escaped in front of her ears, the lobes
pierced with the small diamond studs he'd given her.

"Nice to see you," she said, before smiling a strained
grin.

"Hey." It felt awkward. He hadn't been alone with

her in a long time. He deliberately eased his shoulders, trying to relax. "Nice earrings."

She fingered a stud, as if figuring out which pair she wore. "Oh, these? I can't remember where I got them." She teased with a genuine smile now. She remembered exactly who had given them to her... Him.

The awkwardness was worth it for the smile he hadn't seen in months. "I... No one told me it was your task force."

"Can we sort through the conflict of interest after Mrs. Pelzel's interview? She's watching us out her window."

"Would you like to work with someone else?"

"Of course not." She stopped on the sidewalk, head tilted to the side to look up at him. Physically only an arm's length away, but completely out of his reach. "We can be professional about this. At least I can."

Professional? Sure. Why the hell not?

Her task force. Her lead. Her knock on the door. He turned sideways on the porch to let her pass. The slight scent of ginger and orange filled him with memories. He recognized the smell of her lotion and was getting sentimental. Instead of pulling her into his arms and kissing her until they were both senseless, he tugged off his dark shades and tucked them in his pocket.

He could be professional. If he had to.

Kendall explained who they were when Mrs. Pelzel came to the door. She introduced him as Ranger Murray. No one was the wiser that they were married, since she'd always used her maiden name professionally. Once they were invited inside, Heath quickly discovered Kendall had been on this case for several months. Sitting on one of the most uncomfortable couches in the world, he concentrated on Mrs. Pelzel preparing large glasses of iced tea. A suddenly dry throat couldn't wait to be quenched.

Kendall looked at a message on her phone, and he wondered how they'd drifted apart. More than five years of his life had been devoted to this woman.

How could it all be gone over one wrong question? He didn't want it to be. But getting back to her wouldn't be easy.

Once again, he was close enough to touch his wife, but promise bound to keep it professional. Reminding himself to stay professional. He'd kept that way back when they'd first met. He could do it again now.

Mrs. Pelzel brought the glasses in on a tray. He popped off the couch to help, but she shrugged him off. "Please sit. I have never had a real Texas Ranger visit before. This is so exciting."

She handed them each a glass. He downed his in record time and could only blame it on nerves.

Kendall set down her glass after taking a sip, then straightened her jacket. Time for business. "Mrs. Pelzel, would you be willing to let my computer forensics team take a look at the PC?"

"Can they do that from here? I don't think I could live without my computer for a long period of time," the home owner replied. "That's how I stay in touch with my grandkids, you know."

"We could have someone out here in a couple of days," he answered. "They could check it right here."

The older woman shook her head. "Oh, wait. You know, I should have told you when you first arrived. There's really not a problem, so you'd be wasting your time."

Kendall gave him a look he should have been able to interpret. Maybe she'd just been surprised that he'd given an answer she didn't like. Maybe she thought it strange that Mrs. Pelzel had changed her mind. He didn't know, and that was disappointing since he should, being her husband and all.

"Mrs. Pelzel, what happened that made you call the FBI?" Kendall asked. Her notebook was open. Her pen was clicked to a ready position, but her casual body language told him she wasn't expecting a real answer.

That hadn't changed, at least. He could still read her mannerisms, it seemed.

"I'm afraid I'm just a silly old ninny who made a mistake," the older woman said.

Kendall turned a page in her notebook, sliding her finger across the handwriting as she skimmed the page. "You told us you had a feeling that someone was watching you through the computer's camera."

"I did," the older woman whispered.

To her credit, Kendall the FBI agent didn't roll her eyes or make any facial movement that indicated she didn't believe the older woman. "You also mentioned that the computer seemed to be running slower since they installed the Public Exposure gadget."

"Really, you should believe me when I tell you I made a mistake," Mrs. Pelzel said, her fingers twisting into the loose long-sleeved shirt she wore.

"Will you confirm that you have one of the PE monitoring systems?" Kendall's enthusiasm moved her forward to the edge of the couch. Both sets of law enforcement eyes moved toward the desk, where the older model computer sat.

"They seem like a legitimate company," he said, attempting to get Mrs. Pelzel to share more information.

"I'm not a helpless old woman who doesn't know how to research a product or service. I didn't think it was anyone's business how much time I spent online. But the money they offered was enough to buy a new roof. I just couldn't pass that up."

He'd heard of Public Exposure and their controversial social media monitoring system. The file he'd been sent from the task force stated a strong belief the group was involved in more than the good of the common man.

"I sound old and kooky about someone watching me. But I swear that the camera light comes on by itself while I'm cooking or watching television. I hear a click, and the red light pops on and off." She covered her mouth like she'd said something wrong and then looked at her computer.

Warning bells sounded, and he couldn't help glancing over to see if the light was on.

"It doesn't sound kooky at all, Mrs. Pelzel," Kendall comforted. "In fact, we've had several other residents report the same thing. But we need to take your computer to our forensic team and have them check—"

"I'm sorry. Maybe I'll have my granddaughter look at it. I was wrong to bring you here. There's nothing weird going on." Mrs. Pelzel stood and lifted her hand toward her front door. "I'm sorry, but there's nothing I can do."

"Mrs. Pelzel, I believe you," Heath said. "A start to resolving this issue would be to make certain you log out of your Wi-Fi. Turn everything off before closing the lid and unplugging it. And ask your granddaughter to verify your router has an encryption key. You might want to change your password."

"Thank you. I'll try to remember, and I'm very sorry to have wasted your time."

Kendall stood, defeat written clearly on her face. She flipped her notebook closed and stowed it away inside her suit jacket. They both stopped on the front walk when the door shut. Heath squinted at the noon sun and put his glasses on while she made a couple of more notes.

"The precautions won't make any difference," Kendall told him, following with her sunglasses dangling from between her fingers.

"You don't think this is someone trying to steal identities, like that file sitting in my car states."

"It's bigger than that." Kendall continued to her car.

"How many reports have you taken?"

"Dozens." Kendall leaned on the government-issued sedan, appearing more defeated now than she had inside the house. "And for every person who reports that their camera light is sporadically coming on, there are probably another dozen who don't."

"It's a shame she wouldn't let an expert search her computer. But if you have had that many complaints, why haven't your FBI computer whizzes found what you need from those victims?" He crossed his arms across his chest and leaned his hip against the sedan, close to her.

"What did you think of Public Exposure before this morning?"

"I've seen their public service announcements. They're a group that promotes kids playing outside instead of hanging on social media. How are they involved in potential identity theft?"

"First, no accounts have been affected—bank, credit

card or otherwise. None of these complaints go further than what you witnessed. Mrs. Pelzel doesn't realize that it was me who she spoke with when she called. I take the complaints, but by the time I get to an interview, something has changed their minds and they've all made a mistake."

"All of them?"

"This makes over twenty. Oh, and they all use the word *kooky*."

"They can't all be saying the same thing. You think Public Exposure is threatening them?"

"Yes. Sometime between when the resident calls me and when I get here. All of these people withdraw their complaints or concerns and I can't move forward."

Mrs. Pelzel watched them from her window. Heath saw her drop the curtain back into place. Without moving his head, he looked at the windows of the neighbors. More than one resident peered through the blinds.

"I kind of understand about that feeling of being watched." He barely nodded, but Kendall picked up what he was throwing down.

"There's also a white van at the end of the block." She pointed a finger behind her.

He glanced in that direction. "Two men in the front seat. Just sitting like they were when I arrived."

"Want another chat?"

"I'm game."

Kendall flipped her identification wallet open and held it in her left hand, leaving her right ready to react. Her weapon was at the ready in her shoulder harness, his at his hip. She turned and they took the first steps into the middle of the street toward the van.

The engine sprang to life and the van burned rubber

in reverse. It was around the corner before they could pivot and get back to the car.

"I didn't see a front license plate," Kendall said, pointing for him to get into her vehicle.

"Nope. At least we don't have to wonder if we're being watched or not." He hesitated to open her sedan's door. "My truck is faster than this old heap."

"Yeah, but this is government insured. I'd hate for our rates to go up."

He jumped inside and buckled up. That was his Kendall. Always practical.

And he loved it.

Chapter 4

Kendall concentrated on driving the car. If she let herself get distracted and think about why Heath had been assigned her case, she'd screw up. Driving or talking…somehow she'd messed up one or the other, and he'd shut down.

At the moment, his hand gripped the back of her seat and the other gripped the dash. He'd lowered the window as soon as she'd pulled away from Mrs. Pelzel's home.

"Do you see them?"

"You're about to cross Inwood. Take a right." He was grinning from ear to ear.

A definite improvement from when she'd first arrived. She'd thought he was about to throw up when Mrs. Pelzel went for the tea. She turned right as he suggested with the direction his finger pointed. For a by-the-book kind of guy, he had a good intuition about where criminals went.

"Slow down, Kendall." Heath dropped his hand and pulled his sidearm.

She tapped the brakes and followed the direction of his narrowed eyes, toward the end of the block where the van sat parked in a driveway. She couldn't tell if it actually belonged there or not. She slowed further.

"We need a better view." He rested his weapon on his thigh but kept it pointed toward his door.

"Do you think they've seen us?" She pulled the car to the curb, keeping her foot on the brake and the car in gear.

"Not sure."

"Thoughts?"

"They aren't getting out. We should call for backup. Last thing we need is a chase through a residential part of Dallas."

"Agreed. A high-speed chase isn't ideal anywhere."

"Nope."

At least he was concise. Shoot, he always had been. Heath Murray was a cowboy of few words.

"As soon as I put the car in Park, they'll take off."

"Probably. Backup?"

"I hate to do that when all we have is the suspicion they were watching us or Pelzel's house." She needed proof. Something solid to move forward with. Not a reprimand about pursuing innocent bystanders.

"They did peel out in Reverse to get away."

"True, but we hadn't identified ourselves. I just see a media nightmare when they claim we were coming at them with guns."

"Want me to ask?" His hand reached to open his door.

"Let's just wait a minute and see what they do."

She had no more than finished the sentence when two men exited the van, walked to the rear and removed paint buckets. One of the guys went and punched the doorbell, also knocking loud enough to send every dog on the block into a barkfest.

"You've got to be kidding me." She hit the steering wheel with the palms of both hands. "This is the first nibble I've had."

"Drive slow."

Kendall didn't hesitate and put the car in motion. With his gun resting on his thigh, Heath used his phone as a camera. She didn't have to watch. She was confident that he'd capture as many images as possible. She focused her gaze on the men, switching between them, watching for a weapon or any questionable movement.

They drew even with the house and the man still at the van climbed inside and quickly shut the rear doors. The one at the house knocked again, causing the dog inside to bark once more. She could see it bouncing against the window trying to get out.

"Catch the plate?" Heath asked.

"He stacked paint cans in front of it." Frustrated, she kept the car moving and pulled around the corner.

"We could wait here. See what they do."

"We'll give it a try." She performed a three-point turn, pulled next to the curb and cut the engine.

"Video call me." He plugged a headset into his phone and used one earpiece, dropping the phone into his jacket pocket. "Stay here."

"Heath, no." This went against training, but it was their best option.

"Don't worry. I don't do crazy." With those words,

he was out of the car and tapping the hood as he walked around the front.

She should have been more insistent and demand he return to the car. She dialed and he answered but didn't talk. She could hear his boots on the street, his breathing and then the echo of street sounds after she heard them in real time.

He crossed the street and stood on the grass at the corner house's garage wall. The cell screen finally showed a picture other than the inside of his pocket. He lifted the phone around the corner, and she could see past the neighboring driveways.

"They're standing at the back of the van. One's talking pretty rapidly and waving his hands. Can you make out what they're saying? I can't."

"No," he whispered into his microphone.

"They're both looking in your direction, but I don't think they can see the phone. The driver is opening the doors and putting the paint back inside."

"I can have a conversation," he whispered.

"No. Heath, no. Just wait." She had a bad feeling. A very bad feeling.

Trusting premonitions had never been a strategy for her. She never looked for good luck or blamed a bad streak on chance. More than anything else, she investigated and found the answers through old-fashioned hard work.

But something screamed at her to get Heath back in the car.

"Time to pack it up, Heath."

The screen went black as she heard the driver slam the van doors shut in real time and then on the echo in the video delay. She started the car to be at the ready.

But Heath didn't return to the vehicle. She inched the car forward until she could see her husband disappearing into the front door alcove, getting closer to the van instead of coming back to her.

"Heath!" She called to him without any response. She sank lower in her seat, hoping neither man in the van noticed the car.

The van's engine roared to life.

Kendall braced herself, fairly certain that the next thing she heard would be gunfire. The van peeled out of the driveway and down the street…toward her, passing Heath and turning left. Perfect for them to follow.

"Let's go!" Heath's voice roared at her through the phone.

She put the car into Drive, stopping just as he rushed away from the house and leapt over a small hedge. Even in boots, Heath was across the concrete street and in the car within seconds.

His speed always amazed her. Riding horses, running or taking down a suspect…the action didn't matter. His hat was in his lap, and his hands were waving to follow the van.

"We don't really have a reason to follow these guys," she mentioned as she took the next left, back to the main road they'd turned from earlier. "Why do you want to pursue?"

"Gut feeling?"

Just as she was about to open her mouth to explain how their joint task force operated—that she was in charge and he shouldn't take off like he had—the van sped up and fishtailed around a corner.

"If they really think that's going to work, I guess they don't know much about you, Kendall."

Even increasing their speed and darting around a car, she caught the smile and wink. The natural response was to smile back. So she did. It was the reason she'd fallen in love with him. His gallantry. His bravery. His…okay, everything.

Kendall stopped herself, concentrating on switching lanes and accelerating. She'd confront him later. After whatever they were doing was over.

"Watch out." Heath raised his voice, pointing in front of them.

The van went through a yellow light. They weren't running sirens. And a powder-pink sedan, heading in the opposite direction, turned left in front of them. They were going to hit each other. Kendall slammed on her brakes, as did the sedan. They barely avoided each other as they fishtailed sideways to a stop.

"Gun it. Car to your left."

She heard the words and trusted the Texas Ranger next to her. She floored the gas, trying to look for crossing traffic, getting their car across the intersection. It was a good time of day to be on Northwest Highway. No one was in their path when she heard brakes from one direction and tires squealing from the other.

The SUV they'd passed a few seconds earlier had crashed into the rear of the pink car, stopping where her sedan would have been if Heath hadn't yelled. There was a loud bang and horns.

"Great job, babe." Heath patted her shoulder from where he rested his arm along the back of her seat. "I'll check on the drivers."

She pulled around to protect the drivers from oncoming traffic and hit the hazard lights. Heath got out, leaving his hat in his seat. She dropped her head to the wheel, reaching for her phone to call the accident in to authorities and request a tow truck. She sat back as she gave all the appropriate information, letting out a long sigh.

The van was out of sight. Heath was busy with the drivers, and all Kendall could do was force herself to breathe. That had been close. Too close.

No suspect was worth what had almost happened. She had to be more careful, less reckless. Skylar Dawn needed her parents to come home. Period.

"You okay?" Heath asked, back at the passenger door.

She nodded, still a little stunned by it all.

"I can't say I'm bummed about them getting away." The corner of his mouth barely rose as he leaned on the car.

"What? Why's that?"

"Where's the fun in catching them the first day I get to work with you again?"

He said it with such a straight face that if she hadn't known him, she never would've seen that playful gleam in his eye. Yet she couldn't argue with the logic either. She would've been bummed, too.

Chapter 5

Heath wanted to take Kendall in his arms until she stopped shaking, but he'd jumped out of the car to check on the other drivers. Instead of helping her now, he spoke to her through the passenger door, keeping the entire front seat between them.

Hugging your wife after an accident was allowed, in his book. He just didn't know if it fell under the professional umbrella. He straightened, grabbing his aching ribs, worse now because of slamming into the seat belt. But he swallowed the grimace of pain, keeping it to himself. He wouldn't mention it to the EMTs who would be arriving on the scene, judging by the distant sirens.

Kendall stretched a couple of times as she stood from the car. "I can't believe they missed us."

"You didn't hesitate."

She nodded, letting the statement stand as a compliment about their teamwork. And this time, he didn't add the frightening picture in his head of a different outcome. If she had stopped to question why he was yelling a command at her... Damn, they would be pinned between those two cars right now.

But she hadn't. They were unharmed. Fine to go home to Skylar Dawn. And good enough to work together tomorrow.

"The drivers are fine." He'd walked around the hood of the car before realizing it. His hand opened between Kendall's shoulder blades, and he might have patted her a couple of times if he hadn't seen the tears.

But he had.

Just two, but they were enough to make her curl into the crook of his arm and stand there until they heard the first siren grow close. She broke away like someone had thrown water on them.

"Traffic needs to get through. I should probably move the car." Her voice was awkward and strained as she looked around the intersection.

"I can take care of it."

"Don't coddle me, Heath."

"Whoa there, *partner*." He emphasized the last word to remind her why they were there. "I'm allocating resources. You're the better photographer. I'm going to need every angle possible before the cars move." He stuck his hand in his pocket.

Her mouth formed a perfect O before accepting his phone. Then she was back. Professional. Doing her job as the authorities arrived. Identifying herself as an agent and taking pictures.

Staying out of the way, the Dallas PD officer gave him the go-ahead to move the FBI sedan. It didn't have a scratch on it. Just as he opened the door, in a moment where no one else watched, he caught a glance between the two drivers.

A knowing glance. Like they'd gotten away with something.

It took him a few minutes to get the sedan back on the same side of the street as the rest of the cars. By the time he returned, both drivers stood with officers, giving their statements. After an initial check, they'd both declined the ambulance ride to a hospital.

The woman in the pink car was crying again, her mascara smeared like his mother-in-law's the day his world had turned upside down. It was hard not to think about it—the afternoon Skylar Dawn had broken her arm. But he pushed it from his mind.

Something was off about the accident. Maybe he'd been hanging around Wade too much lately. His friend's intuition seemed to be rubbing off on him. Everything about the SUV guy who had nearly T-boned them screamed that the man wanted to run.

It had to be the highway patrol officer in him. He'd stopped more than his fair share of antsy drivers with drugs or weapons in their cars. The SUV driver shifted his weight from foot to foot. He kept looking around, especially at Kendall.

Okay, Heath admitted that his wife was an extremely attractive woman. Nothing about her shouted married or mom. And seeing her work again was…hot. He got why men would watch her. But this guy didn't have a look like he was trying to ask her out.

Nope. Heath recognized the short glances. The slow quarter turns to keep her in his peripheral vision. The driver must not realize that Heath was a Ranger or anyone else significant. He hadn't given him a second glance since Heath asked if he was okay.

Heath leaned against the pink car's trunk, watching both the drivers through his mirrored shades. There it was again. A specific look that acknowledged the drivers knew each other. One of the man's eyebrows rose, and the woman's chin lifted slightly.

Indiscernible to anyone not watching them specifically. A look that confirmed his gut feeling that something was off. If he'd looked away for a split second, he would have missed it.

If the drivers knew each other, they must know the men in the white van. He took a step toward Kendall, who was wrapping up with the officers. But what would he tell her?

That his instinct told him these two apparently innocent victims had a connection to the group Kendall was looking into? They couldn't hold the two based on his observation. His gut instinct had gotten them into this accident by encouraging her to follow the van.

If he followed any intuition, it would be to keep his thoughts and observations to himself until they could investigate. That's what the Rangers and FBI did. They found the facts and built cases.

He'd wait.

For now, he'd make it clear about his role here. No reason to let Public Exposure know he was working with Kendall. He pushed off the trunk and marched to Kendall's side. He pulled her close to him.

When she turned to him—most likely to express her anger—he kissed her. A full-on-the-mouth, like-she-belonged-to-him kiss. For the moment…she did. Although she may not after the next time they were alone.

"I'll explain when we're alone," he whispered. Then in a louder voice, "You ready to go, babe?"

He could see the fury rising for him embarrassing her. "Gentlemen." She nodded to the officers, excusing herself.

Heath didn't back off. He kept his arm around Kendall's waist as they walked to her sedan. He opened her door and tried to kiss her again.

"No way," she said, dodging his attempt. "You better have a dang good reason for what you just did."

He ran around the back of the car, trying to come up with something. Anything other than the real reason, since he didn't want to explain himself. At least not yet.

She stared at him as he snapped his seat belt into place.

"Well?"

"It was time to go."

She huffed. "That makes no sense at all. If you wanted to go, you could have said something and not embarrassed me in front of the Dallas PD."

He let her vent as he looked through the pictures she'd taken of the scene. Once he was back in the office, he'd be able to run a full background check. Once he had information, he'd explain to Kendall.

"You aren't listening to me."

"What?"

Kendall slowed to a stop beside his truck. "I said, if you're going to get possessive because someone's looking at me, then this joint effort isn't going to work."

"That wasn't… I wasn't…" he tried. *Get your information right before you tell her.* "Professional. Got it."

The awkward pause resulted in an awkward thumb gesture indicating he should get out of the car. She lowered the passenger window from her side and waited until he bent his face down to look at her.

"I'll talk to you tonight when you call Skylar Dawn. We'll decide what our next move is and where to meet tomorrow."

"Good idea."

He stood. The window went up and she pulled away, leaving him in the middle of the street. She had a right to be upset. On the surface, he'd behaved badly.

Back in his truck, he resisted the impulse to bang the dashboard. It sure didn't appear that he'd racked up any points for moving back home. He'd do his research, and maybe his instinct about the drivers would pay off.

Drapes dropped into place at the house to his left. Blinds closed at Mrs. Pelzel's home. There was more to this case than fraud. Every instinct he possessed told him so. Kendall was keeping something from him. He knew that before being assigned to her task force.

Fraud? Or a decision about their life—together or apart? Maybe helping his wife would give them an opportunity to really talk. But now, it was time to work some computer magic to figure out what secrets the residents of Hall Street were keeping.

Chapter 6

"If I weren't a mom, I'd be cussing like a sailor right now." Kendall closed the office door behind her.

Jerry Fisher didn't look up from the paperwork under his pen. "I put in the request as you asked. You must have known there was a possibility that your husband would continue on the task force until they could find an alternate. Do I need to file a furgle conflict of interest and pull you from the case? Oh, sorry. I forgot you're offended by that word."

The witty comeback she'd expected hadn't come. Instead he'd deliberately used that stupid word. Her supervisor sounded…bothered. *Shoot.* She'd been using his listening abilities for her personal venting. That needed to stop.

The pen dropped to the desk, and he covered the papers with a file. Kendall plopped down in the lone chair near the bookshelf, emotionally exhausted. She'd only returned to the office to delay explaining to her mother why she looked like she hadn't slept in a year.

Jerry leaned back in his chair, fingers locked casually behind his neck. "Look, if it's too difficult to work with Murray, I can give this thing to Kilpatrick. It'll die a quick death, and it won't be your responsibility or be on your record."

"Kilpatrick is two months away from retirement. He won't take it seriously." She could handle Heath and the investigation. If she couldn't...well, she deserved to be reassigned.

"We both know this investigation isn't going anywhere, Kendall. I spoke with my supervisor and the DC cybercrime group supervisor. They're still not interested until your victims have monetary losses or receive extortion threats. It's just not a priority for them." He leaned forward, chatting like the friend he'd been when they'd first started out at the Bureau. More like he was doing her a favor by taking the case away.

Did he really believe she was wasting her time? Had he lost confidence in her ability? Or was her desire to crack a big case obscuring the reality that Public Exposure wasn't one?

"We actually had a break this afternoon. The address of the complaint was being watched by two men." She wouldn't remind him that she could manage Heath.

The fact was that Jerry Fisher drank the Kool-Aid. He'd moved up to management. He was her boss. Bosses lived by the rules. Bosses wanted successful investigations. Bosses didn't need to hear about personal problems.

If he needed results...well, that's what she'd give him.

"Were you able to question them?" He picked up the

pen and tapped both ends back and forth on the manila folder.

"We were in pursuit when they— No. No questioning, yet." But the incident strengthened her resolve. She was on to something important. "I won't take up any more of your time."

"Furgle. I have time." He gestured to the files on his desk. "Believe me, I'd rather be in the field with you again."

"I bet." She smiled, in spite of his using that stupid word…again. She left more determined than ever to break this case wide open.

Jerry wasn't the only one who needed results. Climbing the FBI ladder had been her dream for as long as she could remember. She needed a big win in her column. Someday she wanted to be the agent in charge, the boss, the person others reported to.

But, honestly, she couldn't remember why.

Did she want to be behind a desk making all the decisions without the full picture? Did she want to move and take Skylar Dawn away from her life here? And, more importantly, away from her father?

Like my mother did?

God, the realization stopped her in her tracks. That wasn't the plan when their argument started. Well, marrying and having a child had never been a part of her life plan either. She rubbed her palms together as she continued down the hallway. She needed to reevaluate her life. The realization wasn't a surprise. She just hadn't admitted it to herself before this minute.

Even though she'd wanted to have the same evaluation talk with Heath, she hadn't acknowledged it was exactly what she needed to do personally.

She needed more information about Public Exposure, which would mean a late night of research. But her first call was to the house. Her mother picked up Skylar Dawn from day care each day, but she always waited until Kendall got home before serving dinner.

"Mommy!" her daughter answered. She either could recognize the caller ID or knew it wasn't six o'clock and time for Heath's call.

"Hey, sweetheart. How did today go?"

"Bumble the rabbit died, Mommy. It's so sad. I'll miss her."

"That is sad, honey. Is your class all right?"

"Yeah, Miss Darinda says it's part of the circle of life. Like the lion movie."

"That's true."

"I drew a picture. MiMi put it on the frigeator."

"I'll be sure to look at it when I get home."

Skylar Dawn sighed long and very audibly into the receiver. "Working late again? My, my, my."

Her daughter mimicked frequent sayings of the adults around her. This particular one was used by Naomi in an attempt to make Kendall feel guilty or ashamed. Kendall already felt both, since she'd be missing time at home.

"Yes, sweet pea. I'm working late, but I'll be home in time to read a chapter from our book."

"I could get Daddy to read it."

God, she felt guilty enough without letting Heath know she was working late on a Monday. Tuesdays and Thursdays were normally spent in the office. That was Heath's night at the house. For some stupid reason, she didn't want him to know that the late hours were extending to other days of the week.

"I'll be home in time. Can you get MiMi?"

"Love you, bye-bye."

Maybe it was superwoman syndrome or imposter syndrome or some other syndrome working mothers had come up with. Whatever it was could be added to the list of things she needed to face and talk about with Heath.

Not Jerry. Not her mother. And not any other friend or coworker.

It was time she admitted she couldn't do everything.

Right after she proved that Public Exposure wasn't what they claimed.

Heath's phone alarm sounded. Five minutes until his six o'clock phone call. He swiped open the book, getting it ready to read for Skylar Dawn.

"Barlow residence."

Naomi. Not the cheerful voice of his daughter.

"Evening, Naomi. May I speak with Skylar Dawn?"

"I'm sorry, Heath. She's taking her bath. She got exceptionally dirty this afternoon hopping around like a bunny." Naomi described the playful act with disgust.

"Is Kendall available, or is she in with her?"

"She's not here tonight."

"And after Skylar Dawn's done?"

"Returning your call is not my responsibility, Heath."

"Gotcha. She's being punished for getting dirty." He waited, but Naomi didn't respond. "At least tell her I called?"

Again there was silence.

If Heath hung up, it would be the only part of the conversation repeated to Kendall. He kept the line open, waiting until his mother-in-law responded. In fact, he put the call on speaker and looked at the book.

He heard splashing and singing in the background. Naomi had returned to the bathroom.

"I can't stay on the phone any longer. It's time to wash her hair." She disconnected.

"I think Naomi Barlow is in contention for the monster-in-law of the year award," Wade Hamilton stated without looking across the office at Heath.

"Mind your own business. Wait. That's impossible for you, right?"

"I was commiserating with you, man. I know what that phone call means to you."

"You're as bad as an old meddling matchmaker. Admit it. You're the one who assigned me to Kendall's task force." He swiveled in his chair to face Wade.

No one else was in the office. He could speak freely. He had intended not to mention the conflict-of-interest part of his assignment. His anger was actually at his mother-in-law and the phone call. He should shut up. Keep it to himself—his general policy about everything these days.

Too late now.

Wade took a few seconds to smile like a cat skimming a bucket of milk still under the cow. Then he rolled his pen between his palms, shrugging his shoulders slightly.

"I'm not sure if I should slug you or thank you."

"Hey, I'm just looking out for my own self-interests here," Wade said, spinning back to his computer screen. "I'm tired of hearing Slate complain about your bad habits."

"I have a few stories I could tell."

He held up his hand. "God, no. I have no reason to listen to more. Instead, is there anything I can help you with?"

"Thanks, but no. I'm running some facial recognitions and backgrounds. Why aren't you going home?"

Wade shrugged again. "I have my own demons to chase."

Demons? Heath recognized barriers. Several months ago Wade had been brutally beaten, cracking ribs and almost losing an eye. He would have lost his life if it hadn't been for a woman named Therese Ortis warning another company Ranger, Jack MacKinnon.

All traces of the woman had vaporized. Was she the demon Wade chased? Too late to ask. The conversation was over.

It was a good time to step outside and call Kendall. He left a message when she didn't answer, then texted her to call when she was home so he could talk with Skylar Dawn. The light pollution around here didn't block every star in the sky. He perched against the tailgate and just looked out.

There would be rain in the next couple of days. The color around the moon had changed. His mother had taught him that. He should take his daughter for a visit. Soon. But the nine-hour drive to Southwest Texas was hard enough when two parents shared the responsibilities.

That had been the excuse, and his parents had accepted it. The last real trip they'd taken to Alpine had slowed them down further with the horse trailer to pick up Jupitar and Stardust almost a year ago. When had life gotten out of hand?

The day I walked out of my house.

Needing a pep talk, he dialed. "Hey, Mom. How's everything going?"

"It's much the same. The baseball team looks to do

pretty good this year. But you didn't call to catch up on Sul Ross."

"I don't mind hearing about it." And he didn't. Just listening to his mom's voice gave him a sense of inner calm.

"Are you still living…?"

"At the Thompson ranch? Yes. And no, I haven't really talked to Kendall. Skylar Dawn is growing and getting more amazing every day. She made new paintings for everyone. I'll get it in the mail this weekend."

"No rodeo? No busting heads?"

He rubbed his bruised ribs but knew his mother referred to Kendall's mom. "That was this past weekend. Okay, maybe it happened a little tonight, too."

"Uh-huh. You're going to kill yourself and make that woman very happy."

He was pretty sure he wouldn't drop dead, but the pain was a constant reminder that he might not have too many rodeo days left. Maybe he should focus on more rides with Skylar Dawn instead.

"Mom. We've talked about this. I need the money." Yeah, he did. And one crack about his mother-in-law was all either of them was allowed.

The extra work he did around the ranch still didn't repay the Thompsons what boarding his two horses would cost. He was determined to make up the difference and not accept a free ride.

"We could help you out, but you won't let us."

"You already have three full-time jobs. A professor at the university, a wife and a nurse to Dad. You're the one who needs to slow down. I should be sending money to you. Is he okay?"

"Dad is still the same. He's giving everyone what for, doesn't remember doing it, then does it again." She laughed. "I wish we could come see you, but breaking his routine is really hard."

"I know, Mom. I should be there."

"Nonsense. You have a very important job, a family and a wonderful daughter. Concentrate on those precious girls."

"Yes, ma'am."

"I'll call my grandbaby this weekend. You okay? I should get your daddy into bed soon."

"Just that… I'm always better after talking to you." His mother's positive, can-do attitude poured out of her every sentence. "Love you."

"I love you, too, son."

Talking to at least one woman he loved gave him his second wind. He returned to his desk and began the computer searches he needed on Public Exposure. He wanted to know everything.

Making a substantial contribution in the morning would make it much harder to stop his involvement with the case. The last thing he wanted was for Kendall to play the conflict-of-interest card.

Wade finally went home.

It was too late to speak with his daughter. Too late to read to her. He had no reason to text his wife. Again.

"This can't be right." The addresses of the two drivers today weren't only on the same street in Dallas— they were on the same block.

He looked up the owners—not them, a corporation. Now the digging got fun. So fun he didn't notice the time until it was two in the morning.

Time to call it a night.

He had what he'd been searching for. A good, solid, old-fashioned lead.

Chapter 7

Kendall opened the front door and found Heath leaning against her SUV. One hand held a donut with sprinkles, and the other had a large coffee. Skylar Dawn ran past in her pink jeans and matching jacket.

"Daddy!"

Heath set the coffee cup down on the hood and lifted their daughter to his hip. He received his hug and smooches, then set their almost-four-year-old on the ground.

"Is that for me?"

"Yepper doodles." He smiled like Kendall hadn't seen him smile in months. "Jump inside and buckle up first."

He opened the door, got Skylar Dawn settled inside and handed her the donut, complete with a set of napkins to cover her favorite blue bunny shirt she wore in honor of Bumble the rabbit.

Kendall stood there, finishing the last bit of coffee in her travel mug before setting it on the front porch. Without looking, she knew her mother disapproved behind the curtain. She didn't care.

Heath was a great father.

Their baby girl had cried herself to sleep the night before. The tearstains had been apparent on her plump little cheeks. It had been a rare occasion that Kendall hadn't made it home to tuck her into bed. Then she'd noticed her phone battery had gone dead. When she plugged it in, there were numerous messages from Heath.

They'd ranged from upset about her mother to extremely worried about where she was to wondering why she was ignoring him and offering to pull himself from the Public Exposure investigation. She'd texted that her phone had died and received a Great in response.

Of course it wasn't great. Their situation was far from great.

But watching him with their daughter made her knees melt. He showed so clearly how much he loved Skylar Dawn. It brought tears to her already puffy eyes. She hadn't slept. A recurring vision of what could have happened at that intersection had kept her awake most of the night.

"Come on, Mommy," Skylar Dawn said between bites.

"That better be a double shot, skim with a dash of vanilla," she answered from the porch before joining them.

"Why would I order you anything else?" He smiled at her, too.

But as he handed it to her, he glared at the window where the curtains moved slightly. She didn't blame him. Her mother had no right to decide Skylar Dawn shouldn't speak with her father.

That was a direction in which Kendall never wanted to head. No matter what happened between her and Heath, their daughter would never be used to hurt him. She'd made both of those points clear to her mother as soon as they'd gotten up.

"How did you know to bring the donut this morning?" she whispered as she passed him.

"I had a hunch." He cut his eyes toward the window again.

"I did speak with her about bath time."

"Ha. Like that has ever worked before," he said to her over the SUV, then pulled at the booster seat straps to verify they were locked in place. "Mind if I ride in with you?"

Not waiting for an answer, he jumped in the passenger seat and buckled up.

He has a point.

Setting her mother straight hadn't ever done any good. The woman had a habit of behaving exactly how she pleased. Oh sure, her mother helped by picking up Skylar Dawn and spending the night whenever the job required late hours. But she never really let Kendall forget that she'd helped. Or that Naomi Barlow's way was probably the better one.

Explaining why Kendall did something a particular way didn't matter. Naomi just nodded and proceeded as she liked. It was something Kendall had accepted for years.

But not after last night.

Not after seeing her precious little girl's hitched breathing from crying in her sleep.

"It won't happen again, Heath," she said, buckling her belt. She meant it. And she'd told her mother as much.

He placed his hand over hers on the shifter. "Tell Naomi that next time, she'll have to tell me to my face." His voice was low and carefully controlled.

They were all upset. Well, perhaps their daughter wasn't any longer. Her smile had white icing and rainbow sprinkles surrounding it.

"Is that good, sweet pea?" She changed the subject instead of reassuring Heath again.

Skylar Dawn nodded, holding out the now-icing-free donut. "Want a bite?"

"No thanks, Daddy brought me my own treat."

They drove to the day care, listening to stories of Bumble the rabbit. The kids had a memorial service planned for today. Kendall tried to concentrate, but her brain—and body—kept coming back to the surge of energy she'd felt when Heath's hand had covered hers.

The split second of comfort and reassurance had done crazy things to her emotions. She missed that feeling. Missed driving together. Missed family dinners.

Missed him.

This tsunami of emotions set her dangerously close to tears as Heath walked inside the day care with Skylar Dawn. She had only a few minutes to get herself together.

Turn off the emotions. Turn on professionalism. Think professionally.

"Man, those kids are taking this bunny thing seriously," he said, getting back into the car.

Kendall pulled through the drive and was back on a major street before she tried to think of something to say. But her mind was blank. Wiped spotless like a counter top after her mother had cleaned.

"Find anything by working late last night?" he asked. *Professional.*

"I eliminated possibilities, but haven't found anything specific."

"I worked late, too." His voice held a subtle tease that she recognized.

"How could you find something on the first day?"

"I didn't want to speculate yesterday. But I kept getting the feeling that the drivers of the other cars knew each other."

"I totally missed that."

"You were kind of shaken up."

A professional wouldn't admit that she'd been shaken up all night. "Did they know each other?"

"It goes beyond that. They're both members of Public Exposure. Have been for about three years."

Six years ago, she had slammed on the brakes and hugged him after a similar announcement. It had broken the ice, and after their joint case was over, they'd gone on a date. Then another and another.

"It's hard to believe they'd be that bold and try to... to..."

"Kill us? They probably would have liked those results." He took out his phone. "I have their address. They live on the same block off Wycliff, near Uptown."

Genuine excitement. They might be getting a break. She headed the SUV in the general direction that would take them north of downtown Dallas. New nightclubs and restaurants were springing up in the area all the time. Housing was sort of limited and in high demand, barely keeping up.

"You got a lot accomplished last night."

"There's more. They were both convicted of fraud. The Postal Inspection Service brought charges that stuck. The guy's still on probation. He'll see his probation officer next week."

"Why didn't you mention this yesterday? I could have saved you time and run it through the FBI database."

"I got what we needed," he said, pointing out a left turn. "I could just as easily have been wrong and wasted the whole night."

"But you weren't. This might just be the break we needed."

"Are you going to tell me why you feel so strongly about this case? What made you think there's more to it?"

"Maybe I had a hunch myself."

She couldn't admit she needed something big for her next promotion. Or that the promotion might result in a transfer. Not after the night they'd all just had. She wasn't prepared to have that conversation yet. Talk about counting chickens before they hatch.

She glanced at him during a stop light. He was waiting, patiently. Good grief, wasn't there anything bad about the man? Oh yeah, he wanted her to quit her job.

"It bugged me that this antisocial group would be paying people to monitor their social media use. Where's all the money coming from for their so-called study?"

"Have you checked on that?"

"One fund. They actually told me about that."

"You've interviewed them? Been to their offices?"

"I actually made a phone call. I don't have enough to subpoena their financial records. Maybe they thought if they told me, I'd give up."

"But it just made you more curious."

"Exactly."

"If there was an actual social media study, they'd have a variety of participants. Almost all of the people who were accepted are over the age of sixty. They're almost all single-person households and all homeowners."

"I noticed that, too. Wouldn't you want to target social media users under thirty? I mean, if you're trying to change the world and want less use. Why such weird participants? That's what piqued my curiosity. Then I found the odd complaint about being watched or feeling like they were being watched."

"What do you think is going on? You ruled out identity theft, but what else could it be?"

"That was my first guess. But the participants haven't lost money. At least not that they'll admit to me. They receive their payments from the study. I suspect that Public Exposure has a bigger plan. I just can't determine what direction to even look."

"Remember—whatever they're doing, it's big enough to want you out of the way. They must think you're on to something."

Yesterday's car incident came rushing back. "I could have gotten both of us killed."

"It was my fault, babe. I was the one who wanted to follow the van." His palm covered her upper arm, then slid up and down comfortingly before he pulled it back across the console.

"No one's to blame. I appreciate you checking them out. Seriously. Now we have a lead."

"A definite connection to Public Exposure, like you suspected." He adjusted in his seat, looking antsy and uncomfortable.

She turned the SUV a couple of times and realized they were a few minutes away from their destination. She hadn't gone by the office to verify information or follow any of her normal procedures of obtaining another vehicle. The excitement of working with Heath today and all his information had totally distracted her from her normal routine.

Even the drama at home this morning couldn't take away from the excitement of working with this particular Texas Ranger. He believed her. He trusted her instincts.

She stopped and shifted the car into Park with two blocks to go.

"You got me so excited about advancing the case, I forgot to pick up a Bureau car."

"Well, damn. There's not room for them both with Skylar Dawn's booster seat back there." He joked as if he hadn't been waiting for her to figure that out on her own.

He'd never chance someone discovering what car they drove. Neither would she. They'd have to go back. Fortunately, they weren't far from the field office.

"Look, Heath. I might have suggested that I'm totally in charge here. But that shouldn't stop you from sharing your ideas and consulting with me."

"Tell me what you need, Kendall. I'm at your service."

"Advice. Honest advice, not just what I want to hear.

Last night my supervisor was getting in my head, making me wonder if this was truly worth pursuing."

The truth of her words didn't scare her. It felt good to say them out loud.

"Last night you didn't know these people had tried to kill you."

"They tried to kill you, too."

He pressed his lips together and shook his head. "I'm pretty certain they didn't know I was on the case with you. They might now, but yesterday was all about you."

"You're probably right about that." She hesitated to mention the panicked feelings she had the day before, but if they were working together, maybe he should know. But the words didn't form.

"Head to your office. Arrange for backup. Then we can bring both of the drivers in for an interview."

Was he asking a question or giving her a suggestion?

"Why do I get the feeling that you aren't going with me?"

"I don't mind taking a walk and keeping an eye on things until you get back."

"No. You're right. We honestly don't know how these people are going to react. They tried to kill us, Heath. What would happen to Skylar Dawn?"

"I see your point. We wouldn't want your mother raising her." He followed up with a laugh.

Heath had always been honest with her. Even though he'd chuckled, hard truth echoed in his words. Their daughter could not end up an orphan.

"You asked me for my honest opinion, Kendall. I gave it to you." He turned in the seat, picking up his hat from next to the car seat in back.

"You are not going out there on your own."

"I'm just going to verify the suspects are home. Just a little old-fashioned Ranger surveillance while you get things settled. If I have a problem, I'll call Jack. He's close by on assignment."

He opened his door.

"Call Jack on the way. You knock. I'll have your back from the street."

"Good idea. Let's go."

He winked at her like that had been his plan all along.

Chapter 8

Heath made the call to Jack while on their walk around the corner. His voice sounded normal, no overreaction, no urgency. But Kendall could feel the readiness in his determined steps. In the way he moved his badge from his shirt to his suit coat. And in the way he flipped that same jacket behind his holster.

She clicked the lock button on her key ring, and the horn echoed off the gas station behind it. She looked down the block at an array of businesses on Lemmon Avenue, then back in the direction they were heading—full of renovated homes and thirty-year-old apartment buildings. Truly one of the up-and-coming parts of Dallas. One side of the street had gated driveways with stairs leading up to the front doors. The other side had parking along the street.

"This isn't a good place to follow someone," she mumbled since Heath was still talking to Jack.

"I texted the address," he said into the phone. "Yeah, we headed straight here instead of picking up a government issue. Right. No way we're letting them get a look at Kendall's regular ride. Skylar Dawn's seat is in the back... Six minutes is great. We'll be at the corner."

Six minutes. They could wait six minutes. The drivers from the previous day didn't know they were coming. Together with Heath, she could observe, make a plan, get prepared, call her office for backup.

"I can't believe I totally forgot to grab a sedan," she said once he was off the phone.

"We were talking, no big deal. Jack won't be long. This may turn out to be nothing."

Waiting on one of Heath's fellow Rangers would give them time to collaborate. But each minute ticked by excruciatingly slowly. And quietly. The more time she spent observing their surroundings, the less she felt like talking. Heath sent the pictures and information about the two suspects to her phone. She had a good image of who they were looking for.

"Good idea." She tilted her phone's screen toward him. "I can barely remember anything about how they look. Saundra Rosa and Bryan Marrone. I didn't give them a second thought."

"You can't do everything, Kendall. Even though you get close every day."

"Thanks," she whispered. Partly because she wasn't good at accepting praise and partly because of the weird feeling the neighborhood gave her.

Four more minutes.

"About this thing with your mother..."

Heath raised his hat and pushed his longer-than-normal hair back from his forehead. Then he secured his official white hat once again. It was one of his common stall tactics, waiting for her to explain or offer an excuse for Naomi. Then he wouldn't have to talk. But there was no excuse.

"It was wrong and uncalled-for. I told her as much." She did a three-sixty checking the neighborhood again. "Isn't it kind of weird that no one's around? Not a single person."

"You noticed that, too?"

"Do you feel this?" She twirled her finger in the air. "It's like that time at Fright Fest when the zombies were following me."

"Actually, watching you there was a lot of fun for me. But I know what you mean."

"You're getting that prickly sensation like someone's watching you?"

"That would be an affirmative." His voice lowered as his right hand descended to rest on his weapon. "You noticing a theme with these houses?"

They passed Rawlins Street heading to the next block.

"Either they all used the same bucket of paint for their trim…" She counted two houses without the same color. Heath kept walking but managed to turn in a full circle, checking their backs.

"Or they're all owned by the same corporation, which has an odd color preference." Most of the house trim looked the same as the apartment windows from the previous block. She'd seen that specific color every day recently in her files. "Unless you're really into Public Exposure orange."

"You think everyone who uses that color are members? Maybe it's a home owners' association thing." He shrugged. "Maybe they're just weird."

"Or part of a cult."

He cut a disbelieving look in her direction. "Let's talk with the drivers before we draw any concrete conclusions."

She wasn't sure she was off the mark, though. "I don't think Brantley Lourdes leads Public Exposure like a religious cult. But these people all listen to their leader as if nothing he says is wrong. Why else would two people be willing to crash into us, risking their lives?"

"You think Lourdes is capable of an attack?"

"I… I'm not sure." She had no facts to back up her feeling. But just like yesterday, she knew they were being watched. The unmistakable itch raised the hair on the back of her neck.

Heath grabbed her elbow, gently pulling her to a stop. He searched her eyes like he had a thousand times before. "You are sure." He tapped one-handed on his phone, putting it on speaker. "Jack, I'm not sure what's going on here. Stay sharp."

"Hang on, I'm still two blocks away. Don't do anything until I get there," Jack said.

"Man, we've moved past the corner. If I were Wade, I'd say I have a bad feeling about this. Hell, we're heading back to the SUV." Heath hung up.

"Hang on—" She wanted to delay the retreat, but one worried glance from her husband substantiated the uneasiness racing through her blood.

"We both know something around here isn't right, Kendall. How much digging have you done into this Public Exposure group? What's not in the file?"

She faced toward the SUV and began slowly moving down the sidewalk. It was no surprise that Heath took his steps backward next to her, keeping a wary watch behind them.

"Not enough apparently." But that was something she'd correct first thing she could.

"My general research last night gave me the impression they're mostly considered a do-good organization that encourages people to get off social media and interact with others."

Kendall couldn't shake the strange, creepy feeling. Even nature seemed to be in on setting the mood. No dogs barked, no birds chirped. The air hung heavy and thick.

"Excuse me. Can I help you?" A man stood in one of the orange doorways of the corner house.

Heath whipped around, ready for an attack. "Texas Ranger Heath Murray, sir. Sorry if we've alarmed you. Everything's fine."

Heath stopped moving toward the vehicle and didn't remove his fingers from his weapon. The thumb strap was unsnapped, ready to pull.

That creepy feeling got stronger, even though the man looked normal enough and splayed his empty hands for them to see.

"We'd appreciate if you returned indoors, sir." Kendall issued the directive, but the man stayed put. She couldn't force herself to move away.

"I'd rather know what's going on." He put his hands on his hips. "I'm calling the police."

Even though he didn't have a threatening posture, the situation felt off. Everything about it shouted a scenario from training. One where she turned her back and got a rubber bullet bouncing off of it.

"That's your right. Please go inside to make the call."

"I have my phone right here."

"Don't do it. Keep your hands in the air. I'm FBI. Do *not* reach for anything." She drew her weapon keeping the barrel toward the ground, then tapped Heath's shoulder, letting him know she had his back. "My partner is going to approach and verify that you're unarmed."

He was closer, so it was natural for him to check the man out.

"Okay, okay. I'll go back inside."

"You'll stay where you are," Heath shouted. "Keep your hands above your head, turn around slowly then take a step backward."

The man seemed innocent enough, but the uneasy feeling of the neighborhood persisted.

"There's a step. I'll fall." The man stretched his hands higher and took a step inside his open door.

"Stop!" they both shouted.

Heath moved toward the man, who finally froze. A little way down the street, she saw movement—two people running then ducking behind a car. One had hesitated when they'd shouted.

"Movement at nine o'clock," she informed Heath. "It might be our couple."

"One thing at a time. Jack will be here any minute." He took a final step, reaching the man, giving him instructions and letting him know what was coming next in the pat-down.

The neighborhood was still unusually quiet. Out of the corner of her eye she caught a glimpse of a car, heard the doors shut—no matter how quietly they tried to accomplish it. Every sound seemed to echo under the dense trees.

The man now faced her. Heath had explained how he'd watched the glances of the two suspects the day before. From behind her sunglasses, she watched the man who'd gained their attention. Every so often he darted his gaze in the direction of where the people had been running.

Then a crazy gleam was in his eye and the corner of his mouth twitched—just like a person about to smile. He blinked heavily and stretched his eyebrows to relax his eyes before he noticed that she watched.

There it was again—his eyes darted quickly in the direction of a car starting.

"Heath, he's a distraction. Our couple is in a car down the street."

"You sure?"

"Ninety percent."

Heath removed handcuffs from his back pocket, locked one around the man's wrist. He quickly moved him next to the porch post and locked his other wrist around it. The man couldn't run away.

"Let's go." He turned and took off in one motion, getting several feet ahead of her.

They didn't bother keeping to the sidewalk, but simply ran across the lawns to the end of the block. A horn blared from behind, then next to them. *Jack.*

"Where are we running to? Hi, Kendall," Jack casually said through his open window.

A car peeled out, passing Jack's big truck and heading in the opposite direction.

"Go with Jack. Follow the car."

It wasn't her first rodeo. She'd been in charge before. She should be telling the guys what to do. But Heath took off around a parked car and she jumped inside the truck. Maybe her husband had seen something she'd missed, since he wasn't heading in the direction of the car.

"What did this guy do?" Jack asked, quickly following the car down the next left.

She had one eye on the sedan and kept looking around for anything suspicious. Again, there was nothing there, just the spine-chilling feeling that they were being watched. Even while speeding down the street.

"Nothing solid. Yet."

Heath didn't have time to explain why he ran in the opposite direction of the car. He'd seen the woman's pink sweater in the thick shrubbery bordering the apartment complex they were next to. At least he thought he'd seen a pink sweater. Replaying the car's hasty exit in his head, he couldn't visualize two people inside.

Only one.

So he'd taken off. Playing out a hunch.

Hell, he didn't know for certain if he chased the woman from yesterday. How should he know if she dressed in pink every day? What had caught his eye might actually be another decoy. He had no way of knowing. But the sweater happened to be the same color as the car from the day before.

And he didn't believe in coincidences.

He headed to the north side of the house, where he'd seen the top of a blond head before it ducked behind a large oak tree. *Gotcha!*

Grabbing a decorative post to keep his feet under him as he made a sharp right-angled turn, he followed the fluff of pink between two houses. His jacket caught on thorns as he barreled through the narrow path that was basically the width of his shoulders.

As a bead of sweat rolled into his eye, he twisted sideways, wishing to ditch the regulation jacket and hat. He used the sleeve to wipe his face when he slowed at the southwest corner of an old wooden home.

Dang. Rosebushes.

The woman was a lot slimmer than he was to have made it through this gauntlet without getting stuck. The thorny growth on the lattice at his shoulder might appear pretty from the street, but it kept him from scooting next to the house for cover.

Basically, he was sticking his neck out and hoping for the best. He looked around, then pulled back to a position that hid him from the street.

Slowing his breathing, he listened. He kept his movements small and again used his sleeve to wipe droplets of sweat from his face. He wasn't overheating. The humidity was high—like running through a rain cloud.

No matter how much he tried, he hadn't grown used to running in his suit. Boots, yes. Hat, yes. But suit, no. He'd run in boots and a hat his entire life. He'd always had a hat on his head. There weren't many pictures, going all the way back to before he could walk, without one.

And boots? Well, they were safer than tennis shoes where he'd grown up in Southwest Texas. Rattlers, scorpions and other varmints didn't like to be suddenly disturbed by a boy running after a horse or his father.

Funny what went through his head while chasing a subject.

Skylar Dawn on the other hand was dressed in all

sorts of frills. Boots were the exception not the rule—
except on weekends at the Thompson's ranch.

He missed being with her every day, helping her
pick out clothes—frilly girl or cowgirl. He wanted to
sit beside her bed to read, then turn out the light with
a goodnight kiss. Wanting to have memories with her,
but also of him. Just like he did of his dad.

If things between him and Kendall stayed good
today, maybe they'd get a chance to talk about him
moving back in.

Chapter 9

Kendall pulled her phone from her pocket, ready to report what had just happened. Three streets from the original neighborhood, Jack still followed at a distance far enough back not to call obvious attention. At this time of the morning, cars and trucks flooded this part of Dallas. And they basically all looked the same.

Their one saving grace was that Jack's vehicle hadn't been on the street very long. Hopefully, no one had seen her jump inside.

"What did the guy on the porch do?" Jack asked, tires squealing as he turned a sharp corner.

"He was the distraction."

"For the guy who hasn't done anything? That's sort of— Hang on."

She grabbed the handle above the door as Jack followed the path of the car, cutting across two lanes and pulling a U-turn. The bulkier truck required some of the sidewalk.

"I thought you had that light pole for sure." She tried to joke, but her heart raced, causing her voice to shake a little.

The man they followed turned again. Jack hit his brakes, waiting two heartbeats before turning after him, but the sedan was already turning again.

"This guy is acting like he's being followed. Either he's paranoid or his aim is to make us paranoid. I can't tell." Jack securely gripped the wheel and made another U-turn. "I bet he's doubling back. I can get there before him. We'll already be on the street and he won't know we're in position."

"Good idea." She wished she'd thought of it. She wished she could think about anything useful. Her mind kept jumping between Skylar Dawn and Heath.

Focus was definitely necessary.

Truth was, she hadn't been in pursuit of a vehicle in a while. She was out of practice. Most of her work now happened behind a desk or in a lecture hall. Sure, she completed field interviews from time to time, but that wasn't the norm. At least not for her.

Then the file on Public Exposure had landed in her lap. Mysteriously after it had been closed for lack of evidence. She hadn't been able to tell if Jerry had supported her work or not.

"There he is." She pointed to the second car in the left turn lane. "Your hunch paid off."

"This would be easier if we had some backup and could leapfrog tailing him. Anyone around Harry Hines?"

"It wouldn't help. I couldn't catch the license plate number to call it in. Did you?"

"No. It's obscured by the other vehicle. Looks like it's just us for now."

The car passed them on the left with a car between them. Kendall pressed the video button on her phone without physically turning to look in his direction. Definitely their man, and he had no clue they were following him.

Or had been following him. They went straight as he slowed to turn. The sedan waited its turn in the feeder lane for the interstate. Just her luck.

"We're in the wrong lane."

"I got this." Jack jumped the short curb of the median and pulled a U-turn without slowing traffic. "Maybe you should call this in before it gets real."

As Jack sped up to catch her non-perpetrator, Kendall gripped the dashboard, knowing that his definition of *real* perfectly matched her husband's. All she could do was hope it wasn't real yet for Heath.

Heath tugged his slacks higher onto his thighs and knelt, without touching the stone path or garden dirt. He could manage the balancing act for a few minutes. He pulled a blade of grass an edger had missed and almost tucked it between his teeth but thought again.

Kendall wouldn't have let Skylar Dawn mimic his actions. No telling what pesticides might be lingering around. This time he sort of believed there was something in the water. This street was as strangely quiet as the first one everyone had run from.

No dogs barked.

No cars drove past.

Nothing to disturb the heaviness in the air.

Humidity churned with the gut feeling that there was a lot more to Kendall's case than she was letting on. If she ever admitted to acting on her instincts, he might actually get the whole story.

Eventually.

If he earned her trust—no, *when* she trusted him again. He could wait for her. Just like he waited for the woman in the pink sweater to feel confident enough to leave wherever she was hiding.

Two houses with orange trim were nearby. He waited. His gray suit mixed in with the red roses, and he hoped his white Stetson lost its shape against the white house.

Waiting was the only option until Kendall returned. She might have called for backup, but he wouldn't know what type of car to look for. He'd turned his phone to silent, so it wouldn't even vibrate, just after tucking himself amidst the roses.

He wasn't making the mistake of his phone giving him away after the five or six thorns he'd fought.

Waiting was his specialty. But he had little choice in the matter. It wasn't like he had cause to go house-to-house looking for a woman he wasn't certain had even been there. What was he supposed to ask? Is there a pink sweater inside?

At least Kendall and Jack were on the trail of a sure thing. Jack was good. Kendall was better. They'd make sure the driver from yesterday didn't get away.

"Watch out!" Kendall braced herself between the middle console and the door. Her feet worked imaginary pedals. She stopped and accelerated the truck as if she were driving.

"Do you see him?" Jack asked.

"I hate the sun's reflection at this time of day. I can't see the lanes, let alone a gray sedan."

"Same here." Jack moved half of the truck onto the shoulder.

She finally had a better view and tugged at the seat belt to lean forward. "Wait. See the car darting half in the lane and back again?"

"Hang on."

As if she wasn't already.

She made the calls—one saying they were follow-ing a person of interest, then another to Jerry, the boss, who wasn't pleased they were darting through a major Dallas traffic artery during rush hour.

"Even one-sided, that conversation didn't sound good," Jack said when she hung up.

"We're not to put any lives in danger."

"Understood."

Jack drove with skill, taking advantage of a shoul-der or exit lane—when there was one—to illegally pass without putting too many civilians at risk. But it didn't stop her heart from climbing into her throat.

"Looks like he's heading east. Maybe I-30 or south to I-45. What do you want to do?" he asked.

"Do you think he knows we're following?"

"Can't tell." Even behind his mirrored shades, Jack's eyes reflected his excitement. "Right now, he's not showing signs that he knows. He just seems in a hurry to get somewhere. If he heads into downtown proper, we're going to have a problem keeping our cover."

"And if he stays on either highway, we can coordi-nate a safe stop with Dallas PD."

"Looks like it's the Cadiz Street exit. You've got your

direction. It's downtown. How aggressive do you want to get with this guy who hasn't really done anything?"

"When you put it like that…" So Heath hadn't mentioned to Jack that they'd nearly been killed the day before. Or that this guy had been involved. "Before he clearly fled, he was a person of interest. We only wanted a conversation."

With the man who tried to kill us.

"I'll get close enough for a clear look at the plates."

"I'll call it in, making all departments happy."

Jack got the truck just behind the sedan as it braked to exit. She snapped a picture of the plates and of the driver as they passed. Jack turned right at the light and the driver turned left. She made her calls.

The second one was to Jerry, who still wasn't happy.

"I've sent a unit to the address you gave me. No one's on the porch handcuffed or sipping their morning coffee. Did you get the name of this supposed subversive?" Jerry shouted.

"Ouch," Jack said softly.

The last thing she needed was one of Heath's partners cracking jokes. She shortened her breath, deliberately holding an exasperated sigh at bay. "There wasn't time."

"There are two agents cruising the area," her ex-partner said. "No sign of Murray either. Are you with him?"

"Looks like our guy is heading for the interstate. Should we follow or check on Heath?" Jack asked.

"Stay with the sedan," she told the Ranger. Into the phone she said, "Tell them not to shoot the man in the white hat."

Fortunately, there weren't any windows on this side of the house he leaned against.

Heath wanted to move but needed to stay put. Without anyone coming around, the woman in the pink sweater was bound to feel comfortable enough to come back outside. And most likely, she'd be heading down this path back to her place on the other street.

And he'd be there. Easy-peasy, as Skylar Dawn would say.

Unless the rosebush that he'd pretty much flattened caught on his jacket and kept him from moving. Then again, it might be his stiff legs that kept him from chasing someone down. He pushed the brim of his Stetson up with his forefinger, then wiped the sweat into his hairline.

Kendall had shaken her head at that habit more than once. It's why he tied a kerchief around his neck when he worked outside. His straw work hats had more ventilation than the regulation white beaver-felt Stetson. He wouldn't take a chance at drawing attention to himself by digging his sweat rag out of his inside pocket.

Still…he loved wearing the big hat. He loved being a Texas Ranger and all it stood for. Sweat ran down his back. Okay, the suit jacket he could live without.

A door opened.

It had to be close. Maybe even the front door to the building he leaned against. Light steps across the concrete porch headed in his direction. Heath pressed his shoulders closer to the wall and tipped his head back until his hat raised off his forehead.

"I'm sure they're gone now, Rita. Thanks so much for the lemonade. Oh my goodness. I don't need to wear this sweater until I'm back indoors. It's getting warm out here."

"You take care. I really enjoyed the visit. I just need

one more hug. It's going to be a while before I see you again."

There were two female voices. No distinguishable accents. Then additional steps—heels this time. An outer door gently swung shut.

"You guys take care on your trip," the woman who apparently lived there said. "Let us know when you get to Del Rio. That's quite a drive."

"Sure thing. I can't wait until you'll be there, too. Bye now."

More steps. Two doors shut. Humming.

It must be his lucky day.

The blonde he'd been chasing waltzed around the corner of the porch as she swung the pink sweater over her shoulder. She looked toward the street just as she passed him, missing that he stood in the rosebush.

"Howdy," he said with his best twang. He latched onto her elbow so she couldn't run. Then as she twisted to free herself, he said, "Don't do it."

Gone was the polite woman on the porch. She made a disgusted sound, stomped her foot and slung a couple of curse words in his direction.

"Who do you think you are? Let go of me."

He was surprised she didn't have a cell phone in hand, already trying to call for help. "Saundra Rosa?"

"How do you know my name? And what are you doing hiding in the rosebushes?"

"I had a couple of follow-up questions about yesterday."

That got her attention. "What about yesterday? I've never seen you before."

"That's right. I don't think we met at the accident. Ranger Heath Murray, ma'am. We should probably move back to the sidewalk before someone calls the police." He gently and firmly moved the pink sweater lady in front of the house she'd been visiting.

"If I'm under arrest, aren't you going to read me my rights or something? I'd like to contact my lawyer before you cart me off to jail."

"Sure. Is that what you want…for me to arrest you? I was fine with a conversation."

"A conversation?" She looked truly bewildered.

"But if you want me to arrest you…" He reached for his handcuffs, forgetting they were on the wrists of a man almost two blocks away.

"No." She cleared her throat. "Not really. You just want to talk? What about?" She kept looking around, mainly up at the windows trimmed in orange.

Heath took a step sideways, blocking her view of the house behind him. "What were you doing in that part of Dallas?"

"I was delivering some items to a shelter." She stuck out her chin, defiantly, practically daring him to call her a liar.

"I promise this won't take but a minute. You told the officer yesterday that you were unfamiliar with the car you were driving. That's why you accelerated by mistake through the intersection."

"Yes. This is really about the car accident?" She lifted her hand and chewed on her short thumbnail.

"Is it your husband's?"

"What? No, I'm not married."

"Who did the car belong to?"

"Why does that matter? I'm paying for the damage to the other car. But I'm buying the Pink Thing.

That's what my car reminds me of. You know, like the ice cream."

She popped a hip to one side and rested her hand there. It reminded him of when his daughter pretended she was a teapot. Saundra wasn't four years old. The pouting, put-out actions weren't reflecting well on a woman in her twenties either.

A couple of other doors had opened, including that of the home she'd been hiding inside. No one yelled or stepped onto their porch, but he got the feeling they weren't going away.

"That's good, very responsible." He brought his notebook out from his pocket. "This is actually for my office. More paperwork for the higher-ups."

"Are we done, then?" She pointed toward the unofficial path connecting to the next block. "I really have somewhere to be."

"Yeah, that just about covers it."

"Finally." She took steps back toward the house she'd left.

"One more thing." He pointed his finger in the air to stop her, then focused on her face, waiting on a reaction. "Why does Public Exposure want to kill my wife?"

Chapter 10

By the time Jack took the right-hand turn and drove two blocks for the U-turn, the sedan and occupant were nowhere to be found. Kendall received a call that the Dallas PD hadn't seen the car driving down or near Cadiz Street.

"We heading back to Heath?" Jack asked.

"Yes. Hopefully he's had better luck."

She dialed, but knew by now her husband had probably silenced his phone. He was excellent about calling Skylar Dawn, like clockwork. But communicating with the rest of the world…well, he answered when it was convenient. She left a message and sent a text asking for his location and informed him they were ten minutes away.

"Thanks for your help with this, Jack. I won't be caught like this again."

"No problem. I've been helping Dallas PD out with a couple of cases until Wade is off desk duty." He was relaxed behind the wheel, taking morning traffic in stride now.

"I didn't realize Wade had been injured that badly."

"Well, it's his injuries combined with the fact that he went against orders. Of course, I'm not complaining too loudly. I did get a girlfriend because of his misbehaving. Take a look in the console." He grinned, a charming smile that had been breaking hearts ever since she'd met him.

Wow, that had been six years ago. She raised the console lid, where a black jewelry box sat alone.

"Go ahead. Take a look. I'd like your reaction."

"My opinion won't mean much." She reached for it, shutting the console and sitting straight again, both excited and embarrassed at the same time.

"You're a woman, aren't you?" Jack laughed and switched lanes on the interstate. "And this is bling."

She flipped open the ring box. "Oh my, that's a lot of bling."

"I was hoping you'd react that way. I'm a little nervous. Okay, I admit it. I'm a lot nervous." He exited Oak Lawn, very close to the neighborhood where they'd left Heath.

"This is the woman you met last fall?"

"Yeah, Megan Harper. Honestly, I don't know what she's going to say. I mean, I think she'll say yes. It's the logistics of Austin versus Dallas. Who moves, that type of thing."

"No doubts about if she loves you?"

He shook his head. "There's been a zing there since the first time I held her in my arms."

Kendall didn't have any words. The ring was beautiful and she stared at it, missing the ring that normally sat on her fourth finger. She'd removed it and stuck it in her jacket pocket when she'd seen Heath on the stoop of Mrs. Pelzel's house the day before. Things had been hectic and she'd forgotten about it.

"It's gorgeous, Jack. I think she'll be very pleased. When are you going to ask her?"

"Soon. At least I hope to. Her parents are coming from England in a couple of weeks. I think I'll do the whole old-fashioned thing about asking her dad for permission."

The sweet gesture of respect was enough to bring tears to her eyes. It brought back many memories of her and Heath. She quickly closed the lid and stowed them away again.

"I didn't mean to…" Jack let the words trail off. He didn't have to say exactly what he meant. "You're really the only woman I could trust with this. My sister wouldn't be able to keep the secret. And there's no way I want my mom knowing before the ring's on Megan's finger. She'll have the whole wedding planned out without asking either of us for our opinions on anything."

Kendall laughed and dabbed at her eyes. "I know exactly what you mean. Mom had the country club booked in less than two hours. I remember telling Heath that she'd settle down. It never happened."

"I'm afraid that's what my mom's going to be like."

"Of course, I was busy with work, so I didn't really mind. I think Heath was more disappointed that he didn't help choose the cake flavors. The man does love cake."

"I've seen him chow down at office birthday parties."

They were at a stop light, and the truck filled with an awkward silence. Jack tapped his fingers on the steering wheel. Kendall flipped her phone over, checking for messages.

Nothing.

Heath could take care of himself. But in this crazy world, she'd prefer to have his back. Or to know that someone did, at least.

"This is the longest red light ever. Don't you have lights?"

Without a word, Jack flipped a switch and a siren sounded. Cars slowed at the busy intersection long enough for them to get across.

"If he was in trouble, you would have heard from him."

"I'm sure you're right. It's just…"

"It's okay, Kendall. I get it. I remember how I freaked not knowing if Megan was okay." He pressed his lips together and shifted in his seat.

The subject made him just as uncomfortable as it did her. She wanted to believe that Heath was okay. The belief somehow made her feel more professional. And no matter what she'd said yesterday when she'd first seen him, they weren't just professionals. They were married.

No matter their differences, he'd always be the father of her child. She'd never want any harm to come to him. Period.

They were still a couple of blocks away, and Jack was driving as fast as traffic would allow. The lights and sirens were off. He'd only used them to get through the intersection. So she did what she and Heath needed to do more of. She started talking.

"You'll have to tell me what Megan's like. Oh, and

when are you going to ask her? Does anyone else know? I don't want to spill your secret."

"She'll be up this weekend. We could all have dinner if you want," he said before wincing a little. "It doesn't have to be with Heath."

"It's Heath's weekend with Skylar Dawn." As if that was a real answer. She took a deep breath, deciding to be honest. "I know this is awkward. The one good thing about working together for a while will mean we actually have time to talk. We've both been avoiding it."

"That's a good plan." He pointed to her car. "See, he's okay."

He was right. Heath leaned against the brick wall of a 7-Eleven convenience store, as casually as a real cowboy leaned against anything. She was relieved and furious all at once. Thank God he was okay, but why hadn't he returned her calls?

Jack stopped and she quickly jumped from his truck. "Thanks for the help, and I'll see you soon. There's no need for you to stick around and witness me murdering my husband."

Heath looked up from under his hat. He had spotted Jack's truck midway up the block and slid his phone back inside his pocket. He had four texts and a message that he hadn't had time to listen to, but he knew what it contained.

Kendall would be—there wasn't another word for it—worried.

"I guess you didn't catch your guy?" He stood straight, stopping himself from walking to her.

"Well, it looks like you didn't catch yours either." Her voice was controlled and deliberate.

He recognized the compressed lips, the restraints she held on herself. He'd been on the receiving end of the cool wait-until-we're-alone look a few times. She pulled the keys from her pocket, spinning the key ring around her finger and heading for the SUV.

"Um… Kendall. Wait. We're not—" He reached to stop her, but not before Saundra stepped through the front doors of the building with a cup of coffee.

"Holy cow. That's—" She pivoted, doing an about-face toward him and grabbed his arm, taking them to the corner of the building. "What the heck's going on?"

"I was trying to tell you. Saundra ran into me and, after a couple of minutes, she decided to explain something to us about yesterday's accident."

"Oh, that's such a relief."

Dammit. Her go-to phrase let him know that she was more than a little ticked off at him. But at least the words she said loud enough for Saundra to hear were cloaked in a syrupy, concerned tone.

One surprised look and Special Agent Kendall Barlow was back in charge and had herself under control. "Miss Rosa. What would you like to explain? Wait. Should we try to find some place that's a bit more quiet? Is there a coffee shop nearby?"

"I only have a minute. I've explained to Heath that this is all just a big mistake and I need to get to work. I don't really know Bryan Marrone. I mean, I've seen him driving down the street, but that's it. I don't *know* him. You see?"

"Do you want to take her in for questioning?" he asked, crossing his arms, determined to keep a straight face.

"You have to believe me," Saundra pleaded. "I didn't really *do* anything except let him crash into my car."

There shouldn't be anything funny in Saundra's explanation. She didn't know him, but she'd let him crash into her car? He'd heard a lot of explanations over the years—every Texas highway patrolman did. Hers just made his top-ten list. There was hilarious, and then just plain absurd.

"Miss Rosa, I think we'd be better off having this discussion somewhere other than the 7-Eleven parking lot." Kendall gestured toward a couple of men walking inside the store.

"Oh, no. I couldn't possibly go to the FBI building. That's totally out of the question."

"Miss Rosa, please." Kendall opened her arms. One slowly moving behind Saundra and one gesturing more toward him on the corner. "Let's at least get away from the door."

She moved. Kendall moved. He kept his back to the ice machine and glanced around every other minute, making sure no onlooker stared too closely.

"You don't really think I tried to kill you. Do you? I mean, no one was really hurt." Saundra sipped her coffee, stretching her eyes open as large as they could get.

Kendall coughed or choked like she'd swallowed wrong. Heath tried not to look at the varying shades of pink powder on Saundra's eyelids. But damn, she was serious. She really didn't think she'd done anything wrong.

If he'd had a second set of handcuffs, she wouldn't be walking around drinking the coffee he'd bought. This was the very reason they needed backup, or that Bureau-issued sedan. If they'd had it, he would have arrested Saundra Rosa at the rosebushes.

Did Kendall feel the same way, or did she want to

tackle the investigation from a different angle? Standing slightly behind her, he couldn't see her face and couldn't make a judgment call on what she thought.

"Thank you for your honesty, Miss Rosa. Did Ranger Murray get your contact information?" Kendall paused while Saundra nodded. "We'll be in touch."

"Hey, Saundra. You'll be needing these." He returned her cell and ID he'd held onto during their conversation and walk.

"Oh, right. Thanks for not arresting me, Heath." Saundra power walked away from them, retracing the steps they'd taken earlier down the Wycliff Avenue sidewalk. Then she slowed, bending her head over her cell.

"I'd really like to know who she's texting right now."

"What in the world were you thinking?" Kendall turned on him as soon as Saundra was out of sight.

"What?" He honestly didn't know which way the conversation would go from here.

"You couldn't give me a heads-up that you'd not only caught your suspect, but that she was getting coffee?" Kendall vehemently pointed toward the 7-Eleven door while walking toward the SUV.

The key ring was still slipped over her finger. She clicked the unlock button and moved toward it, as if she'd suddenly remembered that she had a car. They didn't need to argue out in the open next to the trash.

Whatever reprieve he'd received from her being upset was apparently gone as they sat in the front seat. She kept twirling her keys instead of using them. She leaned forward, dropping her head on the steering wheel and taking deep breaths.

His hand lifted to drop on her back. After a moment's hesitation, he let it. She didn't shrug it off.

"I was calling you when I saw Jack's truck halfway up the block."

Kendall puffed her cheeks and blew the air out with a slow *wuff*. As much as he wanted to continue to touch her, he raised his hand and rested it on the seat-back. She turned the key, cranked the AC to high and pointed the vents toward her face.

A lot of effort was going into her movements to keep herself calm. He knew her, knew what she did when she was too upset to speak politely. Blasting the AC in her face was just a substitute for fanning herself.

"Why don't you just go ahead and say whatever it is you're trying hard *not* to say? Or maybe we could go collect my handcuffs?"

"You know that the first man is no longer there?"

"Sure. I had to walk past the house with Saundra. Is that why you're sore?"

"Good grief. No. I was—" She put the SUV in gear. "Do you want to see if the man is still in the house?"

"You tell me. It's your case."

"Is that really how this is going to play out? You take off alone, darting through houses that seem to all be part of the same organization where—"

"Yeah? Where what? Did you expect them to ambush me?"

"It wouldn't be the first time. Would it?" Kendall visibly clenched her jaw.

"Are you really going there? I'd prefer to have one argument at a time."

"If it's relevant to this particular argument then I think we—" Her cell rang and she clicked the button, connecting the hands-free. "Barlow."

"This is Special Agent in Charge Lou Grayson with

the Portland office. Have I caught you at a convenient time?"

Kendall pulled into an alley separating Rawlins and Hall Streets. She took the phone off speaker quicker than his mare headed for the barn for dinner. She began to get out, but he stopped her. She could stay in the SUV while he collected his cuffs.

Heath hated to admit as he got out of the SUV that he had another bad feeling. If a Portland agent was calling about the case, Kendall wouldn't have needed privacy.

"Dammit," he muttered to himself. "What the hell is going on?"

Chapter 11

Kendall locked the SUV and followed thirty feet behind her husband.

"Special Agent Grayson, what can I do for the Portland agency?"

"Join us. And it's Lou. Please."

What?

His words stopped her in her tracks at the corner—a good vantage point to have Heath's back if something went wrong.

"I apologize, Lou, but now might be the wrong time. I'm out in the field—"

"I'll text you my direct number."

Heath walked up the sidewalk to pick up his handcuffs.

She needed to get off the phone. "Special Agent Grayson, I need three minutes. Sorry."

She tapped the red disconnect button and stashed the

phone in her pocket. The bright silver still hung around the pole, locked in place. The neighborhood continued to be abnormally quiet and vacant for a block in Uptown. It was just weird to be outside this long and not hear a single bird or dog.

Heath was on the porch, key in hand, as he collected his restraints. No surprises. He didn't knock on the door to see if the man was inside. He did everything she'd asked. Then he retraced his steps. No one left their home. No car drove by. Her husband was ten feet away and she ran back to the SUV, dialing while attempting to be as focused on her duty as possible.

"My apologies, Lou."

"Glad you called back," he said without any irritation in his voice. "I know this might seem like it's out of the blue, Kendall, but you come highly recommended."

"I'm very flattered and honored, sir. But I didn't apply for a transfer."

"Let me give you a better idea of why you were recommended."

Lou Grayson recounted some of the high points of her last evaluation. She heard the words, knowing they were true…but…why her? *Why now?* Those words kept ringing over and over in her mind while Heath turned the corner toward the SUV.

He stopped, took his own cell out and turned his back to her. All the signs were there that her husband suspected something was wrong.

How would she explain the phone call from Portland without lying to him? Her only two options were avoid or evade.

"Kendall? Are you still there?"

Tempting as it was to claim a bad connection and

deal with this another time, she didn't move through life like that.

"Yes, sir. I think I'm still a little stunned."

"As I said, this might seem sudden to you, but we've actually been considering it for quite a while."

"May I ask how long, sir?"

"Since your partner was promoted. You'd be taking over our cybercrime unit, when the group leader retires in three months. Of course, we'd like you here well before then to learn the ropes."

"I'll need time to think about the move."

"How long do you think you need?"

"As long as you'll give me. This is a big change."

"I don't doubt it. How about a week?"

"Sure. Thank you, sir."

Heath stuck his cell in his pocket and placed both hands on his hips, clearly frustrated. She waved at him to return while she exchanged pleasantries with Grayson and disconnected.

"I called for a neighborhood patrol. They'll pick up Marrone when he comes home."

"*If* he comes home. He might be on his way to Mexico."

"More like Del Rio," he said.

"Where?" She couldn't have heard him right. "Del Rio, Texas?"

"Yeah. I overheard Saundra talking to a woman on Vandelia Street. I thought she was just making up the trip. You know, as an excuse. Then again, the woman said she'd love it there. As if she'd been before. Does it mean something?"

"Brantley Lourdes has land there. It's almost compound-like." Practically giddy, she grabbed Heath's arm, shaking it with excitement. "That's where Public Exposure's headquarters are."

"Did you issue a BOLO for Marrone?"

She shook her head, and Heath dialed the Rangers. She flipped open her notebook with the license plate of the sedan they'd been following. He gave them the information needed for the all-points bulletin.

Continuing to smile, she steered the SUV toward FBI headquarters.

She was excited. No. *Ecstatic.*

The couple that had tried to smash their car the previous day definitely worked for Public Exposure. She had a connection. Together they would break this case open. She was sure of it now.

"DPS will get him if he's on a highway out of town to Del Rio." Heath stashed his cell back in his pocket. "Do you want Dallas PD to pick up Saundra Rosa? It might be a good idea to see if she's willing to come to your office on her own. You might be able to flip her there before Public Exposure sends a lawyer."

"You mean *you* might be able to flip her. She seemed very eager to cooperate and kept looking to you when she answered. Sort of like you promised her something. Did you?"

"I've been told that women feel safer with a Texas cowboy around. I simply explained that we needed to file some reports."

"You said 'Yes ma'am, no ma'am.' And you told her we had to file reports. That made her stop what she was doing and let you buy her a cup of coffee while you waited to speak with me?"

Her husband cocked her head to the side and lifted

a finger—a sure sign she wasn't going to like his next words.

"I might have asked her why she tried to kill my wife."

"And her response…?"

"Crying. Full-blown, mascara-running, fall-to-her-knees weeping. As a highway patrolman, I've seen a lot of women cry. I've told you some of the stories. But I've never seen anything like this, Kendall. She even asked me for forgiveness."

"And then she denied everything?"

"Absolutely everything. Even down to knowing Marrone, at least knowing him well. As she said, they wave at each other when they pass each other on the street."

"Do you believe her?"

"Hell, no."

"Thank goodness. For a minute there, I thought you'd totally lost it in the past six months." She pulled into the FBI parking lot. "That woman was lying through her teeth."

"Sadly true."

Heath hated the idea of obtaining a visitor's badge and tagging behind Kendall as she went through her office. He'd been there, done that, and he'd felt like a puppy on a leash.

"I'll wait out here. Make some phone calls."

"You're sure? No coffee or anything else?" Kendall didn't wait long for an answer. She was already out of the SUV and walking fast. "I'll text when I'm coming down. It may be a little while."

"No problem."

Heath didn't want to draw the attention of FBI security. He had other things to think about instead of justifying why he was waiting. He kept the door open and his feet on the parking lot asphalt when all he wanted was to move and get rid of some nervous energy.

His phone began vibrating. "That was fast," he said in answer.

"Hey, Heath. Just letting you know, man. The house you wanted us to surveil has already had four visitors. I texted the pictures. No car fitting the description or plate number you issued the BOLO for."

"I owe you one, Jason."

"Not for long. My daughter wants riding lessons. When she mentioned lessons, I actually told my wife I knew a real cowboy. Me and my big mouth."

"Anytime. We can ride a couple of times and let her see if it's something she really wants."

"That would be terrific. How long you want me to hang around Rosa's house?"

Heath scrolled through the pictures—three men in dress shirts and ties, one woman. "I think we've got a start here. Thanks again."

"I'll talk to my wife and we'll make a date," Jason said.

"You've got my number."

"Let's go with a heavy patrol in the neighborhood."

Heath hung up and first texted, then called Wade at the office.

"What's up?"

"I'm at the FBI headquarters waiting on Kendall to get a Bureau-issued car."

"Thanks for checking in?" Wade asked it as a question, probably since that wasn't the normal routine.

"Okay, what do you want me to do with the pictures you texted? I assume they're surveillance photos."

"You got it. I'm wondering if one of the men is Brantley Lourdes."

"Man, all you had to do was open your smartphone for that answer. He's a pretty well-known guy. But I'll run the other faces for you. While I let the program kick this around, how's it working out with Kendall?"

"It was a rocky start. Then I thought I'd done something good. Now we're back to barely speaking." Enough personal business. "Check if the others have ties to Public Exposure."

"You got it," he said, clicking keys on his computer. "You two are all over the place. Why don't you just tell her you want to move back home?"

"It's not that simple."

"Sure it is."

"It's not like I haven't tried, man."

"For a married man, you sure don't know anything about women."

"And you do? I seem to recall that you're single and haven't had a date in—"

"Yeah. Got it. Minding my own love life. The people in your pictures are all board members for Public Exposure. I'll text you their names and pertinent info. They're from all over the country."

"Question is…why are they all in Dallas? And why are they all visiting a home of a suspect?"

"Good question. When do you intend to find out?"

"Soon. See you, man." Heath hung up.

A horn honked behind him. Kendall had kept her word to be fast.

Just tell her you want to move back home.

The thought was there. The courage…not so much. He was afraid she'd tell him why it wouldn't work.

Instead, he stayed focused on their investigation. "A buddy of mine at DPD is watching Saundra Rosa's place."

"Already?" she asked.

"I had some time while you were on your call. Anyway, he grabbed a couple of pictures of visitors, and I sent them to Wade. One was Brantley Lourdes."

"We only spoke to her an hour ago and he's already making a house call?" She pulled out from the parking lot.

"It gets better. Seems most of his board of directors for Public Exposure is here in town." He tapped a knuckle against the window, giving her time to think.

"You know I'm not someone to play hunches. I like good old-fashioned investigating and facts. But every feeling I have tells me that company is dirty."

They'd played this scenario before, back when they first worked together. His hunches had proved him right after a bet that it couldn't be that simple. That bet had gotten him the first date with the love of his life.

He didn't do a lot of dwelling in the past, but working with Kendall was a constant reminder that he'd been in love from the first time he'd laid eyes on her. She'd been a rookie agent working one of her first cases and he'd been her backup at several remote locations. A little town south of Burleson serving warrants and looking for a handgun.

Following one of his hunches about the gun's location led to their first date. Yeah, he'd won the bet that afternoon and they'd both won that weekend.

"Heath? Yo, Heath!" She snapped her fingers in front

of his face. "Did you have nice trip? Ready to get back to work? So…if they're all here in town, it looks like whatever's going down will likely be soon."

"We'll need a warrant," she said.

"It'll be easier to get it through my department. You have a longer chain of command than I do."

"If I could just get my hands on some hard evidence that this is a cybercrime, they'd give me a lot more resources and a little more leeway."

"Good thing you know someone who has a little leeway then," he answered.

"You know, since we're working together, I don't mind you staying at the house."

That was sort of out of the blue. But he liked it. Riding to and from work, having dinner together… *Wait.*

"I don't want to put you out. I mean, it's only convenient if you don't stay at your mom's."

"True. I… I think it's a good idea. Especially after how upset Skylar Dawn was last night."

Did she want him to stay at the house to work things out? Or was it because their daughter was upset?

Did it really matter? Did he care why he would be waking up with his girls?

Nope.

"Sounds good. I'll even cook."

The BOLO on Marrone paid off. Texas Highway Patrol spotted the car and picked him up south of Waco. He could be transported back to Dallas County Jail soon after she made a request. They could interview him while he awaited a hearing for his parole violation. Again, Kendall owed Heath for arranging the BOLO.

If she hadn't been working the case for more than six months, she might begin to get an inferiority complex.

Late Tuesday afternoon, they easily procured the warrant. Hearing that their suspect had fled the city and had an outstanding violation, the Waco judge had no objections regarding extradition. They could collect it in the morning and question their suspect upon his return.

"I still don't understand why the Public Exposure board of directors met here in Dallas. It isn't the main headquarters, and none of them actually live here."

"It may just be a coincidence," Heath said.

"You've never believed in a coincidence in your life. I don't know how many times you've told me that."

"True. You want to take the munchkin out for chicken strips or pick up food on the way home?"

She smiled. This was the normal routine when it was her husband's turn to cook anything except breakfast. "I think she'd prefer to have you at home all to herself. I'll make myself scarce."

Was that a look of disappointment that he hid by rubbing his face with his hand?

A real look or one she projected onto him? She couldn't let sentiment or wishful thinking get in the way of the case.

"You seem to be thinking pretty hard, Agent Barlow. If you're trying to tell me that my cooking's not so good. Don't worry. No illusions there."

"I wasn't thinking that even if it is true. Would you mind dropping me at the house? I'll send mom home while you take Skylar Dawn to dinner. She'll get a kick out of that."

Kendall turned the SUV onto their street.

"You got it." His agreement sounded like a forced confession.

"You don't have to sound so thrilled about it."

"Not a problem I get it."

"I don't think you do." She parked in the driveway and he practically jumped out of the car faster than stepping away from a bucking bronc. "Wait…"

But he didn't hear her. And she didn't chase him. Instead she sent her daughter skipping to a fast food dinner and her mother home for the night before she could complain too loudly about it.

Then she took advantage of an hour to herself, poured too much bubble bath into the tub and soaked until the water grew cold.

Wrapping herself in her comfy robe, she promised herself the nap would only last a couple of minutes when her head hit the pillow.

And not one time did she think of a way out. She couldn't practice the right thing to say. Whatever was needed to be said to Heath—her husband and her partner on this crazy journey.

Chapter 12

The third day working with Heath began with him in their kitchen if the wonderful smells in the house meant anything. Kendall had never been a night owl. She'd always thought of herself as a morning person. Morning workout or run, coffee and a quick shower had always been her style. Then she'd met a man who fed livestock at the crack of dawn every day and made fun of how late she slept.

This morning she could barely roll over. She'd experienced a total lack of sleep from tossing and turning. The awesome dreams of Heath seemed short-lived, and she struggled to get back to that place where everything was happy…and perfect.

The smell of coffee and biscuits finally had her stretching across the twisted sheets and eager to find her travel mug. Her mother didn't drink coffee. Just tea—morning, noon and night.

Coffee. Coffee. Coffee. The smell beckoned her to get out of bed.

Oh, God. I slept all night.

Shoving the sheets aside, she pulled on running shorts and a sports bra. She needed a couple of miles to work out the kinks and get her blood pumping. But she could start with one of those fresh-baked biscuits—and coffee.

"Hey, good morning." She came around the corner, expecting Heath and Skylar Dawn. Taken off guard, she smiled at her mother setting a plate of food at the bar.

"I told him you don't eat like this in the morning, but he insisted."

"Morning, Mother. Don't take this the wrong way, but why are you here this early?"

"Heath called and asked me to come and take Skylar Dawn to school."

"I can handle that."

"I told him as much, but again, he insisted. He said to check your phone and that you didn't have time for any exercise. He also left you this smelly stuff." She pointed to a pot of coffee.

My hero. Heath had found their coffeemaker from wherever her mother had hidden it. After moving it to the back of the pantry, her mother had bought a single-cup coffeemaker for the counter. It was the perfect temperature for a cup of flavored tea without any mess or boiling teapots.

"Where's Skylar Dawn?" She poured the brewed java into a mug and blew across the top.

"In the tub. In fact, I need to check on her."

"Mother, I'm sure Heath gave her a bath last night,"

she said a little louder, to carry down the hall where her mom was already headed.

"She fed horses this morning and stepped in some— oh good Lord, you know what she stepped in out there. You should listen to your messages, darling. I'm not sure it's really time sensitive, but he said it was about your case."

Kendall laughed on her way back to the bedroom and her phone. She was fairly certain that if—and that was a big if—her daughter had stepped in you-know-what, Heath had cleaned her up. But her mother was her mother.

Another bath wouldn't hurt Skylar Dawn. She'd play in the bubbles and smell like pink bubblegum at day care. No harm done.

She checked her messages. "Another agency— yours—served a warrant on Marrone's rental house. They found Saundra Rosa's body. Don't forget to pick up a Bureau sedan. Meet you there."

When Heath mentioned "body," she scalded her tongue, forgetting the coffee was still hot. She hurriedly dressed, pulling her hair into a ponytail. She scooped her creds, keys and phone into a pocket. Opened her gun safe and holstered her weapon.

"Gotta run, sweet girl." She blew an air kiss to Skylar Dawn. "Thanks for taking her this morning."

"I guess his message was important after all."

"Very." The door shut behind her as she ran to the SUV. *Dang it. I forgot my coffee.*

Heath checked his watch. "Special Agent Barlow is a few minutes away," he told the medical examiner, not really knowing how long it would take.

"I've got a couple of minutes. I know you want her to see the scene, but once transport arrives, I'll have to move the victim."

"I understand."

He kept taking pictures. Every angle possible from where he'd been allowed. Then more of each room he could see.

"It looks like she came for a visit and Marrone dosed her with something. We found a needle mark on her left arm." Supervisory Special Agent Jerry Fisher had mentioned his theory several times to anyone who would listen.

Too many times. An uncomfortable number of times.

There was one problem with his theory. Bryan Marrone hadn't returned to his house. Picked up south of Waco, he was dressed the same as he'd been the previous morning and in the same car. Jerry didn't know that the Dallas PD had been sitting on this house until the BOLO for Marrone had been canceled.

Absolutely a setup.

Yeah, that bad feeling had returned.

Heath kept avoiding direct conversation with Kendall's supervisor. Besides the fact that he just didn't care for his wife's former partner, he didn't want to give the agent an opportunity to tell him his services were no longer needed.

The two players they had connected to Public Exposure were accounted for. One dead—honestly, he was sorry for that. Maybe if he hadn't spoken to her or bought her a cup of coffee… It sounded heartless, but he hadn't killed her. The only justice he could give was to find her killer.

And it sure as hell wasn't Bryan Marrone.

He left the house with orange trim and saw Kendall walking through the police and onlookers, credentials in hand, "FBI" coming repeatedly from her lips.

"Morning. Glad you could make it," he greeted her without saying what he really wanted to say. Okay putting that into words right here wouldn't have worked. But a guy could think about it.

"Any theories as to how she was killed?" she asked, continuing her power walk up the sidewalk.

"Plenty. I'll let you decide for yourself." He stayed put. No reason to crowd the small house with one more body.

She turned, taking a backward step. "Did Skylar Dawn really step in you-know-what?"

He laughed and nodded. "I bet your mother had her in the bath faster than the wicked witch melted."

He stared after his wife, liking the way she flashed her creds at the other staring officers. There had been plenty of times after they were first married that he'd watched men looking at her and simply pointed to his wedding ring. She was definitely a beautiful, confident woman worth admiring.

Returning to his phone, he looked carefully at the body of a totally different type of woman. A young woman who loved pink and had unaccounted-for visitors yesterday.

"Why did you run, Bryan Marrone?" he asked under his breath. "Who were you afraid of?"

"Who's afraid of whom?" Kendall asked, coming to stand next to him. She tipped her head slightly to look at him before blocking her eyes with her sunglasses. "Oh. Well, Jerry's wrong."

"Yep."

"Is anyone checking out her house?"

"Yep." He pointed to three houses down, where a do-not-cross tape had been hung.

"Darn." She snapped her fingers like she'd missed an opportunity. "I don't suppose…"

He nodded. "I took a look at it earlier. Everything looks comfortably messed up."

"'Comfortably messed up'?" she asked with a tweak of her head.

"Like someone looked for something but didn't want us to know they were in a hurry. No phone. No laptop. But the TV was still there." He handed her his phone.

"Oh. I suppose you got pictures?"

"Yep." He stepped aside for the gurney that would remove the body. "I have a different adventure for you."

"The pink car?" She looked at him above her glasses and smiled.

That was the super smart agent he'd fallen in love with—one step ahead of the rest. "It's probably nothing."

"But an adventure nonetheless." She winked. "My car or yours?"

"You drive. Swing by my truck for my laptop. I'll call Jason at DPD and find out where they towed the Pink Thing for repairs."

It took them a good hour to drive to the repair shop. That in itself raised a red flag.

"Why would someone who lived in Uptown have their car towed to McKinney? That's just not logical, unless you have family or someone's doing you a favor." Kendall pulled on gloves before she began looking through Saundra's car. "And Saundra didn't have family."

"No one who works here has seen or heard of our victim. I didn't get the impression that any of them were lying. Did you?"

"No. Darn it. They seemed genuinely upset when you told them she'd been murdered."

"Um. I think that was because she owed them for the work they'd already started."

Kendall flipped the glovebox open. "Papers. Owner manual. Looks like she owned the car."

"She definitely liked pink." Heath continued to take pictures of sneakers, a sweater, T-shirts and running shorts, all in varying shades of pink.

Kendall leaned down to look under the passenger seat. "Candy wrappers, twenty-seven cents and an eraser."

"Eraser?"

"Yeah, it's Betty Boop. A fat Betty Boop, but I recognize the cartoon character." She set it on the seat cushion.

"Can I see that?" Heath asked after taking pictures.

Kendall handed it to him, and he pulled the head off to reveal a USB. "A flash drive?"

"*This* I can work with." He smiled from ear to ear.

"I bet they were looking for this at her place. Perhaps it's a connection to Public Exposure."

Heath took something from his jacket pocket and plugged it into his phone. Then he plugged the flash drive into it.

"I should probably warn you that we shouldn't look at the evidence yet." She waved at him to let her see the screen, too. "You're one of the only guys I know who carries a flash drive attachment for his phone."

"Hey, I resent that remark. I picked it up this morning from the ranch. This case is about computers." He shrugged. "Why wouldn't I?"

"That looks like a complicated encryption. Do you think you'll be able to break it?"

"Looks like it's going to be a tech thing after all. Yours or mine?" he asked.

"This time, I think I have to go with mine. They have a bigger department. If we connect Public Exposure to cybercrime, they'll put a rush on it. DC might get involved."

"Then our adventure would be over."

With the exception of one major thing—they needed a shred of proof for the big leagues to come on board. She didn't know why that was important to her. Maybe it was justification that she hadn't wasted six months of her time and taxpayer resources. Maybe it felt strange, and she wanted a solid explanation.

Or maybe she wanted a big break to boost her career. She couldn't tell. It was probably a little of all of the above.

"Maybe not yet. I'd like to flash this in front of Bryan Marrone to get his reaction."

"It's a long drive to Waco." He bagged their evidence.

"I asked Dallas PD to extradite him. He'll be here in the morning. Honestly, did you think I wouldn't?"

"Nope. Just hoping for more time with you. My couple of days is officially up." They spoke to others in the garage and waited on local law enforcement to take over the car.

"We make a pretty good team, Barlow." He touched the small of her back to guide her through the door first.

"That we do, Murray."

The official call came that Heath would be continuing with the case. The city of Dallas wanted someone local representing their interests.

Avoidance. Who was worse? Him or Kendall? Both of them took the opportunity to talk with as many other people as possible. Right up to the time they were in the SUV and they went over their plan to interview Marrone.

"I like watching you work. I always have." Blocks away from the house…his mouth finally caught up to his heart.

"Right. We only worked one case together."

"Hey, I watched from home."

"Right."

That tone…one of disbelief. Normally it was a good reason to stop and walk away to avoid what would follow. Not today.

"Kendall, I need you to believe me that I don't want you to stop working. Wait a minute before you do the psychological profile and get angry."

"Okay."

"See, I probably did mean it six months ago. But I don't know why. My mom has worked every day of my life. If it wasn't for her, things around me would never have happened. I know you're capable of handling everything."

Seconds ticked by but she wasn't angry. The emotion would have shown up in her movements.

"Then why?"

"I was scared. For you. For Skylar Dawn. Don't get

me wrong, I wanted another kid for the right reasons, but I wanted you around to protect all of us."

"Your dad?"

"Yeah," he squeaked the word out. "Things happen that are beyond our control. Dad is gone because he fell not because he chased criminals through the street."

"I wish you'd told me this earlier. Maybe…"

"It's hard for a man in my line of work to admit he's scared. Even though we know the risks."

They were in the driveway and in a good place. As much as he wanted to stay…she needed time.

"See you in the morning."

His wife waved from behind the wheel without looking at him. He didn't press for an answer just got in his truck. For the first time in months, he might get a good night's sleep.

Chapter 13

Kendall began her questions from the door and slowly moved closer, taking a chair and inching it even closer to invade Marrone's space. Several people watched from the two-way mirror. It was a classic technique.

"Come on, Bryan. We understand if you're scared." Kendall was an excellent interrogator. She had the Reid technique down pat. She'd planned this one down to the minute, or cue. "I mean, they killed your friend. Who wouldn't be scared?"

After she moved in close, after she commiserated, then Heath would enter and say they found proof that Marrone was guilty. They'd discussed exactly what he was to do while returning from McKinney the day before—and again this morning.

"Bryan, you've got to give me something to work with."

"Are you sure Saundra's dead?" He gulped. The

young man's Adam's apple moved up and down his thin neck.

"Yes, hon. I may be alone in thinking you're not guilty." She placed a hand on his knee. "None of my coworkers believe that you left town right after you saw us yesterday morning."

That was Heath's cue.

A light tap sounded on the door. He let himself in, and Kendall withdrew her hand with a guilty look.

"Special Agent Barlow, there's no reason to continue the questioning. The techs found this in Saundra Rosa's car. It proves that Marrone here is guilty. He has one, too."

Bryan might have been watching him toss the evidence bag onto the table, but both him and Kendall stared at the young man's reaction. Everything about his face screamed that he knew what was on the flash drive.

Then he relaxed. He sank down in the chair and acted like he couldn't have cared less what evidence they had. He knew. Whatever was on the flash drive, Marrone knew. It's what he'd been looking for in the apartment.

Kendall's tactics changed. She jumped up from her seat and grabbed the bag. "You know what this is, don't you?"

"You don't have anything on me 'cause you can't read that thing without the key. You'll never get the algorithm before we kick some ass around here."

"You'd rather go away for murder than tell us?"

"I'm innocent."

"Your fingerprints are on the syringe and once we—"

"No. They're not." He tried to bring his arms above his head, but the handcuffs jerked his hands back to the table. "I think I'd like my lawyer now."

They'd gotten nothing definitive. Kendall would be upset.

He wasn't. No one had called to tell him to remove himself from the investigation. That meant another day working with his wife.

Another day to work up the courage to tell her he wanted to come home.

"What do you say? Ready to go home?" Heath asked.

Not Kendall. She was ready to rework everything she had on Public Exposure. "What do you think he meant by 'before we kick some ass'?"

They left the county jail, changed cars and headed out. It was the first time she'd walked to the passenger door and let him drive their SUV home. But it was a silent ride while she scoured her notes, flipping page over page over page.

He didn't bring it to her attention that they'd arrived home. He grabbed his hat and made it to the steps before his daughter threw open the door.

"Daddy, make me fly." Skylar Dawn took a running start and leapt into his arms.

Heath had completely forgotten about his injured side. When she hit his ribs, a smoldering burn kicked into a bonfire of pain. He hid it as best as he could before he lifted his daughter into the air and spun her around like an airplane, complete with sputtering propeller noises.

It didn't last long.

"Hey, sweetie. Let me grab some jeans, then I can play in the backyard with you." Heath used his key and opened the front door.

"Skylar Dawn, come get your bunny and jacket," Kendall called from the car.

Maybe…just maybe she hadn't seen him. Either way, he needed a minute to catch his breath.

He rounded the corner, heading for his bedroom closet. He barely had his shirt unbuttoned and an old pair of jeans thrown on before his mother-in-law appeared in the doorway with laundry.

"Oh dear Lord. You scared me." The stack of clothes fell to the floor as she grabbed her chest with one hand. "What in the world are you doing here? It's Wednesday."

"It…it is my house, Naomi."

"No. You used to live here. It's not your night. Does Kendall know you're here?"

"You know we've been riding together." He bent and scooped up Kendall's laundry. "You're spoiling her by keeping everything together."

It was meant as a half-assed thank-you, but her expression turned deadly.

"I have the right to help my daughter and spoil her if I want. Someone needs to treat her nicely."

"I think I should head back outside." He tried to scoot around her, even with the laundry in his arms.

"I am dead set against you staying here. We have an arrangement and you're breaking it."

He dropped the laundry onto a dresser and turned back to the door. "I don't have an agreement with you, Naomi. There's not even a formal agreement between me and Kendall."

"I beg to differ."

"You can beg all you want, but as long as Kendall's comfortable with me at home, I'm staying. Now step aside, or I'll have to force you."

She did, cowering at the door as if he'd really threatened her.

Five years. For five years he'd been in the house, been around her. He'd never hurt her, and he hoped she knew that.

"I'm truly sorry you don't want to be around me. After all this time, nothing's going to change that." He returned to his walk-in closet, jerked an old T-shirt out of a drawer. "I'm going to play with my daughter now. You can go talk with yours or complain. Whatever you want."

She moved to Kendall's dresser. With her back to him, she began refolding the laundry. He couldn't let her obvious hatred bring him down. Tonight was a plus. An extra night to see his daughter. More time with Kendall, with the possibility of a discussion.

Skylar Dawn was putting things away in her bedroom as her mother had instructed. He wouldn't interrupt her. Pulling his phone out, he texted his own mother. He hadn't appreciated her enough for accepting Kendall as part of their family. He had it pretty good.

His dad may not be capable of remembering things, but his mom was a rock. Just a simple Love you went a long way with her. The return text was a smiley face and heart emoji.

"Your ribs are cracked, aren't they?" Kendall appeared with an armful of kid stuff, probably from various places throughout the house.

"Did I forget to mention that? Yeah, it happened Sunday." He raised his shirt and let her see the darkening bruises. "It's getting better. How did you know?"

"You winced when Skylar Dawn jumped into your arms." She playfully acted like she was about to leap into his arms, too. "Bulls or broncs?"

"Bronc. He caught me off guard. I was thinking about something else."

"Dare I ask? I've seen all those rodeo groupies." She leaned against the doorframe and shook off an offer to help. "Never mind. It's none of my business."

"Wait a minute." He lowered his voice to avoid little ears. "I have never—okay, I can't say never. But since I've met you, I haven't been attracted to anyone else. What about you?"

"Oh, it's not like no one's asked," she teased. "It's just…there's something about touching the person you're in love with. That same kind of touch doesn't come from anyone else."

She smiled thoughtfully. Or maybe wistfully. Words weren't his thing. He'd always used as few as possible. But he'd never thought about what she'd said before. He liked it. She was exactly right. No forbidden fruit was better than a touch from her. No one affected him like she did.

His baby was done putting away her toys. He rushed in the room, squeaking like a monkey. Then he acted like the Wicked Witch of the West from *The Wizard of Oz*, quoting some of the famous lines from the movie. Skylar Dawn quickly imitated the monkeys and wanted to fly like them.

Kendall joined them by cackling and doot-da-do-da-doing the witch's theme. They all collapsed on the twin-size bed, tickling each other. Naomi walked by without a smile. No longer angry, he was simply sorry she couldn't find joy or happiness. He recognized the feeling.

When he wasn't with his family, he felt the same way. The evening went off without a hiccup—not one phone call about Marrone's questioning or Saundra Rosa's murder. No additional complications from Naomi, who left for her own home before dinner. And no last-minute inquiries from work, for either of them.

Heath glanced at his girls, his ladies, his loves. He slid the bookmark into *The Wizard of Oz* and snapped a picture of the page to be able to pick up the story if he read from his place.

Dammit. This was his place. Not the room he used at the Thompson's ranch.

Kendall didn't stir when he picked Skylar Dawn up from her arms. He tucked his daughter in bed, making sure the night-light wasn't blocked by a Lego tower. He kissed her forehead one more time before leaving her door cracked a couple of inches.

She'd be four years old next week.

And he'd missed six months of the past year.

To get to the guest room, he had to cross through the living room again. Kendall had slid down the leather couch and curled into a ball. He reached for a blanket but then tossed it into the chair he'd vacated.

Cracked ribs didn't deter him from lifting her into his arms and carrying her to their king-size bed. He left her dressed, but pulled a light blanket on top of her. He kissed her forehead and got a smile—he could see it from the night-light she now had in their room.

And because he couldn't resist the beautiful temptress in front of him, he brushed her lips with his. He wouldn't be sleeping now. He could sit in her "perfect" chair that matched the "perfect" color of chocolate paint on the walls. Or he could lie down beside her.

Thunder rolled in the far distance as he watched the woman he loved sleep.

Chapter 14

Kendall woke with something all too familiar wrapped around her… Heath. Lightning flashed. A crack of thunder followed.

At some point, Heath had moved them to the bedroom. She'd slept through it. Well, she might have missed him holding her earlier, but not now. His strong arm dropped from her shoulder to her waist.

Perfect. Her world right that minute was perfect.

"You okay?" he whispered close to her hair. His voice was so soft that it wouldn't have woken her. "Want me to go?"

"No. It's too late," she whispered. "You'd just come right back first thing. Stay. But I should check on Skylar Dawn."

"I got it." His warmth left her side as he rolled off the bed behind her.

Heath yawned, using a lot of his vocal chords, as he often did. It always made her smile. His bare feet slid across the carpet, then *tap-tap-tapped* down the hall-way's wooden floor. Minutes slipped by. She closed her eyes, trying to reclaim the dream she'd been in. Heath returned, gently closing the door.

Another lightning bolt struck. The thunder answered more quickly. He sat in the chair they'd specially or-dered to match the paint and bedspread.

"I don't mind sleeping on the couch." He crooked an arm behind his head, supporting it. He still had his white undershirt on along with the rest of his clothes. Another bolt of lightning gleamed off his champion-ship-roping belt buckle.

Kendall pushed into a sitting position, letting the cover drop to her lap. "I need to get out of this blouse and bra."

"I could help with that if you're too tired." He was backlit by the glow of lights outside, so she relied on experience to know he grinned from ear to ear.

He wouldn't make the first move. He wouldn't say the first word, opening a conversation about what they really needed to discuss. When she'd suggested coun-seling six months ago, he'd told her talking had gotten them into this mess. Then he'd asked how it would get them out.

So far their week had been full of polite comments and—*dammit*—professionalism. Just like she'd insisted. God, she wanted to kiss him.

Wanted to lie next to his long body and be wrapped in his protectiveness. In five years, she'd never wanted to sleep alone. Before Heath, she'd never considered herself a cuddler. But she was. At least with him. And she missed it.

She threw back the covers and went to change. Their bathroom was in the opposite corner from where he sat. She didn't need the light to find the door or her things. Her pj's hung on the hook. She slipped them on and crawled across the giant king-size bed back to her side.

If she'd walked over to her husband—still sitting in the chair—she would have sat on his lap, tucked her legs to her chest and wrapped her arms around his solid-as-a-rock chest.

But she hadn't. She pulled the covers up to her breasts, just wishing she had. Wishing for a simple way to get out of the mess they found themselves in.

"You'll be grumpy all day tomorrow if you sleep in that chair."

"I promise not to be grumpy." Heath's nails scratched the stubble on his cheek before running his fingers through his golden brown hair. It was a familiar movement that made her shiver in anticipation. She knew what his chin felt like against the softness of her skin.

"If you don't want to sleep on your side of the bed, just say so." Okay, that came out a bit snippy, but at least she'd gotten it out.

"You scared of the dark now?"

"Oh, the night-light? Your daughter has been coming to sleep with me. I think it's because you let her sleep with you."

Heath cleared his throat. The sound of fingers moving across his scalp seemed super loud in the silence.

"I'd probably be better off on the couch if you don't want me to touch you. I won't be able to make any promises to stay on my half of the bed." His voice was husky and, ironically, full of all sorts of promises.

"I don't recall asking you for any."

"Good. 'Cause I ain't giving any."

The click of the door locking got her hopes up even further. She felt his tall, lean body move through the room instead of heading for the couch.

Kendall covered her mouth, concealing her happy grin. She heard the boots hit the floor—first one, then the other. Another pause where he removed his socks. Heath stood in front of her, pulled his undershirt off, then dropped his old, torn jeans.

He'd lost weight if they fell off that easily. Lightning flashed, outlining his excellent physique. Anything he'd lost had turned to muscle.

"I'll never get back to sleep," she said as he dove over her to land in the middle of the bed.

"Do you need more sleep?"

"Don't you?"

The rain started then, and not a gentle spring sprinkle—it came pounding as hard as her heart. Light from the storm hung in the room long enough for her to see his jaw clench.

"I don't think sleep's in the cards tonight."

God, she hoped not.

They faced each other, both with an elbow propping them up, arms curled around a pillow. She waited for him to make the first move. Had he been serious? Or just teasing? He shifted on the bed, and yearning shot through her entire body at the memory of him lying there.

His free hand reached toward her to catch one of her pajamas' bowed strings. He playfully tugged. Untied, the front of his favorite silky pajamas would fall open like it had many times before. She hadn't thought what that might mean by way of an invitation when she'd hurriedly tugged them on. And now? Now she wanted the invitation to be loud and clear.

An excruciatingly slow pull finally had her top gaping open. The soft glow from outside the windows and the occasional burst of lightning showed her white breast right down to a hard nipple poking the green silk.

She wanted to roll Heath onto his back and take over. He'd let her. She could do what she wanted. But the exquisite turn-on of his exploration was as good as the very first time they'd made love.

She already ached and wanted out of her clothes. She wanted him. And under his boxers, she could tell he wanted her, too.

He gently rubbed the back of a knuckle across her nipple, sending a current through her body. One knuckle turned into four skimming back and forth, making her breath catch.

A half smile brightened Heath's face as the back of his hand slid across her belly, then a veiled touch moved across the inside of her arm, making her shiver. He laughed—a small sound that was full of the fun from torturing her.

She began to do the same to him, but he stopped her, pulling her fingers to his lips and kissing them one by one.

"That's not really fair."

"Nothing about this is fair," he mumbled against the inside of her wrist.

"Hmm? I'm relaxed now and think I can drift off again."

"Is that a challenge?" he asked, already moving to a sitting position and then to the end of the bed.

"Oh, I don't know." She deliberately yawned and

lifted her arms above her head while turning on her back. "I'm seriously tired."

His hand wrapped around first one foot and then the other, dragging her entire body to line up with him at the end of the bed. "Toss it over here."

She slapped her hand backward on her headboard until she landed on the lotion bottle. Flipping it to him one-handed, she grinned to herself at how she'd obtained her foot massage.

Heath wasted no time kneading her tired feet, rubbing each part until she'd melted into the mattress.

"Would you relax?"

"I'm a marshmallow," she mumbled against the pillow.

"Only if the marshmallow's been in the sun and is all dried up." He tugged on her toes, wiggling them back and forth. But he was right. His strokes lengthened into long glides up her legs, with feather-soft kisses on the way back. His calloused fingers skimmed across her skin, exciting her entire body.

He stretched over her, capturing her hands above her head. Nuzzling the base of her neck, barely touching her with his lips, he then dragged the tip of his tongue to her shoulder. She wanted to squeal with delight at the way he caused her body to react.

She tugged at her hands and he let her go. She first pushed at his chest, then began to remove her pajama top. But his hands delayed her action, gently pushing her shoulders to the mattress.

All the while, the storm raged outside the thick-paned window. The lightning was more rapid now, followed by almost-constant rolling thunder. Rugged fingertips traced the outline of her pj top, dipping between her breasts to tease the delicate skin.

"You are absolutely beautiful." He fingered an errant strand of hair from her cheek. "I've missed you."

She parted her lips, about to quip that he'd been with her for four days, only to have Heath pull her quickly to him and slash his mouth across hers.

The temptation had been there each time they were close, but she'd held back. She'd missed kissing him. She didn't have to miss it anymore. They could figure out what would happen in the morning.

This very minute, she really needed him. All of him.

She stretched her arms around his back, wanting skin. Lots of skin. His body stretched on top of hers. He ran his hands down her sides, latching on to her hips and bringing them up to meet him.

He traced her collarbone with his mouth. "I love your legs. Love the fit of you against me." He emphasized his words by dropping his pelvis against hers.

Her mouth opened again and his tongue was there to pleasantly invade, dancing a dance that had stood the test of time. Without words, he invited her to join him.

Or maybe she'd been inviting him all along? She didn't care. She wanted her handsome man, and it was evident he wanted her. She slid her arms higher along his back. He quickly pushed himself up, taking the pressure of his chest from hers and lifting his back out of her reach. She immediately missed his warmth, his weight and…his everything.

His mouth seized her nipple through the silky material. He scraped his teeth gently over it, then captured her sensitive skin again. She bucked into him, wanting more. It didn't work. She could only accept the teasing and absorb the wonderful sensations building inside her.

Lying next to her again, he nudged her chin to turn

with his knuckle. Once more he held her close, kissing her hard and excitedly, then soft and invitingly. Her breathing was fast and ragged. She forced her mouth away, letting the scruff on his chin rub her cheek. She hooked a finger on each side of his boxers and inched them lower on his hips.

Distant thunder. A gleam of far-off light. He quirked an eyebrow, questioning her, stopping his own exploration through her silky pajamas.

Keeping her eyes locked with his, she moved her hands to skim the light dusting of hair across his ruggedly hard chest. Again he stopped her. Was that her hand trembling or his?

"It's okay," she crooned, trying to convince them both. Convince them that everything would be fine for him, and that she knew what she was doing.

"I can still walk away, Kendall. I won't think a thing about this. Well, that's not true. I'll be disappointed, but I can still make it to the couch right now."

"I don't want you to go," she whispered. Then she kissed him, a long luxurious kiss that she had a hard time pulling away from.

"Will you let me stay?" he asked, his voice cracking with emotion.

Stay? As in…stay more than just tonight? As in, come home? Her mind shouted at her that they needed to talk, but her body drowned out the argument.

What really mattered was that she needed him. Wanted him. Loved him.

"Stay."

Chapter 15

Kendall looped a toe in the waistband of Heath's boxers and tugged them off his hips. He drew his breath, stupidly about to object, until she placed her fingertips across his lips.

"Shh."

Then came cool, confident kisses across his chin and shoulders and collarbone. His arms were getting weak supporting himself above her body. The look on her face told him she felt him tremble. The teasing Cheshire cat smile that followed issued a challenge.

It didn't take much to knock his arms aside and force him to drop on top of her. She surrounded him with her arms, using her nails to scrape his flesh in a sexy way only she could accomplish. Immediately, she soothed his skin with the soft brush of her fingertips.

God, her touch charged him with energy, rejuvenating his soul.

His hands grasped both sides of Kendall's hips to remove her pajama bottoms, then quickly shot to cup her face as he got caught up kissing his woman.

His. Everything about her was his. Missing her kept him up at night.

Their tongues tangled a brief moment before Kendall twisted and sat on top of him in the blink of an eye.

"Now, where was I before you distracted me with all that luscious kissing?"

Her hair was still in the tight ponytail like it had been every day recently. He hadn't seen it loose, felt it flow over him, in what seemed like forever. He reached and pulled off the holder.

He captured her surprised mouth and attacked her lips. When she moved, the long lengths of her legs caressed him like the silk of her pajamas.

He grasped her slender hips, his thumbs inching their way to her intimate secrets. She urged him to please her, and when she begged for release, he hesitated, savoring the magic of the way she looked.

Darkness seemed to penetrate everything in the room, but it was the first time in months Heath felt surrounded by light. It followed Kendall wherever she was—especially now. Her eyes were soft, her breasts lush, and the tip of her tongue peeked out between her lips. One last touch, and she cried out her release. The first of many, he hoped.

Lightning flashed, and he soaked in every long curvy line of her. Determined he would take his time, he savored every second of them together. But as the thunder rolled closer, shaking the windows with its intensity, Kendall guided him inside.

He was home…all he could do was feel. An overwhelming amount of love rushed through him, taking him to the only place he wanted to be.

"Don't move," he told her. "Just give me—"

She moved.

In a single motion, he flipped her to her back and let her pebbled nipples rub against his chest. Their hands were everywhere. Roaming, searching and exploring after being apart for six long months. He wanted to memorize every subtle change, wanted to feel her hair—

Kendall tried to move to one side, but he kept her where she was. With very little maneuvering, he slid into her again until the rhythm took care of itself. Kendall pulled him to her until they climaxed like the first days they were together.

Satisfied beyond words, Heath shifted to his side of the bed, bunching a pillow under his head. Kendall turned on her side, propping herself half on him and half on the mattress.

"Storm's moving on." He noticed the lightning flashes were fewer and farther apart.

"I suppose you're tired."

Was that another invitation? He softly dragged his fingers up and down her leg. He loved her soft skin. "Not really."

She nuzzled his wrist. He nuzzled her neck in return. He laughed, and the sound was short but deep from his core. It was an excellent new start, even without an official apology from either of them. But there was plenty of time for that. Now that he would be around every day again.

"What did you have in mind?" he asked after she twined her legs around his.

"We could make up for lost time."

"Actually, I need some food before we go a second round." He twisted a little to get a look at her. "We didn't have dinner. Aren't you starving?"

"Oh." She pursed her lips together in a short pout and kissed him. "Mister, you talk entirely too much. Do you know that?" She turned over, scooting her body into a spooning position.

He'd missed his opportunity to make up for lost time. She was ready for sleep. His right arm was tugged over her body as she pulled her hair out of the way to rest on his left biceps. "Okay, yeah, I get it. You want to cuddle. I can handle that."

A deep type of hunger had been satiated by Kendall. He could wait until morning breakfast with Skylar Dawn to satisfy the other. No food was worth moving away from his wife. He enjoyed her this close.

Life was complete.

It was much earlier than anyone normally got up, but Heath didn't mind. He woke up and decided to run home for a different suit. But that didn't work. As soon as he was out of their bedroom, he heard Skylar Dawn reading under the covers.

Whether she was actually reading was still a mystery. She at least had the book she'd memorized last year with a flashlight pointed at it. She was reading all the parts with different voices for the mommy, daddy and little girl.

Since neither of them could head back to bed, he decided to make breakfast. He still had clean shirts hanging in his closet. Who needed a different suit when he had an opportunity to spend time with his daughter?

"Does MiMi have to pick me up?" Skylar Dawn asked between bites of scrambled eggs.

"Yes. Mommy and I still have to go to work." He flipped a Spanish omelet for Kendall.

"But I like it when you pick me up."

"Why? Want to get dirty?" He gently tapped her nose with his knuckle.

"No, silly." She pointed her fork at him. "We go see Stardust. I love my pony. Can we go today?"

"Sure thing. But we have to go to work first."

"I don't work." She giggled.

"You do your work at day care."

The oven timer began to ring in an old-fashioned buzz. He'd have to replace that ancient thing before long.

"Biscuits ready!" Skylar Dawn shouted.

Heath stuck the spatula over his lips. "Hey, Mom had a late night."

"Biscuits," his daughter whispered, pointing to the oven door. "I want cotton jelly."

"Cotton jelly it is." He laughed. Cotton was short for apricot. They'd all called it that since Skylar Dawn had first asked for it that way.

He spread the jelly on thick, and Skylar Dawn had it on both sides of her cute little mouth when Kendall came into the kitchen.

"What's this? Everybody's up so early." She kissed their daughter's forehead, swiping a finger of jelly off a sticky cheek before turning to him. "You made breakfast."

"Daddy made it special." Skylar Dawn pointed to the stove.

Heath rushed to the pan, pushing it off the burner before the omelet burned. "It's not much."

"I think it's super." She wet some paper towels and cleaned up their baby girl.

Why did he get the feeling something was wrong?

"Everything okay?" he asked, almost afraid of the answer.

"Go make your bed and brush your teeth. Then you can watch TV until it's time to go." She helped Skylar Dawn off the barstool and watched her leave the room.

Heath set down two plates with half of a badly formed omelet on each, then two cups of the single-serving coffee. Then he sat down himself. Kendall leaned against the wall leading to the open living room.

"Going to eat?"

"I'm not really hungry."

"We've got a full day today and might not have time for lunch. You might—"

"I can decide when I want to eat, Heath."

No need for guessing. She was upset. Maybe even angry.

He accidentally dropped his fork on the floor. He bent to get it, but Kendall beat him. She walked it to the sink and didn't turn around to face him.

"Maybe you should take your own advice and just tell me what you want, instead of writing a book in your head to find the best words."

"Okay." She spun around. "I've been offered a promotion. It's an opportunity to lead a cybercrime group."

"And it's in Portland." He should have known.

"How did you know? Oh, the phone call."

"Are you taking it?" His knees hadn't buckled. That was good.

"I… I don't know."

"Are you telling me about it or asking?"

"What do you mean?"

He pushed away from the bar, scooped up the plates and headed for the garbage. He no longer had an appetite either.

"Telling me means you're moving and asking me for a divorce." He rinsed and placed the plates in the dishwasher. "Asking me means you'd like me to come along."

"I haven't… I don't know yet."

"Are you asking or telling?" he pressed again.

He couldn't look at her or he'd lose it. Really lose it. As in yell that she couldn't go. He watched her reflection in the window as she covered her face with one hand and wrapped the other tight around her waist.

Exactly where his arm had been all night.

"If last night hadn't happened, how long would you have waited to tell me you were leaving?"

"That's not fair." She swallowed hard and faced the counter—away from him. "I need to think."

Fair? Think? What about his life had been fair in the past six months? He'd said what he felt at the time, before thinking it through. Before realizing that it hadn't been what he meant.

He wanted Kendall to quit work when *she* wanted to quit. He wanted her only to be happy. As many times as he'd told her that before he'd left, she obviously hadn't really believed him.

Heath didn't have words. How could they work with this hanging over their heads all day? He didn't know what to do.

The hell he didn't. He was taking the day off.

"You know, Kendall. I think this is the perfect day for Skylar Dawn to play hooky. Tell your mom she's got the weekend off."

"You can't—"

"Darlin', I can." He left the kitchen, calling to his daughter. "Skylar Dawn, change of plans. Get your boots, darlin'. Let's go see Stardust and Jupitar."

He got his daughter out of the house quickly by throwing a few things into her backpack and setting her on his hip.

When she asked, he told their girl that her mommy wasn't feeling well. It wasn't a lie. He was pretty sure that Kendall felt real bad about springing it on him like that.

Last night had been a natural reaction. Something neither of them had expected, but they'd both wanted it. Maybe she'd been conflicted. Maybe they shouldn't have made love.

He didn't have the answers, and apparently neither did Kendall.

Chapter 16

"Are we really staying here all weekend, Daddy?" Skylar Dawn kicked the ribs of her pony to keep up with his mare.

"Yepper doodles," he said in a bad cartoon duck voice.

She laughed. "And I get to ride Stardust every day? And not go to school? And I get to stay at the ranch house? And we get to order pizza?"

"Yeppers on everything, but I think Mama Thompson is making the dough. Then you can make your own pizza in her oven."

"I can put as much cheese on it as I want?"

"I'll leave that to Mama Thompson to decide."

"This is fun, Daddy."

"Yepper doodles."

She laughed at him again.

They'd gotten to the Thompson ranch early. He'd

taken care of feeding the other horses and had let Skylar Dawn feed the chickens. The Thompsons had come to the paddock to say hello and get their order for lunch.

Both adults had seen through his excuse that Kendall wasn't feeling well. They told him several times they'd be hanging around the ranch all weekend if he needed help. They'd had a short, knowing look with each other, then Slate's mom had told him she'd make all his favorites.

"Is Mama Thompson my grandmother?"

"Not really, darlin'. But she loves you like a granddaughter."

"I like it here."

By "here" she meant the Thompson ranch, large fields surrounded by trees that cut them off from the housing developments. A secret little stock pond full of catfish. Far enough away from the major roads a person couldn't tell they were twenty minutes from the Dallas suburbs.

He slowed Jupitar to a stop, letting Stardust have a little break. Tipping his hat, he shoved his hair back from his face. Maybe they should go for haircuts this afternoon. Or fishing. Skylar Dawn usually screamed and giggled at live bait, but she was surprisingly patient for an almost-four-year-old.

Shoot, she'd be four in nine days.

Skylar Dawn imitated him by taking off her little straw cowgirl hat, shoving her bangs back and securing it again on her cute little head. He'd been corrected more than once that she was a girl, not a boy.

"Fishing or the barber shop? Which do you want to do after pizza?"

He'd let Skylar Dawn decide. This was her day to play hooky and his to wonder about their future.

"Pizza, then Mr. Craig at the candy shop."

The old-fashioned barber pole looked like a candy cane. He didn't bother to correct her. It didn't matter. How many days would they have like this if Kendall moved them to Portland?

His wife would transfer, get the promotion she'd longed for. He'd have to seek out a new job in law enforcement. Go through more training, be reduced to rookie status—man, he didn't look forward to that.

Dad-blast it. He'd have to give up the horses. Moving them would be too hard. Paying for them even harder. His daughter was just getting the hang of riding, too. They were almost at the edge of the property.

Where had the time gone? Out of the corner of his eye, he caught Skylar Dawn rocking in the saddle. This was probably the longest she'd been in it. No matter, he'd let her ride with him on the way back. That would help.

"My, my, my," she said, sitting back in her saddle like him. "Have you and Mother had another fight?"

"What? Since when do you call Mommy 'Mother'?" He knew the answer. His mother-in-law always said "my, my, my," so this had to be her insistence on proper English. Never mind that. He needed to answer the real question. "Why do you think we had a fight?"

"You're acting funny, Daddy."

He guided Jupitar to face both Skylar Dawn and her little pony. What could he say to make her feel better? No lies. He refused to do it. But he also refused to make his daughter's life miserable.

"Hey, baby. Sometimes things go wrong. So, yeah, Mommy and I argued. But that doesn't mean we don't love you or each other. Remember that time you had a fight with Stacy? What was that about?"

"Bumble. She said he had a stupid name. We aren't supposed to say *stupid* in school."

"That's right. But you still went to play at her house that Saturday."

She nodded her sweet little head. "You and Mommy are still friends, too?"

"Always. No matter what."

"Okay." She shrugged, pulling the reins to go around him.

Dammit. No matter what happened…

Friends, lovers, parents. They'd always be all of those things. There was nothing else to think about. He'd follow Kendall to Portland. He'd live with her or live next door—whatever she wanted. Not just for Skylar Dawn. He'd be there for his wife until she told him differently.

"Daddy?"

Heath wiped the bit of raw emotion from his eyes. Putting a smile on his face, he looked Skylar Dawn in the eyes. "What, honey?"

"What's that?" She pointed behind him.

He turned in his saddle and saw a dust cloud.

Dust? After all the rain they'd had last night? Not dust. *Exhaust!*

"I don't know, sweetheart."

Woah. Engines. The sound of all-terrain vehicles echoed off the stock pond's built-up back containment wall. There were several of them. The Thompsons had only one.

This was not good. Something was off.

"Hey, baby girl, I think you need to ride with Daddy for a while." He guided Jupitar next to Stardust, then reached down to lift Skylar Dawn. Setting her in front of him, he looped his left arm around her.

"You're squeezing too tight, Daddy."

"We're going to go fast, baby. You like fast, right?"

"Yes!"

Excited, she grabbed Jupitar's mane, ready to fly. Now if he just had someplace to go. At the edge of the property, there weren't any back gates close by. Even if he had wire cutters in his back pocket, he couldn't cut the barbed wire before those four-wheelers caught up with him.

He kicked Jupitar into motion. The mud might slow down the men headed their way, but not his mare. She was as fast as the lightning that had cut across the sky in the early morning hours.

"Hang on, baby!"

He'd loped horses with his girl sitting there a couple of times, but not as fast as this. He tugged her to him even closer. There wasn't any doubt the vehicles were following them. Thank God he knew what he was doing.

Riding this land every day had him knowing just where to go. He could make it harder for them to follow. Lead them into small ditches that might be bogged down with mud.

"Stop before you hurt your daughter!"

What the hell?

A gunshot pierced the sound of the galloping hooves. He couldn't slow down enough to tell if they were really aiming at them or not. Mud shot up from Jupitar's legs. The wind whipped their faces as the sun beat down, warming them. His mare darted to the right, causing him to rise in his saddle.

Skylar Dawn screamed. "Daddy, slow down!"

"I can't, baby. I can't."

Public Exposure! The information they'd obtained must have scared them into going after all of Kendall's family. It was the only explanation. He hadn't been on any major Ranger cases. No one was after him. It had to be Brantley Lourdes.

"Haw!" he shouted to Jupitar.

No use trying to get his cell out of his back pocket. Both hands were occupied controlling Jupitar and holding on to Skylar Dawn.

If he could just make it back to the house...

That's when he saw another vehicle. He hadn't turned around to see how many four-wheelers had followed. They'd split up, boxing him in.

He could try to jump the fence, but Jupitar wasn't a jumper. More likely, she'd dump them over her head by coming to a full stop. The vehicle got closer. Two hooded men rode it. One carried a shotgun.

No choices.

No options.

"Whoa, girl." He pulled Jupitar to a stop.

"Daddy?"

He might have halted, but he didn't ease his grip on his daughter.

"First things first. Toss your cell on the ground. Careful-like. Make sure it's face up, and no monkey business." The voice was full of authority and came from behind him.

He slid his hand down the reins, lengthening his grip until he could reach behind him. He tossed it, forcing the man to get off the back of the ATV in front of Heath and pick it up. The man cracked the case, removed the SIM card and then threw it over the fence.

Jupitar startled. He whistled to get her under control. The man with the shotgun jumped off the ATV and pointed it at the horse. *No! Them.*

Skylar Dawn was between the barrel and his chest. There were too many, and he was unarmed. "Down on your own or we can pull you off of there, Ranger," the guy behind Heath said.

There was always the slim chance that the Thompsons had seen the ATVs come up the drive. A slim chance…but a chance nonetheless.

"I don't know who you are, but point the gun away from my daughter."

"There's one way this is going to go. Mine. If you do as I say, we'll be glad to point our weapons at only you. Now, get down," the guy behind him directed.

"I'm scared, Daddy." kylar Dawn had a death grip on his arm. "Why can't we see their faces?"

"It'll be okay, sweetheart."

"Only if you do as I say," the guy doing all the talking said.

"I can get him down," said the one still straddling the ATV in front of Heath.

"Come on, Heath, get off your high horse." A second man behind him chuckled. "Listen to me, or I'll have to kill you in front of your kid."

"Trauma does weird things to kids, man," a third voice said from behind him. "Just look at all of us."

They all laughed and agreed. Skylar Dawn began to cry. He couldn't turn around to see who was there. But looking toward the house, he could tell no one would come there in time to stop these men from doing what they wanted.

No choices.

No options.

Unsure exactly how much his daughter understood, Heath switched her around to face him. "Hold on to Daddy, hon." Her little hands latched behind his neck, and he kicked his leg around until it looped around the saddle horn. It was a tricky place to balance, especially with a small child.

"Steady, girl," he instructed Jupitar.

His left arm held his shaking daughter—who was holding it together much better than he'd ever thought possible. The other held the edge of his saddle. He needed something. Some type of defense. His fingers searched for his rope.

"Whoa there, partner," one of them said. "Keep your hands where we can see them."

"I have to get down, right?"

"Want me to get the girl, boss?"

"That's not necessary. Heath Murray is a champion cowboy. I bet he can slide to the ground from where he's at."

Heath's boots hit the ground, and his horse didn't move. He was out of stall tactics, out of ideas. What did they want? Was it a ploy to scare him or did they—

Stardust came into view, being led by yet another man in a mask. That made six he could now see. Three ATVs with two men each. None of them had identifying marks. No unusual clothing. He couldn't even tell skin color. They either had on goggles, or the skin around their eyes was blacked out like superheroes on TV.

"That's right, Heath. You're surrounded and have no options. Get her." The main guy pointed to one of the men and then to Heath's daughter.

Heath wanted to back up, to run. But the leader was right. He was surrounded.

"Hold on now!" he shouted and put Skylar Dawn's back toward Jupitar's neck. "Why are you doing this? What do you want?"

"Hell, Heath. I thought we were pretty clear about that. We want your daughter. We made a special trip out here and everything," he joked.

"Whatever reason you have for doing this, just tell me. We can come up with some kind of a deal."

"A Texas Ranger like you? Married to an FBI agent? I don't think so." He pointed again—this time at the man holding the shotgun. "Shoot the pony." The man swung the gun from Heath to Stardust.

He tried covering his daughter's eyes, but her little fingers tugged at his hand. She screamed. She twisted.

"No! Stop! Daddy, don't let them hurt Stardust!"

The man pumped a shell into the chamber. It didn't matter. He'd never drop his daughter. How could he?

Three men got to Heath. Two tugged his arms. The third tore his now-hysterical daughter from him. She screamed, "Daddy! Stardust! Don't you hurt them! Stop! Daddy! Help!"

One man locked Heath's arms behind his back. Another hit him. He threw them off. Tried to get to Skylar Dawn. She kicked and twisted herself and bit the man's wrist until she wiggled to the ground and ran. Heath ran after her but was tripped.

He fell, eating mud, as he yelled for his daughter. She was scooped up, her little legs still running through the air. Her hands in little fists beat on the leg of her attacker.

One of the men kicked him in the back of his head. Then again in his sore ribs. White-hot light radiated through every part of him as he heard the rib crack on the second kick. He tried to get his feet under him, but again the toe of a shoe hit him in the side. He began coughing, unable to catch his breath.

The ATV engines revved to life. He couldn't hear his daughter. Maybe because they had gagged her, or maybe because a buzzing sound was shooting between his ears.

One by one the engine sounds faded. He coughed, choked. He couldn't see because of the mud covering his face. Could feel only the pain from his heart breaking.

"Skylar Dawn," he called.

He wasn't alone. Something moved through the brush close to him. One of the men was still there—their leader. He grabbed Heath's shirt, dragging him to his feet and hitting him. How many times, he didn't know.

The world was just pain. It was worse than being trampled by a bull. Much worse. The leader shoved him to the ground. Heath couldn't move.

"We'll be in touch," the bastard said over him. "Follow our directions or you'll never see her again."

The third engine roared loudly to life and then faded across the field. Heath used his shoulder to get a bit of the mud from his eyes. He rolled, taking a long while to get to his knees.

"Oh God." He fought through the pain. Fought to stay awake.

If he could just get to Jupitar. And then what? He tripped over something on the ground and fell hard, taking the brunt of the fall with his chest. He couldn't scream. Couldn't call out. Could barely breathe.

His eyes focused on a small straw hat near his face.

"I'll find you, baby girl. And those bastards will pay."

Chapter 17

"Where is he? Come on, Heath. Pick up." Kendall looked at her phone as if it had the answer. Then she dialed Slate's number and quickly hung up when Jerry walked up.

"Glad you could get here so fast, Kendall." Jerry did a finger gesture pointing to her cell. "Is there something wrong? Having trouble with Heath?"

"No. Did you find something on the thumb drive?"

"Look, I was your partner a long time. It sounded like you were looking for your husband. Is he MIA or do you know where he is?"

"I'm sure everything's fine and he's not answering because he's knee-deep in muck at the ranch."

"Okay. There's nothing yet on the encryption. I came over to see how you were and tell you that you're needed in the conference room."

Jerry left but the creepy feeling didn't as she walked

to her summons. Something was wrong. People could call it whatever they wanted, but she just knew something was off.

"Thanks for coming in, Special Agent Barlow." Steve Woods opened the door to the conference room and gestured for her to sit. "Is Ranger Murray not with you?"

"No, sir. He had…obligations today." She hoped those obligations would allow him to call her soon.

"I wanted to introduce you to Agent Therese Ortis. She'll be taking over the Marrone interrogation. It seems your local complaints have backed into her ongoing investigation."

"Of Public Exposure?"

"Yes," Agent Ortis said. She stood at the other end of the room, arms crossed, mainly looking into a two-way mirror. "I can't go into many details. Sorry about that. I know how frustrating it can be."

Kendall had known from the beginning that the company she'd been investigating had ulterior motives. She just hadn't been able to connect anything except the local dots.

"We wanted you to know that Marrone was released late last night. His lawyer argued it was an illegal stop." The second-in-command of the Dallas field office took a step to the door.

"What about the parole violation? Didn't we have him on that?" She looked from one agent to the other. "This would be one of those things I can't know?"

"You did a good job," Agent Ortis acknowledged.

"Then why do I feel like I'm being punished?" She shook their hands. "Am I off the case?" she asked.

"Therese might have additional—"

"Actually, I'd like to work with Special Agent

Barlow—that is, with your permission—wherever I can." She crossed the room with her hand extended. "There are some things I won't be able to fill you in on. At least not yet."

"Thank you. I'd be glad to help." Her phone buzzed in her jacket pocket. "Is that all, sir?"

He nodded, and she left the room to answer. She returned to her desk and redialed Slate Thompson.

"Kendall?"

Finally. "I've been leaving messages everywhere. I need to talk—"

"Hey, yeah, about that. I got your messages and called the ranch. Mom took a look and found Stardust, Skylar Dawn's pony. She returned to the paddock. Alone. Then Jupitar ran up. I'm on my way there now. I'll call you as soon as I know anything."

It all happened in slow motion.

Kendall looked up to see agents running toward her. She hadn't realized she'd dropped to her knees, taking a stack of files to the floor with her.

Skylar Dawn was gone or hurt? Where was Heath? She'd known something was wrong. She couldn't speak. Her throat seemed to be connected to every part of her body and it was all shutting down, vital organ by vital organ. Someone helped her to stand, and she felt a chair at the back of her knees.

Voices talked over one another. Someone called for assistance. The room filled with men and women. All the dark suits seemed to fade to black.

Kendall took it all in, struggling to think. She stared at her colleagues. None of them could really help. She couldn't keep her daughter safe. Heath might be hurt.

"What happened?" Jerry asked. "Someone call a paramedic."

"Something's wrong. What if they took Skylar Dawn? Heath's… I don't know what's happened and I have a terrible feeling."

"Someone find out what she's talking about. And where the hell are the paramedics?"

"I'm not hurt. I have to get to the ranch." She shoved herself to her feet, rolling the chair backward, hitting someone who stood behind her.

"Kendall, you aren't making sense," someone said. She didn't know who, and didn't have time to figure it out.

She moved through a throng of agents, all clueless how to help. She did an about-face. "I need my Glock." She ran back to her desk and slid her weapon into its holster.

"You aren't going anywhere alone. I'll drive you. That's not a question. You aren't leaving without me." Jerry took her elbow and guided her from the building.

Again, time passed at a snail's pace. Couldn't Jerry drive faster?

Where was the fast-forward button? It had been only a blink of an eye since her daughter was born. One little skip, and now they were planning her fourth birthday party. She needed time to move at the same rate now.

Her phone vibrated in her pocket. "Heath?"

"It's me," Slate said. "Heath's unconscious. We've called for an ambulance."

"And Skylar Dawn?"

"She's not here."

"Are you arranging a search party?"

"Kendall, Heath was attacked. He's really bad off. We found tire tracks."

"Are you saying my daughter was kidnapped?"

There was a long pause. Jerry flipped the lights to warn cars to get out of the way.

"I'm on my way."

Sitting on the porch, Heath listened as Slate tried to issue orders indoors. Jerry Fisher and Major Clements were arguing. Both wanted their respective agencies to be in charge of the investigation. Law enforcement officers searched the area, but they wouldn't find anything. He'd told them that.

Skylar Dawn had been kidnapped by Public Exposure. No doubt in his mind about that. Two hours had passed, and still no word. Drained, his body ran on autopilot, sipping a cup of coffee Mama Thompson had put in his hands.

The idea that someone would hurt his daughter kept replaying in his mind, caught on an endless repeating loop. He couldn't stop it.

"Yes, Ranger Murray is conscious, but the kidnappers wore masks. He said there were six men." Slate was speaking to someone in the living room.

Heath had lost track. Everyone was involved. Local PD, Rangers, Public Safety, FBI Dallas and surrounding departments—they were holding off on issuing an Amber Alert. And he sat there…doing nothing except holding a cup of coffee. He couldn't bring himself to even drink.

"The paramedics said you should go to the hospital, son." Slate's dad laid a kind, gentle hand on his shoulder.

"I'm good."

"You need X-rays. What if you've punctured a lung

or something? What good will you be to your little girl then?"

Heath took a deep breath, letting it out slowly. His eyes met Kendall's. "Nope. I'm good."

He hadn't really spoken to Kendall. He hadn't told her he was sorry for not protecting Skylar Dawn. He took a sip. The breeze across the porch was cool today.

"Did someone find her hat?" he asked. The words came out, but he thought they sounded weird. Maybe it was a weird thing to worry about. "She's going to want her hat."

Kendall moved to sit next to him. "Her hat is with the little bit of evidence they found."

"I told all of them they didn't leave anything."

"They took seven sets of footprints, the ATV tire tracks. But nothing that will point us in the right direction."

"No one knew I was here, Kendall. I should have been working with you. Slate and his parents saw me this morning. That's it. I asked them not to mention us if you called. Sorry about that."

She shook her head.

"Why do you think it was Public Exposure?" Kendall's voice dropped to just above a whisper.

"It's logical after this week. They were organized. They listened to one guy. We know something's happening in their organization. You have the flash drive. They obviously don't want you to discover what's on it. Then they kidnap our daughter."

A cell phone rang. From across the porch, they heard Slate answer. "Ranger Thompson."

Slate ran over to them. "It's the kidnapper. He'll only talk to Heath. No speaker."

The bastard had his daughter. He wanted to curse, rant, say a hundred things, but he kept his mouth shut. Slate placed the phone in his hand.

"Ranger Murray?"

"I'm here. What do you want?"

"Your daughter or your wife. You choose."

During the long pause that followed, Heath wondered if the man had hung up. "You must choose, Ranger. Your daughter? Or your wife? Which will it be? I'll telephone again."

"Wait! Is Skylar—" The call disconnected. "Dammit!"

"What? What did he... Is she okay? Did she say anything?" Kendall stayed next to him.

Others gathered close. He wanted to tell Kendall that everything would be all right, but he didn't know if it was true. He desperately clung to whatever courage he had left. Courage that kept him from collapsing like a desperate father, while Kendall held it all together. Another mother would have fallen apart long before now.

"He wants me to choose between you and Skylar Dawn."

"There's no choice." Her gaze held his.

"You're damn right! I can't choose. I won't."

Kendall cupped his face. "I'm not asking you to. I already have. We're doing everything exactly as he says. We have to if we want to see Skylar Dawn again. She needs to be safe."

Half of him knew she meant it. The other half of him couldn't believe her logical, matter-of-fact response. None of him believed she would've asked such a thing of him.

"Right. How do we convince them?" He nodded toward the men scattered all over the Thompsons' lawn.

"Tell me again what he said. Word for word."

Heath sat on the porch and repeated the short phone call word for word. Then he sat in the living room and repeated it. Then he repeated the conversation in the dining room. He answered all the questions they asked with an "I don't know." He couldn't take it anymore. He grabbed Kendall's hand, leaning on her a bit more than his masculinity preferred.

They left the porch and the crowds. Kendall released his hand and draped his arm around her neck.

"Thanks. Not keeping my feet under me is kind of embarrassing."

People kept reminding him there'd been six men and a gun pointed at his daughter. Hearing it over and over didn't help.

"Where are we heading?" she asked.

"The barn. I don't think anyone's unsaddled Jupitar and Stardust."

"Okay." She didn't try to change his mind, but she did wrap her arm around his hip and take more of his weight.

They walked together and he gained more strength. It was better than sitting around, listening to the different law enforcement agencies argue about who was in charge. Bottom line—he and Kendall would decide how to move forward. Skylar Dawn was their little girl.

"It's going to be hard to fight the bad guys in my current physical condition."

She released him to lean on the corral rail, then pointed to his horses at the water trough. "I don't think you can unsaddle, feed and rub down both horses. But I bet Mr. Thompson would care for them."

"I'll ask him." He reached for his cell. "Dammit, they destroyed my phone. It's somewhere in the neighbor's field, or collected for evidence."

"Sorry, the FBI took mine to trace any possible incoming calls."

"You know that I'm... It was my fault. I'm the one who's sorry." He cupped her face with his hands, staring into the sadness in her eyes. "If only I hadn't brought her here. There just wasn't anything I could do when they showed up."

She wrapped her hands around his wrists, holding him where he was. "I know. We all know. My God, Heath, there were six of them. You're lucky to be alive."

"If anything happens to her..."

"You heard what the kidnappers said. They wouldn't have said anything about me unless I'm the one they really want." She cupped his cheeks like he still held hers. "Promise me you'll go after Skylar Dawn. You do whatever they tell you to do and find her."

She looked at him expectantly. He nodded. The promise just wouldn't come. He'd find a way. He had to.

"Do you hear that?" he asked.

"It sounds like a cell phone. Wait here."

Kendall ran into the barn. Then grabbed Stardust, leading her inside. He waited. The barn had been cleared by three agencies. Nothing would harm her there. It was easier than attempting to catch up. Physically, he felt better than he had two hours ago, but he needed time to recover—something they didn't have much of.

"Heath!" she called.

He limped his way through the door and heard the

cell phone. It was tucked under the edge of Skylar Dawn's saddle.

"There are clear bags in the tack room." He pointed.

"Do you think it's them?" She ran, shouting over her shoulder.

"It has to be. None of the men clearing the scene would have left their cell."

Once back, she carefully slid the phone from the pony as he lifted the saddle.

"We have a choice here, Heath. We answer it and move forward, possibly on our own. Or we let the FBI set up the trace and answer it the next time it rings. And to be honest… I don't know which is the best way to go."

"Does it say there are any missed calls?"

"Not that I can see, but that doesn't mean anything, Heath. It might not be programmed to show that. How could all those agents have missed this?"

The phone stopped ringing. He shrugged while looking into the corners of the barn. He couldn't see anything. There were too many places to look for hidden cameras. But he knew.

"They're watching us, Kendall. I can feel it. They were here." He pointed to his feet. "Probably here in the barn. They waited for one of us to come here to the barn to call."

"You can't be sure—"

The phone rang again. He stretched for the plastic-covered cell.

She met his hand with her own, reaching across Stardust. "That was the FBI agent talking. Kendall Barlow trusts you." She scooted the ringing phone out of the plastic enough to push the green answer button and then speaker.

"It's about time," the same voice from earlier said. "I've got a couple of errands for you. There won't be another call, so you better remember. You with me?"

"Yes," they both answered.

"There are no exceptions. Keep this phone. I'll call you tonight to give you further instructions. You'll need a black suit and a bright red dress. No exceptions. There's a wedding reception at the Anatole Hotel tonight. Be there."

The phone went dead, and they stared at each other.

"They'll never let us do this on our own."

"This guy didn't even ask us not to involve the cops." As inconspicuously as possible, he looked around the barn again.

"It would be impossible to assume we wouldn't find a way."

"Kendall, he didn't ask for anything."

"Except me."

The grip they both had on each other's hand was rock solid. They hadn't been unified in a long time, but there wasn't any question they were now. They'd follow the kidnapper's instructions. They'd get their little girl back.

And somehow, he'd save Kendall, too.

Chapter 18

Fancy red dress? Check. Black suit, white dress shirt? Check. Boots for the suit? On Heath's feet. Small clutch purse with the Cherry Bomb lipstick she'd bought ages ago to match the dress? Check.

Jeans and T-shirts for them both...just in case. And a change of clothes for her daughter. Red high heels?

"Mother, where are my red high heels?" In a flash, she remembered that Heath had given those to Company B to attach a tracker. "Never mind."

Everything was beside their bag. Just like it was supposed to be. She went over the list a second time, unable to accept that it was complete. It was a simple list and a simple task. Her mother had pulled everything together and laid it out on the end of Kendall's bed.

Their bed—hers and Heath's.

In spite of checking the list twice—make that three

times—she had the nagging feeling that she had forgotten something.

"You're forgetting your jewelry," her mother said, coming up behind her and sniffing into her tissue. "You really shouldn't go to a wedding without any jewelry. It will look odd."

"That's it." She removed her wedding rings and walked to her vanity to put them away.

"I meant that you can't attend an evening wedding without jewelry, darling. Not to take your rings off."

"I don't want to lose them."

She dropped her ring set on the porcelain hand Skylar Dawn had given to her. Or, more accurately, Heath had given it to her for her first Mother's Day gift.

"Would they do that? They'd not only kidnap your daughter, they'd steal your wedding rings?"

"I don't know what they'll do, Mother. This is a first for me, too."

Her mother gathered the extra clothes she'd set out, placing them in a garment bag. Kendall couldn't remember owning one. Taking a step toward the door she stopped herself. She'd been heading to Skylar Dawn's room again.

It was silly how long she'd just sat there, staring at the half-built Lego castle. She wanted to finish it for her daughter. But they were working on it together. She couldn't touch a piece without Skylar Dawn telling her where it went. That was the rule.

Kendall returned to her vanity instead and reapplied her eye makeup. It was getting close to the time Heath's partner would pick them up. She should go check on him. But twenty minutes ago, he'd drifted fitfully off to sleep. Obviously still in pain, but refusing to take anything that would impair his judgment.

Her mother watched from the doorway of the bathroom. She was sighing a lot, a cue that she wanted to say something.

"Thanks for staying here, Mother. There will be agents outside. You'll be perfectly safe."

"I'm not worried about that." She lifted a finger, indicating that Kendall should join her in the bedroom.

A sinking feeling hit between her shoulders. She wouldn't like what her mother was about to say. "Are you sure this can't wait, Mother?"

"You've got plenty of time, I think. Heath isn't awake yet."

"It might be better—"

"I need you to promise me something, dear."

"I promise I won't do anything stupid." Used to this promise, Kendall said it without thinking much about it. Her mother required it every week or so. Did it matter that this time she didn't believe that anything would truly keep her out of harm's way tonight?

"No, dear. I need you to promise that when you bring my granddaughter back to me, you'll finally restrict that man's visitation to supervisory visits only."

She could only stare at her mother.

What?

Helpless. Stunned. She couldn't think of words. Her daughter had been taken in order to draw her out without a fight. She might not ever see her baby again. Might not see anyone again for that matter. The demand from her mother struck her as ridiculous.

"I don't understand, Mother."

Naomi Barlow perched on the edge of the chair,

prime and proper with her hands on her knees. "You can't trust that man. This would never have happened if Skylar Dawn had been here, where she belonged."

"They would have taken her from day care or even here. There's no telling how many additional people would have been hurt if that had happened. This is not Heath's fault. How can you blame him?"

"He comes and goes as he pleases."

"It's his house."

"I know he spent last night in this room and not the guest room."

"This is not the time, Mother."

"He took our girl without even telling you where he was going, disrupting her routine."

"Getting her dirty?" The deep voice came from the doorway.

Kendall sent a look telling him to cool it. But she didn't blame him. A lot had happened. Just a few days earlier, her mother hadn't allowed him to say good-night to his daughter. And before they could bring their baby home Naomi wanted her to commit to what? A divorce?

Heath did a one-eighty and left. She wanted to follow, but enough was enough.

"Heath is my husband, Mother. He's the father of my child. If anything happens to me tonight, he has the right to limit your involvement in Skylar Dawn's life. And frankly, I wouldn't blame him. I can't believe you could even think about cutting him out of our lives. How could you?" She headed for the door, but her mother's sobbing stopped her.

"Oh my goodness. I… This can't be happening. It just can't be happening." Her mother cried for real now.

"But it is, Mom. It's not Heath's fault. There were

six men attacking him. He could have been killed." She lowered her voice, almost choking to get the words out. "I… I thought he was dead. I would never have forgiven myself."

She turned quickly to hide the tears. Her gaze fixed on her engagement ring. She'd never planned to marry. Everything about her life had been about joining the FBI. As a little kid, she'd always thought she'd find her father. She'd quickly outgrown that idea as she went through high school and college, each course chosen as a precursor to joining the academy. Every extracurricular activity was carefully chosen for the same reason.

She'd run cross-country for stamina. Even been on the college wrestling team. She'd been in such control of her future, securing the job with the FBI. Then she'd met Heath, and everything had changed.

No more rigid control. Instead, there was joy. Fun. He made her laugh. He made her live. When Skylar Dawn had joined them, she couldn't imagine anything that might be missing. And now…

"If something happens to her, life won't be possible."

"It'll be okay, dear." Her mother gently patted her back. "I shouldn't have said anything, but I know you'll bring our darling girl home safe and sound."

"You don't know that," Kendall whispered.

She'd been in such control of her future, of her life. Now she was helpless. Absolutely helpless.

Facing her mother, she closed her eyes for a second to strengthen her resolve. Now wasn't the time, but her mother had pushed the issue. When she looked at her mom again, Naomi was crying.

It was totally unexpected. Her mother didn't cry.

Not real tears. She sniffed, stayed stoic and normally didn't show emotion.

"Mother, what's the real reason Dad left?"

Naomi looked taken off guard. "I don't believe that's any of your business. Especially right now."

Kendall didn't want to tell her why the thought had popped into her head. Or that she'd known there would never be an answer. It had been a foolish thirteen-year-old's dream to find him. That hope had long been abandoned.

At first she'd blamed herself, but soon her disappointment had shifted to acceptance. Heath had once asked her why she tolerated so much from her mother. Kendall had never pinpointed the answer until right that minute.

Without her and Skylar Dawn, her mother was alone.

Sitting here, listening to her hatred of Heath… Kendall couldn't take it anymore. No matter what happened, he'd always be Skylar Dawn's daddy. Clearly upset, her mother sniffed then patted her eyes with the tissue again.

"I… I'm sorry, Mother. I really do appreciate all the help you've given us—"

"That's what I'm here for, dear."

"Let me finish." She took her mother's hand between her own. "Because of your anger and bitterness, I almost threw out the best thing that ever happened to me."

"That's not true. *He* left. He walked out on you. And now—"

"I'm sure Heath's going to get your granddaughter back home safely. Like I said…if anything happens to me, Skylar Dawn is his daughter. You might want to rethink how you treat him. I know I am."

"Even if he runs to his mother when things get rough?"

"What are you talking about? Are you saying that you overheard him talking to his mother about us? About our problems?"

"I told you that, dear." The tears were gone as if they'd been calculated the entire time.

She wouldn't have gone that far. Would she? Had she deliberately said the one thing she'd confided that hurt Kendall the most? All these months she'd believed Heath had been confiding in another Ranger and shared their problems with the world instead of her.

"Fair warning, Mother. Things will be changing around here when this is all done. You should begin getting used to that idea."

"It's time to get ready," Heath said from down the hall. "Slate's on his way."

Heath tapped on their bedroom door, slipped inside and retrieved his suit. Kendall had been right. It wasn't the time to talk. But there would be a discussion when Skylar Dawn came home.

First and most importantly, his focus had to be on his daughter. The kidnapper said he'd have to choose between them. He'd spent the last three hours staring at the ceiling, his head throbbing, his side screaming that he shouldn't move. His mind was caught in a loop that there was no choice.

No man could choose between his wife or daughter.

Maybe it would be easier to think about his mother-in-law problem? But that didn't take much thinking. Naomi Barlow didn't believe he was good enough for her daughter. A simple cowboy from a failing Southwest Texas ranch would never be good enough.

A Texas Ranger who loved her daughter and granddaughter more than his own life would never be good enough. Not for her. He couldn't change her mind, and he needed to accept it. If he didn't, he'd lose Kendall.

If he didn't lose her today.

Stubborn and smart, his wife would do everything in her power to return home.

She wanted a promise that he'd do whatever the kidnappers said. He couldn't and wouldn't make that promise to her. He trusted that he'd know what to do when the time came.

He was stubborn and smart, too.

After dressing, he opened the front door and checked on the Rangers from Company F, one in a truck and one on the porch. But the man on the porch wasn't in the traditional suit and tie. Tonight Bryce Johnson was dressed in jeans so he'd blend into the neighborhood.

"Just wanted to let you know that Slate's on his way. I assume no one's been sneaking around or watching the house. You guys need anything?"

"We've got you covered, Heath. Don't mind us," Bryce said, standing and shaking his hand. "You guys were there for Major Parker when the twins were kidnapped. Don't worry about anything here."

"I meant to ask when you got here. How's everyone doing in Waco?"

"We're all good. You let us know if *you* need anything. We're here for you, man." Bryce pumped his hand again, and also clapped him on the shoulder.

"Before I head back in, you got the cell numbers of my team. Right?"

"Wade supplied us with everything we need to keep apprised of the situation. If you need any help, just let us know. Otherwise, I can guarantee you that no one's getting in this house."

This time Heath slapped Bryce on the back. "I don't think we've caught up since that advanced computer stuff in Austin two years ago. We should compare notes again soon."

Bryce nodded.

Heath was ready. At least, he was cleaned up and dressed. He hadn't retrieved his black boots from his closet yet. He rarely wore them, except for special occasions.

He stumbled into the wall, his breath leaving him suddenly. Like he'd been hit again. Skylar Dawn had been kidnapped. He shook himself to regain control. He couldn't lose it. Not now. Not until it was over.

"Are you okay?" Kendall asked. "Do I need to call the doctor?"

Damn, she was beautiful. Dressed and ready to go, with the exception of her shoes. With that dress she should have a smile on her face. Her look of concern seemed out of place—but warranted. He was pretty certain he looked like he needed a doctor.

"No, thanks. I got it." He stood, grabbing his midsection, letting her believe the panic he'd experienced was just his sore ribs. "I got a look at my face, though. Looks like the beauty will be attending the reception with a beast."

He pointed to the split on his cheekbone held together with Steri-Strips. The bruise around it had already begun to blacken. He tried to joke, but he honestly couldn't have laughed if he tried.

God, he hoped he could do whatever was necessary tonight. *No!* He would push through the pain and get it done, no matter what it took.

"How much did you hear of the conversation with my mother?"

"You were right. This isn't the best time for that particular talk." He stood straight, keeping his breathing as shallow as possible. "Right now, I need to switch to my dress boots. These look weird with this black suit."

"Sit down. I'll get them."

As soon as she left the front hallway, he hobbled to the couch and eased himself onto it. She returned faster than he could move and caught him just as he leaned against the cushions.

"Maybe we should get a stand-in for you."

"That's not happening, Kendall. I'm resting now, but I'd never forgive myself if something happened and I stayed on the sidelines. You know you'd feel the same."

"It was worth a try. But you're right. I would push through all the pain to do my part." She dropped the boots on the floor. "There is one thing I can help with—getting these boots off and the others on."

"I won't let you or Skylar Dawn down, Kendall."

"No matter what happens, I don't and I won't blame you." She slipped the first boot off. "This is the result of my investigation, not yours. It's exactly what I feared most."

"I remember the multiple conversations about not having kids because we both had dangerous jobs. I meant every word back then just as much as you." He caught his breath from the pain as he forgot to brace himself when she tugged the second boot free. "I don't regret the decision to have our daughter, though. No matter what happens."

She took his hand into hers. "Neither do I. Never. And I'm sorry for what Mother implied."

"Later. But while we have a moment—"

"Ding-dong," Slate interrupted, letting himself inside. "How ya doing, partner?"

Heath waved him off. He wouldn't answer every person who asked him that question. Otherwise he'd be reliving the experience every other minute. It was better to concentrate on the task at hand—rescuing Skylar Dawn.

"Did you bring the phones?" Heath asked.

"Phones? We only need the phone he left in the barn." She looked to both men. "What did you have in mind?"

"This guy is probably going to ask you to drop the phone he gave you. Why not drop two that are old and useless?" Slate said.

"That actually makes a lot of sense. I spent some of the time Heath rested moving pictures off this thing." She set her cell on the coffee table. "That's really smart. Thanks, Slate."

"I wish I could take credit. Totally your husband's idea after his was destroyed." He handed her a grocery sack. "Here are your shoes. Best the techs could do quickly."

"I'm still against this idea. It's likely that the kidnapper will have a wand or something."

Heath raised an eyebrow. "Whatever it takes?"

"Right." She slipped both shoes on her feet. "It's worth the try. They may not actually be as smart as us."

"So what we did is clone your phones." Slate pointed

to the two older versions. "If the kidnappers call your number instead of the phone they left, we'll still be covered. And just in case they allow you to keep the phones, we have you covered with a tracker. Reception begins at seven. Are you guys ready?"

"Give us a minute."

"Sure, man. I'll be in the van."

Heath waited for the door to click closed. He pulled both boots almost all the way on, then stood, slipping them on the rest of the way. When he was done, Kendall threw her arms around his shoulders.

"No matter what—" she kissed his cheek "—I love you and Skylar Dawn more than anything in my life. You two are the most important things in my life. The best things that ever happened to me."

"You took the words right from my heart."

Chapter 19

"Want to dance?" Heath asked her to ease the tension between not only everyone watching them, but the two of them. With his injuries he could only sway. Kendall gently wrapped her arms around his neck. Maybe they'd have a moment to finish talking about the thoughts that had run through his head while he'd been in the living room and van.

"Dammit, Heath, you can't take off like that," Slate said from behind him.

They both ignored him. Kendall drew a deep breath and said, "I need to say something."

He looked at her seeing no one else. Beautiful eyes filled with tears but didn't overflow. Then she blinked them away.

"I'm sorry."

"What?" He was confused. Why would she be sorry? He's the one who lost their daughter.

"Before you moved out, Mother told me she over-heard you talking about our problems on the phone. I was angry you'd talk with someone else and not a counselor."

"Just Mom."

"I realize that now. I should have known."

"I should have told you."

They swayed into the middle of the temporary dance floor at a wedding reception they weren't supposed to be attending. Thinking about wedding vows really hit him in a vulnerable place. No way would he admit that to anyone. But the reminder did its job. Who was he to decide which of their careers was more important?

If she'd have him...he would move to Portland. He bent his head, kissing her neck sweetly, just to remind her he was there. She tilted her face, her eyes closed. For a moment he forgot where they were as his lips softly captured hers. He meant it as a comforting kiss, almost a farewell in case something happened to them.

But Kendall changed it. She kissed him longingly and then drew away, breathless. His body was on fire from the brief encounter.

"You shouldn't kiss me like that," he said into her hair.

"Uh-huh," she mumbled with her head on his shoulder, her breath softly caressing the small hairs on his neck.

"I wish Skylar Dawn was safely at home. Then I could spin you around the dance floor until we forgot all our problems," Heath whispered in her ear. He turned and brought her body closer still, holding the small of her back firmly under his hands.

"I don't need a dance floor to forget," she said, barely

loud enough for him to hear. "I want to be a family again, Heath."

A tap on his shoulder stopped his reply. Slate interrupted, handing him a cell phone.

"It's on mute. But this is our guy. He called me instead of the burner or either of you. He knew it would take us longer to get a lock on him."

They all moved off the dance floor. Slate tactfully blocked anyone from approaching so he could answer the call in semi-private.

"This is Murray."

"Drop your phones in the lobby fountain. A cab's waiting for you. You have four minutes to be at the northwest corner of Elm and Houston. Don't speak or signal the others with you at the reception. Keep the line open, Ranger Murray. You don't want to endanger your daughter."

"Where do we go?"

"I don't repeat myself, Ranger. Take this phone with you and don't disconnect. I'll be monitoring your progress to verify you're following my instructions. Drop your cells in the large fountain on your way out the door. You have four minutes."

The line went silent. Heath was careful not to push the end button. He grabbed Kendall's hand and pulled her toward the lobby.

"That was him?"

"Yeah. We have four minutes to get to Elm and Houston." He dropped the old cell Slate had given him into the fountain. Kendall took her fake phone from her clutch purse and did the same.

"Where are you going?"

He pushed through the revolving door and asked the doorman, "Do you have a cab waiting?"

"I have one for Heath and Kendall."

"That's us." Heath turned to her, pointing to the cell screen to show that the call was still active. "We agreed to do everything exactly as he said. We have four minutes to get there." He put his arm around her, tugging her close. "We might make it if we're lucky."

"One swipe with a wand and the shoes are blown," she whispered close to his ear in order not to be picked up by the phone.

"The guy told me Elm and Houston," the driver said. "Any particular corner?"

"Northwest. There's extra if you get us there in three minutes," Heath told the driver.

"No problem if you let me drop you. The actual corner requires me to circle 'round."

"Fine. Why did he give us only four minutes to get there?" he asked softly. He dropped a twenty on the front seat.

"He had to be watching us. Now we don't have time to contact any of the agencies watching us." Her eyes went to the cell in his hand.

"He told me not to disconnect." He listened to the phone. "Nothing. He's listening and keeping us from contacting anyone."

"He'll probably have another cell waiting for us. We'll jump to another location. He'll try to lose our tail before we can do anything about it. Did you recognize his voice? Could it be Marrone? A high-paid lawyer got him released."

"No, it was the same guy as this morning, but not Marrone."

In a louder voice Kendall asked the cab driver, "How far are we?"

"Just two more turns. You sure are in a hurry to see the grassy knoll."

"The grassy knoll?" they both asked.

"Yeah, man. Elm and Houston is where Kennedy got shot," said the cab driver.

"I didn't recognize the street names." Kendall pressed her fingers to her temple. "That means people, as in tourists."

"Very good, Ranger," said a distant voice and Heath brought Slate's phone to his ear again. "Continue on Elm. The phone's under the tracks. Don't forget to leave your partner's cell in the cab."

"This is going to sound strange, but we need to continue on Elm and be dropped on the other side of the rail overpass," Heath repeated to the cab driver.

"I can't stop there, man. It's a blind curve." The cabby stuck out his hand waiting for extra cash.

"Pull up on the sidewalk," Kendall told him. They left the cab and the phone. "What else did he say?"

The sky was clear, and he could see a few of the brightest stars in the sky. They crossed the dangerous street as fast as they could. Their four minutes were up.

"Hey!" a man shouted from the opposite side of six lanes. "Are you Heath and Kendall?"

"Yes!" they shouted across the busy six lanes of traffic.

"This guy on the phone said to head for the stairs back there." He lowered a cell onto the ledge and pointed toward the way they had come. "Damn. I'm calling the cops. That guy said he'd kill me if I didn't yell for you."

Avoiding oncoming traffic, they moved further

into the underpass and ran across Commerce and Elm streets.

"Good grief, the stench." Kendall covered her nose with her hand.

"It smells like a hundred elephants from the circus relieved themselves."

"I can't believe you're making jokes."

"I thought I was being factual." He guided her along the narrow sidewalk toward the cell.

"We're sitting ducks, you know. The kidnapper has cut us off from our backup with all these one-way streets. We're on a dark walkway that might as well be a tunnel. The car trailing us passed without ever slowing down. We can't be sure they saw us at all."

They exited the semi-tunnel. How many times had he driven through here and not taken a serious look. They both drew clean air deep into their lungs. Heath searched Dealy Plaza on the edge of the city of Dallas. Very few people walked the sidewalks, but the kidnapper could be any one of them.

"How long 'til they realize we're not in the cab?" she asked.

"Until the cab stops for the FBI. Slate will be trailing your shoes. They'll hang back long enough to make it look like they lost us."

The phone rang as they approached the ledge, making it easy to find.

"Walk north through the parking lot, turn east, cross Houston Street, and follow the light rail on Pacific Avenue. Make your way to the West End Marketplace. Don't borrow any phone along the way, Murray. We're watching."

"This way." Heath guided Kendall past a picket fence to the parking lot for the Kennedy Museum.

Mental pictures of President Kennedy's assassination invaded his thoughts. If the kidnapper wanted to give them a feeling of doom, he'd succeeded.

"He more than likely is watching us. What now?" she asked.

"We're to go to the West End."

They began the trek, following the kidnapper's instructions. The light rail street was closed to cars and had no pedestrians.

"At least he can't hear us now," Heath said.

"You hope." She nodded toward the phone. "Try that yet?"

"Password protected. I can answer, but can't dial."

"Figures." Kendall stepped around a shattered beer bottle. She grabbed his hand, causing him to stop and look at her. "Remember your promise to let me handle the kidnapper. You get Skylar Dawn to safety. That's the only thing you need to do."

His tug on her hand got her walking again. "That dress is beautiful. I haven't seen you wear that since we had a night out three years ago. Wow. It's really been that long?"

At his change of subject, she dropped his hand. "You promised, Heath."

"Not exactly. I told you I wouldn't choose. Let's get there and find Skylar Dawn."

He caught her hand in his, seeking anyone out of the ordinary. People walked in both directions. It was a beautiful spring evening to be strolling the West End. And it seemed like everyone was.

They rounded a corner onto Market Street, which

was full of people. They headed toward an open court-yard where a band played. The phone rang, slicing through the dull roar of the street noise. Before he could pull it from his pocket, Kendall stepped in front of him.

"There is no choice, Heath. Skylar Dawn needs you. I know how to handle this creep. Leave him to me."

Keeping his eyes on her face, he brought the phone to his ear as it rang. "Yeah?"

"It is time to choose, Ranger. Your wife or your child."

"Where's Skylar Dawn?"

"She'll be safe for twenty more minutes."

"Damn it, man! What do you want?"

"Your wife. I can see you both. Send her to the Dallas Aquarium. I'll call again to tell you where the girl is when I have your wife."

The line went dead.

"Did he say where Skylar Dawn is?"

He shook his head, frustration keeping him momentarily silent. "I'm supposed to stay here, wait for his call. He'll let me know where to pick up Skylar Dawn after he has you."

"Don't worry about me, Heath. I'm trusting you to find our daughter."

"He wants you to start walking toward the aquarium," he said, pointing behind her toward the building.

They'd taken Skylar Dawn there several times. Seeing the endangered animals section was her second favorite thing to do. The first was riding Stardust.

"You can do this." She squeezed his hand, pushing the phone to his chest.

"I'm not worried about me. He's…"

There wasn't enough time to explain what he wanted

her to know. He should have answered her before they left the dance floor. She was walking straight into the hands of a madman, with a strong possibility they'd never see each other again.

"Come back to me, Kendall."

She turned to walk away, but he caught her off guard and pulled her into his arms. His lips claimed hers with the hunger of a starving man, the desperation of a defeated one. He'd never known a kiss so transparent. He'd never experienced a kiss filled with regret and longing. Regret for what might have been and longing for what might never be.

His wife pulled slowly away, her free hand cupping his cheek.

"I wish you had a gun or I could send backup. Something." His voice rose in frustration. "I can't just let you turn yourself over to him."

"He's watching. I've got to go, Heath. Find our girl."

She lifted his fingers from her arm and kissed him one last time. Then she put one foot in front of the other and walked away from him. Stopping himself from following was pretty much the hardest thing he'd done in his life.

Chapter 20

Heath stood there until she was out of sight. He shoved the phone in his back pocket then ran into the crowd gathered and enjoying a night out. A couple walked toward him and he didn't hesitate—no matter what the kidnapper had insinuated earlier.

"Excuse me, do you have a cell phone? This is an emergency. My daughter is missing."

"Oh my God. Here," the woman said as she handed him her phone.

"I can't tell you how much I appreciate this. Could we walk?" He didn't wait on an answer. Just turned and heard them follow. He dialed Wade's number on the woman's phone. "Come on, pick up," he murmured.

Continuing to move, he ignored the man trying to sell him a bouquet and hit End. He punched the number again. The couple continued to follow.

"Heath? Kendall?"

"The kidnapper split us up. He sent Kendall to the aquarium," he shouted into the phone, looking at the people around him. "Once he has her, he's calling a burner with my daughter's location. Get to the aquarium. Fast. I'll meet you there."

"Where are—"

He heard part of Wade's shout as he clicked the phone off.

"Thanks for your help." The phone was barely back in the stranger's hand before he pushed his way through the crowd, running to find his wife.

But she was gone. No bright red dress anywhere.

Nervous energy kept him running toward the aquarium. A van pulled up next to him.

"Get in!" Slate yelled. "We're tracking Kendall. She's already heading north."

Heath jumped with his three friends and fellow Rangers. Then Slate pulled back into traffic. They were a block away from where he'd been told to stay before he suddenly remembered the phone in his back pocket needed to stay put on that corner. "Pull over." Heath waved the phone at his partners.

"What? Why?" the three Rangers shouted.

"Hell, he's probably tracking you through that thing," Wade said, taking it from his hand.

"Once he has Kendall, he said he'd call and tell me where Skylar Dawn is."

"Who do we go after? It's totally your call, man. Jerry Fisher is standing by, along with a host of other FBI agents. Then we've got the Dallas PD. The other Company B Rangers are posted around the city," Jack said.

"Whichever you choose, I'm with you. I'm your partner. We've got your back," Slate confirmed.

They wouldn't try to change his mind. Not about staying with him to find his daughter and not about chasing after Kendall. The team would do whatever he asked.

"I can stay here, wait on the call. That way the tracker doesn't move," Jack suggested from the front seat.

"You might want this." Wade handed Heath an earpiece communication device, a cell phone and a Glock.

"I can't do this. I can't choose." Heath was torn.

Wade looked at the tracker. "We've got a few minutes before we know where he's sent Kendall. But we don't know what hoops he's going to make her jump through. I don't know if the tracker will remain intact. She might even ditch it herself. She was against it to begin with."

Kendall wanted him to rescue Skylar Dawn. He had to rescue them both. One without the other was still failure. How would his daughter ever forgive him if he let something happen to her mother? The Rangers didn't do failure.

Wade rested his hand on his shoulder. "What do you want us to do?"

"We're going after Kendall." He looked straight at Slate, handing him the phone. "I'm trusting you with my daughter's life."

"I won't let you down."

Thirteen minutes later they'd followed the tracker to the Galleria Mall. Slate had stayed behind with a plan to forward the call and for Heath to speak to the kidnappers himself. Then they wouldn't know he was closer to them than they'd hoped.

Wade dropped Jack, then he drove to the opposite

end of the mall to drop Heath. The phone he'd given to Heath rang.

A text from Slate stated the company phone was set with the forwarded call and he should just answer it.

"Murray."

"Kendall has arrived, and I'm a man of my word. Your little girl loves roses as much as you do."

The phone disconnected.

"What happened? Where is she?" Heath yelled.

The phone rang again. "It's Slate. Do you know what he's talking about?"

"It…it has to be the house on Vandelia Street off Wycliff, where I caught Saundra Rosa. It has bloodred roses on the south side. Orange trim around the windows and doors."

"I'm closer. I'll take a police unit with me," Slate let them know.

"I should be there."

"Kendall needs you. I'll get Skylar Dawn. You can count on me."

Silence. Wade waited to move.

"The bastard didn't give any instructions. His real target has always been Kendall, just like we thought." Had he done the right thing?

"Let's go get her." Wade faced forward and put the van in gear.

Heath slammed the panel door and ran. He hoped and prayed his wife would forgive him for coming after her and leaving Skylar Dawn's rescue to another Ranger.

Kendall stopped at the mall entrance and threw her shoes in the trash. She didn't want to jeopardize anything by letting the Rangers rescue her before she had her daughter's location.

The private car had obviously been sent by the kidnappers. She'd been locked in. No borrowing the driver's phone or talking to him. After the car arrived, the driver had stood at his door to watch her go inside. He'd simply stated that her party would be on the fourth floor.

They knew she was here.

But so did the Rangers.

Now if she could just find another way to let them follow her. The only thing she had in her clutch was that tube of Cherry Bomb red lipstick and two five-dollar bills. She'd refused any fancy gadgets except the tracker in her shoes.

Barefoot and in a tight, short dress, there weren't too many options left. No bread crumbs to leave behind. She leaned on a post on the way to the escalators. Maybe there was something…

Taking the lipstick, she drew a thick *H* on her heel. *H* for Heath. It was worth a shot.

At the bottom of each level of escalators, she left a Cherry Bomb *H*. At the top she'd limp to a bench, discretely reapply the lipstick and then limp to the next up escalator. When she pressed her heel, she left a red spot at each level.

Once on the fourth level, she reapplied and waited on the bench. Good thing she sat down. Her insides were jumping around, making her glad she hadn't eaten. What if Skylar Dawn hadn't eaten? She had to focus, be confident. The Rangers would rescue their daughter. Heath had promised. He never lied. Bringing down the kidnapper was her job. She could do this.

Please, Heath, find our baby.

Chapter 21

"Special Agent Barlow, you've lost your shoes. And you're limping."

When she turned her head, following the familiar voice, she had a moment of pure rage at his release from custody. The man who'd turned her life into a shambles sat beside her like her best friend. The gun sticking in her ribs came as little surprise.

"Bryan Marrone. Public Exposure sent their favorite lackey, I see. I guess I shouldn't have believed you were innocent yesterday." She didn't explain why she was barefoot. Maybe he hadn't seen her with the lipstick.

"True, Kendall. It didn't take much to avoid the cops and kill Saundra. She was a sweet kid, but enough with the pink already. I prefer a lady in red any day."

"I'll put you in jail this time and throw away the key. Where is my little girl? This was supposed to be an exchange of me for her. If anything's happened to her I'll—"

"Stop being so damn dramatic." He poked the gun into her ribs until she began moving to the side of the escalators. His jacket hung over his arm, hiding the gun. To onlookers, he looked like a polite escort with his hand on her back.

"Where's Skylar Dawn?"

"I told your husband." He pushed her toward an alcove. "Don't worry about her. Do as I say and nothing will happen."

"You phoned Heath? Is she here at the mall?" Why didn't Heath recognize this man's voice? "What do you get out of this? Who's in on this with you?"

"Do you actually expect me to tell you everything? I'm not stupid, Kendall. Move to your left. I need to pat you down."

Kendall moved as slowly as she could. The lipstick on her heel smeared a little on the floor. He yanked up her foot, looking at the light trail behind them.

"Dammit, Kendall." He snatched the lipstick from her purse and tossed it into the throng of people, then yanked her out of the group of shoppers. "Show me the bottom of your foot. Your attempt to leave a trail might really get you killed. Do you have any electronic devices that are going to make me angrier?"

"Of course not. We didn't have time." But she did have the side of her other foot. *Thank God.*

"And I'm supposed to believe you?" He rubbed his hands up and down her body. "You know, ever since you rubbed my leg I wanted to return the favor."

The shiver that crept up her spine was accompanied by acid from her stomach. Marrone's hands lingered

over her breasts and hips. Her stomach soured more…
if that was possible.

"Oh, wait. Our modern times make detecting electronic devices easy. Put your hands on your head."

There, in plain sight of dozens of people, he pulled an EMF detector from a backpack and waved the wand close to her body. He smiled and made lewd gestures at a couple of men, who snapped a picture or video.

"I knew you were a smart woman. You wouldn't do anything to jeopardize your daughter. Wipe your foot off. You sure you wouldn't prefer money over the cowboy?"

"Give me my daughter."

He'd made a mistake. One of these people would surely post something to social media. That would help prosecute him. But more importantly, if he made one mistake, he'd make another. That's when she'd make her move, but she needed him to reveal where they were holding Skylar Dawn.

"Head toward the service hall. That way." He shoved her to a back entrance to some of the shops.

Kendall tried to think of ways to stall for time. Surely the Rangers had followed her, but there was no guarantee.

"What did you do with my daughter?"

"Your daughter is safer than you. Those freaks may be weird, but they aren't going to hurt a kid. It'll take some time for the Rangers to determine her whereabouts. Too bad the top brass wanted you out of the picture. I could have saved the day, been a real hero."

Skylar Dawn was okay? Not in danger? Before entering the service hallway, she spun to face him. "You know, every single time a creep on the other side of the table claims they do it for the money, it makes no sense to me. Please tell me there's more to this. Some great cause or reason."

"There's a cause. Huge cause. But you wouldn't understand." He jammed her side once again. She couldn't defend herself against the gun when it was this close. "Turn and walk, or I'll pull the trigger in spite of how long Brantley Lourdes wants this to last. Of course it's about the money."

"Public Exposure is paying you to keep me away from the investigation, and you don't really know anything?"

Another jab. Another sharp pain. "Walk."

His cool, unhurried attitude worried her. Did he really think she came alone? Why didn't *he* think that the Rangers would be here any minute?

Heath slammed the entrance door into the wall and instantly drew the attention of everyone entering or exiting the high-end mall. "Damn. Sorry."

"Your wife tossed her shoes in the trash can," Wade said. "Just like we thought she would. They haven't moved since we arrived."

Where would she be? It had taken three minutes after the tracker stopped for the kidnapper to spot Kendall before he called back with his cryptic message. That was the only clue they had. Skylar Dawn better be at that house.

"Where would he try to take her?" he mumbled, but his earpiece picked it up.

"We've got the closest exits to where she entered covered," Jack said.

"There's too many of them. We need more units," Wade added.

"No. Units outside might put her in jeopardy. Kendall's smart. Look for something. Listen for anything unusual," Heath told them.

The place was packed. Heath searched for a bright red dress on his way, but didn't see one. Lots of dresses, lots of suits, hats, boots, tennis shoes, shorts…but no bright red dress or bare feet.

Maybe he could see from the top. Before he went to the next floor, he had to stop and catch his breath. *Damn ribs.* He leaned on a pole, his eyes scanning for someone with no shoes. There on the floor was an *H*. He bent and wiped the mark. Lipstick.

How many random *H*'s would be on the floor of a packed mall? It had to be Kendall. She'd left a trail of bread crumbs…or red lipstick, in this case.

Several minutes behind her, he rushed as much as he could without pushing people out of his way. If Kendall's trail played out, he might be able to catch up. He looked above his head, barely able to see the escalators to the next floor.

"Stall, Kendall. Stall."

Heath followed the *H* marks at the bottom of each escalator. On the fourth floor, the lipstick led to the hallway with the elevators. "I'm on her trail, near the ice rink elevators. No doubts. I just don't know how far ahead they are."

After he punched the down button again, he slammed his fist into his hand, wishing he were hitting the maniac who had Kendall or Skylar Dawn. The thought of losing either of them forever propelled Heath on. He punched every button, tapping the wall, waiting for the doors to open, checking each floor for her now smeared lipstick mark.

By now they should have police units ready to move in. Hopefully. Except…there was a hotel and bar near taxis or ride-share pickups. Dammit. That was how this guy would leave. "Guys? He's heading for the hotel."

"Are you sure?" both asked.

"Yeah. There's no way he'd use his own vehicle. He's got Kendall for insurance, but he's already admitted he doesn't have Skylar Dawn."

There was no time to wait. The lipstick imprint had been getting fainter.

"You seem like a smart guy, Marrone." Kendall slowed her pace again until he shoved her forward. "How in the world did you get mixed up with Public Exposure?"

Marrone yanked her around a corner. "Money. Lots of money. There really isn't any other reason. Some of those people are 'true believers'. Freaks. Just remember—I will pull this trigger. I can get away while they're trying to keep you alive."

"We could stop right now, if you'd like." The light quip accompanied by a forced smile took control to deliver. The horrifying hatred in his eyes didn't have her feeling lighthearted or in control.

Leaving the elevator, he gestured toward the men's restroom. Ahead of them, Kendall could hear the sounds of loud music and people. A bar? It should be packed at this time of night. The wheels turned furiously in her mind. The small bathroom space was empty except for one man washing his hands. He left, giving Marrone a sly smile.

"Should I call you Marrone? *Perp*, *kidnapper* or *suspect* probably won't go over too well in public."

"Neither would blowing a hole in your gut." He leaned on the door. "I noticed you limping slightly. Heath give that to you while dancing?" he asked with a smirk.

"I'll be fine." She wasn't actually limping, but she wasn't about to correct the jerk. Rolling to the side of her foot, she occasionally left a mark of lipstick. It was her only hope that someone could follow them.

She wanted to scream at him to stop this stupid charade and tell her Skylar Dawn's location. The longing to see her baby girl again wouldn't allow her to lose it. Instead, she needed to get him talking, bragging, something to give her a clue where her daughter had been taken. Or what other men were involved.

"Well, you won't be feeling any pain in a few hours. You'll already be dead when people discover what Public Exposure is really up to. Before they bring Dallas to its knees with the destruction and mass casualties." He said it coldly, with no emotion, as if killing people was an everyday occurrence.

Kendall knew he spoke the truth…and believed it. "Just tell me where Skylar Dawn is. You can go. I won't say anything to Heath or anyone else."

"In the last stall you'll find some clothing. Please leave the door open and change." He made a grand gesture like a butler, then backed up against the door again to keep others out.

The sloppy T-shirt wasn't too bad. The overalls were very large and made moving her legs difficult. The dirty-blond wig needed a good shampoo and brushing.

She left the cherry-red dress on the stall door. As she emerged, he dangled a pair of handcuffs in one hand.

"Are the cuffs really necessary?"

He tossed them at her. She felt like an idiot snapping them on herself.

"Most definitely. Consider it payback." He pulled a small sweater from his pack. "Cover the handcuffs. I wouldn't want to alarm any of the patrons."

The door opened and she stumbled as he pushed her through. Angry enough to take off his head, she had to calm down and think. She had to stop him before he could escape. She couldn't trust he told Heath the truth. If he hadn't they may never find their daughter.

The hotel bar was crowded and dark. People were squished together, attempting to get from one side of the bar to the other. It slowed their progression, giving her a chance to work on Marrone.

"You should be in a hurry," she said, attempting to sound completely confident. "The Texas Rangers are probably hot on our trail."

The loud music didn't drown his demonic laugh. Kendall wouldn't allow it to upset her. She used it to strengthen her resolve instead. This was the last time the creep would harm anyone.

Before he shoved her into another person to get her walking again, she made her move. She waved, then shouted, "Over here!"

He snatched her wrist from the air.

Pulling him forward, she kneed his groin hard enough to make the manliest of men cry. As he doubled over, she brought her knee up under his chin, throwing his head backward. His arm tangled in the links of the cuffs and caused him to bring her to the floor with him.

Several people cushioned their fall. Everything in the bar ground to a halt. She tried to push him from her, but he brought her hand across her throat, pressing the metal against her windpipe. By grasping the cuffs, he successfully held her, and then hit her temple with the butt of the gun.

With an excited smile forming on his thin lips, he pressed the barrel next to her ear. "That wasn't very nice, Kendall. Come with me or I open fire."

Still dazed, she allowed him to pull her to her feet. She splayed her hands and warned the men approaching, "Stay back. He'll shoot you. Stay back."

"Let the lady go!"

They both crashed back to the floor. She hadn't gotten a look at what—or who—had hit them. Through a fog, she saw a man in a black suit lift Marrone off her and raise his fist.

Heath. He'd found her. Thank God for Cherry Bomb red lipstick. He landed his punch, sending Marrone crashing into a table.

Wait! Why was Heath here? The music still blared and the lights from the dance floor flashed, but most of the women were watching Heath.

She didn't blame them. She liked watching him, too. The attempt at standing didn't work well. She settled for leaning on an elbow and watching her husband work.

"Did they find Skylar Dawn? Where's the gun? It must have gone flying."

"You okay?" he asked her.

Heath lifted Marrone by his shirt collar but let him crumple back to the floor. Heath knelt and frisked him. "He's out cold. No keys. Just a cell phone."

"We got him covered for you," a man with the bar's

logo on his T-shirt said. "He ain't going anywhere. Look after your girlfriend."

"Wife." Heath yanked Marrone's backpack off finding nothing of importance.

"You sure did give him what for," someone said, slapping him on the back.

Another man with the bar's logo rolled Marrone facedown and cuffed his hands behind his back. "I knew these would come in handy one day." He grinned. "I called the cops."

Heath flipped Marrone's phone open. "Dammit. Needs a password."

"Nice flying tackle, man. She need an ambulance?" the bartender asked, pointing to Kendall.

"Can you sit up? You okay, honey?" He helped her lean against him. "Helluva stall there, Kendall. Your eye's already swelling."

"You haven't answered me, Heath. You were supposed to get our daughter. Did you find her? Is she safe?"

All the adrenaline left her body with just his look. His rescuing of her would mean nothing without their daughter. Panic pulled her fully to her senses.

"Oh my God. Wake him up and do whatever's necessary to him. We have to find out where they've taken her."

Security guards entered the bar. "Everyone stay where you are."

"He gave us a clue. Slate's heading there along with Jason's DPD units. We should know any minute. Just rest and I'll get us out of here." He kissed her quickly and stood.

"You should have gone for her."

"I'll explain later." He grabbed his broken ribs and sucked air through his teeth, hissing.

But he wasn't the snake. Brantley Lourdes and all of Public Exposure were the cold-blooded creatures who had taken their little girl.

"We're going to be a family again, Kendall. I didn't get to answer you before. Take the transfer to Portland. If that's what you want…then go for it. I'll come with you and stay home with Skylar Dawn until she's okay. We'll figure out how to do this."

Chapter 22

Heath handed the phone to Kendall. The next phone call would be the most important of his life. The seconds ticked by as they waited. Wade arrived and then Jack, who swiped on his phone as he came through the bar door.

"Major Clements hasn't heard anything either," Jack said.

The phone rang with an old-fashioned bell. Heath froze. They all did except Kendall. She answered and immediately switched to speaker.

"I've got her. Skylar Dawn is safe and unharmed."

He heard the words and sank to the floor next to Kendall. No matter what their status—separated, together or moving—they were both her parents.

"Man, that was intense," Wade said, relieving a little of the tension.

Heath helped Kendall to her feet. "Let's go get our daughter." Then he looked at Wade and stuck out his hand.

"Here's your badge. I thought you might need it." Wade placed it in Heath's palm.

Then Jack nudged Wade. "Keys. He's waiting for our ride. But it might be faster if you bring it around to the bar's outdoor entrance. In their shape, it might take them an hour to walk to wherever you parked."

"Good idea," Heath and Kendall both answered.

"Let me get you some ice." Jack headed behind the bar to the men who had helped earlier.

"Your eye's going to be spectacular."

"Why did you come after me, Heath? You were supposed to save Skylar Dawn."

"We did save her. I told you I wouldn't choose. I accepted a plan that worked to save you both."

"What if it hadn't worked?" Kendall's eyes filled with tears.

He wanted to hold her, not debate his decision. He'd argued with himself every step of the way to finding her. What if this…what if that…

"I won't argue about it. You're both safe. That's the only outcome I need to think about."

Jack gave her a bar towel full of ice for the side of her head. Kendall was in good hands. Heath walked away, straight through the outer doors to wait on the sidewalk. Now wasn't the time to disagree. He needed air. He showed his badge and found the Dallas PD.

"A white panel van is on its way to pick me up. Can you make sure someone lets it into the drop-off circle? Thanks."

He was resting on a short cement barrier, when a set of very lovely arms wrapped around his chest.

"I'm sorry." She kissed his neck. "And I'm grateful." She kissed the other side of his neck then moved around to look him in the eye. "And you're right." She took his hand between her own. "We're safe. That's all that matters."

Jack joined them and Wade pulled around. The minutes seemed like hours until the van pulled onto Vandelia Street. Kendall jumped out, meeting Slate for the handoff. Heath moved a little slower, but was right there in time to answer Skylar Dawn's questions.

"I lost my hat, Daddy."

"Mommy found it, baby. It's okay."

"That mean man didn't hurt Stardust, did he?"

"Nope. She's safe and sound with her momma. Just like you." He kissed her forehead. "Let's go home."

"Can we go to McDonald's first? All those people had were carrot sticks."

"Sure, baby, we can do that. Let's go home."

"Oh, my darlings. I can't believe everything turned out okay," Naomi said as they came through the door. She hugged them all. Even Heath. "She is okay, right?"

"Maybe a little dirty and in the same clothes, but she's fine." Heath wouldn't let his mother-in-law take his girl from his arms.

"I'll run a bath." Naomi ran from the room, a tissue covering her mouth.

"I'm not telling her to leave tonight."

"I didn't ask you to. It's safer if she stays here, with the watchdogs out front."

"What do you think?" Kendall asked, looking away

from the Rangers' unmarked cars sitting in front of the house.

"We can rest easy. No one's getting through all the Texas Rangers parked around this house."

"No, I meant…" She gently lifted a strand of hair from Skylar Dawn's face and looped it around a cute little ear.

"We've both had the training, sweetheart," he whispered. "You know that we need to find her a good counselor, talk this out, answer her questions. But from what she's said, they dropped her off at that house and she played."

They caved and let Naomi give her a bath, parking themselves at the open door. Skylar Dawn had lots of bubbles to play with. His mother-in-law would have a mess to clean up, but no one cared.

"I keep going over what Marrone said." Kendall backed up to his chest and lifted her mouth so he could hear her lowered voice. "I thought at the time, this was all a plan to get me out of the picture."

"That was my first thought when he gave me the location to pick our girl up."

"Whatever Public Exposure has been working on, it's happening soon. Marrone said there would be mass casualties. I need to talk with him."

"Call Jerry. Let him handle it. She needs us both right now."

She looped her arms carefully around his neck. "I need you both, too. Maybe you should shower while I get her dried off and dressed for bed."

A breath separated their faces. He wanted to kiss her. He shouldn't kiss her. He was dying to kiss her.

He kissed her.

And she definitely kissed him back.

The perfect fit. The perfect taste. He slipped into the memory of her in his arms, in a sexy sparkly dress with a strap that didn't want to stay on her shoulder. He'd wanted to kiss her from the moment their eyes had met. Even on an investigation, he hadn't waited long. Before the week's end, they were in each other's arms, close enough to melt into the other's soul.

Tonight was no different. It was as if the years had all slipped away last night. His body felt alive again, on fire. He wanted her badly enough that it ached.

A caress across his face slipped down to his shoulders and pressed him away. But his last intention was to stop. They had been close to losing everything. He needed more of her, craved more from her lips. Desire was like an infection in his blood, surging with every pulsing beat of his heart.

But a small giggle from Skylar Dawn reined in his longing. She was laughing at them. They drifted slightly apart, then he lifted her between them.

"I'll only be a minute."

He laid loud, sloppy kisses on both their foreheads and transferred their daughter to his wife. No matter what…they were a family.

Kendall used a giant fluffy towel to cover Skylar Dawn. She put her in pink pj's and braided her hair after brushing it. By the time she was finished, Heath was done and had collected *The Wizard of Oz* from the living room where they'd left it.

She heard Heath begin reading and jumped in the shower. He'd taken a cloth and a bottle of water, then washed her feet clean while they'd waited on transport home.

Scrubbing hard, she scoured every place the filthy Bryan Marrone had touched her, then tossed the exfoliating sponge in the trash. Maybe it was a good thing they wouldn't see him tonight. She might tear his head off for what he'd done.

Tomorrow was soon enough.

She dressed and braided her own hair before slipping into bed with the loves of her life. Then the what-ifs began. Heath's arm was around Skylar Dawn, and he slipped his fingers through hers.

"You can't do that to yourself," Heath whispered. "No one's to blame. We're good. All safe and sound."

How did he even know she blamed herself? Maybe because he'd already had time to do the same?

"It's no one's fault. I…"

"Kendall," he squeezed her hand, "we deal with this tomorrow. Not tonight. Maybe for a while we can just forget."

"You're right," she said, staring at the ceiling.

"Again?" He laughed softly. "This being right thing goes straight to my head. I think I like it."

"Shh, you'll wake the baby." She used her free hand to tuck the light blanket around her little girl's shoulders.

"She's not such a baby anymore," Heath whispered again. "Her birthday's just around the corner. Get some sleep."

He turned off the headboard lamp. She closed her eyes and tried—really tried—to sleep. It didn't work. She switched on the HISTORY channel, clicked the mute button and tried again. She was still wide awake.

The TV glowed, casting eerie shadows over the garment bag. It hung over the chair Heath had sat in only last night. She rolled to her back, stretching muscles she'd forgotten she had.

The room suddenly went dark. She swallowed the moment of blind panic, preparing for an attack.

It took a minute for her to realize she'd moved against the remote, clicking the off button. She wished she could laugh. There was no immediate threat, but for a split second, terror—a too-familiar and unwelcome emotion—had suppressed her intelligence. She cautiously moved from under the covers.

Public Exposure would make a move soon. She hated not doing anything, but their daughter needed them. Needed to know that she was safe.

But was she? Public Exposure was still out there. Planning.

Was anyone safe? Was Marrone telling the truth about a catastrophe? If he was, there weren't many hours left to get the details from him. Who was working on it? Would he talk to them? She should be there, watching the interrogation. It might trigger something she'd forgotten.

Kendall couldn't sleep. She tried to place bits of information into logical categories in her mind. But her mind had other plans. It kept burning the image of Heath's face on the backs of her eyelids.

The image of him smiling as he got on one knee and proposed. He really was gorgeous. Possibly the most handsome man she'd ever met. Her cowboy. It didn't seem possible he could have grown more handsome, but he had.

Some of the cockiness she'd noticed during their first

assignment together was gone. Strange how she missed it. Maybe not strange, since she hadn't thought about working with him in years. But he was much more than that. Even though she'd withheld answers, he'd accepted and offered his help.

Skylar Dawn was so much like him. She had his eyes, his thick hair and that cute little attitude when she slipped on a pair of Western boots. Even the way she stubbornly held her mouth. On Heath it was sexy. But on her darling little girl, it had always been a constant reminder of who her father was.

God, she missed being a real family.

Before she'd met Heath, the closest she'd gotten to settling down was having the same apartment for more than six months. Her mother had encouraged her every step of the way, and she'd accepted the help. But the looks her mom had been sending Heath's way this week were wrong. It was time for Naomi Barlow to accept her son-in-law.

If she wanted her life back—and she did—Heath and her daughter had to come first. She just couldn't imagine life without Skylar Dawn. And the past six months proved life without Heath wasn't a life either. She'd been simply existing. Not living.

In order to protect them both, so they could get on with living properly, she couldn't dwell on what their future *might* be. She needed to determine who had attempted to kill her...and why. Then catch the bastard before he succeeded.

They had a life to live.

Chapter 23

Giggles and the smell of strong coffee awoke Kendall—followed by her daughter's attempt to sneak back into bed. Then came lots more giggles and a few shushes from Heath.

"Ready?" her husband whispered. "One. Two. Three."

"Surprise!" Skylar Dawn shouted in her sweet voice. "Wake up, Mommy. We made toast and omelets."

"Oh my goodness." Kendall pushed pillows behind to prop herself up.

Heath set the tray across her lap, immediately moving the hot coffee to her bedside table. Skylar Dawn twisted around on her knees, grabbed Heath's pillow and carefully plumped it behind her to match her mommy's.

They all sat in bed eating off the same plate until Kendall took a sip from her mug.

"We forgot my coffee, Daddy. My, my, my, what are we going to do with you?"

The "my, my, my" belonged to Skylar Dawn's grandmother and was flawlessly reenacted. Her husband carefully moved from the bed so he wouldn't disturb the tray of food. He bent at the waist and began backing out of the bedroom.

"Your wish is my command."

Coffee for their daughter came as warm cocoa. It had to be in a mug that matched her parents'. Skylar Dawn reached across her and fiddled with the paper towel Kendall used as a napkin. She took her own and tucked it into exactly the same place on her pajamas.

"Do you want cotton jelly for the toast, sweetie?"

"Yes, please."

Kendall handed her the jelly-covered bread. The exchange went a little wonky, the toast flipping jelly-side down from Skylar Dawn's hands. It made a mess on the comforter they had draped over their laps.

"Oh furgle, furgle, furgle."

Kendall's heart stopped. *Jerry?* Her daughter was imitating a man she'd never met?

"Where did you hear that?" She turned to her daughter so fast it scared her.

"I'm sorry. I'm sorry." She began crying and grabbed Kendall's arm. "I know I wasn't supposed to tell anything."

"What's happened? She okay?" Heath asked, returning to the room and setting down the cocoa.

"I didn't mean to scare you, sweetie. I'm not mad." Kendall pushed the tray past her feet to the end of the bed.

"They said I couldn't ever tell or we'd get hurt. Bad hurt."

She held on to her daughter, wanting to forget everything. But she couldn't. *Those bastards.* "They can't hurt us, honey. I—I—I promise. Just tell me where you heard that word, okay?"

"I don't know. I think it was the house." Skylar Dawn sniffed.

"What house?" Heath asked.

"The one I didn't like. Please don't make me go back." She turned and buried her face in her daddy's chest, then pulled the covers over her head. "I'm sorry. I won't say it again. Promise."

"It's okay, baby. No one's making you go anywhere. You'll stay right here with us."

Heath looked over their hidden daughter's shape. Kendall moved her breakfast to the bedside table, then scooted close to her family. She and Heath soothed Skylar Dawn until she fell back to sleep. Heath tucked her in tight and nodded his head toward the doorway. Kendall joined him at the open door.

"I promised Skylar Dawn she wouldn't be alone." He lowered his deep voice. "Will you wake your mom up to sit with her while we talk about this?"

"I should check in and see if they've discovered anything." Her mind was spinning. *Jerry? How could that be?*

"Check in with who, Kendall? The only man we know who says *furgle*?"

"There has to be a different explanation. What if she heard it after he arrived? He's an FBI agent and used to be my partner. He can't be dirty."

"Agents can be bought just as easily as a store clerk. Who better to point your investigation in the wrong direction?"

She turned her face into his chest. "He knew every move we were making. Oh my God, Heath. Jerry kidnapped our baby. What are we going to do?"

"We're going to send that bastard to jail."

"How? Who's going to believe us?"

"We'll need a plan."

"Still, Heath. We have no real evidence. How can we convince someone he's responsible because our daughter learned a new word?"

He pulled her into his arms, surrounding her in love and confidence.

"I know three men who won't hesitate to have faith."

Chapter 24

With another long day ahead of them, Wade wished he had someone to call and talk to, like his fellow Rangers. Maybe it was because his three best friends each had a special someone now. He had watched Skylar Dawn go into her mother's arms and wanted…something. Anything.

"He's quitting," Slate announced as he walked through the office door.

"Who are you talking about?" Jack asked, right behind him.

"You mean Heath," Wade tried to confirm.

"Yes, I mean Heath. The guy I've been calling partner since I came to Company B."

"This is about you?" Jack said. "Not the fact that he almost lost his daughter and wife?"

"It's not for personal reasons." Slate sat on the corner of Jack's desk, looking at everyone around them. "Kendall has an offer in Portland, and he told her he'd quit the Rangers."

"How do you know this?" Major Clements asked, coming from his office.

"He said it to her after he knocked Marrone what's-his-face on his back."

"Through his comm? That was private." Jack frowned.

"I can't help it if you guys didn't listen after they left the club and I did." Slate shrugged.

"You're not supposed to know this. He hasn't resigned yet, Slate." Major Clements waved everyone back to work. "It ain't over until he actually does it."

"Yeah, he's going to. I know how much he wants to be with Kendall and Skylar Dawn. He's been moping around here for six months," Slate said.

"Hell, you're the one who's been complaining about how horrible he's been acting." Jack replied by pushing Slate off his desk.

"We have work to do, boys. We still need to find out what Public Exposure is up to. Why did they need Kendall out of the way? What had she discovered, and why did Bryan Marrone say a lot of people would be finding out what they were all about? Do we have a ticking clock?"

"As in a bomb or something?" Slate asked.

"We have no idea when, or if, this threat is actually going to occur." Jack began looking at his computer. "How are we going to narrow down what this event could be?"

"Right," Wade said.

"So we have access to Kendall's notes?" Major Clements paced between the desks.

"I don't, but I think we have something better now." He pointed at the door, and the couple who should have been at home.

"What the hell are they doing here?" their commander semi-yelled, but hugged Heath and Kendall as they entered. "We're glad you two have Skylar Dawn back safely. You guys should be home with her. We've got this covered."

"She's actually bouncing back pretty well. And she's in excellent hands. Josh and Tracey Parker brought their twins up to play." Heath wrapped his arm around Kendall's shoulders. She didn't pull away.

"Actually, Tracey brought the twins. Josh brought three Company F Rangers. They're at the house and not leaving until this is all behind us." Kendall laced her fingers with Heath's free hand.

Wade leaned back in his chair. The question on his mind was which Ranger called which Ranger. Josh offering to keep an eye on them was probably a safe bet. He probably didn't count on both Heath and Kendall coming back to the case.

"Why do you think we can't handle this without you? And why didn't you take this to the FBI since it's your case, Kendall?" Wade crossed his arms, waiting for the bomb.

"Because the FBI is in on it." Kendall dropped the words like an explosion.

"My office. Now," Major Clements commanded. "Slate, bring chairs for these two."

Wade grabbed the back of Heath's rolling chair, and Slate grabbed his own. They exchanged glances, and true to form, Slate smiled—most likely at the possibility of saving someone. He loved to be a hero.

In the major's office, Heath didn't hesitate to sit. The beating he'd taken trying to protect his daughter had left him with two broken ribs and a hell of a lot of bruises.

Kendall waved off the chair and rubbed her bruising cheekbone. "I prefer to stand, thanks."

The last one inside the office, Jack closed the door. "Maybe you guys should start at the beginning."

"Agreed," Major Clements said.

"For months I've wondered how Public Exposure always seemed to be one step ahead of me. I could never get a break." Kendall paced, but kept her eyes on the major. "I was handed this case by my former partner. He'd been monitoring it, but kept saying nothing was there as the complaints grew. There was an immediate reluctance to give me resources or support."

The major sat on the corner of his desk. He'd known Kendall almost as long as they all had. He'd been at the wedding and at the hospital when Skylar Dawn was born. He'd cursed right along with all of them when she'd been kidnapped.

Wade didn't have to wonder if everyone believed Kendall. All they were waiting for was enough proof to act on it.

"I know now that Jerry Fisher, the supervisory special agent, asked to waive the conflict of interest regarding Heath helping the task force," the major said.

"He bet on us being at each other's throats and not making any progress," Heath said.

"Right. The thing is—" Kendall looked at him with admiration and love "—Heath's a damn good detective. We made headway that Jerry wasn't counting on.

That's why he arranged to distract us by abducting Skylar Dawn."

"Distract?" Jack asked.

"Heath said from the beginning he thought the whole thing was a ruse to really get Kendall," Slate said.

"It was. Bryan Marrone stated he was instructed to keep me under wraps—"

"Or dead," Heath interrupted.

"—or dead," Kendall agreed.

"Other than his assignments, you haven't mentioned why you think Supervisory Special Agent Fisher is working with Public Exposure," the major pointed out.

"This is the part that's really thin." Heath wrapped his arm around his midsection and took a deep breath.

He and Kendall looked at each other. "Paper-thin," she agreed.

"Skylar Dawn has a habit of mimicking people she's around." Heath twisted in his seat to make eye contact with everyone. "For instance, she says 'my, my, my,' when imitating my mother-in-law. Or 'that's a relief,' which is something Kendall says."

"That's true. She even does my mom and dad after riding," Slate threw out.

"She hasn't been around Jerry since she was born. He's never been to the house. I've never taken her to work," said Kendall.

"And what's she saying now?" the major asked.

Kendall moved to stand behind Heath again. "Furgle."

"Paper-thin," Major Clements mumbled. Then he looked straight at the couple. "We can't march into the FBI headquarters and arrest a man because he says 'furgle'. What does that even mean?"

"I'll let you look that up, Major. It's an obscure word from *Catch-22*."

Heath stood. "Agreed, sir. But without him," he continued, "my family isn't going to be safe. I believe Marrone knows something, but I also think he'll never tell us. He talks about freaks being true believers. Yet he's bought into whatever they're selling."

"We know we're the only people who can get Special Agent Fisher to admit he was behind the kidnapping." Kendall moved to stand closer to the major. "He was one of three people who knew where Heath was on Friday. I remembered that early this morning. The other two are in this room. Slate wouldn't even tell *me*."

"In my defense, Heath asked me not to."

"I appreciate your loyalty. Even if it almost got my husband killed." Kendall laughed halfheartedly.

At least she could joke about it. Things could have gone in an entirely different direction if Slate hadn't called his mom to check on Heath and Skylar Dawn.

"Paper-thin," Major Clements said again. "If we get the warrant to search Special Agent Fisher's apartment for a device to read the flash drive…then and only then will we move forward."

"I suppose you two have already determined a plan of action?" Jack asked.

They both nodded. Kendall put her hands on Heath's shoulders. It was good to see them together. Really together.

"Kendall and I will go to his apartment and see if we can find the information," Heath began. "I could grab the devices, but then the encryption key might also be in the apartment—we'll have to make sure the warrant covers looking through items, etcetera."

"You don't need to do this. Any of us can plug in a flash drive," Slate said.

"When it comes to computers, I'm the best this Company B's got. You've all come to me for help. Sorry, but I'm not leaving it to one of you guys."

"Now all we need is the flash drive," Slate said. "There's no way Jerry will relinquish that into our custody," he added.

"I think I know a way." Kendall paused, and everyone looked in her direction. She looked only at Heath. "I didn't have a chance to tell you that the Public Exposure case has been moved to another agency. The agent in charge said she'd work with me if possible."

"Great. How do you contact her?"

"I'll need to contact Assistant Special Agent in Charge Steve Woods, and hopefully he'll tell Agent Ortis to contact me."

Agent Ortis? It couldn't be the same woman. The rest of the planning had lots of discussion and objections on both sides. Wade didn't hear much of it, until Slate punched him in the arm.

"What's up with you?" he asked behind a cupped hand. "Are you really going to let these two go after yesterday? That's a good idea?"

"Was I able to stop you or Jack from finishing what you started with your girlfriends? This is Heath's wife, his daughter. If he can walk, he's going to see it to the end."

Everyone looked at him. Yeah, everyone in the office had heard him.

"Damn straight," said Heath, Kendall and Jack while Major Clements nodded.

Wade leaned against the door, waiting. He opened it

for Kendall when she stepped out to call Woods, and he stayed in the doorway of the break room while she dialed. She raised an eyebrow, silently asking if he wanted something. He did.

He couldn't think straight until he knew if this Agent Ortis was the Therese he'd been looking for since last year.

Kendall finished up with a smile on her face. "He's going to pass along the plan and see if they go for it. He wasn't surprised about Jerry. I wonder if they already knew."

"It might make the warrant easier if they did."

She pointed her finger toward the major's office. "Is there something else?"

"First…is Skylar Dawn okay? Do you guys need anything? I could watch the house after Company F leaves."

"We'll have to see, but thank you. Today, my mother promised to spend every minute with her. I think she's okay. Josh Parker's twins were kidnapped, and they took them to a counselor. They're calling a couple of people for a recommendation."

"That's good. That's good." He scratched his chin while Kendall looked at him strangely. "This might seem out of the blue but I was wondering…is the agent who took over the case *Therese* Ortis?"

"Yes, do you know her?"

"I believe we've met a couple of times."

"Small world, isn't it?" She scooted past him. "I should get back in there. Special Agent Woods said he'd have an answer pretty soon."

She turned around a few feet from him. "Would you like me to tell her to give you a call? That is, if I see her. She seemed a little on the top secret side."

"No. No. That's okay. She knows how to find me."

Chapter 25

Kendall entered Jerry's high-rise apartment building and issued the warrant to the supervisor. Heath entered covertly through the basement. They each took a different way to Jerry's apartment door. Major Clements was meeting with Steve Woods at the Dallas field office.

None of her coworkers had known the details of how they'd gotten Skylar Dawn back. They had to be right. It had to be Jerry. Therese hadn't reacted with surprise, and had been instrumental with the warrants coming through so quickly.

Everything inside Kendall told her Jerry worked for Public Exposure. It hadn't been easy, but they'd managed to get through most of the morning without tipping him off. Hopefully.

"We're keeping it quiet," Heath reminded her. "Remember, if he comes back before we're done, we wait for backup. No heroics. And no bashing the jerk's head in for what he did."

"Are you reminding me or you? Public Exposure can't know we've got him. I agreed to the plan, Heath. I'm fine with it. Even if I want to rip the man's head from his shoulders."

Once inside the apartment, the laptop was in plain sight. The password took a little longer to find. Heath pulled out desk drawers and looked on the bottom of small statues, pin holders, the stapler and tape dispenser until he found the current version inside a notebook.

"How did you—"

"A guess. He seems like the kind of guy who would use something complicated. But he doesn't seem like the type who can keep it in his head."

He began to access the information on Jerry's computer. She touched his shoulder before leaning in close to see what he found. With each screen, she was sure they were getting closer to arresting one of the men responsible for kidnapping their daughter.

"There it is," he said with an exaggerated sigh.

"That's a direct email from Brantley Lourdes. We've got him." She almost giggled in delight. "Are there any others?"

A noise in the hallway brought her back to earth super fast.

"Dammit. That's a key. Make the call."

Heath dialed his phone, connecting with Wade.

"What are you doing in here?" Jerry said as soon as the door swung wide. "I thought you were giving your statements. Why are you on my laptop?"

Kendall looked at her friend, her boss, her former

partner. There wasn't any reason to pretend. Not any longer. "Why?"

"Why what?" Jerry asked innocently. But the recognition was there in his eyes. He knew they were on to him. "You have no right to be in my home."

Heath nodded in her direction, poised to plug in the flash drive. Hopefully the laptop would decrypt the file.

"Actually we have a warrant for your personal computer and cell phone, and to search your residence. Someone's at your office." She stuck out her left hand, leaving her right on her Glock. "I think I'll take your weapon while I'm at it."

"Slow down, Kendall. Are you going to arrest me? On what charge? You have no proof anything's been done," Jerry spouted as he looked back into the hallway.

Maybe. But at least with those words he sounded guilty.

Kendall flexed her fingers for him to hand over his weapon. "Heath and I already tossed a coin to see who took you down. Too bad for you that I won. Hand it over—now. Or I'll drop your face onto this expensive Italian tile."

Heath pulled his weapon.

"Okay. Okay." Jerry raised his hands.

"You messed up, Jerry," she told him. "While I was waiting on Heath to call me yesterday morning, you interrupted my phone call to Company B. You pointedly asked where I thought he was. You were the reason I stayed at the office instead of looking for him. And then you insisted on driving me to the ranch putting you at the scene so you could plant the phone."

"You're right, babe. But I think Jerry's smart enough to know that's all circumstantial. But wait," Heath nodded. "As hard as you might have tried, there was a fingerprint on the cell phone left on Stardust."

"Not yours, unfortunately," Kendall continued. "The kid who placed the SIM card inside and activated the bogus account? Turns out he's in the system and was oh too willing to pick you out of a photo lineup."

They might have been gloating. Just a little. But they had a right to be proud for doing their job. Both of them could have stayed home. They could have buried their heads under the covers and just been thankful they were all alive.

That wasn't what men like Heath did. Because he was a better man, he made her a better person, too.

"I really don't understand how you got into bed with that vile piece of slime. You stole my daughter, Jerry." She advanced a step, really wanting to plant his face in the floor. "Hand over your gun or I'll consider it resisting."

"Don't do anything stupid, Kendall." Jerry splayed his hands. He drew back his jacket and took his service weapon from its holster with two fingers. "There's definitely been a mistake."

"We know you were one of the kidnappers."

"Skylar Dawn mimicked your idiotic use of *furgle*," Heath threw out. "Got it. I'll have files open any minute. The file might take longer."

"Okay, okay. I was hired by Brantley Lourdes. You should be thanking me for saving her. They wanted you both to disappear. At least I put the kid someplace safe."

"She was safe with me." Heath stepped from around the desk.

"We've got him, Heath. All of them."

"I don't think you know exactly who or what you're

up against. This won't end with you taking me to the Bureau. Public Exposure is bigger than Brantley Lourdes."

"Save it for later." She took handcuffs from her jacket pocket. "We'll nail Brantley Lourdes *and* Public Exposure. You should start worrying about the deal you're going to broker."

He turned around, but only one hand came behind his back. Before she could say furgle, he'd reached out and grabbed a hidden snub nose revolver. He spun again, aiming it at her head.

"Drop it, Heath. Or I swear I will shoot out her control center and your kid will have a vegetable for a mom if she's not six feet under."

Heath dropped his gun on the desk.

"Now, pull the flash drive and join your wife." He directed them toward the open door. "Uh-uh. Keep those hands up."

Their backup would be there any minute. But Heath's phone that was relaying all the information to them was still on the desk. Moving as slowly as possible, they made it to the elevator.

"How could you have betrayed us? Betrayed your country?"

"There you go getting all dramatic again, Kendall. Money, and knowing where the nonextradition countries are." Jerry laughed. "Basically lots of money."

Heath looked from Jerry to her and reluctantly backed onto the elevator when the doors opened. Standing closest to the panel, Jerry pushed a button, and then pulled a second gun strapped around his ankle to point directly at Heath's chest.

"No." She moved between Heath and the barrel. Jerry might be reluctant to shoot her, but not her husband.

The elevator began its descent. Heath's hands were on her shoulders, trying to push her to the side. She stood firm.

This was her fault. She hadn't cuffed him soon enough. Could he get to the second Beretta under her jacket she'd put there for just this reason? She crossed her arms to disguise any movement he might make.

"Don't try it. Keep your hands up exactly where I can see them, Heath. Turn around and put your hands on his shoulders, Kendall." Jerry held his gun steady.

She turned her back to the traitor and held Heath's steady gaze. The pressure in his hands exuded trust and confidence. Jerry pulled her gun and his cell, then stuck his snub nose into her back. She continued to look into her love's eyes.

"What are you going to do when we get to the ground floor?" She meant it for Heath, not Jerry. She'd need his help to take this bastard down before he shot both of them.

Heath frowned and pressed four fingers into her right shoulder, then three, then two... He'd understood her question. She needed to know what floor they were on if they were to do this together.

"You are the only *one* for me, babe," she said to let him know when they should act. Now they just had to survive the ten-floor descent.

"Believe it or not, Kendall, you've brought this on yourself by being too damn good at your job," Jerry said. "If you had just walked away. I gave you a lot of opportunities to shut the file on this thing."

Heath's fingers pressed into her shoulder, counting

down the floors. It was risky, but the close quarters could work to her advantage. They had to act before they reached the basement.

"I'm afraid I'm going to have to get rid of you both." The basement floor indicator dinged.

The doors began to open. She let the rage, terror and love all mix together to create a surge of energy. She leaned forward against Heath and kicked backward, hitting Jerry's chest. Heath shoved her aside, and she hit the wall as he rammed the traitor in the chest. The momentum carried the men down, and they fell to the hard elevator floor, between the doors, keeping them from closing.

The gun blast made her ears ring. Heath pounded Jerry's wrist against the floor until the gun skidded down the slick garage floor. Heath kept Jerry down with his weight. She added his strength to hers, but soon pulled back, taking Heath with her.

Jerry didn't move. He was out cold. Heath pulled them away from the traitor. He checked for a pulse, then rolled Jerry to his stomach, pulling Jerry's arms behind him and resting his knee and body weight there.

He stretched out a hand and pulled her close for a hard quick kiss, then his hands were searching her arms. "You okay? You weren't hit or anything, were you?"

"I'm fine. His shot didn't get you?"

"No, I'm good." He gave her another quick kiss.

"You really are." She pulled her badge and pointed to her Glock as the second elevator doors opened, and a security guard ran toward them. "Special Agent Kendall Barlow. He's a Texas Ranger. Could you direct our backup down here? We're taking this man into custody."

The guard didn't move, but the second set of elevator doors opened again and Heath's team was there for the save.

"Took you guys long enough."

"Did you find the elevators kind of slow here?" Slate said.

"Did you get all that on tape?"

"Right up until you left the apartment."

Heath put an arm around her, pulling her farther away. "First off, I regret not getting to hit you for what you did to my wife and daughter. And basically the hell you've put me through. Keep that in mind before I get on that elevator to escort you upstairs."

"Heath," everyone cautioned.

"You've got one chance, man. Where is Public Exposure attacking this afternoon, and where is Brantley Lourdes?" He lowered his voice so that only Kendall and Jerry could hear. "One shot to answer, or you're mine. Alone with me for as many floors as this building has, and then back down."

Chapter 26

Heath let the Rangers talk around him and over him in the apartment garage while he sat in Wade's truck. He was actually too tired to think about anything. He didn't know whose back seat he occupied. He just needed to close the windows and not move for a month.

He was too exhausted and in too much pain. He'd been holding it together on aspirin and having his ribs bound with an ACE bandage. But damn, he and Kendall looked as bad as they felt for once.

"Here, take these." Kendall dropped two extra-strength somethings in his palm and handed him a bottle of water. "It's all I could find. I think you could still take a painkiller the doctor prescribed when you get to the house. Wade and Slate both volunteered to take you home."

Bruised and broken physically, but not down and out.

They'd won. They had Skylar Dawn. They had the man who had orchestrated her kidnapping. So why didn't he feel that it was over?

"What's wrong with my truck?" He pushed himself to a sitting position, waiting for her to explain. Images of someone swiping it raced through his head.

"We're in no shape to drive, remember?"

"I'll wait around until you finish. We should both see Skylar Dawn together."

"That's just it—"

"One down, one to go." Slate swooshed his hands together like he was dusting off. "The threat of being alone in the elevator with Heath really scared the pants off your boss. He talked a little, but lawyered up."

"I'm sure all the Rangers standing behind Heath helped convince Jerry to disclose where Brantley Lourdes was staying."

"What do you mean, 'one down, one to go'? Are they arresting Brantley Lourdes?" Heath looked at Slate for the answer.

"You ready to go, or should I let you guys talk?" Wade pointed toward his truck. The one Heath was currently using.

"Were you trying to get me out of here before you took off to follow another lead?" Heath turned to Kendall. "Are you trying to question him without me?"

"Actually, you're both heading home," Major Clements informed him. "You have only two options—the hospital or the comfort of your own bed. Which is it going to be?"

Heath slid across the seat, attempting to hide the winces and groans.

"Give up, Lieutenant. You can barely stand. You

won't be any good out there if you pass out. Time to go home to your little girl," the Major said.

"He's right." Kendall extended a hand to help him from the truck.

He had to admit defeat by sitting on the edge of the seat. "What about you? Somehow I'm getting the impression that you have different plans." He wouldn't let her go without him. "At this moment, Lourdes is still out there and you're at risk."

"I'd be fine, but I told them I need to head home. They're sending the new agent who's in charge of the case here. She has a couple of questions."

"Why didn't you say so?" He tried to push himself to stand on his own.

"We've had a couple of interruptions," she whispered.

Most of the time he was a tough guy. Now…not so much. Wade and Slate each claimed a side, ready to help. Wade's fingers began clenching his biceps as a dark-haired woman walked into their circle.

"Kendall. Heath…if I may? I'm Special Agent Therese Ortis." She stepped forward to shake his hand. "I have a few questions for you both. Then you can head home. I'd be glad to catch you next week for your full statement."

That look. The shy moment when two people who know each other try to keep it a secret. It happened between Therese and Wade. Heath had a hunch, but he'd respect their bare acknowledgment of each other.

"What can we do for you, Agent Ortis?"

"I'd like to face Brantley Lourdes with a little more knowledge of his group. Why did you think the word *furgle* was so unusual?"

"Jerry used it on Kendall more than once when he

was her partner." Heath's dislike of the man had begun as soon as they'd looked up the meaning.

"It's a word used in the book *Catch-22*. Jerry always used it out of context, and I didn't appreciate it," Kendall said.

"We found the book upstairs in his bookshelves. But you never reported him for his actions?"

"She told me, but she took care of the problem herself," Heath answered.

"Did Special Agent Fisher read a lot?"

"Not really," Kendall said.

"Would it surprise you to know we found at least thirty top literary titles?"

"Yes. He doesn't talk about reading. I'm not certain what that means, though." She thought of something important. Her mouth formed a perfect O before she pulled out her phone. "Heath, what's your password to your backup file for your phone? You know, the one where your photos are stored automatically."

"The same as it's always been." *K-n-H-4ever.* He still believed that could happen. "What did you remember?"

"The pictures you took of Saundra Rosa's crime scene. There's one." She rapidly swiped through the pictures. "There's the other."

She flipped the phone toward Agent Ortis.

"They have the same books. This is great. The books are their key. I can work with this. Good work. I'll be in touch."

"Let's get out of here." He lifted his arm and waited for Kendall to dip her shoulder under it to hold him steady while they walked to his truck.

Once out of the apartment garage, they continued

around the block to where he'd parked and his partners were waiting to drive them home.

"You made the agency come to you," he said once they reached the truck. "I didn't think you'd ever walk away from a case."

"One thing I think we've both realized this week is how important our family is. We're needed at home."

He handed her the keys and she helped him into the passenger seat.

"Did you see the way Wade looked at Therese Ortis?" Kendall sounded lighthearted and teasing by the time she had her door shut. "I swear, I think he's got a thing for her."

"She has to be the informant who saved his life after that beating he took. Before we left, Jack told her that Megan would be in town this weekend." He could play along and avoid the all-important question of which room he'd be sleeping in tonight.

"Oh my gosh, so much has happened that I forgot to tell you Jack is supposed to propose. I guess those plans are on hold."

"Good for him. He's been head over heels for Megan since they met."

"What about Slate and his new love life?" Kendall turned onto the highway, heading home.

"Vivian wants to get back on her feet, but they're still exclusive. Is that the word nowadays? I've been away from that rodeo for a while now and was never that much into it before I met you."

"Really? Come to think of it, you've never mentioned any old girlfriends. Surely you had a girl in every city." His wife smiled. Teased. Winked and smiled some more.

He shook his head, afraid to break the relaxed atmosphere inside the truck's cab.

"Not even in college?" she asked.

"I think I told you things got hard about that time. I worked at the ranch in Alpine every spare minute I had. Mom needed my help so I lived at home."

"Unlike my mother, who has never needed help. Sometimes I wonder…"

"Wonder what?"

Kendall stopped at the corner of their street. "I wonder if she did…you know, if she needed someone, she might actually find a person who makes her happy."

There were four Rangers guarding her house and visitors inside. Kendall hesitated to drive the truck into the driveway, wondering how to tell Heath she needed a little time. He reached over and took her hand. Maybe he'd sensed her hesitation. Maybe she needed some type of explanation for how well he knew her.

"I need time to figure this out. Alone. My emotions are all mixed up."

"Take all the time you need. Moving is a big decision for all of us."

"I'm just an emotional wreck right now," she finished with a long involuntary sigh, shutting the engine off in their driveway.

"I get it." He caught her hand, bringing it to his lips and making her smile. "Wait. Before we go inside, I've been trying to say this all week. So bear with me."

"I just need a little time—"

"Sweetheart. It's my turn. I'm going to respect your time, but I think I need to move back in for a while. I love you and Skylar Dawn more than life. I thought my biggest fear was if something happened to the two of you because of work."

"But it was my job."

"Just hear me out." He scratched his chin. "I found out that's not my biggest fear. That would be living without you."

"And Skylar Dawn."

The squeals of children at play inside the house brought her statement home.

"Honestly, she'll always be my daughter. Nothing will be able to take that away. No matter how far away she is or whether or not I live in the same house. I don't want to grow old without you. And believe me, I'm feeling the creaking bones earlier than I thought I would." He rubbed his ribs with his free hand. "You don't have to say anything now. I'm sorry for all the assumptions and for leaving you alone. I should have just told you that a long time ago."

Her hand shook. "For one of those strong, silent cowboy types…you know just what to say."

They got out of the truck. He stood on his own, not needing her help. She liked helping him, enjoyed him leaning on her—literally. It was a reason to touch him and feel safe.

More sounds of children playing had her feet moving up the steps. She waited at the top for him.

"I'm going to talk to the guys before I head inside. But—" His brow crinkled in concentration.

"What?"

He stepped up and pulled her into his arms, kissing her like it was the first time. Exploring her mouth, accepting her passionate response.

"I love you, Kendall. I always will."

He waited as she turned and quietly opened the door and then clicked it closed. No one heard her come inside. She let him go without telling him. She leaned against the door with her hand on the knob about to return to him.

"Real pretty speech." Bryce, the Ranger who had stayed at the corner of the porch, had hung back until she'd come inside. "She'll come around."

She waited. There was a long pause before Heath responded. "I don't know. There's been a lot of space between us in the past six months."

"I have the first shift on your porch tonight before your partner takes over. He's ready to take you to the ranch. If that's really where you want to go."

"Need. Not want."

"Like I said, she'll come around before you know it. See you in the morning."

She ran down the hallway away from the door, away from Heath.

Did she really need to think about their situation? She was emotional and out of control. Waiting was the logical thing to do. And she'd always been logical. Waiting to make a choice—that was the way to go.

So why was her heart breaking again without him by her side?

Chapter 27

Why had he come to the rodeo? He'd gotten up early to feed the horses after a restless night of tossing in his bed alone. But he'd needed to get away from the ranch. Needed to get away from everyone really. Needed to be with people who weren't worried about him.

His parents' house was too far away to visit and be back to work in a couple of days—if he could concentrate on anything. It had been less than a full day. He couldn't go by himself, and he didn't want Kendall to think he was pressuring her for an answer. Instead, he reassured his mom that he was okay via text…about every three hours.

Hell, maybe he *should* pack up Jupitar and take a trip home to see his mom and dad. The major had looked him in the eye and told him he'd put him on desk duty for six months if he showed up for work sooner than a week.

But the major didn't know Heath was sleeping on the couch. Officially…he didn't have a home at the moment. Maybe that was the real reason he'd come to help at the rodeo. He didn't want everyone to know he wasn't with Skylar Dawn and Kendall.

Dammit, he was a chicken after all. Even his morning ride had lost its appeal.

"What are you out here for, Heath? Did that bronc throw you a little softer than we thought last week?" the manager of the rodeo asked.

"Afraid I've got some broken ribs, Bobby Joe."

"And you're spending your free time here? Don't you have a life, kid?" He cupped Heath's shoulder before he walked off to the next thing he had to do.

A rhetorical question that shot straight through his heart. He didn't want to think. His thoughts would only land on Kendall. And who knew how long she'd take. He might not know what to say or when the right time to say it was…but she always needed time to think.

And he always gave it to her.

"So what do you say, cowboy? What are you doing after you're finished?" asked a sweet voice he recognized but didn't expect to hear.

Heath dropped the edge of his Stetson to block the sun from his eyes. "Kendall?"

"I had to come down here to make sure the rodeo groupies were behaving themselves." She wore her tightest, lowest-cut jeans and had her shirt tied in a knot just under her breasts.

"I'd let out a howl but it might draw attention to you."

"And that's bad?"

"Sure it is. No way do I want to share your company."

"Oh. Really?" She turned to face him.

"You can't be surprised."

"I'm just… I'm not very good at flirting anymore."

He looked around, searching for their daughter. She was with the Parkers, heading for the stands. Two additional Rangers from Company F flanked her and his mother-in-law. Bryce hung back, waiting on Kendall.

Her shy mannerisms reminded him of his ability to get tongue-tied. He tried not to crowd her when cowboys passed by and needed more space. But he liked crowding in close to her.

"I see Skylar Dawn found her hat," he said, tipping his up a little to see her better.

"Actually, Josh's twins asked to visit Stardust. You know they have their own horses. I agreed because I thought you went to the ranch." She stuck her fingers into the front pockets of her jeans, but they didn't disappear very far because they were super tight.

It had been awhile since he'd seen her in his world. Jeans and boots looked great on her. The wolf whistles would start pretty soon if he didn't get her shirt untied from under her breasts and tucked into her waistband.

"Anyway, we went out there this morning. We might have to get her a bunch of farm animals after what the Parkers were telling her about baby pigs and chickens."

"We?"

"Dammit. I'm going to sound crazy, but I don't need time to think about whether I love you or not." She threw her arms around his neck.

"You sure? You seemed to have a plan to wait yesterday. Waiting is sort of your thing."

"That's ridiculous. If I knew what I was doing, don't you think I'd be doing it right now? I'm stumbling around in the dark."

She switched her hands into her back pockets, drawing even more stares from the cowboys.

"Hey, babe. It's kind of chilly out here. Do you have a sweater?" Heath didn't wait for an answer, he took his jean jacket off and draped it over her shoulders.

The men behind them laughed. Kendall waved, flirting a little more by dropping the jacket off one shoulder. The wolf whistles ensued. Bryce covered his laugh behind his hand. Heath glared then looked up toward their daughter to smile.

"Changing the subject, Skylar Dawn seems to be doing okay. She's walking around without you and laughing." He waved at the stands.

"Jackson and Sage have talked a little about how scary it was to be kidnapped. They've been a big help. Our daughter is bouncing back faster than I thought possible." She turned to wave at everyone in the stands.

"Enjoy the show, Bryce. I can take care of my wife for a while," he said in a louder voice. "Maybe we should go somewhere we can talk?"

"Home?" she asked.

"I was thinking about a walk around the pens. That is, if you don't mind the smell." Heath wrapped his arm around her waist and guided her behind the staging area.

Kendall tugged his arm to head to a secluded corner. "What do you say, Heath? Will you give me another chance to get this right?"

"I don't want to go through life without you, sweetheart. I love you."

"I love you, too. And I'm *asking* you to help me decide about our future."

Heath took off his hat, circled it in the air and let out a big cowboy holler. He grabbed his ribs and winced, but not for long before he pulled her into his arms and kissed her.

When he let her up for air she told him, "I'm ready to ride off into the sunset, cowboy."

* * * * *

Danica Winters is a multiple award-winning, bestselling author who writes books that grip readers with their ability to drive emotion through suspense and occasionally a touch of magic. When she's not working, she can be found in the wilds of Montana, testing her patience while she tries to hone her skills at various crafts—quilting, pottery and painting are not her areas of expertise. She believes the cup is neither half-full nor half-empty, but it better be filled with wine. Visit her website at danicawinters.net.

Visit the Author Profile page
at Harlequin.com for more titles.

HIDDEN TRUTH

Danica Winters

To Mac,
thank you for teaching me the meaning of true love.

Acknowledgments

This series wouldn't have been possible
without a great team of people, including
my #1k1hr friends, Jill Marsal and the editors
at Harlequin—thank you for all your hard work.

Also, thank you to my readers. You keep me writing.

Prologue

She clicked open the tabs of the gun case, exposing the M24 sniper rifle. It was a thing of beauty. Even without firing a single round from this particular gun, Trish Martin could recall the precise feel of pulling the trigger, smelling the spent powder and watching as her enemies fell to their knees.

There was no greater feeling in the world than a justified kill. The men standing around her, those dealing in death, would be easy to strip from this earth.

She ran her fingers down the synthetic stock, taking in the slight imperfections on the newly manufactured gun. This one would be for a different kind of kill, a long-term tactical assault, rather than a one-and-done straight to the head.

Some people were only too happy to judge her and her family for the work they did, but she didn't care.

She didn't care that she was out there protecting the ones who didn't appreciate it right alongside the ones who did. She was a hunter, a predator, who fought for her territory and for life as she knew it.

The shroud of darkness wormed its way around her as she waited for the Bozkurtlar, or what some people called the Gray Wolves. To call them a Turkish crime syndicate was an understatement. No, they were so much more.

They were the reason she and her family were here in Adana, the reason she couldn't sleep at night, and the reason there were so many unmarked graves scattered around the Turkish hillsides. Their name suited them. No matter where in the world they were, death and mayhem followed.

That would all end soon.

She heard the sound of footsteps on the concrete floor and the clink of the metal door closing behind the group. From the sound, there had to be at least ten men. If anything went wrong...

She looked around her. They had made a mistake in agreeing to meet them in this shell of a warehouse. There weren't nearly enough hiding places or corners where she could find cover if she needed to. And there wasn't anywhere for her brothers to hide within the building. Without a doubt, the group's intention had been to isolate her and to strip her of any way to double-cross them.

"Ms. Stone," a man with a thick Turkish accent said from behind her. "I hope you aren't planning on brandishing that weapon. We're here to buy new, not used."

She stood up to face Fenrisulfr Bayural. He was nearly a foot shorter than her, but what he lacked in height, he made up for in his stance. When he stared at her, his golden-hued eyes took on the darkness that surrounded them, making her instinctively twitch for the gun at her side.

She stared down at him, forcing herself to act far more confident and self-assured than she felt in his presence. He couldn't sense weakness in her. If he did, he and the bodyguards around him would certainly pounce. When it came to running guns, buyers tended to get skittish.

Two years ago, in Egypt, one of her team's sting operations had ended with a shipment of American weapons falling into the wrong hands—and the men on her team being murdered. They were part of the reason she had ended up here—men, especially those with a Napoleon complex, tended to be more than happy to play nice with a hot brunette. But she'd be crazy to think her looks would keep this from becoming a firefight.

"We sell nothing but the best. You'd be a fool to think anything less," she said.

"Good. But will you also be providing more advanced weaponry or just the ARs?"

He wanted the launchers. Of course he did. But rocket launchers weren't something that they readily had on hand. Yet what he didn't know wouldn't hurt him. For now, she just had to play along and make it out of this room alive.

"How many did you want?"

"Four thousand RPGs and ten thousand ARs. I need my men to have adequate coverage when they attack Ankara."

As he spoke the name of the city, she felt the warmth of the mic strategically stitched into her jacket. They had their location and an estimated number of enemy combatants—admittedly, a number far greater than they had anticipated. But perhaps it was Bayural's plan to inflate the numbers. In the event any of their dealings leaked, he would appear far more powerful than he and his group really were.

"What do you have available for us?" Bayural crossed his arms over his chest, covering his vital bits as he prepared to negotiate his price.

No matter how he tried to protect himself, once her brothers bore down there would be no protection great enough. His life would be theirs for the taking.

"The Type 91 Kai MANPAD rocket launcher will do everything from annihilating a door to wiping almost an entire city block clean with its shoulder-launched surface-to-air missiles. They're easy to carry, cheap and fast to reload. Everything you want." She chuckled slightly as she realized how much she sounded like a used car salesman instead of a trained killer. Her mother would have been so proud.

Bayural squatted down and picked up the sniper rifle. He lifted it up as he stood and shifted the gun in his hands as though he was weighing it. "Hand me a round," he said, turning toward the guard to his right.

The man pulled a round from his pocket. Bayural jacked the round into the chamber, smiling at the metallic click and slide sound the gun made.

No. He couldn't be allowed to actually shoot the rifle. It would be too dangerous. They were here to keep the general public from falling into harm's way, not to place them into greater danger. "The gun is solid. The shipment will be solid. Our team, Black Dragon, will get them to you by tomorrow." She tried to sound nonchalant as she slipped in their fake name, the code word. Her team would be here any second to strike these bastards down.

Finally, they could cut off the wolf's head.

"Tomorrow? I want them within the hour." He lifted the rifle, pointing it directly at her center mass as he peered down the scope. "You can do that, can't you?"

She glanced toward the far wall, hoping like hell that she would see the laser signal letting her know her brothers were in place, but there was nothing.

"When can we expect your shipment?" Bayural pressed.

"First, I want my ten million."

Bayural smiled. "Ten is too much."

"With everything happening in Syria, prices have gone up for your standard RPGs. You know as well as I do that the market is at least two Gs per RPG. As for the ARs, you are getting a screaming deal. That's less than two hundred a gun. We could get five if we went somewhere else."

He nodded slightly. "I'll give you a G per RPG."

She laughed. Even if she had really had the weapons, there would be no way she would go for such a ridiculous deal, but she had to keep up the negotiation until her brothers arrived.

"Or we will give you two if you can have our shipment to us within the hour." Bayural's pitch rose, like he was growing more nervous with each passing second.

His bodyguard leaned in and said something in his ear, something far too quiet for her to hear. Bayural's eyes widened and his brow furrowed. Whatever he said, it wasn't good news.

Her chest tightened, and her Kevlar vest suddenly seemed all too heavy.

Her brothers should have been here by now, at her side. "We can do the hour, but I'll have to talk to my team. Your order is larger than we were anticipating."

This was falling apart. Fast. She had to get out of there. She scanned the room for her planned exit point. The door to the alley was closed, barred from the inside. There was nothing to use as cover. It would take at least three seconds for her to get to the location, two to get the door open. Five seconds. Basically, a lifetime if they opened fire.

He clicked off the safety, the gun's barrel steady as it pointed at her. "Is something wrong, maybe you have something you want to tell us?" His voice threatening.

"No," she said, trying to appear relaxed as she took a step back. "But if you wish to have the deal go through, you need to lower that gun."

Bayural lowered the weapon slightly and motioned toward her with his chin. His guard took a step closer.

"What are you doing?" she asked as the guard grabbed her wrist and pulled her arm behind her. Her shoulder pinched as he lifted her hand higher, forcing her to submit.

Her instinct was to struggle and pull free, to launch into an attack. To get the hell out of there. But no, she had to trust her team. If they were waiting, there had to be a reason. They were trying to get more information. They must have needed more. She had to believe in her family.

"Back off," she growled at the guard. "Let go of my arm or the last thing you will see is me ripping it off and shoving it down your goddamned throat."

He lifted her wrist higher, forcing her to lean forward from the pressure.

"Bayural, get your man—"

"To stand down?" Bayural said, finishing her sentence. "Hardly. Who the hell do you think you are to command me?" He dropped the rifle to the ground and looked to his guard. "Break the stock."

She looked at the base where she had just run her fingers. The imperfection suddenly seemed so much larger.

The guard picked up the gun and smashed it against the floor again and again until cracks formed in the plastic. He batted it against the concrete one more time, sending the small GPS tracker her team had planted in the plastic skittering across the floor.

"You, your brothers, your sister, your team… You're dead."

"You may get me, but you'll never get the rest of them. We're survivors."

"Even if I have to spend the rest of my days on this earth hunting every one of your family members down, I'll do it. When I'm done, you and your kind won't even be a memory. You will be nothing."

There was a smatter of gunfire outside the corrugated steel building. A round pinged against the metal siding, the sound echoing through her.

With her free hand she reached down and pulled the knife from her boot. She jammed it deep into the guard's foot. The man screamed, letting go of her arm in a panic to remove the blade.

She grabbed her sidearm, taking aim at Bayural and pulling the trigger. The round ripped from the barrel, striking the man in the chest. Buyural didn't seem to notice the hit. He must have been wearing a vest.

The guards around him pulled their guns as she turned to find cover. Anything. Anywhere. She had to get the hell out of there. Now. She rushed toward the door as the sound of gunfire rained down upon her. The first round struck her in the thigh, ripping through her muscle with a searing heat, but there was no pain. Her ravaged thigh tripped her, the muscles failing to follow her brain's command. Her body fell to the floor, but she pressed on, dragging her injured leg behind her as she crawled toward the back door.

The door flew open, and standing in the nearly blinding light was her brother. "Trevor!" she screamed. "Get the hell out."

He ran toward her in what seemed like slow motion, but as he took two steps, the next round struck. Wetness. Warmth. Something had splattered her cheek.

She stopped struggling as she pressed her fingers to her face and traced the spatter to the gaping hole in her neck. No. This couldn't be real. This couldn't be happening. Not like this. Not now.

She sank to the floor as the blood poured from her.

The concrete was cold against her face as she watched the pool of red grow. The world narrowed to a pinpoint until all she saw was Trevor. His face. He'd always been so handsome. So dangerously handsome. She'd miss her brother.

She'd miss them all.

Breathe. All she had to do was breathe. But as she struggled to fill her lungs, there was only a strange gurgling sound.

She had been wrong to think this operation would

be easy. Nothing in their lives had ever been simple. And now that misjudgment—and her desire to trust— would prove fatal.

Chapter 1

There was a single question that Trevor Martin hated above all others: "Who do you think you are?" It only ever meant one of two things—he was about to get slapped by a woman or he was going to have to knock some sucker out.

It wasn't the question that bothered him so much. On the surface it was just some retort people came up with when they didn't know what else to say, but when he heard it, he heard it for what it really was—a question of who he was at his core. And when he thought about that, about what made him the man he was, he wasn't sure that he liked the answer.

That self-hatred was one of the reasons he had taken a leave of absence from his contract work with the CIA. His entire family needed a break from the family business, so they bought the Widow Maker Ranch in Mystery, Montana. It was supposed to be an escape he so desperately needed from the thoughts of all he had done wrong in his life. Instead, it was as if the rural lifestyle and the quiet mountain mornings only made the self-denigration of his character that much louder.

He'd only been there a few days, but he couldn't help but wonder if maybe he'd made a mistake in coming to this forsaken place where he was constantly shrouded in clouds and imprisoned by the brooding mountains. Everything about the ranch made him long to stretch and push the world and his thoughts away—if only it were that goddamned easy. No matter where he went or what he did, his memories of the days he'd spent in his family's private security business, one they called STEALTH, constantly haunted him.

And here he was the bearer of bad news once again.

If he were being honest, pulling the trigger and tearing down an enemy combatant was a hell of a lot easier than what he was going to have to do. He spun the motorcycle around in the dirt, kicking up dust as he screwed around and tried to focus on something he loved instead of something he was going to hate.

After a few more doughnuts, he got off his Harley and pushed the kickstand into place with his foot. Taking off his helmet, he set it on the seat, though a part of him wondered if it wouldn't have been better for him to wear it as some kind of shield from the battle that was likely to ensue.

Running his hand over his too-long locks, he pushed them out of his eyes and tucked them behind his ears.

There were times, just like this one, that he wished he were back in a war zone and had a staff of people under him who could handle this kind of thing.

All he had to do was say his piece, give them the letter, and he could get the hell out of there. He just had to go in and do his duty. The moment he and his brothers and his sister had purchased the land, they agreed that this would be a part of the work that would need to be done. Unfortunately, he had drawn the short straw.

He had never seen a picture of the house in question, but the shack in front of him was a squatter's paradise and far from what he and his family had imagined. The roof was a collection of corrugated steel in a jumble of different colors, and the siding, what was left of it, had started to rot and several pieces were only half-attached. Even the front door was cockeyed, listing to the left so far that there was at least a two-inch gap at the top.

Whoever resided there must be hard up. Maybe they had been hoping they were far enough out of the way at the farthest reaches of the ranch that they would go completely unnoticed. Thanks to the neglect of his cousins, the Johansens, whoever was living in this place had pretty much free rein—and their plan for disappearing in plain sight had worked. And from the state of the house, it was clear it had been working for a long time.

The forest around the house was filled with junk, everything from antique wringer-style washing machines to the rusted-out shells of farming equipment. From the state of disrepair, it seemed likely that this had once been the dumping ground for the ranchers of years past.

He walked toward the door. Behind him a twig snapped and the sound was answered by the chatter of a pine squirrel high up in one of the trees.

He wasn't alone.

If he turned around now, it would give away that he was aware he was being watched. For all he knew, the inhabitants of the shanty had taken to the woods at the sound of his bike as he'd made his way down the makeshift road that led up to this place. If he just kept walking, it would give him time.

He started again, looking for a window or something he could use to catch a glimpse of whoever was lurking in the shadows around him.

They couldn't get the drop on him; he wouldn't allow it. He'd made it through years of toeing the line between danger and death, and he wasn't about to get tripped up and find himself on the losing side now. Not when he'd come here to make a real home and a real life for himself.

He stopped at the front door of the squatters' shack and started to knock.

"They're not home," a woman said from somewhere in the distance, her voice echoing off the timber stands around them and making the source of the sound impossible to pinpoint. "And they would have been long gone regardless, thanks to your crappy driving."

He turned in the direction the voice had come from and relaxed a bit. She probably wasn't going to try to shoot him—if she had wanted, she already could have drawn on him—but some habits died hard, and he lowered his hand to the gun that was always strapped on his thigh.

Standing in the shadows at twelve o'clock, her back against the buckskin-colored pine, was a blonde. She was leaning back, her arms over her chest like she had been there for hours getting bored. Even feigning boredom, she was sexy as hell. She had the kind of curves he had spent more than one lonely night dreaming about. And the way her white T-shirt pulled tight over her leopard-print bra... His body quivered to life as he tried to repress the desire that welled within him.

"You know where they went?" he asked, trying to be a gentleman and look at anything besides the little polka dots that were almost pulsing beneath her shirt.

She smiled as though she could see the battle that was raging inside him between lust and professional distance. "Have you met the Cussler boys before?"

"How many are there?"

She pushed herself off the tree. "If you stop thumbing that SIG Sauer at your side, maybe we can talk about it. Men playing with their guns make me nervous."

"You around men and guns a lot?" he asked, but the question was laced with a provocative tone he hadn't intended.

She walked toward him, and from the way she moved her hips even he, a man who had slept with only a handful of women, could tell that she had heard the inflection in his words as well...and she intended to do something about it.

He raised his hands in surrender. That's not what he'd come here for, not that he would have minded kissing those pink lips, not with the way they gently curved in a smile but hinted at something dangerous if they were allowed free rein. With the raising of his hands, she stopped and her smile faded. There was a small cleft in her chin, and damn if it didn't make her look even cuter than she had before.

Once, when he'd been young, his mother had told him, "Dimple in the chin, devil within." From the look in her eyes when she was staring at him and that damn bra she was wearing, there was plenty of devil within her.

"Are you Trevor?" she asked, not moving any closer.

He took a step back, surprised that the woman had any idea who he was. "Who are you?"

This time, she was the one to wave him off. "Your brother hired me to keep house—starting here. He didn't tell me that I was going to need a backhoe and a dump truck."

Either she had accidently forgotten to supply him with her name, or there was a reason she was keeping it from him.

It hardly seemed fair she should know anything about him when this was the first he was hearing about her.

"You from around here?" he asked, motioning vaguely in the direction of Mystery in hopes she would loosen up with a little bit of small talk.

"Actually, I'm kinda new. Was looking for a slower pace of life."

"Well, it doesn't get a whole lot slower than here," he said, a darkness flecking his words. He hoped she didn't read anything into his tone. He didn't need to get into some deep discussion with a stranger about the merits or pitfalls of a place where he doubted he was going to stay.

"If you think it's slow in town then you haven't spent enough time in the mountains. These mountain men are about as fast as cold molasses and a little less intelligent. If you ask me, their family tree is more of a twig."

He laughed. "So where are you from…and hey, what's your name again?" he asked, trying to play it off like she had told him and he had simply failed to remember it.

She gave him an impish smile, and he could have almost sworn that she fluttered her eyelashes at him.

"Sabrina. And I'm from all over. Kind of an army brat, but my last stop was Schofield."

Instinctively, he glanced down at her arms. She was pale and far from the buttery color of someone who had spent their days in the Hawaiian sun. She had to be lying.

On the other hand, maybe he was reading far too much into her and her answer. Maybe she just valued her privacy like he valued his. Besides, if he was going to transfer into the civilian world, he would need to stop thinking everyone was out to conceal the truth from him—not everyone was his enemy, especially a house-keeper in the little town of Mystery, Montana.

But he'd been wrong before, and that failure to see danger had gotten his sister killed. He couldn't let his guard down. Not now. Not ever.

"Your father in the marines?" he asked.

"Schofield is an army base. I wouldn't make that mistake around a vet, if I were you." She sent him a dazzling smile.

She had passed the first test, yet something about her just didn't feel right—just like everything in his life since his sister Trish had died.

"How long have you been waiting on the Cussler boys?"

She shrugged. "I only got here a few minutes before you. To be honest, I was trying to figure out where to start the cleaning."

"So, they're gone?" His job of kicking the family out of their shanty was proving to be a whole lot easier than he had expected.

"They're not here, but I thought you had already

come to kick them out. At least, that's what your brother led me to believe."

He was supposed to be here an hour ago, but he hadn't known his brother was sending a crew behind him or he would have been on it. "And you haven't seen any sign of activity?"

She shook her head. "But like I said, I only got here right before you."

He walked up to the door and knocked. There was the rattle of dishes as the mice, or whatever vermin it was that lived in the place, scurried over them. He went to knock again, though he was almost certain they were alone, but as he moved the door creaked open.

"Hello? Someone home?" he asked, walking in.

The place was dark and as he entered, a putrid smell wafted out—the brothers mustn't have been there in some time, or they were even worse at keeping house than they were at building one. He stepped in and the cobwebs in the corners of the front door clung to his face. He tried not to be squeamish as he wiped them away. No matter where he went in the world or what he was doing, he'd always hated that feeling. No amount of training or conditioning could get rid of the instinctual revulsion—and that was to say nothing of the inhabitants of the webs.

"Trevor," Sabrina said breathlessly from behind him. "Look."

He dropped his hands from his face and gazed into the dark shadows where she pointed. There, sitting against the corner, was a man. His face was bloated and his lips were the deep purple color of the long dead.

Trevor clicked on the flashlight on his cell phone and pointed it toward the man as he moved closer. Above his right ear, at the temple and just below the dead man's ruddy hair, was a small bullet hole. There was no exit wound on the other side. The man's eyes were open, but they had started to dry and shrink in the socket, in sharp contrast to the rest of the man's features.

"Do you see a gun anywhere?" Trevor asked, flashing the light around as he looked for the weapon that could have killed the man.

"No," she said, but she stood in the doorway staring at the man. She covered her mouth with the back of her hand as though she were going to be sick.

Trevor rushed over to her and wrapped his arm around her. "Come with me. Let's go back outside. It's going to be okay. You're all right. Everything is going to be fine."

She turned her body into him, letting him pull her into his arms as he moved her out the door and to the fresh air of the forest. He had been right—she would be just fine; from the way she felt in his arms, he was the one who was truly in danger.

Chapter 2

Sabrina had no idea why she had reacted that way. The man was hardly the first dead body that she had come across, and yet it felt like the first time. Maybe it was the way he seemed to be looking at her through those cloudy eyes or the smell of the body that had been left sitting in the heat of the fall, but she just couldn't control her body's reaction.

Damn it. Every time she started to think that she was strong, she did something like this.

Although maybe it wasn't a bad thing that she had reacted as she had. She had gotten to play up the lady-in-distress angle. If she had to be undercover for any amount of time, it was going to be immensely easier if she had one of the brothers under her spell.

She just had to remember to keep him at arm's length; the last thing she needed to do was let her emotions come into play. Emotions only had a way of getting her into trouble, and she was in enough as it was. They were the reason she was stuck in this place…and out of the direct line of sight of her superiors. Though she was certainly under their thumb.

Trevor was just another case, another investigation she had yet to complete. In a month, if everything went according to plan, she would be out of here and set down in a new little nowhere town in the middle of America investigating another possible threat to homeland security.

Trevor rubbed her back and as he held her, his chest rose and fell so rhythmically that she found herself mimicking his movements. He was like a man version of a white noise machine, and just as soothing.

If she had to guess, between his dark brown hair, his crystalline blue eyes and a jawline that was so strong that it could probably cut glass, he was all women's kryptonite. He probably was the kind of man who had a woman every time he went downrange.

She pushed herself out of his arms and sucked in a long breath as she tried to completely dissociate herself from him. The last thing she needed was to share anything with him—even his breath.

"Are you feeling better?" he asked, looking at her like she was a bird with a broken wing.

She nodded. "I don't know what that was about. I'm sorry."

"That was about a dead man," he said, shock flecking his voice. "It's not something one sees every day. I would have been more worried if you hadn't reacted that way. Shock can be more dangerous than most flesh wounds."

Crap… She couldn't give herself away. Of course he would think she was a newbie to this kind of thing. She had to remember the role she had been sent here to play. A role that required that she be seen little and heard even less. What a joke for her superiors to play… they knew just as well as she did that silence wasn't her strong suit. She wasn't the kind of woman who was going to let anyone push her around, tell her what to do or require that she "let the men do the real work."

Her skin prickled at just the thought of the last time she had heard someone mansplain to her.

Trevor touched her arm. "Sabrina, you with me?"

"Huh? Yeah." She looked at him and forced a smile.

"Why don't you go and sit down," he said, pointing toward his motorcycle. "Or I guess you can lean." He gave her a guilty smile, realizing what an absurd idea that was.

"I'm fine. Do you think you should call the police?" She motioned toward the shack with her chin.

She would rather not have any local officers running around the place and mucking up her investigation or compromising her position.

Yet they couldn't hide a dead body…

Or could they?

If they swept this under the rug, it would give her more access to Trevor and his family without the threat of outside interference. It would definitely speed things up for her. If the police started poking around, the Martins would clam up and go even deeper into hiding.

And really, who would care about one mountain man who had turned up dead? He was totally off the grid, and as far as the government was concerned he was a nonentity. In fact, the only thing that his brothers, and folks like him, were known for were extremist ideals and a penchant for causing trouble.

Yet she couldn't be the one to bring up the idea of hiding the very dead Cussler brother.

Trevor stared in the direction of the shack. "We should call somebody…"

The way he spoke made her wonder if he was thinking along the same lines as her. No doubt, he didn't want anyone poking around, either.

"But?" she asked, prodding him on.

"I bet his family would go bonkers if we brought law enforcement out here. And the last thing this ranch needs is more craziness from the locals." He frowned. "We are just trying to fit in here. We don't want to draw unnecessary scrutiny from our new neighbors."

"Well, if you think that the Cusslers would appreciate us not—"

"Yes, I'm sure they would want to keep this a family issue." Trevor sounded sold on the idea.

She wanted to point out the possibility that the other members of the Cussler clan may be lying dead somewhere out in the timber as well. Otherwise wouldn't they have already buried their brother's body?

Yet she didn't want to press the issue. Not if it meant there was a possibility he would change his mind and call the police. Not that he would. She had the definite feeling he wanted to sweep this man's death under the rug just as much as she did.

"I'm going to go back in and take a look around," he said.

"Why?" she asked, before thinking.

He looked at her as though he was trying to decide how much he should open up to her. "If we're not going to call someone out here, we need to make sure that this isn't the work of some serial killer or something. You know what I mean?"

"You think he was murdered?" she asked, trying to play up the innocent and naive angle.

"My hope is that this is nothing more than a suicide. I just need to make sure."

She doubted that was really why he was going back in. He was probably looking for something more, something that would guarantee they wouldn't find themselves in deeper trouble if any of this ever came to light.

"You wait here. I'll be right back."

She grimaced. He hadn't really just tried to tell her what to do, had he? If he thought she was some kind of chattel that he could just order around, he had another think coming.

"Okay." She sighed as she tried to calmly remind herself he wasn't bossing her around out of some need for control; rather, it was his need to protect. "But be careful in there. If I know one thing about these kind of recluses, it's that they have a reputation for hating outsiders. They may have set up some kind of booby trap."

He stared at her like he was trying to figure her out. The look made her uncomfortable. "Got it, but I promise you have nothing to worry about when it comes to my safety. I have experience with this kind of thing."

His alleged role in peacekeeping and his family's Blackwater-type company was known, but she was surprised he was admitting any of it to her. Maybe her investigation wouldn't be as difficult as she had thought. Hell, if things went her way she could have all the answers she needed in a matter of days.

Then again, things would have to go her way, and life hadn't been playing nicely with her lately.

Trevor slipped back to the shack, holding up his phone as a flashlight as he made his way back inside.

She moved quietly after him. Maybe she could see something that he would miss, something that would prove the brother's death was nothing more than a suicide so they could put this all to rest.

As she walked toward the shack, she stopped. No. She couldn't pry. She couldn't get any more involved with this. If she went in there and did find something, there was a high probability that she would slip up and say something that would give away her background. He couldn't know anything about her position in the FBI.

She walked around to the back of the shack to where an old push lawn mower sat. There, on the ground beside it, was a puddle of dried blood. Pine needles had collected at the edges, making the pool look like some kind of macabre artwork.

She opened her mouth to call out to Trevor, but stopped. No. She couldn't tell him.

From the state of the body in the house, there was little possibility this blood belonged to the dead man. If someone had shot him out here and moved him, there would have been drag marks or some indication that the body had been staged. Though she hadn't spent long in the room with the dead man, she had noticed the blood leaking out of the wound at his temple. If she closed her eyes, she could still see the trail as it twisted down his ravaged features and leaked onto his dirty collar, staining it a ruddy brown. He couldn't have been moved postmortem. No, the blood pattern didn't match.

Which meant this blood had to belong to another person. And based on the volume of it on the ground, they were possibly dealing with more than a single death.

Crap.

She stared at the dried blood. Kneeling down, she scooped up a handful of the sharp, dried pine needles that were scattered around. What she was about to do could end up going all kinds of ass-backwards, but it had to be done for her, for her investigation and for her chance at getting her future back. There was nothing she wanted more than to rise in the ranks, and sometimes that meant that sacrifices had to be made.

She threw the needles atop the blood and stepped onto them. She kicked away at the dried blood, earth and needles until there was nothing.

It felt wrong to destroy evidence, but at the same time a sensation of freedom filled her. It was refreshing to break the rules and to make her own in name of the greater good.

Walking around to the door of the shack, she poked her head inside. Trevor took a step deeper into the shadows around the dead body. He knelt down and moved aside a piece of discarded cloth on the floor. He chuckled.

As he stood up, she saw a gun in his hand. He wiped the grip and the barrel down with his shirt, as though he was stripping it of any possible fingerprints.

There was only one reason he'd wipe the gun down—he was trying to protect the person who had pulled the trigger. Maybe that person was him.

Hell, he had probably come in here and killed the brothers in an attempt to get rid of them once and for all. Then he had waited for her to arrive before he rode up on his Harley like some kind of badass playboy.

He'd probably wanted her to see the man's body first. He'd wanted to come off as innocent. He'd wanted to take her in his arms and act the hero.

And she had allowed the bastard to set her up.

Chapter 3

Trevor walked up the front steps of the ranch house and waited as Sabrina parked her car and made her way over to him. He had told her that she could have the rest of the day off. She didn't need to come back to the main house with him—she could return to the old foreman's place, which was hers now—but she hadn't accepted his offer. Instead, she had only said that she had work to do.

Actually, it was the only thing she had said. The words had rung in his ears the entire ride back to the main house. There had been something in her sharp inflection that told him she was angry about something, something he was missing—and that there was danger afoot—but for the life of him, he didn't understand.

It was like he was married all over again, his life awash with unspoken anger and resentment. The memory of standing at the front door of his apartment, watching as his wife bedded another man on their once-pristine leather sofa, made a sickening knot rise in his belly.

Once again, just like before, he was forced to be an unwilling participant in things unspoken.

Hopefully this time he would be able to stop his life from falling to pieces in front of him.

She came to a stop beside him, but she was putting off a distinct "don't touch me" vibe.

He must have crossed some invisible barrier when he'd pulled her into his arms back at the shack, but it hadn't been his intention to make her feel uncomfortable. He had just been trying to help, to lend a shoulder to a woman in need, not to tick her off.

"Did you talk to Chad yet?" she said, glancing down at her watch like she was checking just how much time he'd had before she arrived.

He shook his head. Truth be told, he had been hoping she would keep driving instead of turning off on the little dirt road that led back to the ranch. It would have made sense, her running away after seeing the Cussler brother rotting in his chair.

And if she had kept driving, he could have had the real conversation he needed to have with Chad without worrying about what she would hear. Now he'd have to play it cool until he could get his brother alone and he had the chance to find out exactly what he knew. No doubt, Chad would have dealt with that man's remains as he had and left them out there for the Cussler family to handle.

They didn't need to draw undue attention. They

needed to fly under the radar and off the grid for as long as possible.

He cringed at the thought of having to move again.

Getting out of Adana had been a nightmare after Trish's death. When they made their move to Montana, they sent misinformation on the dark net to make it seem like they were moving east to Thailand. They had no doubt that Turkish mobsters were just waiting for their chance to kill the rest of the family.

As long as nothing came out, they'd be safe for a while. It was the reason they had chosen this speck on the map. Plus, they'd have the cover of the United States and the amnesty that it offered if anything blew back on them. He and his family had done so many covert ops for the former president that they would always have government backup.

Or so he hoped.

Chad came sauntering out of the kitchen, a hot dog in his hand. He glanced from Sabrina to Trevor and gave him a raise of the brow as he stuffed the rest of the hot dog into his mouth, leaving a blob of mustard on his lip.

"I see you're already living the high life, brother," Trevor said with a laugh. "You want me to go in and get you a Budweiser, too? Nothing says American like a hot dog and a beer."

Chad swallowed the bite. "Not all of us developed a taste for world cuisine. You can't tell me that dolma is better than a good hot dog." He wiped off the speckle of mustard at the corner of his mouth with the back of his hand. "What do you think, Sabrina? You vote American food?"

She shrugged like she couldn't give a damn less. "Either, so long as I'm not cooking it."

"And that right there is the reason I hired you. I've always liked a woman who was as smart-mouthed as me. You are going to fit right in." Chad laughed. "Did you guys get the squatters handled?"

"Not exactly," Trevor said. He cocked his head toward Sabrina in a silent message to Chad.

Chad's smile disappeared. "Sabrina, do you mind getting started with your cleaning up here in the kitchen? 'Fraid I may have made a bit of a mess in there."

She opened her mouth to speak, but stopped and instead gave Trevor a look as though she hoped he would step in and allow her to take part in their conversation.

"Uh, actually…" Trevor stammered. "Sabrina, you must be pretty tired. Like I said, if you wanted to head back to your place—"

"No," she said, taking off her jacket and hanging it in the coat closet just inside the door. "I'll get started in the kitchen. I have a job to do, and this place isn't going to get any cleaner if I just go back to my place."

Sabrina strode into the kitchen and the door swung shut behind her.

"Let's step outside," Trevor said.

Chad followed him out and Trevor made sure to close the door behind his brother. He glanced in the front window of the house to make sure that Sabrina wasn't anywhere in sight. Thankfully, it looked as though she was in the kitchen.

"What in the hell were you thinking sending that woman out there?" Trevor asked, turning back to his brother. "Do you know what the hell I found in that shack? And because you were in some freaking hurry, Sabrina saw. Now she's a possible loose end."

"First, you were supposed to get out there long before her. You don't get to make this my fault. You should have stuck to the schedule."

"Had I known you were sending someone out behind me, I would have. How about you learn to freaking communicate?" Even as he said it, he couldn't help but feel that he was the pot calling the kettle black.

"What exactly did she see?" Chad asked, taking a step back from him like he was afraid that Trevor was going to take a swing.

"That damned Cussler guy was splattered all over the walls. Been dead at least two or three days." He pointed in the direction of the shanty. "I had to convince Sabrina that the dude was better off if we just left him and waited for the family to come back and collect his remains."

Chad turned around as he ran his hands down his face. He stomped as he turned back. "Are you kidding me? We haven't been here a week and there's already a dead bastard in our back forty?"

"You should have just left me to handle my end of things, man. I had this taken care of. All I needed was a little time. But no, you wanted to rush things. To make sure everything was cleaned out and taken care of before Zoey and Jarrod arrive."

"You know how they can be—they were even more adamant than I was about the absolute need for privacy here. This family is all we have, Trevor."

"You don't need to tell *me* that."

Chad took in a long breath as though he were trying to collect himself. "So, was the guy's death a suicide or what?"

"There's no goddamned way. Someone shot him." He

thought of the handgun he'd left sitting on the ground beside the dead man. "The gun was too far away from the body. No major stippling around the entrance wound, and the bullet had lost enough velocity that it didn't even travel through the entire skull—there was no exit wound. I'm guessing whoever pulled the trigger had to be at least ten to fifteen feet away."

"And where did you say you found the man?"

"He was sitting up in a chair, like someone got the drop on him. He didn't even have time to stand. He didn't see it coming."

"What about the rest of the hillbilly clan...did you find them? They alive or dead?"

"Hell if I know." Trevor threw his hands into the air. "I'm hoping that they just ran off. We don't need a dead family on our hands."

"Did you get a chance to look around?" Chad asked. "Wait, did you and Sabrina call in the locals?"

Finally, Chad was beginning to understand the implications of his screwup. If only he hadn't been in a hurry, they wouldn't already be compromised.

"Sabrina went along with keeping it quiet, but I don't know how long she'll be up for maintaining that." He glanced back inside, but the beautiful and stubborn woman was nowhere in sight. "She hasn't been acting right, ever since..." *I held her in my arms.* He didn't finish his thought.

"Huh? Ever since what?" Chad pressed.

"Since she saw the body. I'm afraid she may be a liability."

"What are you saying?" Chad asked. "You think she needs to disappear?"

"No," Trevor said, almost the same moment his

brother had uttered the question. "No. We can't harm her. She hasn't done anything wrong. And who knows, maybe I made a mistake in thinking she can't be trusted. Maybe she won't be a problem."

Chad shook his head. "What if she does tell someone? What if it comes out that we tried to cover up a man's death at our new ranch?"

Trevor stared at his boots. "She wouldn't…"

"Dude, if she tells anyone… First, we are going to look as guilty as hell. Second, our faces are going to be spread across the world in a matter of hours."

"She won't say anything."

"And how are you going to know if she does or doesn't? For all we know, she's in there texting her mother's brother's cousin about what you guys found. Hell, she could be sending pictures of the dead guy." Chad paused. "You know that I don't want to hurt an innocent woman. Not after what happened in Turkey… And Trish…" Their sister's name fell off his brother's tongue like it was some secret code, some unspoken link between past and present.

"Then let's leave her be."

Chad shook his head. "No. If you don't want to neutralize the threat, you're going to have to watch her like a hawk. Every move she makes, you need to be there… hovering."

"And what about the squatters? The body?"

Chad sighed. "What about it? Like you said, let that guy's family handle it."

"And what if they do, and they call the police?"

"If they haven't already, they aren't about to now." Chad stared at him. "For all we know, one of them is the one who pulled the trigger—or else they're lying out there in the woods somewhere, too. Either those bastards are on the run or they aren't going to be spilling any secrets any time soon."

"Do you think I should go back out there? See if I can find them? Make sure that they're going to stay quiet?"

Chad stared out in the direction of the main pasture, but Trevor could tell that he wasn't really looking at anything. "I'll talk to Zoey and see if we can find out a little more on these Cussler guys. I want to know how many hillbillies were living out there, and who would have wanted them dead. I want to make sure that whoever is responsible for pulling that trigger isn't about to bear down on us."

His brother was right. They needed to make sure they weren't about to be ambushed.

"Most importantly," Chad continued, "I want you to keep Sabrina quiet. If you don't…you know what's at stake."

"She won't be a problem." Trevor paused, thumbing the gun at his side and letting it comfort him from his barrage of thoughts. "Hey…you don't think these Cussler guys have anything to do with STEALTH, do you?"

Chad shook his head, but from the way his face pinched, Trevor could tell that he was wondering the same thing. "Bayural and the Gray Wolves couldn't know that we are here. Zoey has made it her business to make sure of it. Everything we did has been in cash, or through Bitcoin. We're covered."

"Just because our sister is a computer whiz, it doesn't mean that we are safe. You know how easy it is to find someone, especially a group like our family. One stupid random selfie with us in the background and we're in danger. They are using the same facial recognition software that we are."

"Zoey has this under control," Trevor said, trying to give them both a little comfort—it had always been his job to keep the peace within the family, a job that had proven harder than ever thanks to his failure with Trish. His mistake was something that neither he nor the rest of his siblings would ever forget. "Besides, Zoey has made it her personal mission to keep them chasing fake hits around the globe. From what she said this morning, she currently has us pinging at a marketplace in Cairo."

Chad chuckled. "God, can you imagine those bastards' faces when they realize that they've been set up? I would almost pay to see it."

There was the clatter of pans hitting the floor from inside the kitchen.

Chad bounded up the porch steps and cracked the door. "Sabrina, you okay in there?"

"Fine, just fine!" she called back, sounding harried.

"Where did you find this woman?" Trevor asked, motioning toward the house.

"She came recommended from Gwen when we bought the ranch. They hired her when they were getting the ranch ready for us to take it over."

"So, just because our cousin—whom we barely know—thinks this woman is trustworthy, you took her word for it?" Trevor was surprised. Chad wasn't one for details but he was normally careful about who they brought into their lives.

"Brotato chip, you seriously have to pull the stick out of your ass. You're starting to act like Jarrod."

He was nothing like their oldest brother. Jarrod had been a lone wolf since the moment he called upon them to take their positions within the business. After he had set up STEALTH he hit the road, looking for assignments from various governments.

"I hope Zoey looked into her background," Trevor pressed.

"Of course. Zoey said she was clean, nothing too much to tell. Looks like Sabrina had been travelling around the world with her military family until she turned eighteen, just working odds-and-ends jobs since then."

It was in line with the little Sabrina had told him, but something still felt wrong. Trevor glanced toward the kitchen where Sabrina was working. Maybe someday, if he could just ease himself back into being a civilian, something might start feeling right.

A man could only hope.

Chapter 4

She sat in the corner of the barn, letting the streak of morning sun that was leaking through the siding spread over the tips of her boots. Though the beam had to be warm, she couldn't feel it through the leather. Maybe the sun was just like the rest of her life…pretty to look at, but completely devoid of feeling.

Then again, yesterday had been full of them—at least when it came to Trevor. She glanced down at her phone and his picture. The photo was sharp, black-and-white, typical of the FBI. And yet it didn't really capture the man she had met. No, in real life he was far less imposing than he seemed in the picture. The photo failed to show the way it felt to stand there encircled in his arms, and then to realize that he had been playing her from the moment they met.

She flipped to the email from her handler, Agent

Mike Couer, and stared at the man's instructions. She'd have to play nice, get along and then get out of there. If she didn't screw this up, she could be in and out without the Martins even knowing who she was or what she did. She'd made it this far; as long as she didn't get wrapped up in another set of arms, she'd be just fine.

For a moment she considered calling Mike and telling him about the body they had found, but she stopped. There wasn't enough evidence to track this back to the family. Sure, she could probably take Trevor down for the murder, but that wasn't what she was here for; no, she was here for them all. They had to be stopped before they put any more weapons into the hands of terrorist organizations…and that was to say nothing of the lives that they themselves had snuffed out. This family was likely responsible for the deaths of thousands of people, if not tens of thousands.

The thought made the anger bubble up inside her. These days that feeling, that fire, was her only constant companion. Without it, she wouldn't know who she was. It was that feeling that propelled her forward, past the crap in her personal life, and helped her to focus on her prime objectives. Her life wasn't hers to live. Her life belonged to the people of the world, people who deserved to be kept safe and out of the line of fire of the Martins.

Stuffing the phone back into her pocket, she made her way into the house.

She just needed to get her hands on as much information about the incident in Turkey as possible. There were reports of photos, pictures proving that the STEALTH team had been involved in the illegal gun trade, and during the event civilians had been shot and killed. If she could just prove it, or find evidence that the family was part of organized crime, not only would her past indiscretions at the agency be forgiven, but she might also find her way out of the remote offices and back to DC.

The house was silent as she weaved between the moving boxes. Trevor and Chad had been vague in their plans for the day, but she expected nothing less. No doubt, they were at the shanty taking care of their mess. She should have been out there with them, getting information about their possible involvement with the dead man and his family, but she hadn't found a way to get herself invited along. And really, even if she caught Trevor red-handed with this murder, where would it get her?

He was good at keeping people in the dark, but his family wasn't as good as they thought they were. She'd get what she needed. She always did.

Trevor's bedroom door was closed, but his room seemed like as good a spot as any to start. She opened the door. The room had nothing but four boxes, a desk, and a mattress and box spring on the floor. At the head of the bed, there was a rolled-up mummy bag sitting on a large body pillow.

Apparently, even though he had nothing, he was a man who still liked to make his bed in the morning.

Grabbing a box, she set it on the bed and pulled off the tape. As it opened, the scent of sand and sweat rose up and met her—the smell of war.

Well, she could fight, too.

She pulled out a set of fatigues. They were green and brown, a throwback to what Americans once wore in the jungles of Vietnam—not what she would have expected from desert warfare. The last time she'd seen an operative wearing this was in northern Africa. Some of the insurgents there loved to use the fatigues almost as their own personal calling card. They had even taken to calling themselves al-Akhdar, or "the Greens."

It didn't surprise her that this man would have found himself alongside such an infamous group. From what little she knew about them, the Martins had a way of being in prospective war zones even before the leaders of the country knew they were under fire.

She lifted the uniform out of the box and hung it up in Trevor's closet. Though she never had time to clean her own apartment back in Washington, coming in undercover as a cleaning lady had its benefits. She could almost openly go through whatever she wanted under the guise of her newfound job.

It didn't take long to empty the box and move to the next, putting away things as she came across them. Though she hadn't expected to find much in the boxes, she had hoped that maybe he'd tucked something away—a picture, some sentimental token—but there was nothing. In fact, aside from his picture and the few boxes that were in the room, there was little to prove that this man truly even existed.

The only things she'd been able to glean so far, thanks to what she'd managed to overhear from the brothers this morning, was that the rest of the family— Zoey and Jarrod—would be arriving sometime soon. When they got there, she would have little time alone in the house. She'd have to work fast.

After going through what amounted to four boxes of random clothing and a set of encyclopedias that she was sure dated from the 1980s, she folded up the boxes. Carrying them under her arm, she stepped toward the door. As she moved, she noticed a gap between the head of the bed and the wall. It wasn't much, just a couple of inches.

Making her way over to the gap, she pulled back his pillow, exposing a long black gun case.

Now we're talking.

She pulled out the case, gingerly setting it on the bed and clicking open the tabs. In the belly of the case sat an M107 .50 caliber. She'd only seen a few of these in her days, and they were always in the hands of snipers—army snipers, to be exact. She snapped a quick picture of the gun and its serial number, but made sure not to touch the weapon. She sent a quick message to her people at the Bureau, hoping that one of them could pull up something.

He had played her when he'd brought up Schofield. He must have been testing her. Which meant there had been something about her that made him think that she couldn't be trusted. Or maybe he mistrusted everyone. She racked her brain trying to think of something she had said or done that could have blown her cover, but nothing came to mind. She'd played it pretty cool...except for the girlie bit.

Or perhaps he wasn't Army after all. If his family had in fact been running weapons, as they assumed, then maybe this was just one from their catalog. There was little reason for Trevor to have such a specialized weapon out here in the Middle of Nowhere, Montana. Unless he feared for their safety, or he thought he was one phone call away from having to kill someone.

She was probably right in assuming he was the type who was always looking over his shoulder. It probably came with his kind of game.

Maybe it was that she simply saw some of her own life mirrored in his. Over the last year, thanks to her little slipup—okay, major setback—she had been away from home and the Bureau nearly the entire time. In fact, there had been only three days that she was in the office. One when she went in to see *him*, one when she was called into her superior's office and told she would henceforth be working remotely, and then when she was packing up her desk. Ever since then, she'd been living out of hotel rooms around the world. Everything in her life had been temporary and single-use.

She ran her fingers through her smooth hair. Since she'd taken residence at the Widow Maker Ranch she'd finally gotten the chance to buy and use real shampoo again, and not be stuck with the cheap stuff that was always in the guest basket at the hotels where she stayed.

Compared to Trevor's constantly on-guard life—a life that required high-caliber rifles and owning nothing but a smattering of dusty old clothes—a few split ends seemed to pale in comparison. At least she had a certain amount of freedom. For the most part, she could check out when she was off duty.

For a split second, she felt a niggle of pity for the handsome Trevor Martin. He was never going to be able to live a normal life, not doing what his family did. They would always be hunted. And forget about having a love life.

The pity turned to something else, something entirely too much like disappointment.

She was just being silly. What was going on with her since she met this man? It was like she had never been around a good-looking, dangerous, Harley-riding, perfectly built badass before.

She closed the gun case, slipping it back in exactly the same position she had found it.

No doubt with her unpacking his room and all, he would probably assume she had seen it, but she didn't want to make it blatant. And hopefully he would brush it aside, thinking she was the kind of woman who knew nothing about guns.

Her secret made a smile flutter over her lips. There was just something thrilling about being something and someone that no one expected at first glance. It was almost like a superpower…if she were a superhero, she'd have a cool name. No, better than cool—she'd want something enigmatic, mysterious. Something like the Shadow Defender, keeper of secrets and protector of the innocent.

She giggled as she walked out of the room, running smack-dab into Chad. Looking up, she tried to cover the guilt that was no doubt marking her features. Damn it, how had he gotten in without her hearing anything?

"Hey," she said, stepping around him. "I thought you guys were out for the day."

Chad glanced toward his brother's room. "Uh, yeah. What were you doing in there? Does Trevor know you were planning on going in there?"

She gave him her most alluring smile, hoping that she could bring down his suspicions in true female superhero style. "I just thought I'd get a move on unpacking all the boxes. I was going to go ahead and hit your room next. That way you guys have a comfortable safe haven to come home to at the end of the day." She shifted her weight, subtly exaggerating the curve of her hips. "There's nothing worse than a barren room."

Chad's eyebrow rose.

Crap, hopefully he didn't think she was making a move on him; she hadn't meant anything. No, not when it came to him. Chad was good-looking enough, but he wasn't nearly as handsome as Trevor. She thought back to the way Trevor had taken off his helmet and swept the long hair from his eyes. If he had a fan blowing on him, she might as well have been watching a freaking modeling shoot.

She turned before Chad could get any clue as to what she was thinking. The last thing she really needed was either brother assuming there was any possibility of something more than an employee-employer situation.

"Sabrina?" Chad called after her. "If you don't mind, I'll go ahead and unpack my things. No need for you to worry about it."

She waved behind her, not bothering to look back. There went her chance, at least for now, to get into his room. At least she had a starting point to her investigation. If she ran the serial number on the .50cal, maybe she could pull up something. If she was lucky, there would be some agency out there tracking the gun, but based on what had just happened, luck wasn't on her side.

She made her way to the newly remodeled kitchen, which still smelled of paint. As she pulled a box of Cap'n Crunch out of the pantry, the back door opened and Trevor strode in. He was sweaty and shirtless, wearing only a pair of running shorts and tennis shoes. He stopped and stared at her for a moment too long before he shut the door. Apparently he hadn't been planning on bumping into her, either.

He wiped his forehead with the back of his hand as he walked over to the cupboard by the sink and grabbed a glass of water. Since his back was to her, she could make out a droplet of sweat slowly twisting down the thick muscles along the tanned skin of his spine. The bead moved slowly, making her wonder if it tickled.

"I see you're one for a healthy start to the day. I like it," he said, filling up his glass and turning around with a cheesy, oh-so-cute smile on his face.

"The Cap'n and I have a long-term relationship," she said, hugging the box to her chest like it was a bulletproof vest. "He knows just how to make me smile."

"I hear you. I'm a sucker when it comes to food."

"You know what they say about the way to a man's heart," Sabrina said, but as the words escaped her, she just as quickly wished she could rein them back in.

Why couldn't she just be normal around this guy— flirty, yet out-of-bounds? Instead, here she was saying things that she couldn't have imagined herself saying when she was forced to take this assignment.

"In that case," Trevor said, grabbing a towel and dabbing at his forehead, "would you mind pouring me a bowl? I'll be right back, just going to go put on a shirt." He flipped the kitchen towel over his shoulder.

Hold up, had he really just implied she could make her way into his heart? No. He couldn't have meant anything like that.

As he walked away she once again found herself staring at the little bead of sweat, which now sat at the subtle indent that marked the place where his hips met his back. Her gaze moved lower as he walked away. His shorts moved in perfect harmony with his round, toned behind.

Yeah, she could touch that. Chances were, he would fit perfectly in the cup of her hand.

Wait, he was playing her. She couldn't fall for his abundant charms or his easy grace. No.

She turned around and grabbed a bowl from the cupboard and poured him some cereal, carefully setting the milk on the table beside it so he could add it in when he came back.

Her phone pinged with an email. Checking around her to make sure no one was near before opening it, she unlocked her phone. There was a message from Mike. Just seeing his name pop up on her screen made her stomach clench. Just once, she would have liked to not have that feeling. It was stupid, really. His name would always pop up. He was too involved in her life for him to just disappear. If anything, she was foolish to think she would just get over him and be able to go back to work and pretend that nothing had happened between them.

Maybe she would have been better off quitting her job and moving on to something else, but she had told herself she was a big girl—able to handle anything that life threw at her, that she would just have to accept the consequences that came with her choices…and yet she seemed to always die just a little every time she saw anything to do with her former flame.

She hated him. Everything emotional he represented. He was the embodiment of all of her worst flaws—her inability to say no, to make people unhappy, and the weakness she felt when it came to the needs of her heart. If only she could turn the damned thing off, be cold, distant, professional.

Opening the email, she read the encrypted note:

Dear Ms. Parker,
In regard to your findings at your current posting, we

are and have been aware of your assignments' past—
including jobs dealing with long-gun usage. I'm glad
to see you are finally making headway. Too bad it has
taken you this long.

If you fail to meet the goals and standards set forth
in your proposal in a timely manner, the SAC has let
me know that they will be forced to look elsewhere for
a UC who is better qualified. You have a week.
—M.C.

What a bastard. Mike had known what Trevor was
and he'd left it out of the case files he'd handed her. He
was trying to get her fired.

Of course.

What had she been thinking, assuming her sentence
would be simple banishment to a remote office as an
undercover agent along with her former flame? The special agent in charge, or SAC, whom they'd been forced
to report to regarding their relationship had put them
together out here in the middle of nowhere, hoping that
they would learn to get along and develop a new sense
of trust with each other. But the move had been ill-advised. As it was, she had a feeling she was in a dog-
eat-dog battle with her ex, and only one would leave
this kennel alive.

No big deal. She could do this. In fact, there was no
better impetus for her to kick butt and take names than
someone thinking she was incapable—or, in this case,
Mike thinking he had the upper hand and assuming he
could get rid of her that easily. She would show him, and
the rest of the Bureau, exactly what she was made of.

The door to the kitchen opened and Trevor walked
in. His smile had disappeared.

"Were you looking for something in particular?" he asked, the playful edge in his voice completely gone.

"Excuse me?" she asked, feeling the blood rush from her face as she stuffed her phone in her pocket.

"You went through my things. Why?" he said, staring at her.

She paused, thinking about every syllable before she spoke. "Your family hired me to do a job. I am here to help you get this house in order." She walked to the drawer and pulled out a spoon for him and set it down on the table beside his bowl like it was some kind of olive branch. "I have no interest in disrupting your life or invading your privacy," she lied, forcing her face to remain unpassable.

"Then why?"

"I told you why. I want to help." She sat down at the table, hoping he would recognize her contrition. "Look, I understand you're nervous. But about the man we found yesterday…"

Some of the anger disappeared from his face. "Did you tell anyone about the body?"

She shook her head. "Like I said, I am here to make your life easier, not cause more problems. If you don't want me to go in your room anymore, I won't." There wasn't anything in there she was looking for anyway.

He sighed. "No, don't worry about it. I guess I'm just a little jumpy. I'm not used to civilian life."

"That's okay. We're just going to need to start learning to communicate a little better with each other—especially when it comes to our boundaries." She motioned for him to sit.

He picked up the spoon as he sat down, finally a bit more relaxed in her presence.

Maybe she wasn't so bad as a UC after all—given time, she would get exactly what she needed.

Chapter 5

Trevor didn't quite know what to make of her. On one hand, Sabrina seemed to be everything a cleaning woman would be—focused, driven and into all of his things. On the other hand, the mere thought of someone poking around his house made him clench. He hadn't had a woman taking care of his life for him since... well, he was a child.

Done with breakfast, he walked back to his room. He hadn't had a closet, at least one that wasn't in a hotel or rented room, in forever. It was strange to think he actually owned something. In a way, it felt like a leash tying him to this place.

He had spent entirely too much time being out in the world and on his own to adjust to this kind of lifestyle overnight, but he had to admit that it would be nice to just hand things over to someone else for a while. For once, he could just focus on living.

A pit formed in his stomach. He'd been working in the shadows for so long he wasn't quite sure what living actually meant. The only thing he knew for sure was that he didn't want to be alone.

He thought of the way Sabrina had looked over breakfast, her long hair falling down in her face like gentle fingers that longed to caress her cheeks. He'd wanted to reach over and brush the tendrils out of her face, but as much as he had desired it, to touch her seemed wrong…especially after what had happened at the Cusslers'.

No matter how beautiful she was, she was clearly not interested in him. And yet if there was one reason he was glad to be leashed to this place, it was because of her.

But could he trust her?

He closed his bedroom door and walked to the head of the bed. Lifting out the gun case, he looked at the latch. The hair he'd left tucked in the lock was gone. She'd seen his gun.

No wonder she had been so strange with him, nervous even. He could only guess what she thought of him. Hopefully she thought he was just some redneck with a penchant for high-end weaponry. Or better yet, she hadn't a clue what she was looking at.

He pulled a hair from his head and put it back in the latch, setting the booby trap again. If she came back… well, they were going to have to have a longer talk. He'd show her exactly how well he could communicate.

Slipping the gun case back, he sat down on his bed and pulled out his phone. Zoey had sworn that she'd

looked into the woman's background, and he trusted
his sister's judgment and aptitude when it came to tech-
nology…and yet, every cell in his body was telling him
that Sabrina wasn't all she seemed to be. Zoey had to be
missing something. He didn't know much about housekeepers, but it couldn't have been normal for them to
open a gun case…that was, unless they were going to
strip it down and clean the gun, or if they were looking for something.

Whatever she was looking for, she wasn't going to
find it in his gun case. The only thing she'd find there
was a recipe for disaster.

He unlocked his phone and went to his secondary
email. Ever so carefully, he wrote:

Dear Ahmal,
My team will be in place Wednesday night for the hand-
off. Johnson and Beckwith. City Centre. Seven o'clock.
T

If Sabrina was a spy, she'd have it read within the
hour. If she was a decent spy, she'd have men in downtown Seattle Wednesday at seven.

He emailed Zoey using his private server, letting her
know to keep eyes on the fake drop.

The pit that had formed in his stomach started to dis-
sipate. For now, he'd done all he could to put his mind
at ease…at least when it came to Sabrina.

He still needed to get to the bottom of the Cussler
murder.

Crap. What if she is tied to the murder?

No. He shook his head at the very thought. She was
suspicious, but she didn't seem like the type who would

kill people. He'd seen those types more than he could count, and she didn't carry the same darkness in her eyes.

If anything, her blue eyes were like the sky…open, bright, and full of promise. And the way she sometimes looked at him, when she was unguarded it was like she wanted…well, she wanted *him*.

Yep, he was definitely losing his edge.

He needed to get to work.

As he made his way from his room and the traps he secretly hoped she wouldn't step into, Sabrina was whisking her way around the living room, dusting.

"I need to head up to check out the Cusslers. You wanna go with me?" he asked, trying not to notice the way her jeans hugged her curves as she bent over to dust the bottom of the built-in bookcase next to the television.

"Sure." She turned and smiled. "I don't know if you know this, but there is only so much of a mess that a man and his brother can make in a house. I swear, I've dusted this room at least three times in the last day. I could use a break."

He chuckled. "I can't say that I've dusted three times in my entire life. What's the point? It's just going to get dusty again."

She laughed, the sound high and full of life, and it made his longing for her intensify. It would have been so easy to take her back into his arms. She was…incredible.

Maybe being around her today was a mistake, not only professionally but personally as well.

"I…" he started, but the sound came out hoarse and he was forced to clear his throat. "Sorry. I was just going to say, I was thinking about running over to see our cousin at her family's ranch, Dunrovin. Maybe we could borrow a couple of horses and ride around the property and maybe a bit up the mountains behind the squatters' place…see if we find evidence that could help us get to the bottom of this guy's death."

Her face pinched for a moment, but then her smile returned…this time not quite reaching her eyes. "I haven't been on a horse in years, but I'd be happy to help you out. Investigating a murder is far more fun than cleaning a house." She walked to the coat closet and grabbed a jacket before turning back to him. "Wait, should I not say that? You being my employer and all?" She gave him a melting smile.

It worked.

"I'm not your employer…that would be my brother." He took her jacket from her and lifted it so she could simply slip her arms into it. As she moved under his hands, his fingers grazed her skin, sending sparks shooting through him.

He tried to ignore the way she made him feel, but the more he ignored it the hotter the sparks seemed to burn.

He walked a few steps behind her on the way out to his motorcycle. For a moment, she stood staring at it. "Um, do you just want to take my car?"

He checked his laugh. "What? Are you afraid of a little danger?"

Sabrina gave him a cute little half smirk. "There is a difference between danger and a death wish. Do you know how many people die each year on these things?"

Though he couldn't deny her logic, she wasn't seeing the bigger picture. "I've always thought life should be lived to its fullest. Sure, you can stay in a safe little bubble and live an extra day, or you can grab life by the horns and ride it for all it's got."

She laughed. "Of course, you would say that…if you want to ride, feel free, but I'll be following you in my car."

In a strange way, he found comfort in her refusal. Clearly, she wasn't the kind of woman who sought an adrenaline rush…or who wanted to court danger. Rather, she seemed to want to play by the rules. No one who lied for a living played by the rules all the time. There was a certain level of gray that just came with the life. He couldn't count the number of times he had been forced to break the law in order to serve the greater good. It was one of the things he had missed most about standing in the countryside of Turkey, running guns over militarized borders and taking down men who deserved to die a thousand painful deaths in recompense for the horrendous crimes they had committed.

Trevor had always considered himself to be on the side of righteousness when he'd been in the thick of things, but now…looking back, he couldn't help but wonder if he had made mistakes. There had been plenty of times when he didn't have to pull the trigger, when he could have let his target go…and yet, he'd never flinched. For him, there was never any hesitation. He was just there to do his job, do right by his family and get home safely. He'd never questioned his orders or his assignments. But what if he should have? What if he had killed innocents?

"Let's go ahead and take your car. I don't have a helmet for you anyway. And the last thing I'd want is for you to get hurt." He motioned toward her beat-up Pontiac. The paint was chipping around the wheel wells, and what paint remained was bubbling with rust. Clearly not a Bucar—a Bureau car—so she couldn't have been sent here by the Feds. That was, unless they had put her in this junker so she wouldn't fall under any unwanted scrutiny.

They did undercover well, but they weren't this good.

Besides, what could he possibly be under investigation for—they worked for the CIA. However, in the US government, they were notorious for the right hand not knowing what the left hand was doing…and it had only gotten worse with the new leadership in the Oval Office on down.

Then again, she could have been working for a foreign government. The Gray Wolves were known to have people planted throughout the Turkish government, and he wouldn't have doubted that they also had government allies in and around Europe.

He sighed as he opened her door and helped her into the car. He was making something out of nothing. Though he wasn't completely innocent, he wasn't guilty, either. He just needed to relax.

He walked around to the passenger side and stopped for a moment, trying to contain the writhing ball of snakes that were his feelings. Even if an innocent person had been killed, it hadn't likely been by him. He'd only fired on his enemies, but…they had been in an enclosed space. What if a round had ripped through the building and somehow struck someone outside? It had been known to happen.

In his time in the military, they'd touched on the topic of collateral damage time and time again. He'd always told himself that he was above making mistakes, especially ones that involved lives… but now he couldn't help questioning himself.

He'd let his sister down. He'd let her die. What if he'd killed someone else's family member in the process?

He closed his eyes, but the second he closed them he saw Trish's face, looking up at him as the pool of blood around her grew. He'd tried to save her. He'd killed at least five men getting to her, but by the time he'd gotten her to safety, it was already too late.

Every night since he'd gotten back to the States, he'd had the same nightmare—him doing those damned chest compressions on Trish. Waiting for her to take a breath. Checking her pulse. And watching in terror as he realized she was gone.

He was living in his own personal version of hell.

He'd never forgive himself.

All he could do now was protect the family he had left. And that started with making sure this Cussler guy's family wasn't going to come after them or bring the law down on them. They didn't need any more trouble.

As they drove to Dunrovin, he caught himself glancing over at Sabrina again and again. She seemed to be concentrating entirely too hard on her driving. Her eyes were picking up the light as it streamed in through the windshield, making them look even brighter. And now, in the sun, he could see the fine lines around her eyes and at the upturned corners of her mouth—the lines of someone who loved to laugh. In a way, it made her seem even more beautiful. Whoever had her on his arm was a lucky man.

"Have you been to this place before?" he asked, forcing himself to look away.

She nodded. "Yeah, I helped Gwen move their stuff to the new place when she and her mother decided to sell you all the ranch. Dunrovin is really nice. They've had some trouble in their past, but now they are up and running and doing well as a guest ranch."

They must not have the same problem with squatters that they were having at the Widow Maker. "Hey, you never did tell me what you knew about the Cusslers. I tried to look them up this morning, but it doesn't appear that they have left much of a paper trail."

"I don't know much, just what Gwen told me in passing."

"So she knew there were people living out there in the boondocks?"

Sabrina passed him a guilty look.

He wasn't sure if he should be annoyed that his cousin hadn't taken care of the problem before they arrived, or if he should be concerned. Gwen must have known the danger. Maybe she had avoided them out of fear.

He just loved walking into a hornet's nest.

"Do you know how many folks we should be worried about out there?"

"From what I know, which isn't too much, it sounds like there were just some brothers. I'm assuming that the man we found is one of them."

"Were any of the brothers married?" he asked.

"I don't know. They were all pretty reclusive, but with that came an ability to live off the land. Whoever is left out there, they are certainly more than capable of surviving."

He nodded. He wasn't worried about their ability to survive—in fact, he was about as far away from that concern as humanly possible. They were just looking for more potential threats. Hopefully he wouldn't tangle with the remaining brothers, their wives, kids, grandkids, dogs and who knew who or what else. He had been in that situation before. Family dynamics always had a way of complicating any situation.

When they found the rest of the clan—rather, if they found them—he could speak to them and discover what happened. Maybe he was making something out of nothing. Maybe the Cusslers had gotten in a fight, and the man he'd found had been on the losing end. Hopefully, this had nothing to do with the Gray Wolves, or Trevor's family's long-term safety.

"I'm not sure if you're aware," Sabrina started, sounding nervous, "but Gwen's husband, Wyatt, is the local sheriff's deputy here."

"Sabrina, can I ask you something?" As he asked, he second-guessed himself.

"Hmm?" she said, looking over at him and away from the road.

"I appreciate you not wanting to make waves with this guy's death…but why—"

Her face pinched as she interrupted him. "Let's just say that I don't want to draw any unnecessary attention."

"Why? Are you on the run from the law or something?"

She laughed, but the sound was tight. "Hardly. I just don't like drama. I've had enough of that over the last couple of years." She tapped her fingers on the steering wheel nervously. "And as much as I think murderers should be held accountable, this guy didn't seem like the type that would want someone digging too deeply into his life."

To a certain degree, he agreed with her. However, everything just felt off about her answer. She was hiding something.

"If you don't mind me asking, what kind of drama have you been going through?"

She nibbled at her lip, like she was deciding whether to tell him the truth. It all came down to this—if she opened up to him he would finally be able to trust her. If she didn't, well...

"Let's just say I found myself in a relationship with the worst possible man."

Oh.

She was wounded. Now she was beginning to make a little more sense to him. He could understand some of the fear and pain she was feeling.

"I get it." It was the only thing he could think to say. What he really wanted to do was to pull her into his arms and make her feel better. Together, they could heal from the traumas of their past.

Sabrina chuckled. "What about you—any skeletons in your closet?"

He visibly twitched but tried to cover it up by casually scratching at his neck. He wasn't sure he was ready to tell her about his own failed relationships. "I... I used to be married."

Instead of coming at him with questions, as he assumed she would, she sat in silence for a long time letting the road roll by.

"I hope you know you can trust me," she said, finally breaking the silence between them.

This time he didn't even try to cover up his twitch.

There was no way she could possibly read his mind, and yet here they were. "The rifle at the head of my bed…"

She tensed, her hands wrapping tight around the steering wheel until her knuckles were white. "Yeah, I was going to ask you about that."

At least she wasn't denying or trying to hide the fact that she had gotten into his gun case. He could respect her honesty.

"I spent quite a few years in the army before we started in the investments game. I guess some old habits die hard."

He was grateful as a ranch came into view in the distance. There was a long row of stables, a main house and a bright red barn. The place looked like something out of *Town & Country* magazine. "Is that Dunrovin?"

Sabrina nodded. "You should see this place at Christmas. Gwen showed me some pictures of last year's Yule Night Festival. There were Christmas lights everywhere, the whole shebang."

He had no idea what the Yule Night thing was, but he was glad they were no longer talking about their pasts.

As they drove up and parked in the gravel lot of the ranch, a group of mutts ran out to greet them. Well, mostly mutts. Among them was a small Chihuahua barking maniacally at their approach. In fact, the little dog seemed to be the leader of the pack, egging on the rest of them in their cacophony.

"Looks like we got the royal greeting," he said with a chuckle.

An older woman walked out from the ranch's office, waving at them as they approached. Behind her was a woman with long, wild blond hair whom he recognized as his cousin Gwen. He hadn't seen her since they were children, but even the way she moved, with an air of confidence and grace, hadn't really changed.

The older woman called the dogs off and herded them into the office, closing the door behind the pack and then turning back to Trevor and Sabrina. "Welcome to Dunrovin. It's a pleasure to finally get the chance to meet you, Trevor. I've heard so much about you from Gwen," she said, extending her hand as he made his way up the steps.

"The pleasure is all mine…" He shook her hand as he waited for her to supply him with her name. Hopefully all she had heard about him had been positive.

When he and Gwen had last met, when they were both about eight years old. He had pulled her pigtails, which had quickly devolved into a wrestling match that ended with them both muddy messes. He could still distinctly remember the hay sticking out of Gwen's French braids and the stupid, victorious smile on her face.

"Eloise. Eloise Fitzgerald," the silver-haired woman said, giving his hand a strong shake.

"Hey guys," Gwen said with a nod. "I already have the horses waiting for you in the trailer. Are you sure you don't want me to go along with you on your ride? I know some great Forest Service trails. There's one up Elk Meadows you would love."

Eloise jabbed a sharp-looking elbow into Gwen's ribs and looked back and forth between him and Sabrina, like she was seeing something between them that wasn't there.

"Oh," he said with a chuckle. "We…no…"

"It's not that kind of ride," Sabrina said, finishing his sentence for him. "We are just going to go out and check some fences, then maybe head up the mountain for a couple of hours."

Gwen frowned. "The fences were in good order when I left."

Eloise looked over at her like she was clearly not getting the hint. "Don't worry about it, Gwen. You and I have plenty of things to do in the office today. In fact, I was hoping you could call next week's guests and confirm their reservations. Then we need to finalize the menus and talk to the kitchen staff."

Thank goodness for busy work.

"I'll be waiting for you in the office," Eloise said, motioning inside. "Shortly."

Gwen nodded as Eloise gave them a quick, knowing wave and made her way into the office. She was met with a barrage of barking.

"I hope you don't mind taking the old ranch pickup," Gwen said, walking them out toward the barn where a white pickup and horse trailer were waiting. As they grew nearer, there was the thump of hooves coming from the trailer. "I already put their saddles on, but you're going to need to cinch them tighter when you get there." She looked him up and down as though she doubted his abilities. "Are you sure you can handle this? If you need, you can give me a call and I can help you out."

He waved her off. He hadn't been riding in a long time, but he was sure that after a couple of minutes he'd be more than comfortable back in the saddle. "Nah, but thanks. If I need something, I'll just give you a ring."

"Just so you know, about half the back side of the Widow Maker is without cell reception—or it's sporadic at best. Make sure you're careful out there," Gwen said, giving Sabrina a look of concern. "If Trevor is anything like he was when we were kids, he's going to go all out and get himself into trouble. He tends to act first and ask questions later."

He laughed, the sound coming from deep in his core. "I'm not a kid anymore. You don't need to worry about me."

"I'm not worried about you," Gwen said, stepping closer to Sabrina. "I have this girl's life and the welfare of our horses to be concerned about."

Though she was just teasing, he couldn't help being rankled by her ribbing. "Look, if you don't want us to take the horses, it's okay. We can find some other way to do the work. Chad and I have been talking about getting four-wheelers. I was just putting it off until we knew exactly what—"

"Stop. It's okay," Gwen said, interrupting him. "I just want you to remember that we are in Montana, not New York. Everything isn't just a phone call away. I don't want you to go messing around up there and find yourselves in trouble. Believe it or not I love you, cousin."

"I love you, too, even if you are still a pain in my ass." He laughed as he wrapped his arm around her and gave her a quick side hug. "Hey, about the Cusslers... Sabrina said you knew a bit about them."

Gwen nodded, smoothing her shirt where it had wrinkled under his touch. As she moved, he spotted the band on her finger. "They would come to mind with the mention of a pain in the ass, wouldn't they?" Gwen sighed. "What did they do now? I want you to know, I tried to talk to them when I found out you were going to take over the ranch. They were less than welcoming."

Apparently, they had all been alive, which was more

than he was currently working with. Yet he couldn't let Gwen know anything that would implicate her should something leak to the authorities.

"I believe it," he said, stabbing the toe of his boot into the gravel of the parking lot. "How many are living out there?"

She shrugged. "All I know for sure is that there were four brothers and a couple of women. But there could be more or less. They were a bit like rats, scurrying around and hiding whenever we went out there to try to talk to them."

Which meant that they may well have been around when he and Sabrina had gone out to evict them. He could understand exactly why they had been living out there for so long. It was hard to catch their kind.

He glanced over toward Sabrina, who gave him an acknowledging nod. Her face was pinched, like she was working hard to keep a secret, and somehow that simple look made something shift inside him…something like trust clicking into place. No, it was something else, something deeper, a feeling much too close to desire.

Like before, he wanted to tell her to relax and that everything would be all right, but if he'd learned anything in the last few months, it was that no one close to him ever walked away unharmed.

He couldn't allow himself to fall for her. And if he couldn't stop himself, he most certainly couldn't allow her to get any closer to him than she already was. If he could, he would fire her and send her far from this place…but Chad would have his hide.

"Do you know about how old they all were?" Sabrina asked.

Gwen shook her head. "The oldest brother was probably around forty. And the women... I don't know if they were wives or sisters, but they could have been anywhere between their twenties and forties. From the state of them, it was hard to tell."

"What do you mean?" Trevor asked.

Gwen twitched. "They hadn't bathed in a long time. Their hair was in mats. They looked absolutely wild. We wanted to help them, but what could we do? We were barely making it as it was. And like I said, the Cusslers were well beyond wanting or taking help."

"I get it, Gwen. After seeing their place..." Trevor stopped as he tried to prevent the memory of the dead man's sallow face from creeping into his mind. "Do you know if they get along?"

Gwen nibbled at her bottom lip. "From what I know and what my husband has said, it seemed as though they do. But there are whispers that there are other groups out there—families like the Cusslers who take to the hills."

"Do you know where they're living?"

She shrugged. "Nomads for the most part. The Cusslers just managed to find a spot to squat where they didn't face too much trouble."

"So they don't move around at all?" Sabrina asked.

"I think they may have a hunting cabin farther up the ridge. I assume they went up there whenever they were needing a fresh supply of game."

Trevor checked his excitement. Just because they found a possible location for the rest of the Cusslers didn't mean they were any closer to finding out who had killed the man.

"Now, I don't know if there is any validity to it, but I heard rumblings from Wyatt that the Cusslers were fighting another family out there. From the sounds of it, it was a real Hatfields-and-McCoys kind of thing—doesn't sound like there were ever any kind of winners." Gwen glanced toward the mountains that loomed over them. "It was just another reason for us to keep our distance, the last thing we wanted to do was get wrapped up in a never-ending war."

He held back a chuckle. His entire life was just one unending war. Whether it was here or on the banks of the Yangtze River, he'd always be fighting some kind of battle, but at least these kinds weren't the ones inside him.

He relaxed slightly.

If Gwen was right, they had nothing to worry about. The man was a victim of nothing more than a hillbilly civil war. But if she was wrong...if the Gray Wolves had planted a false rumor...

No, they wouldn't. It was too far-fetched. The Gray Wolves were smart, but like him, they wouldn't just walk into this community and start stirring up trouble. They would want to fly under the radar.

But he couldn't make another catastrophic mistake when it came to his family's safety—he couldn't live with himself if he lost someone else because of his failure to understand his enemy.

Eloise poked her head out of the office door. "Gwen, you coming?"

She tossed him the keys and he scooped them out of the air. "Thanks, Gwen."

She dipped her head. "Not a problem. Just be careful out there. I don't have a good feeling about this." She turned to walk away, but looked back at them. "You aren't planning to go out there to see the Cusslers today, are you?"

Sabrina slipped her hand into his, their skin brushing as she took the keys from him.

"Nah," he said, but even to his ears it came out sounding tinny and fake as he looked down to the place where Sabrina had touched him. "Fences today. Just wanted to know what to expect."

Gwen gave him a wide smile, like she actually believed his lie.

Denial just might have been his most powerful ally—especially when it came to his own feelings.

Chapter 6

Sabrina gripped the steering wheel hard, carefully maneuvering the truck and horse trailer down the bumpy road leading straight to the Cusslers' shanty. Every time the truck hit a bump and the mud splattered against the windshield, she cursed last night's rain, and she couldn't help but to look over at Trevor to see if he was silently judging her.

Truth be told, she hadn't driven a truck carrying such a heavy load before, but she would never be second to a man. She could do anything he could. She was tough. And what she didn't know, she would learn.

"Are you sure you don't want me to drive?" Trevor asked, holding on to the dashboard like it was his lifeline.

She gritted her teeth. "I've got this." As she spoke, the front right tire connected with a giant rock in the road, jarring them so hard it made her jump in the seat.

"Dude," Trevor said, looking back at the horse trailer they were pulling. "If you're not careful, you're going to end up rolling us."

Though she was only going ten miles an hour, she slowed the truck down even more. "Look, Trevor, if you think you can drive better than I can on this crap, be my guest. But it's not as easy as it looks." She motioned toward the muddy, pitted road in front of them. "Have you ever even driven a truck and trailer before?"

He opened his mouth to speak, but paused for a long moment as he stared at her. "I've done more of this kind of driving than I care to admit."

This was her chance—finally she could learn more about this man in a way that wouldn't seem suspicious.

"All that driving have anything to do with that gun I found in your bedroom?" she asked, raising an eyebrow.

He snickered. "You're awful curious, aren't you?"

Or maybe it wasn't her opening, after all.

"I just like to know who I'm working for...and whether I need to be concerned for my safety or not."

He slowly blinked, like he was trying his hardest to control every single muscle in his body. "The only people who should be scared of me are my enemies. You've already shown me that we are fighting on the same side. In all honesty, it's been a long time since I've been around somebody—other than my family—who hasn't wanted to use me to achieve their own gains. It's a bit of a relief."

A wave of guilt washed over her. Sometimes she hated the duality of her job. Here she was making strides professionally, and yet she found herself personally compromised. It would've been so much easier if she didn't like the man she been sent here to investigate.

Then again, perhaps his little speech was nothing more than a subtle manipulation, a tactic to lull her into becoming complacent. Well, if he thought she would be that easy to manipulate, he was wrong.

Or maybe she was just looking for a reason to stop herself from falling for Trevor. It was unprofessional in every way, to even think about having feelings for the handsome man sitting beside her in the truck. Yet a heart wanted what a heart wanted; if her heart was easily controlled by her mind, she would never have found herself in the backwoods of Montana.

This time had to be different. She couldn't let herself be sucked in by a man's charms; she had to remain distant. Untouchable.

"With time, Trevor, you'll find that I'm a woman who is different from the rest. I'm not the type to pander to a guy."

Trevor took his hands off the dashboard and leaned back in his seat, like he was trying to avoid the ricochet of her words within the truck's cabin. "You don't think I was already aware of that?" Trevor asked.

"Well, I just don't want you thinking that I was…" She paused as she searched for the right word. "I guess I don't want you to assume that I'm weak. You know, after what happened the first time we came down here to the Cusslers' place. I don't know what came over me. This time when we see this guy, I'll be ready."

Trevor looked at her for a long moment, almost as if he was trying to decide how to proceed. "Sabrina, it's okay to have a weakness."

There was a softness in his voice that made her wonder if there wasn't another layer of meaning to his words.

"Weakness is unacceptable. Weakness means we

have to depend on those around us. Doing something like that means you open yourself up for disappointment, for hurt. Strength is the only way to survive."

"Do you mean in dating, or in life?" Trevor asked, as his hand slid slowly to the center of the bench seat.

"Both," she said, jerking the wheel as she dramatically tried to avoid another pothole, secretly wishing he'd be forced to hold on again so his hand wouldn't be so accessible. A girl only had so much restraint.

"Don't take offense, but…" Trevor sighed. "Well, you sound like a woman who's been hurt…a lot."

She answered with a dark chuckle. "If you had grown up in a family like mine, you'd see the world from my perspective, too."

"You mean because your family was military?" Trevor asked.

She was surprised he remembered anything about her. She'd have to be careful about what exactly she said to him. "The moving around and constant change was fine. Sure, it takes a special breed to be able to live that kind of lifestyle, but that wasn't what our problems really stemmed from. My dad was the kind who always wanted to be in control, and sometimes that meant acting in a way that is completely unacceptable by today's standards."

"Is that why you took the truck keys from me—you wanted to remain in control?"

"I took the truck keys because I saw you driving the other day. I wanted no part of that." She laughed.

The smile returned to Trevor's face and his hand moved a bit closer. "One time is not indicative of anything." He reached over and took her hand, like he finally was giving up on her making the first move.

His hand felt cool against hers, and she wasn't sure if it was because he was cold or if she was just blazing hot because of her nerves. She thought about disentangling their fingers, but as he started to caress her skin she couldn't find the willpower.

It felt so good to be touched. It was strange, but besides their hug the other day, it had been a long time since anyone really touched her. More, she was being touched by Trevor...the only man she had ever been instantly attracted to.

With most men, her attraction to them only occurred after months of them being securely planted in the friend zone. She hadn't really taken Mike's advances seriously for at least six months; that was until Mike had finally kissed her after a lunch meeting, and something inside her changed.

This thing with Trevor, it was...disconcerting, uncomfortable and strange. And yet so right. When she looked at him, she wanted to move closer. To touch more of him. To feel his arms around her. It was like he was the sun on her face after months of winter gray. As much as she loved the sensation, that spark, she hated it.

Many of her friends had told her stories about the elusive spark, and how they knew the instant they met someone that they loved them. All their talk had made her wonder if there wasn't something wrong with her—aside from her atrocious taste in her past boyfriends. She had tried to make herself feel better by telling herself that her friends were crazy, that nothing like that ever existed except in movies. Those sparks were just weakness...their body's way of opening itself up and revealing its most vulnerable part—the heart.

Right now, she wasn't sure if she was right or wrong,

but she wasn't ready to give her heart to anyone...not after all she had put it through in the last few years.

"I'm a good driver, regardless of what you think." She forced herself to let go of his hand.

A silence widened the gap between them.

"Uh-huh," he said, sounding dejected as he put his hand in his lap.

Maybe it had been wrong to pull back from him. If she had stayed put it might have made it easier to learn everything she needed to know about his family, their work, their role in the murders and their gun trade. And for a while, she could have just lied to herself and told herself that this really was her life. She could play the housekeeper who was falling head over heels for the man beside her.

She groaned. Why did he have to make her feel this way? It was so much easier to live within the framework built by the FBI—where he was nothing but her assignment and she was safely detached.

If feelings didn't have a way of muddling everything in her life maybe they wouldn't be so bad, but as it was, feelings sucked.

As the little shanty came into view, with its rusty, corrugated steel roof filled with holes, she relaxed. She'd never been so happy to get to a dead body in her life. At least she'd have something to think about besides her feelings.

That was, if she could just control her reaction when she saw the man again. She couldn't be weak in front of Trevor. She had to prove to him that, like he said, a single event wasn't truly indicative of anything—it was an anomaly.

She pulled the truck and trailer down the drive leading to the pathetic shack and turned to Trevor. "I'll get the horses together and buttoned up if you want to go take a look around."

He gave her a look of disbelief, like he questioned who she thought she was giving orders to him. She'd have to reel that in a bit. No matter what she personally felt, she had to remember that she was supposed to be doing a job...a job that didn't include leading the charge in getting to the bottom of a hillbilly's murder mystery. She had bigger fish to fry.

"If you don't mind, I'll give you a hand," Trevor said. "With things out here so up in the air, I don't want to leave you alone. We don't know where those other Cussler boys are, or the women. For all we know, we're walking out into some kind of mountain men's civil war."

He wasn't wrong, but she couldn't seem to think straight thanks to his presence.

"You think his body's still inside?" she asked.

Trevor shrugged. "I'd be lying if I said I hoped his body was still in there. It would make things a lot easier if his remains are buried somewhere out in the woods."

Once again, they were skating down the slippery slope between right and wrong, but she couldn't disagree with him.

The horses nickered as she and Trevor stepped out of the truck and into the mud. Theirs were the only fresh tracks.

"It's okay, guys, we're gonna get you out," Trevor cooed to the horses as they stomped inside the trailer.

He walked around behind the trailer and opened the door. Carefully, they backed the horses out and walked them around and tied them up. He helped her put on the horse's bridle and cinch her saddle tight. He may not have gone on a horseback ride in a long time, but he seemed right at home taking care of the animals.

"Here, let me give you a leg up," he said, holding out his hands.

She didn't want to take his help. Not after she'd made such a show of taking over the driving. But the last time she'd ridden on a horse the owner had kindly given her a set of steps in order to get up.

She put her left foot in the stirrup and he helped her with her right. For a moment, his hand rested on her thigh as he untied the horse and handed her the reins, unclipping the lead rope.

"You got him. You gonna be okay?" he asked.

She nodded. She'd forgotten the thrill that came with sitting astride a horse. It didn't escape her that she was sitting on an animal who weighed a ton more than she did, but was just as stubborn. Hopefully today would go well and she wouldn't make an idiot of herself. All she had to do was pretend she knew what she was doing and soon enough she would.

At least she hoped.

"What's her name?" she asked as the horse took an unwelcome step away from the trailer. She checked the reins, trying to pull her to a stop.

"First off, he's a gelding, and I think he goes by Zane."

She wasn't off to a great start.

She ran her hands down his whiskey-colored coat. "You and I are going to get along great, aren't we, Zane?" She tried to sound more confident than she felt.

The horse took another step, and she tried to relax

into the saddle. It was going to be okay; she just had to play it cool.

Trevor rode up alongside her. "And this is Donnie. They're both supposed to be great horses, so I think you're gonna do fine." He reached back and slipped something into the saddlebag.

Apparently, he could see exactly how uncomfortable she was. She readjusted herself in the saddle and tried to recall what she had been told about sitting up straight. She couldn't remember exactly how she was supposed to move with the horse. No doubt she looked like a sixth-grade girl at her first dance—gangly and out of rhythm.

And just like a sixth-grade girl, she wondered when she would finally get over her awkwardness. She was tired of always feeling like she didn't quite fit into any situation. Just once, she would've liked to let herself go and fully give herself to the world around her.

Thankfully, Trevor and Donnie took the lead and Zane moved in step behind them. They rode over to the shanty, where Trevor stepped down from his horse and handed her his reins. "You guys stay here and I'll go check on our friend. I'll be right back."

She looped the reins in her hand and stared at the cabin's blacked-out window. For a second, she considered getting down and going in with Trevor, but she stayed seated. Maybe it was weak of her to not want to see the dead man, but it saved her from making a fool of herself. It was probably the same reason Trevor had left her behind.

She couldn't deny the fact that he was thoughtful and kind, but she forced the thoughts away. No, he was a fugitive from the law. Her enemy.

She pulled out her phone—no signal. She hated the feeling of being cut off from the world around her. There probably wouldn't be a cell signal again until they were back at the ranch. She reminded herself that they'd be back tonight. Besides, Mike had made it clear that he wasn't keen on the idea of her checking in too often. If she was out of contact, at least she would be off Mike's radar.

And yet the whole situation made the hair on the back of her neck stand on end. She was completely on her own. If Trevor caught even a whiff of what she was up to, he could kill her and dump her body without anyone ever being the wiser.

She took a calming breath. No, she hadn't made him suspect anything. This would go fine. It would be suspicious if she tried to leave now. She just had to blend in and play along, gleaning information as they went.

There was the rattle of dishes from inside the cabin. "Everything okay in there?" she called.

"Yeah, everything's fine," Trevor answered. "The body's gone. Aside from him being missing, everything else seems untouched." Trevor walked out of the cabin and got back up into the saddle. He was frowning, and there was a distinct look of concern on his face.

"I bet it was one of the brothers. They probably saw us here the other day and as soon as we left they came in and got the body."

She thought back to the puddle of blood she'd destroyed behind the shanty. More than likely, the blood had belonged to one of the other Cusslers, and it wasn't until he'd been treated for his wound that the family could come and recover the body. And yet she couldn't tell Trevor what she really thought.

Trevor rode toward the trail that led up the mountain. "The only way we can be sure to know what is going on here is to find them. We need to talk to them and make sure they know they aren't welcome back. I can't have my family involved with whatever's going on out here. We don't do chaos."

She nearly chuckled. Her life was often nothing but chaos and one crazy event after another—just another reason they didn't fit. Not to mention she would be constantly keeping secrets from him. A relationship and life built on bedlam and secrets wasn't viable—she had learned that lesson all too well. And in her line of work, all she had was secrets. She could only imagine what would happen if she truly had to keep everything about her work away from the man she loved.

Wait, did she love him? No. It was impossible.

She had to pay attention to the work at hand and remember that she was going to bring chaos to his life no matter what he wanted.

"What else have you found out about their family?" she asked as they started ascending the trail.

"My sister, Zoey, she's a super nerd. Anything on the computer, she can do it," he said, his tone filled with unmistakable love and pride for her. "She's been looking into a few things for me, and so far, we haven't found anything of use. Though I can't say I was surprised."

"She found nothing. That's odd."

"There was just one headline, must have been from forty years ago—a man who might have been the dead guy's father was convicted on a murder charge. Apparently, he suffered from what the paper called insanity, but from what I can make of it, it sounded like he had undiagnosed schizophrenia. He spent ten years in an institution, then disappeared from the records."

She cringed as she thought of the antiquated institutions where those with mental health issues had been stuffed away. They were the thing of nightmares—corporal punishment, physical labor, isolation, lobotomies and even sometimes practicing eugenics. She could barely imagine the horror and the terror those who were forced to live in such a place must have experienced.

"As in he died? Or do you think he escaped?"

Trevor shrugged. "I would guess he died, but who knows."

Even if the man was alive, by now he'd have to be in at least his late sixties, and the last thing he would do is kill his own son. But then again, humans—and the atrocities they committed—constantly surprised her. Filicide wasn't that uncommon, even if she wasn't accustomed to seeing it. She'd heard about it in many other investigations—and it was increasingly common in cases where large amounts of money or corporations were involved…or in cases of mental illness.

On the other hand, she'd read study after study that had found that only a small proportion of schizophrenics were dangerous to others…and yet this man had already proven that he was in the small percentage that was willing to kill.

She nibbled at her lip. If she remembered correctly, children of a person with schizophrenia were 13 percent more likely to develop symptoms of the disease.

"Do you think he was killed by family, or do you really think it was someone else? One of the other squatter families?"

The leather of his saddle creaked as he looked back at

her. "I hope it's one of those things. If not, we're going to have a significantly bigger problem on our hands."

"What are you going to do if these guys come back to the shack?" she asked.

"We will make sure they know they aren't welcome…we can't have people being murdered left and right on our land and we can't be compromised—" He stopped and glanced back at her to see if she was listening. "We can't have anyone or anything living at the ranch that is going to be a liability."

She tried to keep from cringing. "Gwen and her mother lived here for a long time. They managed to coexist peacefully with the Cusslers. Don't you think it's strange that all of a sudden people are turning up dead out here?"

"Gwen didn't tell you everything, did she?" He laughed. "Gwen's crew called the cops out here more times than I can count to evict the family. When that didn't work, they came out and bulldozed their little shanty—more than once. These suckers are like gophers. They just keep popping their heads up."

In a way, she couldn't help but feel sorry for the people who had been living out here on the land illegally; no doubt, if they had other options, they wouldn't have found themselves in the situation they were in. But perhaps she was giving the Cusslers too much credit. They were knowingly breaking the law, indifferent about the rights of others, disrespectful and possible killers.

She shook her head as she thought of the moral pluralism they were facing. Why could nothing be cut-and-dried? What she would give to go back in time, to live in her early twenties when she was smart and resourceful enough to be independent, but still naive enough to believe that everything in the world was simply black or white, good or evil. She longed for the days when she just made a decision and didn't second-guess herself or think of at least nineteen other ways to answer the questions posed to her.

"I'm sure Gwen doesn't feel good about what she was forced to do," she said, thinking of the moment she covered up the blood, and when she had come inside the shanty to see Trevor wiping off the gun.

"Like Gwen said, they were well beyond help." Trevor slowed down so they could ride side by side.

The terrain had flattened out and they were surrounded by a thick pine forest, a forest where anything or anyone could have been hiding completely undetected. Chills rippled down her spine as she thought of the danger that may well have been surrounding them. Trevor reached down and ran his fingers over his gun's grip as he also must have realized the farther they rode, the farther they were from help.

"Had you ever been to the house before, you know, before we saw *him*?" she asked.

Trevor shook his head. "No, but I'd heard about the place and I had been tasked with cleaning it up—just like you."

Was that what he had been doing with the murder weapon—cleaning up the place?

She wanted to ask him why he had wiped off the gun, but if she revealed what she had seen, it may well place her in danger. Trevor would never hurt her, but she didn't know if she could say the same thing about the rest of his family. If it was known she could act as a witness and testify against him—if push came to shove—they may decide to take her out. As it was, he had already hinted that they saw her as some kind of liability.

She was the only one outside the family, and outside the Cusslers, who knew about the murder.

She had known she was in danger before, but as she worked through her thoughts, the fear within her swelled.

"Is that why you picked up the gun and wiped it off?" If she was going to be in danger, she might as well at least find out the truth.

Trevor pulled his horse to a stop and she followed suit. He stared at her for a long moment, like he was thinking about exactly what he wanted to say. He had to realize there was no use in lying; obviously she had seen what he had done, and he was likely weighing the consequences and ramifications of her revelation.

"I don't know why I did that. I just—"

"Wanted to cover your brother's tracks?" she said, finishing his sentence.

"Look, I don't know where you got that idea, but Chad isn't the kind of guy who would just come out and murder somebody. We aren't that kind of people… we're just looking for a quiet place to retire and get out of the public eye." Trevor raised his hands, like he was submitting to her.

She wanted to believe him, but he and his family were likely nothing but a deadly force.

"But you weren't sure, or else you wouldn't wipe down the gun. There was no harm in just leaving it there if you knew he wasn't responsible."

He looked down at his hands as he rested them on the saddle horn.

"From the little time I've been here, it's obvious to

me you guys aren't all you say you are—you're not just some investment bankers or hedge fund family or whatever." Her entire body tensed as she thought about how much danger she was putting herself in.

"Who is it that you think we are?" Trevor asked, catching her gaze. He looked torn.

"I don't know, but I want you to tell me." She was forcing him to completely trust her or else get rid of her.

She was playing the odds that he had strong feelings for her, feelings that he would give in to. It was just too bad that if he did open up to her, he'd end up getting screwed.

Chapter 7

The last person who started asking questions about his family had ended up dead. It had been three weeks before the body washed ashore on the coast of North Carolina. They handled security breaches in such a way that he was surprised anyone had ever found the body at all.

He couldn't let anything happen to Sabrina. She wasn't like the man before, who had been investigating the family for the French government. She was innocent and unfortunately too observant and smart for her own good—and for his as well.

"My family and I are from New York. Last year, our tech company VidCon went public and we sold our shares to an investor. We all had been working together for so long it just didn't make sense for us to go our separate ways, and we all loved the Widow Maker. We came here a lot as children and had so many good memories. Here, we could be together as a family, each building our own houses on the property."

He looked over at her to see if she was buying his story. From the sour look on her face, she wasn't.

"I know that's who you say you are, but most tech junkies I've met don't have sniper rifles in their bedroom. Not to mention a closet full of military gear." She looked at him like he was growing two heads. "I'm not an idiot, Trevor."

"Yes, I was in the military. Where do you think I learned how to run logistics for a company?" He had to make her believe the story he was selling, otherwise she'd be toast.

She nudged her horse forward, making him wonder if she just couldn't stand being so close to him any longer. He wanted to reach out and pull her back to him, to tell her to stop thinking what she was thinking, that she was wandering down a dangerous path—but he couldn't.

"I know you're not telling me something, Trevor. You don't have to keep lying to me. I want to help." As she spoke, he couldn't help but notice that she wasn't looking at him.

They rode in silence as they moved off the property and onto public lands, Sabrina leading the way, for at least three miles. He didn't know exactly where they were going, but it didn't matter; he needed all the time he could get in order to make a decision about what to do with her.

If he were smart, he would take care of the problem that she was becoming with a single shot. He'd hate himself for it, but he needed to protect his family. They had to come first—they always came first. The dedication and loyalty they had for one another was the reason they had survived in the business as long as they had. He couldn't let a woman come between them.

And yet there was something about her that he was inexplicably drawn to. Sabrina was the last thing he had expected when he'd learned that she was the family's housekeeper. She didn't seem to fit the bill of someone who would want to make her living by cleaning up after people. She seemed like the kind of woman who would find that monotonous. If anything, she seemed like a fit for a job like a district attorney or something…a job that would require she be able to speak her piece and then back it up with statistics and charts.

He could imagine her up in front of a judge and jury, arguing for the greater good. She'd definitely put him on the spot about that gun…and in doing so, she seemed to understand that she was going to draw scrutiny. And yet she still had the strength to face him head-on. That ability both captivated and terrified him.

"Sabrina," he said, finally breaking the silence between them as he rode up alongside her, "don't be upset with me. I'm sorry about what happened with the gun. I made a mistake. Just know it was made with the best intentions."

She sighed, letting the clatter of their horses' footfalls against the rocky scree path fill the air. "I appreciate your apology, but I don't like feeling like I'm being lied to. And if you're like me…or if you're feeling what I'm feeling…" She reached over and took his hand, the simple action surprising him. "You have to understand that all I really want is for you to open up to me."

He wanted to do that, to tell her everything about who he was, what he'd seen and where he'd been. He wanted someone to tell his fears to and his dreams, but that wasn't his life. It wasn't something he could offer another person. His life was complicated, so much so that regardless of what his heart wanted, he couldn't risk bringing another person in.

And yet he couldn't deny that he was feeling something for her—something he hadn't felt for a woman in a long time.

Not for the first time since her death, Trevor wished he could go to Trish to ask her advice. She would've known exactly what to do and the kinds of questions to ask. He missed her so much. His brothers and Zoey were great, but none of them had a relationship like he'd had with Trish. With her, he'd always been able to talk about anything—even feelings. He didn't delve into them often, and now that Trish was gone, he wasn't sure he was really up to talking about feelings ever again. They were just so damned complicated, especially when it came to the other sex.

"Sabrina, have you had a lot of serious relationships? I know you said you'd had a rough time with the last guy you dated, but have you dated anyone else for a long time?" *Ugh*. That had not come out at all like he'd wanted it to. It sounded so stupid.

She glanced over at him with a cheeky grin on her face. "I do know what a serious relationship is, Trevor." She laughed. "And yes, I've had a couple serious relationships. Why?"

"When you were in these relationships, did you always tell them everything?"

The grin on her face twitched. "What are you getting at, Trevor?" Her voice lost its playful edge.

He'd struck a nerve. She must have been hiding something about her love life. Maybe that's why she had come to the middle of nowhere to disappear. He'd dated enough in his lifetime that he could certainly understand the desire. There was nothing worse than heartbreak.

At least he wasn't the only one with a secret.

"I'm not saying that I think you're a liar or anything," Trevor said. "I'm just asking if there are things you choose not to tell—" *the person you love.*

He didn't dare finish his sentence. He was already close to implying that their relationship was something more. She didn't love him; she barely knew him. And yet…ever since they'd met he hadn't wanted to be without her. It was like her presence both comforted him and made him question everything. It reminded him of the first time he'd fallen in love, but then he'd been merely a teenager—he couldn't go back to being the boy he once was. He'd had too much happen in his life, too many heartbreaks and failed relationships. He couldn't allow himself to repeat his mistakes.

Her grin reappeared. "I admit nothing."

"Admit it or not, we both know that no relationship is completely without secrets. Sometimes in order to keep a friendship or relationship, or to make another person feel better, we omit things. It's human nature."

"Human nature or not, what you did at the shanty was more than just omitting a detail." She paused. "But here's the deal, I don't want you to lie—ever. I don't want you to omit anything. I want to be able to trust you."

Here he'd been worrying about trusting her, and apparently she'd been worried about trusting him as well. That made him chuckle. Maybe they were more alike than he thought.

As they moved higher up the mountain, snow dusted the scree. Even in August and September, snow was common in the high country, and it wasn't unheard of to get fresh snow in the higher elevations every month of the year.

Though he had brought a few essentials, in case of emergency, he didn't have enough supplies to last more than a day or two at most. When it got dark, and colder, the snow was likely to become a problem.

He didn't want to put Sabrina at risk. If something went awry, or if he got hurt, he didn't want to burden her with all that it would take for them to survive.

He thought back to his days in Afghanistan. At that time, he'd just gotten into the private security game with his family. They'd been at it for some time, but he'd finally reached an age at which his father agreed to bring him along. Being out there, in the countryside of a foreign nation where he didn't speak the language or know the customs, had been intimidating. It hadn't taken him long to learn that what they did tended to get people killed.

He winced, remembering the al-Qaeda hit man who got gunned down right in front of him for failing to light his commander's cigarette. Later his brothers had explained to him the commander had done it as a show of force, as a reminder that they were to do as he wished and play by his rules. The man had died because they were there.

He'd had to stay at that camp, pretending to be a bodyguard for the al-Qaeda commander, for two months. Luckily, he had gotten out of there alive. It had been one hell of a welcome into STEALTH.

After he left, they had traced the terrorist group

coordinates thanks to the implanted GPS trackers in the weapons they had supplied. Some of the guns had spread as far north as Mirzaki and as far south as Bahram Chah. With the information they had accumulated, they gave the coordinates of the largest and most active terrorist cells to the DO, or directorate of operations. The next day, eight of the ten cells had been wiped off the map.

It wasn't the easiest or the cleanest way to track the movements of their enemies, but it had been highly effective. They were proof that boots on the ground were truly their government's most effective weapon. He was sure that they had saved thousands of lives.

What he'd done then was a thousand times more challenging than what he had to do now. And yet finding himself alone with Sabrina seemed to create an entirely new level of difficulty. Maybe it would be easier if they just dispelled the sexual tension that reverberated between them. If they just kissed, things would get easier, and hell…maybe he could go back to focusing on the task at hand. He kept finding himself thinking about them, about her, trust and feelings and not thinking about where they were or what they needed to be looking for. At this rate, unless the hunting camp had been built right in the middle of the game trail, he doubted he would notice it.

"Do you want to turn back?" he said, his breath making a cloud in the cold.

Her cheeks were red, like they had been nibbled at by the chill of the later afternoon. "No, I'm fine." Her words were slow.

"Let's take a little break." When they came up to a

flat clearing, he got off his horse and held out his hand to Sabrina. Her fingers felt like ice.

He had to build a fire before hypothermia got the better of her. It had to be in the twenties, with snow starting to accumulate around them. While the snow would prove helpful in tracking, he had to get his head on straight before he was ready to continue.

Heck, maybe he was right in thinking about turning back. She was cold; he wasn't at the top of his game.

She hugged her arms around herself and did a little two-step move as she tried to get warm.

Yes, fire first.

He tied the horses up to a couple of pines and set about collecting anything dry that would burn. He made his way back to her with a collection of pine needles, pitch wood and branches. She had built a little teepee-shaped stack on the ground with her own collection of fire starters. A tendril of smoke was already puffing from the top of the stack, and there was a split log sitting beside it.

She looked up at him as the fire got going. "Oh, hey, thanks," she said, motioning to his redundant work. "You can set those right there," she said, pointing to the log.

Sometimes she had a way of making him feel so inept.

He dropped the kindling within her reach. She had her hands up, warming them.

"Where did you learn to do that?" he asked.

"Anyone worth their salt knows how to start a fire."

He raised a brow. He wasn't sure she was entirely right, but the comment intrigued him. She was definitely from a military family. Most people were vaguely curious about that kind of skill, but when it came to practical use, few had actually gone so far as to learn how to do it—especially in a wet environment.

"Did your dad teach you?"

"Are you asking me that because I'm a woman?"

"No." He sighed. "I'm asking because my dad taught me. When we came here for vacation, my dad loved to take us all out and spend time in the woods like this. When we got older, we were allowed to set our own camps, just so long as we were within yelling distance."

"Sorry, I didn't mean to be all defensive. It's just…"

"You're a feminist. There's nothing wrong with it. I can understand why you don't want to be underestimated."

"I don't know if I'd call myself a feminist or not. There are so many stigmas with that…but I do know that I'm tired of being put on a lower tier because I have ovaries."

He laughed, the sound echoing through the surrounding woods. "You are hilarious."

"There's nothing funny about being treated like you're not capable or that you should be subservient to a man. I think I should stand beside whomever is in my life, not behind him."

"That's not why I think you're hilarious," he said, picking up a log and moving it over by the fire so they could sit down together. "I guess *hilarious* is the wrong word. I just think you are amazing." He patted the spot next to him on the damp log. "I'd love to have you at my side."

She smiled, but it looked like she was trying not to. She sat down beside him. "You're not so bad yourself." She leaned against him, putting her head against his shoulder.

The action surprised him. He could make out the smell of the horse on her skin and the floral aroma that perfumed her hair, and the effect was perfect—a woman and a warrior.

"What about you?" she asked.

"Huh?" He tried to sit still, not quite sure if he should let her simply lean against him or if he should make a move and put his arm around her. The last time it hadn't ended so well.

It wouldn't be to his advantage if he made a move and it resulted in them riding back in silence. It would be one heck of a long ride.

"Were you really in the military?"

"Uh." His body went rigid. She had just given him a speech about opening up and being honest, but he wasn't ready for her to start asking questions. "I was in the army."

"So you were toying with me about Schofield being a marine base?"

He gave her a guilty smile. "Maybe a little?" He tried to sound cute and semi-repentant.

"I see. Okay." She nodded. "When did you get out?"

He shook his head. "I've been out for about eight years. I only did a four-year tour—that was more than enough time."

"What didn't you like?"

He didn't want to answer that question. Something about it was so private. It was like in telling her, it would bare some of his soul. And yet… "I loved the travel, but I found that it was too *political* for my liking." He thought of all the times he had traveled in order to fulfill contracts and take out foreign leaders.

She was quiet for a long time. He leaned over and put the log on the fire.

"Chad didn't send hot dogs with you, did he?" she asked with a chuckle.

The reminder of food made his stomach rumble. Though he wanted to sit there forever with her, he got up and grabbed his go bag. Coming back, he dug through it. "Here, I've got a granola bar. And there's vodka." He pulled out a silver flask.

"Vodka?" She laughed. "That sounds like the meal of champions."

"The granola bar is complex carbs. The vodka— aside from being the beverage of the gods—is great for medical purposes as well as for relaxing." He tried to sound serious, but his voice was flecked with playfulness.

"I see. In case we needed to get drunk and eat carbs, we're totally covered. You don't have a steak in there, do you?"

"I wish." He laughed as he sat down beside her and she put her head back on his shoulder.

Handing her the flask and a bar, she took them and then opened the canteen's cap and took a long swig. As she handed it back, he followed suit. The vodka burned on the way down. He wasn't much of a drinker, but being this close to her it felt like it was called for. Maybe, for once, he could just relax around her.

They munched on their bars and he threw the wrappers into the fire, watching as they melted into nothing. It could have been the alcohol, but he was mesmerized by the flames as they danced. They were so beautiful, and he was reminded of the fleeting nature of it…and the life that succumbed to its force. In a way, Sabrina reminded him of the flames. She was so wild, free and alluring. He could have happily gotten lost in her for hours.

She reached over and into the breast pocket of his jacket, took out his flask and took another pull. Reaching back over, she slowly put it back, letting her fingers move over his chest. His body sprang to life, and as she touched him, he longed for more.

He took her cheek in his hand, caressing her fire-warmed skin. "I was serious when I said you are amazing. You…you are something special."

She looked at him and he watched the flames dance in her eyes. As their lips met, it was as if the entire world lit up around them.

It was happening. Really happening. Sabrina couldn't remember exactly how they had gotten there. As his tongue caressed her bottom lip, she gave herself to the moment and decided not to dwell on it.

He held the back of her neck, his thumbs caressing her cheeks as they kissed. The world dissolved around her. The only thing existing was him, his lips, his warm touch on her cold face and the feel of his breath against her skin.

If she could, she would live in this moment forever.

Unfortunately, he pulled back, ending it far too soon. His cheeks were flushed, and there was a thin gleam of sweat on his skin even though it was bitterly cold.

"I…we…" she stammered, trying to be logical about what had just transpired between them, but all she could think about was how she wanted more—so much more.

Instead of saying anything, he reached into his go bag and pulled out a hatchet.

"Uh," she said, looking at the gleaming blade. "I didn't think the kiss was that bad. In fact, I was hoping you'd want to do it again."

He laughed as he put the blade behind his back and out of sight. "Crap, sorry! That's not it… I was just going to build us a little shelter."

"We kiss and you think *shelter*?"

He was such a dude. There she was thinking about feelings, and he was thinking survival.

Apparently, her kiss didn't carry the same magic it once had. In the past her kiss would have left a man thinking about nothing more than wanting the rest of her.

"I promise you…that's not it." He pulled his coat down a bit, covering his crotch. *Oh.*

Maybe she had a gift after all.

"You don't need to be embarrassed. I take that as a compliment." She gave him a coy look.

He laugh nervously. "Oh, believe me, I'm not embarrassed about anything I've got going on down there."

"Oh my goodness…" She laughed so hard her stomach hurt.

"If I have my way, you will see exactly what I mean."

"You have no shame, do you?"

He reached out and took her hand, giving it a squeeze. "Actually, I was thinking I'd build us a shelter so we could…get a bit more comfortable." He looked up at the sky where there were stars peeking through the dusk. "It's getting dark. Even if we turn around and start making our way back to the truck, we're going to be packing out in the dark. Our horse skills being what they are, I think it's best if we just wait out the night."

"That's the only reason you want to stay out here?" she asked, raising her brow.

"I have to take care of my lady first, then we can have the rest of the night to see where things go." He kissed her hand. "If you want, there's a couple of Mylar survival blankets in the bag. We can start setting up the lean-to." He started to say something else, but stopped. From the guilty look on his face, she could tell he'd been about to start giving orders.

He was learning that she didn't appreciate being told what to do. And the realization made her like him that much more. It was a rare man who wasn't intimidated by an independent woman.

"Don't go too far. If the Cusslers are close they'll come to investigate the fire," she said, looking into the shadows that surrounded them.

"I guess we'll need a door for our lean-to if we want our privacy."

The way he spoke sounded like he was joking, but she liked the idea. The last thing she wanted was to be spied on by a group of hillbillies in the middle of the night. Especially if things went to the place she wanted them to go with Trevor. She'd like to see exactly what he had been trying to cover with his coat.

They collected a few poles and set up a frame for their shelter. Trevor chopped off fresh boughs from the surrounding pines and, using them for the insulating materials, set them around the frame and on top to stop the snow from getting through. It didn't take long, but by the time they were done, she was starving. The granola bar had done little to keep the pangs of hunger at bay, but she could make it a day or two without food.

She sat down on the log by the fire and opened his bag. At the top was a handgun. The black steel immediately reminded her of why she was there in the first place, and all that hinged on her investigation of Trevor and his family.

If they had sex, it would compromise her in an entirely new way. If she did it, would be she doing it because she wanted to, or would there be a part of her that had sunk so low that she was willing to use her body to get ahead?

She hated the thought.

She pushed the gun aside and pulled out the Mylar blankets. Opening the crinkling, tinfoil-like material, she set the first sheet on the pile of soft boughs that would act as their bed for the night. If this was what they were going to sleep on, it was going to make for a loud night.

Trevor came over and took the second blanket from her. Using a bit of duct tape, he lined the top of the shelter with the Mylar sheet so the fire's heat would be reflected down on them as they slept. As he worked, she could make out the scent of saddle leather and sweat and the sweet aroma of campfire on him. She'd never thought she was the kind of woman who would find that to be an aphrodisiac, but it was just that…especially when a bead of sweat worked its way down his temple, slipping into the corner of his lips.

She wanted to take those lips again. Thankfully, one of the horses chuffed. Getting up, Trevor followed suit, and they made their way over and readied them for the night.

As they finished, Trevor put his hands on his hips and stood admiring their work. Darkness had settled in on them, and with it came a whisper of tiredness. It had been a long, exhausting day, but she wasn't going to let it stand in the way...*if* she decided to act on her baser instincts.

She slipped her hand between his; her fingers were icy in comparison. "What, no door?" she teased, looking at their shabby-chic survivalist paradise.

"Well, I was thinking something in a teak...maybe mahogany." He let go of her hand and gave her butt a playful pat. "You are freaking funny, aren't you?" There was a brilliance in his eyes as he looked at her that made him appear even more handsome.

She had found herself an Adonis. Yeah, Mike had definitely set her up to take this fall.

But she was no Aphrodite and she couldn't fall in love with this ill-fated man. However, maybe just for one night, she could give in to her desires.

Stepping into the lean-to, she pulled him after her. The sheet crinkled under them as he lay down beside her. He unclicked his SIG Sauer P226 from his thigh and set it above their heads like an ominous reminder of the reality that awaited them when they stepped out of their silver wonderland. Wrapping her leg around his, she scooted into his nook and put her head on his chest. Maybe she could be satisfied with just this...the simple pleasure of lying in his arms.

Then again, there was something that seemed more dangerous about sinking into the comfort and safety of his arms...sex was intimate, but listening to the beat of his heart would be far more bonding. And that bond, the sacredness that came with letting someone into her heart, terrified her.

He ran his fingers through her hair. If she hadn't been so nervous, the sweet comfort of his touch would have put her to sleep. And yet all she could think of was where her hand rested on his abs. As he breathed, she could feel the muscles expand and contract. A warmth rose up from his core, growing steadily warmer as her hand eased down his stomach. She was so close to him. All it would take would be one little flip of the button and everything between them would change. For one night, he could be hers and she could be his…in every way.

One little button. How could she have let her future come to rest on one little brass button? She'd been playing this game long enough that she knew what she was setting herself up for; she couldn't claim ignorance now. And yet she was still surprised how *authentic* it felt being with Trevor. If she was just *her* and he was just, well, *him*, they could have made the world theirs.

He cleared his throat and stopped playing with her hair as her hand moved down until her fingers grazed the rough fabric of his blue jeans. "Sabrina?"

She stopped moving and looked up at him, gently resting her chin on his chest. "What?" she asked coyly.

He gave a light nervous cough and didn't seem capable of continuing.

"Shhh," she said, pressing her finger to his lips.

He drew her finger into his mouth and gave it a playful nibble. Her thighs clenched at the pleasure of the slight pain. She withdrew her hand and rested her fingers on the fateful button. Reaching down, he stopped her for a moment.

"Are you sure you want to do this?" he asked, giving her a look that was a mixture of desire and concern.

She understood exactly how he must have been feeling, but at this moment logical thought was failing.

"I want you, Trevor. I've wanted you since the first moment I laid eyes on you." She moved atop him, straddling him as she flipped open the button and unzipped his jeans. She looked into his eyes. "What about you? Do you want me?"

"More than you can possibly know." He emitted a slight growl, running his hand over his face. "But you are going to be the death of me." He took hold of her hips and she ground against him.

She giggled, but at the back of her mind she questioned if he was right in his assumption—literally. She forced down the thoughts. Now wasn't the time to worry what would come of their forbidden relationship. Now was the time for pleasure.

Sitting up slightly, she wiggled down his pants. Standing over him, as much as she could in the enclosed space, she slipped off her pants and black panties and let them drop on the Mylar beside him. The fire reflected off the silver sheets around them, but the chill of the night pressed in against her nakedness.

He sat up, taking hold of her. His hands were warm against her ass. He gave her a wicked smile as he kissed the soft skin of her inner thigh. His lips were hot against her cold skin, and as he inched his kiss higher up her leg, she was sure he was hotter than the flames that danced on the Mylar.

She reached up as his tongue met her, and her hands brushed against the world of fire around her.

"Trevor," she gasped, as his fingers found her. "I

need you. Please," she begged, running her fingers through his long hair.

He kissed her again, then took her hand and leaned back, leading her atop of him. She pulled him inside her and in one slow movement, he filled her. There was nothing more glorious than this night...*their* night. It would be one memory she would cherish for the rest of her life.

Chapter 8

The sun was breaking through the trees, but as they rode deeper into the backcountry, all Trevor could think about was the taste of Sabrina. He sucked at his bottom lip. He'd never known a woman could taste exactly like peaches.

And the face she had made when he'd pressed inside her. Just the thought made his body spring to life. Dang, he would give just about anything to be back in that lean-to, holding her against his chest and listening to the sounds she made when she was satisfied.

Ever since they'd loaded up and hit the trail this morning, she had been quiet. If she was like him, it was lack of sleep catching up with her, but it still surprised him. Not that he'd ever done this kind of thing before, but when he had slept with women in the past, normally the next day they opened up and wanted to talk. Sabrina was certainly a different kind of woman, and she definitely kept him on his toes. It was one of the things he loved about her—she challenged him.

As they rode up onto the top of the saddle that bridged two mountains together, in the distance he could make out a muddy game trail. Thanks to the pristine snow around it, the muddy mess looked like a snake slithering through an Arctic playground. The trail had probably been made by deer and elk, but it seemed out of place in the high country.

While animals were sometimes at the top of the mountains this time of year, it seemed like they would have moved lower to wait out the cold snap. Unlike humans, they heeded nature's warnings.

If he and Sabrina had been smart, they would've never spent the night up in the woods. It had been an ill-advised decision. Even without the possible ramifications of sleeping together, the weather alone could have been extremely dangerous. Luckily the storm hadn't been that bad, but if it had, they could have been stuck out in the wilderness for days. Even now there was no guarantee they would make it back unscathed.

The cold air nibbled at his nose as they rode toward the serpentine game trail. The distinct odor of campfire drifted toward him on the gentle breeze. "Do you smell that?" he asked, unsure if it was his clothing that he was smelling or if it came from some unknown source.

"Smoke." She looked around, pointing toward the east. "Look over there."

There was a fine tendril of wispy smoke drifting up and over the edge of the mountain. They were close to someone. But in the millions of acres that spread around them, it was impossible to know exactly who awaited them. Hopefully it was the Cusslers, and they could finally start making heads or tails of the situation they found themselves in. Then again, it might also be the second hillbilly family. Either way, they could be walking straight into a trap.

The people who lived in this kind of environment weren't stupid about survival. If they had any indication that he and Sabrina were coming up the mountain to find them, they wouldn't have built such a visible fire. In the event it was an ambush, they were ill-equipped to succeed.

Or at least one of them was.

He'd fought this kind of battle more times than he could count. It always seemed like the odds were stacked against him when it came to looking at something like this on paper, but his training and his level of expertise always gave him an advantage. They just had to play it smart.

He motioned for Sabrina to stop, riding up alongside her and climbing down off his horse. To their left was a small drop-off. He led his horse down the embankment and into the small stand of timber. Sabrina followed suit. They tied up their horses and he grabbed the go bag. Pulling out the gun, he handed it to her.

"You need me to explain how to use it?" he teased.

She smiled at him, but there was a sassy look on her face. "Isn't someone feeling feisty this morning?"

"That's not the only thing I'm feeling," he said, pulling her close and pressing his lips to hers. She wrapped her arms around his neck and dug her fingers into his hair, making him nearly groan.

"Hey now," she said, pulling back from him. "This isn't the time or the place for fooling around."

He didn't want to point out that last night was just as questionable, so he stayed quiet. She slipped the gun in the back of her pants and covered it with her jacket. There was something about the way she moved that made it look like she had done that a million times before. There was no hesitation, no shock at the feel of the cold steel against her skin and no second-guessing herself before she put the gun away. She was some kind of housekeeper.

"How accurate are you thinking you can be with that gun, if it comes down to it?" he asked.

"Let's just say starting a fire and working a truck and trailer weren't the only things my daddy taught me to do," she said. "If I were you, I would make sure I wasn't the one standing on the other end of my barrel."

He laughed quietly, looking over toward the smoke as he realized that up here, with as little cover as they had, it also meant that sound would most certainly carry.

His phone buzzed in his back pocket. They must have found a tiny service signal. Moving to take it out and check, he stopped himself. "I need to take a whiz before we get started. Do you mind waiting here?"

"No problem," she said, waving him off.

It wasn't a great excuse, or charming, but it was the only thing he could think of to be alone for a few minutes.

He walked away from her and sat down behind a small knob on the hill where he couldn't be seen from above or below. Taking his phone out, he looked down at the screen. Chad had texted at least twenty times. Zoey had set up the fake drop in Seattle. They'd have at least a dozen eyes watching the place; if there was even a chance Sabrina wasn't who she said she was, he'd know.

Saying a silent prayer that he was wrong, he stuffed the phone back into his pocket. Last night had been inimitable, but he would love to try again.

But if Sabrina were working for some foreign government or the Gray Wolves, what had occurred between them would never happen again. More likely than not, his family would require that he take care of the problem. He couldn't stand the thought of hurting her.

He sat with his knees up, and he pressed his forehead against them as he closed his eyes. The cold snow was starting to melt and leach into his pants, making his butt cold, but he ignored the feeling. The biting cold was nothing compared to the gnawing he felt in his chest.

Hopefully he hadn't misplaced his trust when he'd put it with her.

For now, he could rest in the naive hope that he had found the one woman in this world to whom he could truly give his heart.

MEN. Sometimes they were so uncouth…it was like she was back in the good old boys' club that was a FBI resident agency.

As he walked away, she made her way down the embankment from the horses and found a little bush. As she unbuttoned her pants, her phone buzzed from inside her breast pocket. The sensation caught her completely off guard. She hadn't had service in the last day and it was a surprise that she even had any battery left, considering her phone had likely been searching for a signal since then. She pulled out her mobile, and looking over her shoulder to make sure Trevor was nowhere in sight, she punched in the code to unlock it.

Front and center in her inbox was an email from

Mike. She opened it, and as she read, excitement and then a sense of dread filled her. Her team had intercepted an email sent from the Widow Maker. Apparently, Trevor and his team were supposed to make a drop in Seattle at seven tomorrow night. Mike wanted to know whether or not they were to move on the information.

She stopped reading and pressed the phone to her chest.

If that were true, then it was likely the reason Trevor had been only too happy to spend the night out in the woods. He'd probably wanted them to spend the night out here again so she was completely out of the equation. Maybe he still saw her as a security risk and wanted her as far from his dealings as possible. Then again, she hadn't given him any concrete reason, that she knew of, for him not to trust her. Besides, he would have to be at a meeting like that, wouldn't he?

She glanced back in the direction he had gone, but he was nowhere in sight.

Maybe Chad and the rest of the family were taking the lead on this one.

If the intelligence was legit, she needed to have a team there. Between the email and what they could glean from the handoff, her team would likely have more than enough for whatever prosecutor was put on their case. They could take down the family and put an end to their illegal gun trafficking once and for all. Then she could move on to another UC position. Maybe she could even get transferred away from Mike. She'd heard of some of her people taking remote location gigs; maybe she could get a little sunshine in and see the beaches of Colombia.

Going back to her phone, she told them to move on the intel.

If she was wrong, and Trevor or someone from his family had planted this for them to go on some wild-goose chase, her job would be on the line. The Bureau hated spending money and resources on anything that proved to be a dead end, but her gut was telling her that this was something they had to do. If she didn't act, and the Martins were in motion for a trade, then she'd miss her opportunity. Maybe it was a bit aggressive to jump on their first big break in the case, but if they could one-and-done this, she could go back to the agency with her head held high. Mike would have his deadline met and she would be the resident hero.

Besides, Trevor had probably set all this up…he'd brought her all the way to the backside of the moon knowing they were unlikely to have any digital reach. If he thought she was a threat, it was one heck of a plan. She'd been completely at his mercy. Why had she been so stupid in letting him take her on this ridiculous trail ride? She should have trusted her gut and found a way to stay behind. If he had gone without her, she could have been right there and dug deeper into the lead the IT crew had picked up. As it was, she might as well have been sitting on her hands.

She stuffed the phone back in her jacket and after doing her business, careful to keep the gun from fall-ing in the snow, she made her way back to the horses. Trevor was already there, waiting for her. He had a worried expression on his face and after what she'd just learned, all she could do was stare at him. He was probably thinking about the deal he was going to miss.

The last thing she should have done was sleep with

him. Heck, he'd probably even had that planned, too. Be cute, joke a bit, tell her she was beautiful, and she had turned to putty in his hands.

Why was she so stupid sometimes? She knew better than to let herself fall for a man like him.

She stretched, as if by doing so, she could wedge herself back into the box that was her role as a UC for the Bureau. There was a job to do. If she didn't think about the way his lips felt against her skin, or the way he sighed when he fell asleep, it wouldn't bother her too much.

He turned away from her and as he moved, there was a dark blue patch on his ass like he'd wet his pants. "You know," she teased, trying to relieve some of the stress that filled her, "most people take their pants down when they use the restroom."

"Oh…yeah…" He dropped his hands to the back of his jeans and gave a constricted laugh. "I slipped and fell down in the snow when I was trying to find a place. Nothing like a cold, chapped ass to remind you how good life is back at home." As he said the word *home*, his face pinched like there was something painful about the word itself.

She couldn't help but wonder if he really meant how good life was back where he could run guns once again.

She set her jaw. He was a killer. He put guns into the wrong hands, hands that were more than happy to pull the trigger even when the guns were pointed at the innocent.

He could act as endearing as he liked, but that didn't make him any less guilty.

She just had to remember not to be a fool—no matter how tempted she was to take on the enticing role as the woman on his arm.

No doubt he had one incredible, fast-paced and thrilling life. If only it was on the right side of the law.

Chapter 9

She was acting weird. Or maybe he was, he couldn't decide. As they hiked toward the smoke, he couldn't make heads or tails of his thoughts. This was all driving him mad. At least he would soon find out one way or another if she could be trusted. He would have his answer and then they could move forward—or not.

The snow crunched under their feet, the sound reminding him of what needed to be done. All they had to do was get to the bottom of the Cussler brother's death for now. He could deal with the rest when he got home.

Yes, shoving the thoughts of her possible deception away...yes, that was the best answer. If he was acting weird, at least he could put an end to it this way and slide back into his role as one of the Martin brothers—tech billionaires extraordinaire, complete with a fictionalized military backstory...well, sort of fictionalized. Some of his experiences with the military had been all too real.

That's all this feeling was, his past coming back to haunt him. He was out of that game. Now he just had to look to the future.

If only it were that simple.

Becoming a civilian was proving to be far harder than he had expected it to be. He'd always thought that the people who had the biggest issues were also the ones whose egos wouldn't allow them to step away from the game. He'd never thought that *he* would be one of those people. Sure, his identity had been all spook all the time, but that wasn't who he *was*. He had always thought of himself as so much more…and yet he was constantly proving himself wrong. Even the way he made his bed every day spoke of his passion for a life that was no longer going to be his once he retired completely.

There was a click and slide in the distance, just like the sound of a round being jacked into a bolt-action rifle. He glanced in the direction of the smoke. They had to be at least a half mile away from the possible camp. They were surrounded by a blanket of white, interspersed with dots and jags of gray and black and trees that had fallen victim to a recent forest fire. In the world of white, nothing moved. Yet the sound had been nearly unmistakable.

He'd heard that grind of metal too many times in his life to get it wrong.

"Get down," he said, moving behind a piece of deadfall and motioning toward Sabrina to follow suit.

She looked at him like he had lost his mind, but she did as he told her and squatted down beside him. "What is it? Did you see something?" she whispered.

As the last syllable fell from her lips, a bullet whistled by them. Without thinking, he pushed Sabrina all the way to the ground so she was lying behind the log. Based on the sound and the percussive wave of the shot, whoever was shooting at them was uphill, not far. He knelt as low as he could, using the tree for as much cover as possible. He pulled his phone and using the selfie angle, he looked behind him.

At the top of the trail, he could make out the black tip of a rifle barrel.

They couldn't move. If they dared to go anywhere they would be an easy target for whoever was holding that gun. Their adversary literally had the upper hand.

"Can you see who it is?" Sabrina asked.

"Can't see their face, but whoever it is, they are using a high-caliber rifle. Any closer, and a tree just might not be wide enough to keep us safe." He moved to pull his SIG Sauer out of his thigh holster, but then he realized it was already in his hand. He had no idea when he had taken the gun out, and yet he was impressed by his body's autonomous reaction to gunfire.

Maybe being a trained mercenary really did have its advantages after all.

"Take out your—" Before he could say the word *gun* he noticed that, just like him, she had her weapon drawn and ready. The gun was pulled close to her chest and high, the position of a law enforcement officer or a well-trained marksman.

She had said she'd been trained to use weapons by her father, but she didn't appear to be a Sunday shooter.

She rolled and moved to look over the log. As she readjusted, another round pinged through the air. This time, it sounded like it struck something to their left.

"Do you think they're really that bad a shot?" he asked. "Or are they messing with us?" The question was as much a legitimate question as it was a test for her.

She looked up the hill, like she was gauging the distance. "The gun's caliber is too big to be using open sights—they have to have a scope on it. And if they have a scope on it, they could hit the hair on a gnat's ass at this range. They have to be messing with us. Either they're trying to flush us out, or they're sending us a message that we aren't welcome."

Test failed. She was definitely no Sunday shooter.

"You're right," he said, crestfallen. "Which leaves us with two options. We can fight—and turn this into a shooting gallery—or we can sit here and wait for them to get bored and leave. But if we wait, and they really are out to kill us, then they may well get the drop on us and move around until they have a better angle. We could be sitting ducks."

In a way, regardless of what the person shooting at them chose to do, he couldn't help feeling like he was a sitting duck with Sabrina. It seemed all too likely that she wasn't the woman she was pretending to be. Hell, she probably had gotten pinged on her phone the second he'd gotten pinged on his. Maybe she had heard something that had turned her off of him… Maybe she was already making plans for the fake drop in Seattle. That would explain why she was acting so weird.

He grumbled aloud. He couldn't fall back down that chasm, no. No more second-guessing himself. No more second-guessing her.

He had bigger things to worry about right now. He was being ridiculous by allowing his mind to wander. He had to focus.

The wind kicked up as quarter-size snowflakes cascaded down from the sky, making the entire world look like something inside a snow globe. It was his chance. Though they only had small arms, he'd have to make a break for it.

"Cover my six," he said, moving his chin in the direction of the shooter.

"Are you crazy?" Sabrina asked. "If you go out there, you'll be an open target."

She wasn't wrong; there was little cover. "That's what you're here for," he said, smiling in an attempt to downplay the danger they were in and put her mind at ease. "You're going to have to put your money where your mouth is. You said you're good marksman."

"I didn't mean I was *this* good. They have to be at least fifty yards away—way outside my comfort zone." She grabbed his hand, stopping him from moving. "Don't go." There was a deep well of concern in her eyes.

He had to act for the same reason she didn't want him to go—he had to shield her, the woman he loved.

Not that she could ever know that.

Though if she thought about it, she'd probably quickly realize that he wasn't the kind of man who would risk his life for just anyone.

He moved his hand out of hers and snapped a round into the chamber of his weapon. "Start shooting in three...two..." He stood up and raced up the hill, firing as he zigzagged haphazardly over downed trees and rocks. The brush pulled at his feet, threatening to bring him to his knees and welcome him to his death.

Taking a hard right, he watched as the gunman's barrel came into view above him. He hit the ground as the muzzle flashed. The bullet thumped as it ripped into the tree base just inches from his head.

Gunfire rang out from Sabrina's direction. There were twenty-two rounds in each of his guns' magazines. They'd have to be smart about this.

As Sabrina fired, he jumped back to his feet. A couple dozen yards in front of him was a large boulder. It was a long way to go without cover, but he had to go for it. He sprinted as hard as he could up the hill. The shooter fired. The bullet pinged off a rock, ricocheting into the air.

He slumped down behind the boulder. His breath came in heavy gasps, but he barely noticed as adrenaline coursed through him. Sabrina was out of sight, tucked behind the deadfall. *Good.*

For a moment, the world was silent. Fat blobs of snow coursed down, one landing on his nose and quickly melting, like some warning to him about the impermanence and fickle nature of life. He needed no reminder.

Trish flashed into his mind. She would have loved this. There was nothing she jonesed for quite like a good firefight. She was probably looking down on him from heaven. The thought came with an ethereal bit of warmth.

He smiled up at the sky, knowing full well that it was probably nothing more than his mind playing tricks on him, but he didn't care. If there was even a tiny chance she was here with him now, he needed her to know he loved and missed her. Maybe he could even make things right by saving Sabrina now.

Raising his gun, he charged from behind the rock and ascended the hill. He expected gunfire to rain down on him, but as he ran there was nothing except the crunch of his boots in the snow. As he breached the crown of the mountain, he stopped. There was no one there. A little way down from where he stood was a stand of timber, thick and dense as it had somehow escaped the ravaging effects of the fire that had taken down its sister side.

Near him on the ground was the packed snow where someone had been lying down. A smattering of brass casings littered the ground. From the patch of packed snow, there was a set of tracks leading into the timber and then they disappeared between the trees. The shooter was probably watching him right now. The hairs on the back of his neck stood up as he realized how easily the shooter could set up again from behind a tree and take an open shot at him.

He moved to the patch of boulders they had been using as coverage. Whoever had been shooting must have planned out this location. In defense and offense it was literally perfect—high point, great coverage and the ability to blend in with the background. He couldn't have done a better job himself.

Whistling down, he motioned over the hillside for Sabrina. She stood up and he waved her forward, surveilling the area around her as she hiked up the steep hillside. His breath made a cloud in the air as he guarded her and the cold bore down upon them. It was colder up here, even more frigid than it had been the night before.

They'd gone a whole day without food and the water supply was running low; soon they'd have to start thinking about boiling snow. They couldn't afford to chase after whoever it was that had been trying to gun them down, but they were so close. They couldn't stop now.

Sabrina plopped down beside him, her breathing

heavy. "Holy crap, that hill didn't look that steep from the bottom. How did you run up it?"

He chuckled. "Someone taking aim at you tends to give you an extra incentive to move."

"You're hilarious," she said sarcastically, nudging his arm as she slipped her gun back into the waistband of her pants. "I don't see any blood."

"And I haven't seen anyone moving. Either they are hunkered down somewhere in that timber—" he motioned toward the stand down the hill "—or they high-tailed it out of here."

She motioned toward the curl of smoke rising up from the center of the timber. "Do you think we have enough rounds to go down there, poke around and see if we can flush anyone out?"

"I can't put you in danger. At least not more danger than we're already in—up here, in the middle of nowhere, if one of us gets hurt, we may never make it out."

"From the moment we left the ranch, we've both known that this was a high-risk situation." She moved closer to him and put her hand on his knee. "Even when things are hard, I'm not one who gives up."

"But this isn't a battle of wills, or resilience." He put his hand atop hers and traced the length of her finger with his. "This is possibly life or death, and I don't want anything to happen to you."

She gazed into his eyes, and as she looked at him he could see the start of tears. And yet the look on her face wasn't happiness; it was like she was torn. Maybe she was feeling just as confused as he was about this entire situation and how unlikely it seemed that they would end up together.

"Trevor, you...*we* are amazing. I know I shouldn't

say this, but I've never met anyone like you. I don't know what it is about you, but even now just sitting here close to you, with bullets raining down on us at any minute… I dunno why, but I feel safe. More than that, I would be the happiest woman alive if I could stay out here and avoid going back to the real world if it meant I could spend another second with you." The expression on her face seemed to darken as she spoke, in contrast to what she was telling him.

"But?" He waited for the ax to fall.

She huffed. "But…" She paused, suddenly taken with her pants' stitches. "But I don't think we should be worried about it right now."

That wasn't what he was expecting her to say. He'd assumed she was going to tell him she wanted nothing to do with him once they got out of the woods, that she was quitting the ranch, or she had some deep dark secret that would keep them from coming together, but not this. As much as her avoidance was a relief, it was going to nag at him. There was something she wasn't saying, that she must not be ready to tell him. And yet he had to respect her needs and not push her to open up more than she was comfortable with.

She reached down in the snow beside them, digging in the white fluff like a nervous tic. Her fingers reddened as she moved them around in the snow, and it melted and stuck to her skin. Even though it was not his own hand, he could feel the sting of the cold, and he wanted to take her fingers and warm them for her so she wouldn't feel any pain. But he stopped himself. It seemed like perhaps he wasn't what she wanted.

She gasped, pulling her hand from its icy diversion.

In her grasp was a spent casing. She flipped it over, reading the caliber stamped into its base.

"This came from an HK416," she said, staring at the brass in her hand.

There was no way she could possibly know about the Heckler & Koch assault rifle. It wasn't a particularly common gun, though they could be bought on the black market. "What do you mean? How do you know?" The knot in his stomach returned, larger than ever.

"This brass is nearly identical to a .223, but here." She handed the casing over. "If you feel the weight, it's significantly lighter."

He took the casing and rolled it around in his hand, but he wasn't thinking about the cold metal thing; rather, who the stranger was sitting next to him. He stuffed the round in his pocket and stood up.

"Why would it be lighter?" he asked, even though he already knew the answer.

"In 2012, the army commissioned manufactures to reduce the weight of the brass casings in this type of round by 10 percent. That means that this weapon most likely belongs to someone who is either active military or FBI." As she looked up at him and their gazes met, her expression changed from focused to guilty.

"Sabrina." He said her name like it was just as much of a secret as whatever she was hiding from him. "Tell me the truth. Who sent you?"

Chapter 10

She had screwed up, royally. Her hubris had caught up with her and she had no one to blame but herself. Why did she have to open her stupid mouth?

Her investigation was over. She was done. Her cover was blown.

Sure, she could lie about why she was here, but even if he pretended to believe her he would never really trust her again. And if she came out with the truth, he'd inevitably run her out of his life like the infiltrator she was.

But she had to try to cover her ass and buy more time with him. Maybe she could salvage something from this investigation—maybe even clear his name and keep his family out of federal prison.

He opened his hand and helped her stand. "Just tell me." There was a deep sadness in his voice, and it broke her heart.

It hurt more than she ever would have expected. This wasn't her first investigation to go off the rails, but it had never happened like this before. In this moment, it was her life—her *real* life—that was most impacted.

If she told him the truth, maybe they could work together and come through this—but that seemed like one heck of a pipe dream. To hope for something like that was like having faith in humanity—a great philosophy, but rarely worked in practice.

She had been sent here to stop him from putting weapons into the enemy's hands, and yet as the minutes slipped by it was like her objectivity had collapsed. Her heart had come into play and she hated it.

"Trevor, I want everything to work out for everyone involved." She reached over and cupped his face in her hands. "None of this is what I expected when I came to the Widow Maker Ranch. I'm hopeful everything is going to play out all right, but I need you to tell me some things."

He nodded but remained stoic. "Is your name even Sabrina?"

She huffed. Of course he'd be questioning her from the ground up. If she was in his shoes she would be doing exactly the same thing. "Yes."

"And what happened last night… Were you just playing me?"

She stepped closer to him, their bodies brushing against each other. She ran her hand down his neck and rested it on his shoulder. "I'm not the kind of woman who jumps into bed with a man. Ever. There has to be something there, really there, before I'll even consider being intimate."

His lips pursed and he nodded, remaining silent.

Stepping away from her touch, he turned around and slowly made his way toward the smoke rising up from the stand of timber. His hands were limp at his sides, and the gun nearly dangled from his fingers.

He was in shock, hurt and probably analyzing exactly how this was going to play out. She had admitted nothing, at least not directly, but he had to realize what a liability she was for him and his family. He made it clear from the very beginning that his family was the most important thing to him, and she had no doubt he was willing to do whatever it took to keep them safe. And that placed her in more danger than when an unknown gunman had taken aim at her. At any moment, Trevor could decide to take her out.

It was unlikely anyone would ever find her remains if he chose to kill her.

She started walking after him, following his footsteps in the snow. The trees moved in on her like brooding sentinels, as if they, too, were judging her for the role she had taken on with the Martin family. Trevor, more than anyone, should've understood what it meant to do a job like hers. He had a life filled with secrets as well. Secrets that she still wasn't privy to. And yet those same secrets could save them.

Trevor was growing ever more distant, and the shadows of the timber threatened to help him disappear. Right now, that was probably exactly what he wanted to do. In fact, it was almost exactly what she wanted to do as well. However, she didn't want to lose him. She wanted to keep on living this fictional life—a life in which she was free to love and she could put aside the possibility that he was her enemy.

"Trevor," she called after him.

He turned and waited for her to catch up. As she neared, she could have sworn there were faint marks on his cheeks where tears had fallen, but she hated to think she had elicited such a response from him—the warrior.

"Don't say anything." He raised his hand. "I need some time to work through all of this."

She nodded. "I'm serious, just know that I want to help you. We can be on the same side."

He turned away from her and kept walking; the subtle evasion amplified her pain. They walked in silence until they came upon a small clearing. At its center was a dying campfire. There was a collection of pots and pans, mugs, and blue plates. It looked as though at least five people had struck camp and had been eating breakfast when they suddenly fled.

The footsteps in the snow went off in all directions. If they followed each trail, they would be tracking for hours.

Trevor walked to the right, moving around the fire as he searched the ground. She made her way left, as she tried to focus on the work at hand instead of the conversation that Trevor didn't want to have.

Not far from the back side of the camp there was a smattering of blood upon the snow.

"Trevor, can you look at this?" She pointed at the ground.

He made his way over. A faint smile played across his lips. "Looks like we may have hit the shooter after all."

"Maybe we don't make such a bad team," she said, but the sentiment came out sounding more like a question.

He didn't respond, squatting down beside the bloodied snow. "This is definitely fresh. It's still melting. But based on the little amount of blood, I'm thinking we just winged him—or her."

"If we did hit one of them, they're going to be moving slow." She looked out into the timber. "We could probably catch up to them if we move fast."

Trevor sighed as he stood up. "Nah, I think we should head back." He brushed by her as he looked around the camp.

She should have been following suit, looking around to see if they could find anything to give them a clue about who had been shooting at them, but all she could focus on was Trevor.

The second they got out of the woods and headed back to the ranch everything would be completely over—her investigation, the case, her job and their relationship. But she couldn't blame him for wanting to get out of the woods and away from her.

They walked around the timber near the deserted camp for a bit longer, but time seemed to lose any reference. She kept looking to him, hoping the right words would find her, but none came. Between them there was only awkward silence smattered with unspoken feelings.

It felt like a breakup, even though there was nothing formal to end.

Maybe this kind of work, as a UC, wasn't something she was cut out for. Normally she was fine, but her emotions had never come into play. If she couldn't keep her heart out of her work, she had no business doing it.

She'd have to give Mike her notice as soon as she got back into service. Not to mention the fact that she'd have to tell them she had let them all down. Mike was going to have a field day with this. He'd always told her she was weak, and now it turned out that he was right.

Trevor finally stopped as they came back to the edge of the timber and to the camp. He looked in the direction of the shooter's perch. "How did you know about the HK416 being a FBI weapon? Is it because you're an agent?" He turned to face her, but from the emotionless look on his face she couldn't tell exactly what he wanted her to say.

A lump formed in her throat. She tried to swallow it back and to replace her nervousness with bravery, but it didn't work. She was scared for so many reasons, the biggest being that if she walked away from Trevor, she would be walking away from the love of her life. The thought tore her apart.

"I…" She struggled to find the right thing to say. There was no easy way out of this. "Yes, I was sent here because of what happened in Turkey. We have reason to believe that you were responsible for several civilians' deaths… That, and a few other things."

He reached over and braced himself against a tree. The bark crumbled under his fingers, littering the ground with the ashy remnants of what had been so beautiful only moments before. Everything was disintegrating.

"So you came here believing that I was some kind of monster?" There was a pained look in his eyes.

"No, I came here to find out the truth. And the moment I met you, I knew that things weren't going to be as black-and-white as I'd hoped. You are nothing like the man I expected to meet." She wanted to reach out and touch him, to reassure him that everything was going to be okay—but the truth was, she didn't know whether everything would be all right or not.

"And you know about Trish's death?"

She nodded. "What happened to her...from what I know, it wasn't your fault."

He leaned against the tree, crossing his arms over his chest. "You're only saying that to create a bond—empathize with your target, make them feel safe. I know your game."

His words tore at her, ripping away what little was left of her defenses. "I'm not playing a game. If I were, I'd never have told you the truth about me being an agent. Until very recently, I wasn't sure about you. But I've come to believe that you are incapable of hurting an innocent person." She couldn't stand it; she reached over and put her hand on his chest. His heart was thrashing beneath her touch. "Don't think I didn't notice that you weren't shooting earlier. You could've gone in there guns blazing, but you took the high road. That takes an entirely different level of bravery."

"That wasn't bravery, it was curiosity." He looked down at her hand but didn't move to take it. "I didn't want to kill the one person who could have possibly known about the Cussler brother's death. I have to know how close all my enemies really are." He moved away from her.

She'd broken the bond they'd had, irreparably.

"I know you probably don't believe me, but I'm not one of them. I have the power to condemn you—if I'd found evidence—and I also hold the power to clear your name. But I need to know some truths from you, something I can take back to my handler to prove that you're the man that I know you are—and not the gunrunning terrorist the FBI believes you to be."

His indifferent expression changed to one of complete shock as he opened and closed his mouth like he was struggling to find the right words. "How much do you know about me?"

The way he asked made her wonder if she had missed some glaring detail.

She'd already admitted her truth to him, so all she could think of was the old adage *in for a penny, in for a pound.*

"I know that you and your family are in fact a group called STEALTH. You've been running guns around the globe for a number of years now. I know, and the FBI has proof, that you are involved in the trade. I don't know to what degree, and I'm hoping our intelligence was wrong—that you are just the little fish and we are going after the whales. From what I've seen, you don't seem like the type of man who would put guns into the hands of those who wish to do the most harm."

"You're right, I don't want to hurt anyone who doesn't deserve to be taken to their knees. But being in the FBI, you have to know as well as I do that there are truly wicked people out there. And the only way to bring those kinds of monsters down is to send monsters after them…and just like you first assumed, I am that monster." He sat down on a log next to the dying campfire.

She didn't know what to make of what he was saying. Was he admitting his crimes? If so she had no choice but to turn him over when they got back to the ranch. Perhaps that was what he wanted, to fall on the sword and go to prison…otherwise, why would he have so easily admitted to his mistakes? And yet there was something about the way he spoke that made her wonder if there was more to the story.

"Why, Trevor?" She sat down beside him.

"Why what?"

"Why do you think you're a monster?" She tented her fingers between her knees as she leaned forward and looked back at him.

"I had nothing to do with civilian deaths in Turkey. Yes, I took down my enemy combatants—I've killed. And if you asked me if I'd do it again, I wouldn't hesitate to say yes. Especially when it came to trying to save Trish. I'll do anything to save the people I love," he said, a deep sadness in his voice. "But I'm also the man who is willing to run into a burning building and save the innocent. I'm the man people call in the dead of night when the demons seep out of the cracks and wish to do them harm. So you can judge me however you wish. I'm guilty of plenty of things that society deems wrong, but in my heart, I know that I'm the man who is doing what many others can't. I make the hard choices."

She sat in silence, trying to come to terms with the things he was saying. He wasn't like any gun dealer she'd ever met before—not that she'd met many. He didn't seem to be after money or driven by greed. Instead he seemed almost like her, focused on humanitarian need and the prospect of justice—but in the most unconventional way. And she still didn't understand how giving guns to warlords was saving the innocent. Was this an elaborate rationalization?

"Trevor, why were you running guns?"

He smirked and ran his hands over his face. "That's past tense. We don't do it now. We got out of the game after everything with Trish. So if you think you're going to help the FBI and federal prosecutors by coming after my family, it's nonsensical. We're out of the game."

She didn't know whether or not to bring up Seattle. He was lying to her—they were still very much active in the trade—but she couldn't reveal everything she knew. Not if there was a chance he was playing her for a fool. "But you admit you have been putting guns into the wrong hands?"

"Just like you said *trust me*, now I ask the same of you. What I did, I did because I had to. Yes, the ethics were somewhat ambiguous, but there were greater things at play than even you know."

"What do you mean?"

"I mean that you don't have all the answers, and neither do I. But I'm not the bad guy here. Just like you, I do what I have to do—sometimes at the cost of others."

"You don't care that civilians are dying because of you?" The question came out and slashed like a sword. She hadn't meant it to be as harsh as it sounded, but she needed to know exactly where he stood. Both of their futures depended on it.

He shook his head. "I know it doesn't look like it from the outside, but I wanted to keep people safe just as much as you do. When I realized I couldn't, that's when I came here. If I can't even keep my own sister safe, then I have no business out there. Thinking I could make a difference, it's almost the definition of stupidity."

"You're not responsible for your sister's death. I've seen the reports. Maybe they didn't have all the facts, or the answers, but I saw the forensic analysis. From where you were standing, you could have never gotten there in time to help. The shooter had the advantage."

"You may have seen the science behind everything, but what you didn't see was someone you love looking up at you and knowing that they needed your help, and yet all you could do was watch them die."

She wanted to hold him and tell him it would be okay, that time would heal. And yet he wasn't hers. They were enemies, at least in his mind. If she even tried to console him, it would come off as false—and only drive them further apart.

She couldn't make his heart feel something toward her that his mind wouldn't allow.

And as much as she knew she shouldn't reach for him, she did. She took his hand in hers and lifted it to her face. "Trevor, I'm so sorry. For everything. For Trish. For this. For the investigation. But you're not alone in your suffering. When I was young, I lived in Redmond—"

"On a military base, or was that a lie, too?" he asked, pulling his hand away.

He had every right to snap at her. "Some of what I told you was backstory, but there is some truth to it. I find it easier to have an identity that I can actually relate to. My dad was in the military. He was controlling and passionate about his Second Amendment rights— until he and my mother were found in a parked car at the bottom of Mount Rainier, murdered. I was sixteen."

They sat there in silence for a long moment. "I'm sorry, Sabrina. I know how hard it can be to lose people you love." He turned to her. "Is your parents' murder the reason you decided to become involved in the Bureau?"

She nodded. "After their death, I had nowhere to go. I was shipped around foster homes in the area for a while until I ended up in a nice couple's house in Redmond. The guy worked for a local law firm and the woman worked at the federal office. My guardian set me up with an interview at the FBI after I graduated from college. Go Huskies," she said, raising her hand in the air in feigned excitement.

"Did they ever solve your parents' murder?" he asked.

She shook her head. "And the files are buried. I've tried to look into them a few times, but I don't have the clearance."

"It sounds like there's more to your parents' murder than the Bureau wants you to know."

She chuckled. "We live in a world full of conspiracy theories, don't we?"

"They're not always theories. Sometimes the most outrageous things I see and hear are the truth." He picked up one of the blue camp plates like he was inspecting the edges. "As much as you want to get to the bottom of your parents' murder, you probably need to let it go. You're chasing ghosts, and when you do that you open yourself up for a lifetime of disappointment. One ghost leads to another, which leads to another, and then all you end up with is heartbreak and a life haunted by questions you'll never have the answers to."

"Sounds like that's something you have a little bit of experience in," she said, looking into his eyes.

"I don't want to talk about it, but people don't lead lives like ours if they have a healthy childhood." Trevor threw the plate he'd been holding and it hit the exposed ground opposite them with a clatter.

"Why did you do that? You know that had to echo throughout the entire forest." She motioned toward the plate.

"They wanted us to come here. They'll be glad to know we took the bait."

She looked around. From what she could see it looked like a regular old campsite. There were no booby traps or any other evidence that they'd been set up, so she wasn't sure where he was coming up with this idea.

Almost as if he could read her mind, he continued, "Did you notice everything around here is brand-new? If you look at our guy's tracks, his boot marks are still in perfect diamonds and squares. And that plate, and all the dishes, barely have any marks on them. And if you look at this makeshift camp, everything has been moved here within the last day or two." He pointed toward the ground. If they'd been here long, the ground would be trampled well beyond this.

"So what? Maybe they just got here. These people are travelers."

"If these are the Cusslers, or their enemies, they aren't the type to be running to Walmart to get cookware and boots very often. Either they aren't who we've been thinking they are, or we're chasing the wrong ghosts."

She couldn't think of anyone else who could have been behind this.

"While I have my fair share of enemies, they aren't people who would shoot at me and miss. The people who want to kill my family are the type who can kill from two miles away, like our friends in Turkey. Which means it's likely that whoever is behind this is after you. Who have you ticked off lately?"

No. He was grasping at straws. There was no way she was the target here. He couldn't turn this back on her. This was his mess. His family's drama. Not hers.

Unless everything wasn't on the up and up with Mike.

The brass they'd found, the new plates, the manic deadline and the threatening emails…the evidence wasn't in the Bureau's favor, but everything he was pointing out was circumstantial. Sure, she had enemies—who didn't? It didn't mean that anyone was after her.

And yet she had a sinking feeling Trevor was right.

Chapter 11

Trevor wasn't sure if he had assumed correctly or not but he could tell he had planted just enough doubt about her team to create a distraction. As soon as they got back, he would alert the family that they were under investigation. In just a couple of hours, they could bug out—and disappear once again. He'd always heard Crete was beautiful. He could use a little bit more of a tan, and he certainly wouldn't miss snow.

As they walked back to the horses, he tried not to feel guilty as he took in the view of her walking ahead of him. He would be lying if he didn't admit how much he enjoyed that picture. He loved the way her hips swung back and forth as she picked her way through the under-brush that led to the serpentine trail. He'd miss that al-most as much as he'd miss feeling her breath on his skin when she fell asleep with her head on his chest. It had been a long time since he'd made love, but the things she had done with her hips were unlike anything he'd ever experienced before. He couldn't risk losing her.

If the situation had been different, she was definitely the kind of woman he could imagine settling down with. Then again, he was never planning to settle down again. Maybe she was more the kind of woman he could imagine traveling the world with. A scene from the movie *Tombstone* came to mind—with Wyatt and Josie slipping away into the sunset aboard a cruise liner and setting out on a life of adventure together.

But she was his adversary. She was trying to take down his family. Or at least she *had* been. It had to count for something that she had outed herself to him. Working with the CIA, he knew exactly how much was at risk in doing so—and exposing the truth to him may have put her job on the line. She certainly couldn't continue their investigation—but just because she left didn't mean that his family wouldn't still draw scrutiny from the Bureau. Just for once he wished he could call his friends in the CIA and have them whisper the truth into someone's ear in order to get this all to stop.

He'd end up dead long before the truth reached the right people. The Gray Wolves had their men everywhere, and where they didn't have their own people, they had paid informants. There was a lot of money to be made if a person was the type who was willing to sell state secrets.

"Sabrina, can you think of someone who wants you gone at the FBI?"

She stopped walking and turned around to face him. "There's always someone who is breathing down your neck behind closed doors."

The pinched expression on her face told him he had struck a nerve. She definitely had enemies.

"Is there anyone you can trust inside the Bureau?"

She looked off into the distance, as if she were contemplating her answer. "I know you think you're onto something, but I just don't see anyone working this hard to get me fired. If my enemies wanted to see me go, all they had to do is fudge a little paperwork."

"It isn't that easy. I *know* it isn't."

She quirked her eyebrow. "And how would you know? Did your family do an in-depth study of the Bureau?"

He chuckled. "You and your BuCrew aren't nearly as secret as you all would like to think you are. Sure, you have great people in tech, but when it comes to the truth I'm learning that you guys are at least ten steps behind."

"And yet we knew all about you and your family's dealings." She gave him a smart-ass tilt of the head.

If only she knew the truth, she wouldn't be so glib. And yet he could never reveal his truth to her. It wasn't just his to reveal.

"At least you can find some comfort in the fact that your enemies don't want you dead, or else they are just crappy shots," he teased her. "If this is someone from the FBI taking potshots at us, with all your long gun training through Quantico, I'm sure your instructors would've been so proud." He laughed. It felt good to be able to joke with her once again.

"Hey now, we don't know for sure whether or not those were my people shooting at us. In fact, if those were *my* people then I guess they weren't really mine after all, were they?" she pondered aloud.

"You are ridiculously cute when you're being asinine.

You know just as well as I do that it was your enemies up there—FBI or not."

"I just think it's too far-fetched. It seems more likely that it's someone who wanted to make it look like FBI or a government agency. Plenty of these off-the-grid types are anti-government. It's easy enough to get your hands on those types of weapons. You know all about it." She gave him a judgmental look.

He walked up beside her and slipped his hand into hers. "How about we put a bet on this? If we get to the bottom of this and it's someone close to you, you have to spend another night with me—we'll order room service."

She gave him a playful grin. "Since you seem so certain, if it ends up being someone involved with your family—which by the way, seems far more likely—then you owe me two things. One, you have to keep my secret, under threat of penalty of death, should you expose me."

He loved that she could threaten him with death and it turned him on. "And your second ask?"

"A favor yet to be named. Do we have a deal?"

"I don't make bets when I don't know what's at stake."

"It's a deal, or there's no deal at all." Her playful grin grew even more impish. "It all comes down to how much you believe in your theory."

She was calling him out—testing to see exactly what cards he had up his sleeve. "Okay, deal...but the second ask can't be for something I don't want to give."

"Again," she said, a look of pure innocence on her face as she cajoled him, "all or nothing."

"Then _all_ it is." He didn't like the deal, but something

deep in his gut told him that he was right and there was more to this than what they had first assumed.

The ride out of the woods took far less time than it had taken them to ride in. As they passed by their make-shift lean-to, he found himself once again wishing they could go back in time.

He wasn't angry at her admission of working for the FBI, not as he watched her ride in front of him. She had a job to do, just like he did. And the fact that she had finally admitted the truth to him went a long way. She certainly didn't have to do that. And it proved to him, more than anything else she could have done, that he could trust her. In a way, it also made him wonder if she was just as emotionally invested in what happened in that lean-to as he was—which meant, she must have realized how impossible their relationship would be.

If nothing else, at least they could walk away from each other knowing that somewhere in the world there was a person who really cared for them.

The ranch was dead quiet as they rode up with the truck and trailer. Unsaddling the horses, they barely spoke. It was as if she knew just as well as he did that things between them were about to come to an end.

There was no way they could go back and pretend they weren't the people they truly were, the people they had revealed to each other up on the mountain. If only he could have told her his truth as well, that he was working for the CIA, and yet…he couldn't. If he did, it would serve nothing. She would still have to leave, but when she did she would be in even more danger than when she arrived. The people he worked for weren't the kind who liked leaving loose ends. They made Trevor and his family look like teddy bears in comparison.

Instead of taking the horses straight back to Dunrovin Ranch, they'd decided to head home. It could have been all the riding or all the emotions he experienced over the last few days, but when they hit the front door, he was exhausted.

When he walked in, Chad was sitting on the couch, watching ESPN. He looked up and his expression darkened as though he could see from their faces that something was up.

"How'd it go? Did you find them?" Chad asked, flicking off the television.

Sabrina glanced over at Trevor. "Hey, I'm going to run out and unload the horses and put them in the barn. You guys go ahead and talk." She gave him a pleading look, as though she didn't want him to tell his brother what she had told him, but also understood he couldn't let a secret that big just stay between them.

He hated being in this position.

"Okay, I'll be right out and I can help you grab the rest of the stuff out of the truck." Stepping closer, he was going to give her a quick peck to the forehead, and then stopped himself. Chad didn't need more fodder for the fight they were likely about to have.

As the door closed behind Sabrina, Trevor walked over and sat down on the couch beside his brother. His knees ached from all the riding, making him feel old and tired.

Chad leaned forward looking him in the eye. "Are you going to tell me what that was all about?"

And so it began.

He couldn't look his brother in the eye, and he wished Chad hadn't turned off ESPN—it would've made things easier.

"What do you mean?" he asked, trying to buy himself more time.

He had been trying to think of ways around this conversation for hours now, and yet at zero hour, he still couldn't decide exactly how he wanted to handle things with his family. They deserved to know the truth about Sabrina, and they absolutely had to learn that they were under investigation. In fact, if he were under investigation, it was likely that other UCs were trying to break into their lives—other UCs who probably weren't as softhearted and kind as Sabrina.

And yet it would be immediately clear who the UC was in their lives as soon as he started talking. He wouldn't be able to hide her identity. At least Chad wouldn't want to kill her since she was an agent for the FBI…hopefully. Even though she didn't have a clue, they were all playing for the same team.

He would just have to figure a way out of this that worked for everyone and kept his family and Sabrina safe.

"You know exactly what I'm talking about, Trevor." Chad motioned toward the barn. "What happened up there on the mountain? Did you kill the family—is that why she's acting all weird around you? Or did you guys bump uglies?"

"Dude, seriously?" Trevor said, trying to look as innocent as possible. "Would I be this quiet if I'd taken the family out?"

"Good point," Chad said with a nod. "So then, you banged her?"

Trevor shook his head but was careful not to look at his brother. His eyes would give it away. "Sabrina? She's a nice woman, but I have a feeling that she's not going to stick around here too much longer. Especially after what we found," he said, a bit proud of the way he'd maneuvered around lying to his brother. Some things were better left unsaid.

"Which was?"

"Somebody up there decided to spark a few rounds off at us. They were just warning shots, but somebody wanted us to get the message we weren't welcome."

He told him about the shooter and the campsite but left out his theory about who had been pulling the trigger and why. There was no use getting his brother up in arms about something he wasn't sure of just yet. All Chad needed to worry about was making sure that the affairs of the ranch were in order and that the Gray Wolves didn't find out where they were.

If nothing else, at least he could be fairly certain that it wasn't his family's enemies who were behind this and the Cussler guy's death.

"What, are you surprised that our squatters would have a problem with you chasing them down? Nobody likes being kicked out of their house," Chad said.

Now would've been the perfect time for Trevor to tell him the truth and explain all the problems they were facing, but he held back. "Chad, do you think we made a mistake coming back here?"

"What makes you ask that?" Chad asked with a worried expression on his face.

"Nothing," Trevor said with a shrug. "I've been thinking maybe the US isn't the best place for us. I know we thought we had amnesty here, but what if we don't? What if we peed in the wrong person's cornflakes, you know what I mean?"

"Clearly you're not telling me something," Chad said.

"When you left here yesterday, you are all gung ho and ready to start making a new life here—even though it was boring. And now it's like you had a complete change of heart. You have to tell me why."

Trevor got up from the couch and strode over to the bay window that looked out toward the barn. The lights were on and the sliding door was open. Sabrina was unloading Zane. He watched as she backed him out of the trailer. "Call it a gut feeling or whatever you want, but I just think that maybe it's best if we bug out for a while—go somewhere in the Cayman Islands or something. Think about it, we could be lying on the white sand beach and drinking a cold one."

Chad stared at him like he was trying hard to figure him out. "Dude, Trevor, if you did something to upset Sabrina, we can figure it out—we don't need to get out of here. There a lot of housekeepers we could hire."

"Have you talked to Zoey at all while we were gone?" Trevor asked, trying to change the subject.

"Zoey said she's been watching all the channels, but so far she hasn't seen anything that would indicate the Gray Wolves have any idea where to find us." Chad got up and walked over and stood beside him at the window. "I know you're nervous, maybe that's what's going on with you, but I'm telling you this ranch is about the safest place we can possibly be. At least out here we have less of a chance of the Gray Wolves buying out some government agency in order to find us. I mean who is out here who would give two craps about us?"

Trevor's stomach dropped. What if Bayural had bought out someone at the FBI? Maybe they had sent Sabrina here to make sure they stayed while they got everything in place to take them out. But then, if that were the case, wouldn't they have just taken out a contract with a merc?

"Let's get the hell out of here," Trevor said, turning his back to the window.

"What? And what about Sabrina?" Chad asked, not stopping to ask him what he was thinking. His brother knew him well enough that if he said it was time to go, it was time to go. He could explain it to him later.

"We'll take her with us—if she wants to go."

"I knew you banged her," Chad said with a satisfied laugh as they rushed down the hall to their bedrooms to grab their bug-out bags.

Trevor was pulling out the .50cal from behind his mattress when the front door of the house slammed open.

"Trevor!" Sabrina yelled, her voice frantic.

The Gray Wolves were coming for them; he could feel it even though everything hadn't yet quite clicked into place. "What?" He dropped his bag and his gun case and sprinted out of the room, pulling his SIG Sauer from his holster and readying himself for whatever—or whoever—he was about to meet at that door.

Sabrina was standing at the front door, her hands over her mouth.

He lowered his weapon when he saw no one was behind her. "Are you okay? What's going on?" he asked, the words rushing out like it was a single syllable.

"There…" She motioned behind her. "There's a man out there, inside the last barn stall. He…he's been shot."

"Is he still alive?" Trevor hurried to her as Chad came running down the hall and to the living room.

She shrugged. "There was blood everywhere. I didn't stay to check him out."

"How long have you been home, Chad?" Trevor asked.

"I got back last night at midnight. Haven't left since then."

"And you didn't hear anyone coming or going, any cars?" Trevor asked.

Chad shook his head. "It's been quiet. No one."

"Stay in the house," Trevor said. "Make sure you watch our six. Whoever shot the guy is probably still out there—and they are probably gunning for us as well."

As he ran toward the barn he couldn't help but wonder if he was wrong and their shooter was already long gone—he had to hope, but he wasn't going to risk it.

If Bayural or his men were here, they could have easily taken Chad out while he'd been sitting watching television in the living room. From the right vantage point, Chad would never have known that anyone was ever even out there.

Whoever was behind these killings was doing their best to frighten them into submission. He couldn't let the killer get away with their murderous rampage any longer.

"Did you recognize the guy?" he asked Sabrina as he followed her into the barn.

Sabrina shook her head as she pointed toward the last stall. "He's in there."

Zane was nickering, his sound high-pitched and scared as he trotted nervously around the stall. Just like Trevor, he must have been able to feel the danger in the air.

Trevor walked to the last stall, half-afraid of what he would find. The blood was splattered over the wood paneling and there was a bloody handprint smeared down the far wall. "Hello?" he called, hoping that the man would answer. But there was little chance that the man was alive on the other side of the gate.

There was no answer.

He unclicked the latch and opened the gate, stepping into the stall. There, against the wall closest to him and tucked back into the corner of the room, was the man. He had scraggly gray locks and hair was sprouting from his ears. On his neck was a long, puckered scar as though someone had once tried to cut his throat but failed.

His hands were covered in blood and palms up in his lap, and his head was leaning haphazardly to the side. There was something about the man's face that looked familiar. He'd seen those same eyes and that shape face before—in fact, he looked almost identical, albeit slightly older, to the man in the shack. Trevor had to be looking at another of the Cussler brothers.

He walked over to the man and placed his fingers against his neck, hoping against all hope that there would be some faint pulse, but he found nothing but a sickening chill. He pulled his hand back. Algor mortis had started to set in.

Trevor moved to the man's feet and pulled back the leg of his pants, careful not to touch too much and leave behind any trace evidence. The guy had been sitting with his knees up and, even though Trevor pulled at his jeans, his legs stayed bent due to the effects of rigor. He'd definitely been down at least a few hours. Around twelve and he would have been completely immobile, but there was still a bit of pliability in his limbs.

Who in the hell was killing this family? And had they planned to murder the man here or had the man come here to die after he had been shot—making it look like Trevor and his family were responsible for his death?

"Is he alive?" Sabrina asked, but there was a resignation in her voice that told him she already knew the answer.

He didn't respond. Sabrina stopped behind the opened gate and looked inside; her gaze moved to the dead man. Maybe the poor light in the barn was causing him to see things, but he could have sworn that her face had grown a shade paler.

"You don't have to be in here," he said, moving closer to her and taking her hand. "You don't have to pretend to be tougher than you are with me."

She opened her mouth to speak as she looked up at him. There was a renewed softness in her eyes, and the look reminded him of when they had been making love and her body had begged him for her release.

"It's okay," he said, giving her a soft kiss to her forehead. "I've got this."

She took a step back so the man's dead body was out of her view, but she didn't leave. "What are we going to do, Trevor?"

He hadn't gotten that far yet.

This really should have been a case for the local cops, but calling them in would lead to a whole slew of questions he wasn't ready or willing to answer. It would only land them in deeper trouble. Yet they couldn't just wait for this body to disappear like they had the last, not with so many possible variables.

His first thought was for her to call her people at the FBI, but if they were in any way connected to this case, they wouldn't be coming in as allies. They weren't an option.

He'd have to call in a few of his friends at the CIA. They didn't typically work within the borders of the States, but undoubtedly his people knew some folks who could help him sweep this man's death under the rug.

Though sweeping it under the rug last time had certainly done them no favors. They needed to find answers and fast.

"You don't think your brother has a hand in this, do you?" Sabrina asked, her voice soft and smooth as though she was trying to be careful and not sound too accusatory.

He appreciated her effort, but her question still ruffled his feathers. "Chad wouldn't be stupid enough to kill a guy and leave his body sitting out here."

"Unless he wanted to set us up. He doesn't have a reason to want to drive you off the ranch, does he?" Sabrina asked.

He tried to control the anger that rolled through him. "No. He didn't do this. He wouldn't do this. My family are the only people I can really trust."

She visibly cringed at his unintentional jab.

"I just mean that he wouldn't have let us walk out here and work in the barn if he'd left this guy to cool down before getting rid of his remains."

"But you admit your brother is fully capable of pulling the trigger?"

"Look, Sabrina," he said, running his hands over the stubble that had grown on his cheeks over the last few days. "Anyone is capable of killing under the right circumstances. My brother is perhaps more likely to find himself in those kinds of circumstances than most, but that doesn't mean he is an evil man. He doesn't just go around killing people."

"I'm sorry, I know you're right," Sabrina said, leaning against the doorjamb. "I'm just...tired."

"I know you want to find an answer to this that doesn't point back to your people at the FBI, but you need to stop looking in my direction in order to figure out who is behind these killings—at least in the direction of my family. I'm telling you, we aren't the ones keeping secrets from one another."

She nodded. "I'd be lying if I said I wasn't a little jealous. Your family...it's one of a kind. I would like to have a group of people who I could always depend on."

His anger dissipated. He knew what it felt like to be lost, so he could empathize with what she was going through right now. In fact, he had to wonder if he was the only one she could really trust.

It seemed crazy how far they had come since they first met each other. He would never have guessed that this was how they would've played out. Aside from the dead guys, he wasn't sure he would change anything. He liked the fact that she was nearly as dangerous as him.

"Did you figure out where he was shot?" she asked, clearly trying to change the subject.

That was something else he appreciated about her— she was just as avoidant of feelings as he was. Sure, it may not have been the healthiest response, but it certainly kept one from getting hurt.

He stepped closer to the man. There was a small hole in his jacket just over his heart. Flipping back the edge of the coat, there was a small wound in his chest. Blood had seeped out and run down from the wound and had pooled at the top of his large belly before slipping down onto his jeans. "Looks like it was a single shot. Likely at least ten feet away."

There was the crunch of tires on the gravel of the parking lot just outside the barn. Trevor flipped the man's jacket closed, and as he did so he noticed the smear of blood on his own hands.

As he turned away, he saw a small hole in the wall. Lodged in the soft wood was a bullet.

Sabrina looked at him. "You think we should go out there?"

There was the sound of footsteps in the gravel as somebody made their way toward them.

Trevor rushed out of the stall, wiping his hands on the backside of his jeans. As he turned to face the door, a man came into view. Not just a man, but a deputy sheriff. He was all brassed up, complete with a Kevlar vest underneath his uniform. He looked to be in his midthirties, maybe. His hair was shorn and starting to recede just above the temples, and his forehead was littered with the wrinkles of someone who worried often.

He forced a smile as he walked toward the man. Zane's whinnies intensified from inside the horse's stall.

"Hey, Deputy, how's it going?" Trevor said, trying to sound amicable.

The deputy gave him a two-fingered wave. "Good," he said, sounding as tight and rigid as the vest he was wearing. "Anything going on out here that I need to know about?"

Sabrina gave him a confused look. "Nothing I can think of, Deputy."

The man chuckled. "May I ask your name, please?" The question was more of an order than a nicety.

Trevor strode toward him, moving with as much confidence as he possibly could. He extended his hand. "The name's Trevor Martin, you?"

The man gave him a strong shake of the hand, so strong it came across as an act of dominance—as though he wanted Trevor to know that he was at the head of the hierarchy here. "The name's Wyatt." A smile broke across the man's face. "Did Gwen tell you I was coming?"

Sabrina stepped between them as she shook her head. "Trevor, this is Wyatt, Gwen's husband."

"Oh," Trevor said, a wave of relief crashing over him. "Nice to meet you, man. Gwen's a fantastic woman. I'm proud to have her as a cousin."

"She is that." Wyatt glanced around the barn. "It's been a long time since I've been in here. I helped Gwen and her mom get this place together so you guys could move in. Hope you found everything in order."

Trevor nodded, but his mind went straight to the dead man in the last stall. "Everything's been great, but we are still getting organized on our end. I'm thinking my sister and other brother should be descending upon the ranch in the next few weeks."

Wyatt nodded. "That'll be great. It'll be nice to have some more family close. I know Gwen's been awful lonely since her sister passed away. She's been looking forward to getting to know you guys a little better."

Trevor nodded. "I was so sorry to hear about Bianca's death. At least they caught the person responsible."

"Yeah, best part of my job is getting to watch the guilty pay for their crimes."

Panic rose within him.

Zane nickered as he stuck his head out of his stall door and looked toward them.

"Ah," Wyatt said, looking toward the horse, "my old boy's here." He walked by them to the horse and gave the gelding a good scratch under the mane. The horse seemed to soften under Wyatt's touch.

"This your horse?" Sabrina asked as she stepped around Wyatt like she was trying to keep him from walking farther into the barn.

"Yep," Wyatt said. "He and I have been buddies for a long time. Gwen told me you had taken them up riding, but I figured you had brought them back to Dunrovin by now."

"Actually, we just got back from our ride. We were gonna take a rest, and then bring them back to you guys in the morning." Trevor motioned outside. "In fact, we haven't even unloaded the other horse yet. If you wanted, since you're here, we could load up Zane and—"

"No worries. Gwen and I both know how it is." Wyatt waved him quiet. "Did you guys just run the fences or did you go up the mountain a bit?"

Trevor wasn't sure if Wyatt was testing him or not, but he didn't want to give him the wrong answer. "Yeah, we ran up to the top of Rye Creek. Nice area up there."

"When you get up there in those high mountains the last thing you want to do is come back to real life." Wyatt looked to Sabrina and then back to Trevor and gave him a knowing wink. "And you can keep the horses here as long as you like. Zane isn't our main guest horse, so he's not in high demand. It does him some good to get in some trail time."

Why did everyone assume that something had happened between him and Sabrina out there in the woods? Not that they were wrong. It just hardly seemed like it was anyone else's business.

"Zane is such a good boy," Sabrina said, bridging the gap for him. "It was a nice ride."

"Did you run into the squatters?" Wyatt pressed.

Did the man know something he didn't? Or was he looking for him to supply him with some kind of information? Regardless, his questions were making him unsettled.

"Nope, but we saw a camp they may have been using as a base."

Wyatt nodded. "Good thing. That family can be a wild bunch. And they like to take potshots at people they don't know or don't like."

"Good to know."

Sabrina smiled, the effect dazzling. "Was there something we could help you with, Wyatt?"

He turned and looked toward the end of the barn like he was some kind of damned bloodhound. "Actually, I was here because we got an anonymous tip."

"What?" Trevor asked, his voice taking on an unwanted higher pitch.

"Someone said they heard some shooting coming from out here. They said it sounded like it was coming from inside one of the buildings." Wyatt turned to them. "You guys know anything about that?"

There wasn't anyone within earshot of this place, and certainly shooting at a ranch wouldn't have rung any warning bells. Someone had called in the tip on purpose—they probably wanted Wyatt to stumble onto the body.

They'd been set up.

"Don't know anything about that. Like we said, we just got back from our ride," Trevor said.

Wyatt looked to Sabrina and she nodded in support. "Anyone around here while you were gone?"

If Wyatt looked outside and toward the house he would have likely seen Chad standing near the front window. They couldn't lie and cover his brother's whereabouts—but as far as Wyatt was concerned, he seemed to be out here for nothing more than some suspicious activity. There was no use in lying.

"Actually, my brother Chad was here. He didn't tell me he'd heard anything. And I'm pretty sure he's been watching old football games all day."

Wyatt laughed. "Dang, I want your brother's life. That is just so long as he was drinking beer and eating Doritos as well."

"You know it," Trevor said, giving his cousin's husband a jovial slap on the back. He started to move toward the barn door in an effort to get the man out of the death zone. "You want to come inside and ask him about it?"

"Sure thing. It'd be nice to meet the rest of the family." Wyatt walked toward the front of the barn.

Trevor was careful to stay behind the man so he couldn't see the blood that was likely smeared on the seat of his pants. That would be hard to explain away.

They walked back to the house and Chad met them with an open door. "Hey, bro, this is Wyatt Fitzgerald, Gwen's husband."

Chad wiped his cheese-dusted fingers on the legs of his sweatpants and gave Wyatt a quick shake. "Nice to meet you, man. What can we do for you?" Chad gave Trevor a worried look, and Trevor shook his head in an attempt to convey the fact the deputy knew nothing about the body.

"We have a report of some shooting going on out here. You know anything about it?" Wyatt asked.

Chad nodded for a moment, and Trevor could see the wheels turning in his brother's head. "Hey, yeah… Sorry, that was me. I saw a coyote out there. Wanted to scare 'im off."

Wyatt nodded. "It work?"

Chad laughed. "Not gonna lie, been a lot of beers in the belly today—that, or the aim was a bit off on the old .22."

"I hear you, coz," Wyatt said as he started to warm to them. "If I was retired I would probably be doing just about the same thing—though Gwen may have something to say about that."

Chad laughed. "There are some benefits to being a single guy."

Sabrina's brow lifted as she gave him a look of disdain. "If you keep up the sweatpants and Doritos fingers, the last thing you have to worry about is some poor woman falling in love with you."

"Oh, burn." Wyatt laughed. "It's funny how women have a way of making us step up our game, isn't it?" He looked to Trevor.

The game—that was one word to describe exactly what was going on in their lives. And this game of murder was one game he couldn't lose.

Chapter 12

What in the name of all that was holy was going on around here? Sabrina wished the answers would suddenly appear and everything would make sense.

As the guys continued to talk, her mind wandered. It seemed possible that the Cusslers and the other hillbilly family could have been in some kind of backwoods war, and this was their way of telling the Martins they weren't welcome at the ranch. Maybe it was the second family, and they were figuring they could kill two birds with one stone—the Cussler man, and the Martins' chance of having a peaceful life out here.

But they couldn't have known the Martins wouldn't call the police—unless they been watching them dance around the issue of the dead body in the shack. They must have been watching, and had pieced it together that the thing Trevor and his family feared most was drawing attention from the cops. And they had set the boys up to take this fall.

The thought of being under surveillance made the hairs on the back of her neck stand on end. And yet it made her feel like a hypocrite as she had been doing almost exactly the same thing to Trevor and the Martins for the last little while.

Wyatt gave her an acknowledging nod goodbye as he made his way out the door and toward his patrol unit. "If you guys need anything, or want to meet up for supper sometime, give us a call. Gwen's looking forward to getting together." Wyatt opened the door to his car and the small Chihuahua from Dunrovin jumped out and scurried off in the direction of the barn.

"Francesca," he called after the dog, and as he called the animal's name a look of embarrassment crossed over his face. "I swear I didn't name the dog," he called as he chased after the little thing.

Sabrina ran after them in hopes of catching the dog before she could make her way too far into the barn. The opportunity to tell Wyatt about the body had already come and gone, and if he found the man's body they'd all be arrested for obstruction of justice and possibly tampering with evidence.

She'd have to expose who she was and why she was here to Chad and Wyatt, and what little chance remained of her finishing this investigation and clearing the family's name would go up in dust.

"Here, pup!" Trevor called, his voice frantic.

Wyatt rushed ahead of them into the barn and disappeared.

She hurried to the door, but it was too late. The deputy stood beside the small dog, who was sniffing manically at the base of the last stall. Francesca barked, panting as she looked up to her master. The little dog looked proud of her investigative skills. It almost would have been cute if it hadn't have just blown her cover.

Trevor slipped his hand into hers and gave it a squeeze. For a second, she considered running and getting out of there, but she wasn't the kind who was going to run from her problems. She had to face whatever was coming thanks to that little dog.

She never really considered herself a full-blown cat person until now.

Wyatt stood there in silence, simply staring into the stall for a long moment before turning to them, a dark expression on his features. "How long did you guys say you been back from your ride?"

Trevor took the lead. He shrugged. "Not long. Like we said, we just unloaded Zane. Why, what's up?"

Smart. Feigning ignorance was the only plausible excuse for what the deputy had just found.

Wyatt turned back toward the stall. "I hate to tell you guys this but it looks like I'm gonna need to call out a few more friends of mine."

"Why?" Sabrina asked, she and Trevor took a few steps toward him.

Wyatt held up his hand. "Stop right there. I can't have you coming any closer. Not until I can get my team out here to investigate."

Trevor was already close enough to see the body from the open gate. He motioned for Sabrina to back up. "You don't need to see this." She wasn't sure whether Wyatt wanted to keep them away from the body to see exactly how much they knew, or if he just wanted to protect them from seeing something traumatic.

"Trevor, run inside and get Chad. He needs to know what's going on out here," she said, and leaning in close she whispered, "Don't forget to change your pants. Put them somewhere safe." She gave him a peck on the cheek in hopes it wouldn't look like she had been whispering directions.

Trevor looked unflappable, and his stoicism made her chest tighten with something much too close to love. She had to respect a man who held a great poker face even under the most strenuous of circumstances.

"I'll be right back," Trevor said, but Wyatt was focused on the body.

As Trevor rushed from the barn, she walked toward Wyatt, ignoring his request for her to stay back. She had to pretend to look at the body for the first time.

She stopped beside Wyatt as the man's body came into view. She clapped her hands over her mouth in an attempt to look as surprised as she had been a little while ago. "Do you know who this man is?"

Wyatt turned to her. "I told you not to come back here. You need to leave the barn, right now. Don't touch anything."

Reality came rushing in and Sabrina realized what she had to do. "Wyatt, we knew about the body. We had just found him before you arrived." Before Wyatt ran away with this, she had to tell him the truth…no matter how badly she didn't want to. "I'm a special agent with the FBI, currently I'm investigating a series of crimes. I'm close to cracking the case, but if you pull your men out here, I'm afraid that my cover and my investigation will be blown."

"That can't be true," Wyatt said, staring at her in disbelief.

"Call your sheriff. My people have been in contact with him throughout the investigation. He's the one we briefed when we came in, so he knew what was going on. I wasn't planning on being here too much longer. The Bureau is breathing down my neck. They want results."

"And are you going to get them?" Wyatt asked. "Did you get everything you needed?"

"I'm starting to figure things out. But with this guy's death, I'm afraid there's more going on here than I had anticipated. I need to talk to my handler about what's happened. However, I doubt I will get an extension on my assignment."

"How much longer do you have?"

"Less than a week," Sabrina said. She scuffed her boot around in the spent hay on the barn's floor, kicking up the scent of dirt and horse manure. "It's my hope that I can clear the Martins' name and head off to my next assignment."

Wyatt nodded, but he didn't say anything. The barn door squeaked as Trevor and Chad pushed it open a bit wider and walked in. Chad had the look of a deer in the headlights as he stared at Wyatt.

Wyatt cleared his throat and turned toward the brothers. "Did your brother tell you what we found?"

Chad nodded.

"I'm going to have my crew come in and investigate this man's death. It would make it a whole lot easier if you tell me what actually happened here before my team lays this on you." Wyatt stepped over to the pile of hay bales and leaned against them, crossing his arms over his chest. "You're my family by marriage and I'm going to do everything in my power to make sure you guys stay out of harm's way, but you have to tell me the truth." He looked directly at Sabrina and gave her an almost-imperceptible wink.

It did little to quell the nerves that were building within her. From what she'd heard about the Mystery, Montana, sheriff's department, their forensics team left much to be desired. Hopefully, that would work to her advantage.

But she still couldn't have anyone blowing her cover.

"Let's try this again," Wyatt said to Chad. "Was this man the coyote you were shooting at today?"

Chad rubbed his hands over his face. "I only found out about this dead guy about four seconds before I walked out here. If I had shot him, I would tell you it was in self-defense or something. But I haven't even seen the guy yet." He waved toward the end of the barn.

"The man's name is Earl Cussler. He's the second oldest of the Cussler boys. They are all as mean as rattlesnakes, so if you had admitted to shooting him in self-defense, I would've believed it. However, as it stands, this isn't going to work for me or my department." Wyatt took out his cell phone and glanced down at the buzzing device. "I want you to all go inside before I call in my team."

She turned to leave the barn, but Wyatt motioned her back. "Trevor, I'll be along in a second."

Trevor frowned at her as he made his way out of the barn. "Are you sure?" he whispered, glancing at his cousin's husband.

She nodded. "It's going to be fine."

She watched as Trevor and Chad went back to the main house. They were chatting as they walked, but she couldn't hear exactly what they were saying. No doubt it was something about how much trouble they were going to be in once everything broke. She was afraid she wouldn't be able to help them.

"Who's your handler?" he asked, pulling her attention back to him.

"His name's Mike Couer," she said, a bitter taste filling her mouth. "If you talk to him, take what he says about me with a grain of salt. He and I used to be a thing."

Wyatt chuckled, the sound out of place and haunting in the impromptu crypt. "I thought the Bureau looked down on that."

"They do, but it didn't last long—only long enough to make us realize it was a mistake."

"And to dislike each other?" Wyatt asked.

She couldn't deny it. "Let's just say, if you call him about me, I can't guarantee exactly what he's going to say. I was hoping to use this case to get out of the trenches and into another field office."

Hopefully Wyatt wouldn't judge her unfairly for the mistakes she had made. He was the only shot they had at keeping things under wraps for a bit.

"If that's all true," Wyatt said, leaning back on the hay, "then I understand why you're in a rush to end this investigation. There's nothing more fun than having to deal with your ex's crazy behavior all the time. My family knows exactly how far an ex will go to wreak havoc on a person's life."

"Yeah, Gwen told me what you guys had gone through." She hoped this commonality would act as a bridge between them, a bridge that would lead to her getting her way. "I'm sorry to hear about the mayhem. Sounds like a lot of people died." She hadn't meant to sound so crass and un-empathetic, but her tone came out all wrong.

Wyatt looked at her with surprise, as though he had heard the hardness in her words as well. "You weren't investigating my family, were you?"

She didn't want to lie to him. "Your family drew a bit of scrutiny thanks to your recent run-in with the law, but you were all cleared. However, your name was scattered throughout my files. Just like the Martins, upon coming here and digging a bit, it was easy to see that you weren't criminals—just at the wrong end of someone's sights."

"That's an understatement. It was one hell of a Christmas."

"I can only imagine how you guys must've been feeling."

"Yeah, but even with all the upheaval, a lot of good came from my family's legal troubles."

It was no secret that everything had worked in his family's favor financially, and they had added several family members to their tree. Again, she was witness to a family that seemed to figure out how to stay together, no matter what. She'd never know what that would be like.

"Then I'm sure you can understand—maybe better than anyone—what I want to happen for the Martins." She brushed her hair out of her face. "I know what I'm about to ask isn't aboveboard, but I want you to consider it just for a couple seconds before you give me your answer. Deal?"

The darkness returned to his features, but he nodded.

"All I'm asking," she continued, "is that you give me twenty-four hours. Tomorrow at this time, regardless of if I have this figured out or not, I will call you and report this guy's death and your crew can come and get the body. You and your team will have access to everything I can give you, and I'll talk to Chad and make sure he had nothing to do with this. However, for the time being, I need you to turn a blind eye. Call this a favor for the FBI, a favor I will happily return if the need arises."

"I knew that's where you were going." Wyatt stood up and readjusted his Kevlar vest. "If I don't hear from you in exactly twenty-four hours, I will be standing on that doorstep. I will come after you, and your ex won't be your only enemy in law enforcement. Got it?"

"You can trust me, Wyatt. Thank you for this. I know it's hard to do something like this, but know you're doing the right thing."

"I hope so. I hope you realize you're not just putting your own ass on the line, but mine as well. I don't need this kind of trouble, but I've learned having friends in high places can make all the difference. Don't you be forgetting you owe me."

She had expected some of the weight to be lifted off her shoulders, but as Wyatt walked out of the barn, it was like the entire world was upon her. They'd have to get to the bottom of this fast, or her entire world—and everyone else's around her—would come crashing down.

Chapter 13

Trevor hated that he'd had to leave Sabrina in the barn alone with Wyatt. He could only guess what they'd talked about, but no doubt she'd had to let him in on her secret.

Wyatt walked out of the barn and got into the squad car. Starting it up, he drove away. *Holy crap*, what had she said to him? The deputy hadn't seemed like the type who would walk away from a case like this. Family or not, he hadn't expected any sort of favors from the man.

"Dude, did you see that?" Chad asked, pointing out the window.

"I'll be right back," he said, already half out the door.

Sabrina met him halfway; her hands were up like she was surrendering to him. "It's going to be okay, Trevor. I made a deal with him."

"Is he dropping his investigation?" he asked, taking hold of her shoulders and looking her in the eye.

Her whole body tensed underneath his touch. "Far from it. We have twenty-four hours. That's it. Then all hell's going to break loose. And I would guess that at least Chad will be arrested. And you wouldn't be far behind…nor would I."

"Are you kidding me? We barely have a clue about what's going on out here. And yet you think we can solve this in a day?" She must've lost her mind. He was going to jail. They had to run. And yet if they did, it would make them look incredibly guilty. And she would have to answer for their leaving.

"Trevor, there's something I didn't tell you before. I didn't think it was important, but now with this…" She nibbled at her lip. "My handler at the Missoula resident agency, his name is Mike. He's my ex."

As she said the man's name, it looked as though she was in pain. She must hate the man. He could only imagine the kind of drama that would unfold inside the close quarters that was the FBI. It was known for being fraught with varying levels of corruption and mistrust—none more so than the last few years. Lately, it was as if everything had gone crazy in the Bureau. It was a wonder that she even had a job if she'd made the mistake of falling for her boss. In fact, this Mike guy was lucky that she hadn't gone after him for any sort of predatory behavior. The man had to be one hell of a winner if he was preying on women within his agency in order to get some.

On the other hand, perhaps she really had loved the guy and it was a relationship built upon real feelings. It was easy enough to see how something like that could come about, with forced proximity and all, but he would have thought a man in an authority position would have made the choice to not put them both in jeopardy. Then again, Sabrina was of her own mind. She had made choices—this wasn't sitting on just the shoulders of her boss. She had to have understood what kind of position she was putting herself in.

He needed to distance himself from her. Not that he didn't already know that. He just couldn't get over how sweet her lips had tasted, and how it felt when her body was pressed against him. In a weird way, his heart had felt as shriveled and emaciated as a starving man, but when she'd entered his life it was like it had started to beat again and grow stronger thanks to the nourishment that came with her presence.

Ugh, he was being so ridiculous.

"Do you still love him?" he asked without thinking.

From the look on her face, the question had clearly come out of left field. "No."

Her curtness didn't help him feel any better.

He counted his breaths until he reached ten and his heart rate lowered. He had to keep his wits about him. "Okay, so do you think this guy is gunning for you… for us?"

She chewed on her lip until a tiny bit of blood dotted its pink curve. "I want to say no, but the truth is I'm not sure. He's been pushing me hard throughout this investigation. He rushed it through the bureaucracy. What normally takes six months to get approvals for, he did in a matter of weeks. I don't know how he did it, but it may be part of the reason he needs us to get to the bottom of this so quickly."

"*This*—as in my family?" Even he could hear the hurt in his voice.

"I meant my investigation." She gave him an apologetic smile. "Mike is probably on the warpath. He likely overextended himself and promised results that, frankly, I'm not sure I'm going to be able deliver on."

"Do you think if you went to the offices that you could get a better feel for what's going on with Mike?" Part of him wanted to go with her, to ensure she was safe. Yet the last place he needed to be seen was sitting outside a federal building. Even with his connections with the CIA, those watching wouldn't appreciate his suspicious behavior.

"Mike is not the kind of guy you can get an easy read on. The FBI has trained that out of him. He's like talking to a wall."

With that kind of description, he wasn't sure how she had ever found herself falling for such a guy. Though if he looked at himself closely, he was probably cut from the same cloth as Mike. Again, he found himself lacking. He had to hope he was nothing like a possibly crooked agent. Though Sabrina hadn't always thought him capable, he was a man guided by morals. Which only made all of this more difficult.

"I think we should go, but I'll need stay out of sight. The last thing we need is you showing up to the regional headquarters with the man you are in charge of investigating." Trevor pulled the keys from his pocket.

Sabrina sniggered. "I can't even imagine how badly that would play out."

"Well, you don't have to as long as things go smoothly. In and out, okay?" he said with a raise of the brow.

"All right, but no matter what happens you have to stay out of the limelight."

He nodded. "I'll unhitch the trailer if you unload the other horse."

They made quick work of it. Sabrina wiped her hands on the leg of her pants as she closed up the barn and turned to him. "What about Chad and the cops? You don't think he'll blow my cover, do you?"

"Chad is a knot head, but he's not stupid. You're safe when it comes to my family and them keeping their mouths shut." He lifted the keys. "You want to drive?" he teased.

"If we want to get there in one piece, I better."

He threw the keys to her with a chuckle.

It wasn't too long a drive to Missoula. With each passing mile, more nerves started to fill him. It felt almost as if he was back in Adana, and the gun trade was just about to go down with Trish. This same sense of foreboding had filled him then. If something happened to Sabrina, like it had to Trish, he wasn't sure he could keep on living. The crushing blow of losing his sister had been all the tragedy he could bear. He couldn't lose someone else he loved.

"When I get out, I want you to take the wheel and drive over to the Staggering Ox. Order a sandwich, and I'll get an Uber and catch up."

He didn't like the plan, but he was in no position to argue. If something happened inside the federal building, he'd never get access in time to save her. But Mike didn't sound like a guy who would get caught making a visible threat against another agent.

Regardless of how uncomfortable it made him, he had to trust her judgment. She was going to do what she had to do for them and for their investigation. Though he had never intended on them working together, in this moment, he realized that was exactly what they were doing—inadvertently, their relationship had morphed into something new…something that *fit*.

No. He was just seeing things that weren't really possible. Sure, they could work this thing together, but that didn't mean anything for the future. This was nothing more than an isolated incident including some extenuating circumstances—circumstances that, for this moment in time, had them working toward the same goal. Once they got to the bottom of this and found their murderer they would be forced to go their separate ways.

She pulled the truck to a stop about a block away from the Fed office and got out.

"Be careful," he said, ignoring the apprehension that was gnawing away in his gut. "If you need me, I can be back within a couple of minutes."

She nodded. Her features were tight, as though she were feeling some of the same nervous energy that he was—it did nothing to make him feel better. He wanted to tell her to stop, that they could do something else, something less risky, something that wouldn't put her square at the center of Mike's radar. And yet, the leads—which all pointed at corruption—had brought them here.

This was the only way…anything else would take them far longer than the time they had been allowed.

In the meantime, he had some work of his own to do.

He watched for a moment as she walked down the sidewalk. She was still wearing her dirty clothes from the trail ride, and there was mud on her boots. She looked like anything but a special agent.

He put the truck in gear and looked up the sandwich shop on his phone, then made his way across town. The hole-in-the-wall restaurant comprised about a dozen tables, all of which were covered in inlaid comic book pages. It carried a certain charm. And as he walked toward the register, the scent of warm bread and fresh lettuce filled the air. It made his mouth water as he realized that the last time he had eaten was when they were up on the mountain. His stomach grumbled and twisted in his belly.

He ordered a couple of sandwiches and went outside to make a phone call while he waited for them to be ready.

He pulled out his phone and dialed his point person within the CIA.

She answered on the first ring. "Trevor, what's going on, man?" She sounded excited in her normal, brusque way.

"Hey. I'm working a case and I need your help."

"I thought you had taken a leave of absence," she said with a chuckle.

"You know full well that even when we're not working, we're working."

"I wouldn't know. I'm never blessed with free time, you lucky bastard," she teased.

He'd always appreciated Tina's ability to not delve down the dark and disturbing rabbit hole that was the past—she knew exactly why he had taken time away from the CIA, and why he was likely going to choose to retire, and yet she avoided bringing up his sister.

"I'm what we're calling lucky now?" He laughed. "I'd hate to see what it means to be one of the unlucky ones."

Tina laughed. "What do you want? I know you didn't call me just to be an ornery ass."

"I've been dealing with some DOAs."

"Because of course you have," Tina said, interrupting.

"Ha ha, you know if your job ever craps out at the agency, you can always become a comedian."

"I'm not half as funny as your face is looking."

"Anyone ever tell you you're a real pain in the butt?"

"Every day."

"Actually, I was calling about a friend of mine in the Bureau. We have reason to believe that there's some interoffice corruption going on."

There was a long silence on the other end of the line.

"Dude, Trevor, if you're right, you don't want to get within a thousand miles of that kind of thing. Politics has a way of ruining even the best reputations."

Tina was right, but in this instance, he didn't have a whole lot of choice in the matter—he was already deeply involved. "I hear you. I do. However, that ship has sailed. What I need from you is for you to help me run some ballistic tests. I have reason to believe that the rounds may belong to a federally issued weapon. I just need to know for sure. That something you can help me with?"

"Are you serious? Are you really asking me to stick my neck out and take part in defaming an FBI agent? You'd be putting my job at risk, you realize that, right?" Tina asked, but from her tone he couldn't decide whether or not she was being serious or kidding around. Either way he wouldn't have been surprised.

"Is that a no?"

Tina chuckled. "Pfft, come on now, you know we're supposed to be all buddy-buddy with our FBI brethren, but nothing would make me happier than knocking the hierarchy down a peg or two. Get them to the Montana State Crime Lab. I have some friends there who owe me a favor."

"I knew I could count on you," Trevor said. "I'll get the samples there as soon as I can. They should be to you within the hour. And hey, thanks."

"I've always got your back. And next time we work together, I'll make sure you get the first crappy detail that comes along."

"I'd expect nothing less."

She hung up. He sent a quick text to Chad, asking him to run out to the barn and pull the round that was embedded in the wood of the stall.

The waiter walked out of the sandwich shop, carrying a paper bag of sandwiches. "Thanks," Trevor said, handing him a ten-dollar tip.

He walked back to the truck and sat down with his sandwich. He'd forgotten to order drinks, son of a gun. He slipped his sandwich back into the bag and was just about to get out as his phone rang. It was Sabrina. Just the sight of her name made the bite of sandwich he'd eaten sit poorly in his stomach. Hopefully she was okay.

"Do you need help?" he asked, bypassing any pleasantries.

"Mike isn't here. No one has seen him in the office in a couple of days. But they were acting strange, like they were hiding something." She sounded worried.

"And no one knows where he's at?" Trevor put his phone on speaker, sat back in his seat and slammed the truck door closed. He revved the engine and screamed out of the parking lot, hurrying back to get to her.

At least he didn't have to worry about Mike taking

potshots at her, and she wasn't in immediate danger, but that didn't mean they were out of the woods yet.

"It doesn't sound like he's been seen or heard from in days. People are concerned and looking into his disappearance. This kind of behavior is very unlike him."

Something was going on in her office. Something that surely wouldn't play out in her favor.

"You didn't talk to anyone about our investigation into your team at the FBI, did you?"

"No, never. I couldn't."

Trevor ran through a yellow light as it turned red. Right now, he didn't care about following rules. He just had to get to Sabrina and make sure she was safe.

"You're not driving like a bat out of hell, are you?" Sabrina asked, but there was a hard edge to her voice as she teased him.

"I have no idea what you're talking about." He glanced at the road signs. "I'll be out front to pick you up in a minute. Be outside."

She laughed, but he could hear the echo of a stairwell and her footfalls as she must have been running down stairs. "It's okay, Trevor. I'm fine. You know you don't need to worry about me."

"I'm not," he lied. "I'm approaching one block due east of the front entrance."

The front door of the building opened and Sabrina walked outside. There was a muffled cry as she dropped her phone and it clattered onto the sidewalk. The line went dead. A group of agents surrounded her. She put her hands up and said something. She glanced in his direction, terror in her eyes. Her mouth opened, and from the distance it looked as though she was telling him to stay back.

He pulled the truck over just as the agent closest to Trevor took Sabrina down to the ground.

What in the hell is going on?

He couldn't just rush in there and fix things. If he did, it would likely only end up with him getting arrested and Sabrina getting fired for misconduct. But that didn't stop him.

He got out of the truck, only half-aware of the traffic that was passing around him. He ran down the street. "I demand you tell me what's going on here."

An older man, probably in his midfifties, sent him a dangerous smile. "I know exactly who you are, Trevor, and if you think your connections give you any right to know what is going on here, you are sorely mistaken." The man had to be Mike, Sabrina's ex. He seemed like exactly the jerk that she had described—with his salt-and-pepper hair, his silver fox looks and his arrogant swagger.

"What do you know, jackass?" Trevor sneered.

"Oh, I heard all about how you got fired from Spookville for your role in getting your sister killed." Mike stepped away and waved back the agents around him. "Sounds like you have your hands in all kinds of pots. I just wish it could have been us that found the information that proved it. As it was, Agent Parker here... Well, she lost her edge."

He didn't know what the hell he was talking about. Just like everything else about this investigation, it appeared as though he only had half the information—the half that made him want to punch Mike in the face.

"Sabrina," he said, pushing the arresting officer back and helping her up. "Are you okay?"

"Trevor, it is far from your best interest to get involved. I have it on good authority that you're just a few days away from this happening to you as well." Mike put his hand on the gun at his side, threatening him. "Actually, I bet I'd get a slap on the back for bringing you in for your role in the murders of Earl and Owen Cussler. Former CIA or not, murder is murder."

There were a lot of things that Trevor was guilty of, but not that. "And what genius came up with this theory?" He looked directly at Mike. "I'm sure this is your handiwork."

"Sounds like the words of a guilty man." Mike looked around the group of agents like he was looking for some sort of validation.

"That's the dumbest thing I've ever heard, Mike." He glanced to the agents standing around them. "What kind of motivation do we have to kill those guys?"

"It's no secret that you're trying to evict the family from your land." Mike sneered. "Sounds like one hell of a motivation to me. Not to mention Sabrina's hatred for me…she's been trying to make me look incompetent from the very beginning. She's been setting me up. I just couldn't believe it when I learned of her role in the shoot-out that took place with her fellow agents. I assume she must have thought she was shooting at me." He glared at her. "In case you were wondering, Agent Heath is still recovering at St. Pat's hospital."

He had been right. The people they'd been fighting on the mountain had been none other than the men from her own agency. But it didn't make sense. She should've known they were up there. Mike should have informed her that they might run into friendlies.

"Thanks to your mistakes, we have more than enough evidence to take you and your whole family into custody." Mike gave him a weighted look, like he was sure he had the upper hand.

It took all of Trevor's strength not to get up in the man's face and tell him exactly where he could stuff his theories. In fact… He pushed his way toward the man and started screaming obscenities like some outraged hillbilly. While his mouth ran wild, he lifted Mike's gun from his holster and slipped it under his jacket.

"Trevor, stop!" Sabrina said. "Just go. Before you get into trouble. I'll get this figured out. I'm innocent. We both know that. We'll get this sorted."

He stepped beside her and gave her a long, passionate kiss. Their public display of affection caused some of the agents to look away. As they did, Sabrina slipped a gun into his waistband. She leaned in close like she was whispering something sweet into his ear, and said, "This is mine. Send it to ballistics along with the one from the cabin…and Mike's."

She must have seen him take the man's gun.

She moved back from their kiss. "Now get out of here before Mike does something stupid."

As far as Trevor was concerned, Mike had already done something extraordinarily idiotic when he decided to screw over Sabrina. And now his stupidity was going to come back to bite him. Trevor would not rest until he cleared the name of the woman he loved.

Chapter 14

She was innocent, and he was the only person who could prove it.

From the truck, he watched as the agents paraded Sabrina into the building—like she was some kind of prized cattle that they just couldn't wait to take to slaughter. He would've thought that there would be more comradery within the FBI, but then it shouldn't come as such a surprise. It was a dog-eat-dog world.

Loyalty was a commodity in short supply.

Which made him think about Seattle. He couldn't be completely sure, but he had a feeling that the Bureau had taken the bait—if it hadn't, Mike would have certainly arrested him when they'd arrested Sabrina. As it was, they were probably still hoping to bring him down for gunrunning. He was probably still being watched.

If he caught a plane now, he could get to Seattle with

a half a day to spare—hours in which he could put his plan into action.

His first stop was to the crime lab. When he arrived at the bland brick building he was reminded of a generic apartment building in New York—maybe in the low-rent district.

Chad was just parking when he arrived, and he parked beside him. As he got out Chad flashed him a little Ziploc bag; inside was a piece of shrapnel.

"What kind of mess have you gotten us into?" Chad asked.

"If I told you, you wouldn't believe me. But on a positive note, it looks like you and I will be flying to Seattle. We need to be there before the morning. In the mood for some spoon-melting coffee?" he asked with a chuckle.

Chad sighed and handed him the bag. "And here I thought moving to Montana would give us a chance to live a slower paced life. You just love proving me wrong, don't you?"

Trevor slapped his brother's arm. "It's not about proving you wrong, it's just about keeping the standard of living to which we've grown accustomed. I'd hate for you to get bored."

"I can't say life with you has ever been boring," Chad said with his trademark half grin.

"Good, then I'm not about to let you down." Trevor flashed his brother the two guns tucked into his waistband.

"Where did you get those?" Chad asked, giving him a look of concern.

"You're not gonna believe this, but I just lifted one off of one of our local FBI agents." Trevor smirked. "Best part, I doubt he even noticed it's missing."

"You have got to be kidding me," Chad said, each word like it was in independent sentence. "No wonder you have us running. We're going to be jumping borders in no time, aren't we?"

"It all depends on what happens in that building," he said, pointing toward the crime lab.

"Please tell me that there's a Get Out of Jail Free card somewhere in there." Chad frowned. "If I end up going to jail for you, I'm going to be irate."

He would have liked to tell his brother he had nothing to worry about, but the truth was that their butts were hanging way too far out in the open for him to feel comfortable. Mike, and the agents working with him, were going to be out for blood once they figured out what he had done.

"I'm going to run in. You need to call Zoey and have her arrange for a private jet to take us to Seattle. Got it?"

Chad nodded, already reaching for his phone.

As Trevor made his way into the crime lab, he looked back. Trish would've loved this kind of thing. She'd hated FBI agents even more than he did. Though now it seemed like he may well have fallen in love with one.

Trish would have given him such crap for Sabrina. But when push came to shove, his sister would have loved Sabrina just as much as he did. In fact, Trish would've probably helped him figure out a way to make everything work, not only with Sabrina but with this cluster he found them in.

He had no idea what he would do if this didn't work.

It wasn't just Sabrina's career that hung in the balance. If this failed, not only would he likely lose all credibility within the CIA and secret services, he'd also probably end up in jail, just as Chad had predicted. He would hate to prove his brother right.

In all of his years as a independent military contractor, he had never thought he would find himself in such a compromising position. He'd done many questionable things in the line of duty—but this was by far the craziest. It seemed like some kind of karmic slap that his greatest adversaries wouldn't be some terrorists abroad, but rather American law enforcement agents.

It didn't take long to hand the guns off to the tech at the lab; apparently Tina had already made the call.

When he made his way outside to Chad, his brother pointed toward his car and said, "Get in. We will have a jet waiting for you in the morning." Chad walked around to the driver's side.

Maybe this was all going to go better than he hoped, but he had a sinking feeling that he was in some deep water.

The next morning, the flight took just over an hour, and when they arrived Zoey was standing out on the tarmac waiting for them. Even in the overcast gray sky that seemed to always hover over the city, Zoey's black hair picked up what little light there was, and the effect created dark blue streaks. Even with her dyed locks, she looked so much like Trish.

There was a town car and a driver waiting beside her.

"Wipe that look off your face," Zoey said. "Stop worrying. I already hacked into the FBI mainframe. This Mike guy was bluffing, but he's hoping that they can bring you in for running guns. As such, I made sure he got orders from the top to intercept our 'trade' this evening. I also contacted the DOJ. they are sending someone to look into things and find out how deep this corruption runs."

"And what about Sabrina? Is she going to be cleared?" Trevor asked.

"Depends on her level of involvement. From what Chad was telling me, sounds like you and this woman have been hitting it off."

He shot a disapproving look at his brother, but Chad just shrugged.

"What can I say, man? We're a family that hates to keep secrets from one another." Chad's half grin reappeared.

As ridiculous as his brother could be, he couldn't be mad at him. It was this open policy that was currently in the process of saving their butts.

"Sabrina and I have grown close since I got to the ranch," he admitted.

Zoey smiled. "Yeah, I knew she would be right up your alley when I vetted her for the housekeeping job."

"Oh yeah," Chad said. "I forgot that this was all your fault. Thanks a lot, sis. Maybe next time worry less about being our virtual matchmaker and worry more about whether or not the people we bring into our lives belong to the FBI."

Zoey held her hands up in surrender. "I admit, I may have overlooked the fact that her background seemed a bit sparse, but I just thought she was the kind of girl who didn't get out much."

"Well, you were definitely wrong." Trevor walked to the town car and threw their go bags into the trunk. "Then again, who am I to start pointing fingers? I assume Chad told you everything?"

Zoey nodded. "One thing for certain, you are gifted

when it comes to getting us into highly unconventional situations."

That was one way to put it.

He once again thought of Trish. Zoey gave him a mournful look. "Hey, Trevor, I know what you're thinking... It wasn't your fault."

He wasn't sure he believed her, or if he ever would.

"The family...we...none of us are upset with you about what happened back there. It was outside your control. You need to start forgiving yourself. Trish wouldn't want you to hang on to her death like you are."

It was easy enough for her to say, but she wasn't living in his shoes. "I hear what you're saying, but until we get through tonight unscathed, I'm not gonna forgive myself for anything."

Some tragedies were just too great to overcome...all he could do now was try not to repeat history.

Chapter 15

Sabrina paced around the interrogation room. She couldn't even begin to count the number of times she had brought people in rooms like this one in order to get them to bend to her whims. And now here she was, on the other side of the table. There was a box of tissues and a stack of magazines at the center of the table. In the corner was a percolating coffeepot. The scent of coffee was there to promote a sense of safety, reminding people of being home and in the comfort of their own surroundings, but the aroma only made her more anxious.

At least they hadn't forced her to wear the cuffs around the building when they brought her up from her holding cell to the interrogation room this morning. It was already embarrassing enough that she had been brought in here like she was nothing more than one of their normal, run-of-the-mill murderers.

She was never going to be able to show her face around Missoula or the county again. Everyone in law enforcement knew, or had found out by now, that she had been arrested for murder. No doubt, they would have to call in an outside investigation team to review her case, but knowing Mike, he had gone out of his way to make sure she looked as guilty as hell.

What she couldn't understand was how. She'd had no intuition that they'd been watched or set up. Everything had seemed relatively…*normal*. Well, as normal as her days at the Bureau could be. Sure, not everybody came across dead bodies every few days, but in her line of work it was par for course.

Mike had to have been plotting this for some time—probably from the first moment they were sent to this remote agency from Washington.

She hadn't expected Mike to remain her friend, or even an ally, after they broke up. Things hadn't ended on the best of terms but they owed each other some amount of respect, especially after all they had been through. Instead here she was, standing on the other side of the glass thanks to his denigration of her character.

Even if she could prove her innocence, it would take some time. Certainly, the damage to her career would be nearly irreparable. Maybe she really would have to become a housekeeper. Maybe, just maybe, the Martins would hire her full time. But she had likely burned her bridge with that family, once the rest of Trevor's siblings found out about her role in the FBI.

As of the last she knew, Trevor had protected her secret, but now he'd have to out her in order to ask his family to help. Unfortunately. Even if his family did help, she wasn't sure that they would be her best allies when it came to standing in front of a judge and jury.

However, she could have sworn she'd heard Trevor say he was working with the CIA, but she couldn't believe it. If he had been working with the CIA like he said, there was no way that Mike would have sent her in to investigate the family. He had enough clearance to have that information.

But documents and proposals for the investigation had been fast-tracked through the Bureau. It was possible that either someone hadn't fact-checked properly or that Mike had known all along and had wanted her to disappear at the hands of the trained spook.

The CIA and their operatives, especially those who did not wish to be found, had been known to use their connections to make sure anyone who stepped in their way would fall prey to the shadowy nature of the agency.

There was a soft knock on the interrogation room door. "Yep," she said, awkwardly.

It didn't feel right to say anything at all, given the situation. But remaining silent also seemed equally odd. Speaking of remaining silent, she'd need to call in a lawyer.

"Good morning, Agent Parker," a female agent whom Sabrina didn't recognize said as she stepped into the room.

The woman had a pixie haircut that did nothing for the wrinkles that creased her forehead and were scattered around her eyes. Even her lips carried deep creases, like she spent one too many years smoking. As the woman walked into the interrogation room, Mike followed behind her, looking like a pit bull. He was out for blood, her blood, and seeing him made her skin prickle.

She wanted to go toe to toe with him and call him every obscenity that was rolling through her mind, but it would do no good. She couldn't deal with the situation proactively by being angry. All she could do was play his game—a game of logic and manipulation. Hopefully, she hadn't entered the game too late.

Actually, there was no time left for hope. She was already under arrest for crimes she hadn't committed. She'd already lost.

"I want my lawyer." The words tasted like the ocean, salty and smattered with the remnants of tempests.

"I bet you do," Mike said.

The woman gave him a look to shut up—it was the same look Sabrina had given him entirely too often when they were dating.

"Agent Parker, my name is Rowena Anderson. I'm the special agent in charge from your sister agency, the Madison County resident office," the woman said, an air of authority in her tone.

"Pleasure," Sabrina said, unsure whether or not she should play nice or say nothing. It didn't seem as though it would be in her best interest to be an ass.

"Yes," the woman said. "I hope you slept well. I'm sorry it took me so long to get here."

She hadn't slept a wink. Instead she had spent the entire night staring up at the ceiling of her cell and thinking about all the ways her life had gone wrong. For both their sakes, she said nothing.

Agent Anderson pointed toward the chair beside the table and motioned for her to sit down.

She did as instructed, but she couldn't take her eyes

off Mike's smug face. Looking at him, and the way he seemed to have no remorse for what he had done to her, she couldn't understand what she had ever seen in him. He was nothing but a weasel.

"Agent Parker, it is with my deepest regrets that we have to meet under such circumstances. However, I'm sure that you understand, thanks to your many years of dedicated service for the FBI, that we all must do our duty. Today, my duty is to talk to you about your role in the two deaths that occurred while you were representing the Bureau undercover." The woman walked over to the coffeepot and poured herself a cup. "Would you like some?"

The woman was stalling—it was a common interrogation technique. It was the same reason they had kept her locked up in this room for four hours before anyone had even acknowledged her presence. They wanted to make her nervous, to drive up her anxiety level to the point where she'd be easier to manipulate.

By the same token, Agent Anderson had to know that Sabrina was fully aware of her tactics.

The woman took a long sip of her coffee, staring at her through the steam—she was trying to get a read on her. No doubt, she wanted to feel her out in order to determine how she would play this interrogation.

"Sabrina, it's in your best interest to just admit you killed those two Cussler guys. We found your fingerprints all over the murder weapon." Mike smirked.

Oh, that bastard.

It was a good thing she had sat down. Her hands fell limp into her lap as the shock worked its way through her body.

Her fingerprints had been found on the murder weapon?

It was impossible.

She'd never even fired her gun—only the one that Trevor had given her on the mountain, a gun she had returned to him. Her own firearm she'd given to Trevor, so Mike couldn't have sent it off to the lab for analysis. This didn't make sense.

She wanted to cry out and to tell Agent Anderson that she had no idea what he was talking about. But she knew that they must have had concrete evidence well in advance of her arrest. Which meant they had a different gun...a gun she had likely never actually touched.

At the shanty, she had watched Trevor pick up the gun that had killed the first brother. He'd wiped it down and left it there. She'd never touched it—or even gone back inside the shack. But that didn't mean someone hadn't tampered with the evidence. If the FBI, or Mike, had gone to that shanty they easily could have planted her prints on that gun. Or maybe there was an entirely different gun. She just couldn't be sure.

If only they had just called in Wyatt and the sheriff's department when they found the body. Wyatt was probably going to have a fit when he learned where she was. If he admitted to his role in her supposed cover-up of the second Cussler brother's death, his future would be in jeopardy. Everything she had done, every choice she had made, had been wrong.

"Nothing to say for yourself?" Mike said, taunting her.

"Agent Couer, I told you that if you wished to stand in on this interrogation, you were to remain silent," the woman said. "As you seem incapable of such a daunting task, and given your familiarity with Agent Parker, I think it best that you leave." She pointed toward the door.

Mike opened his mouth to argue, but quickly shut up. It was the smartest thing she'd ever seen him do.

If only she could tell the woman the truth. And yet this woman had no reason to believe anything she said. It was normal for the accused to immediately start blaming others. A perpetrator rarely admitted fault. And even if they did passively admit to some wrongdoing, there would always be some extenuating circumstance that explained their misdeed away. She couldn't be like one of those people. But she also couldn't sit here and be accused and do nothing.

Mike stepped out of the room, but not before giving her one last sidelong glance and an accompanying smirk. The door clicked shut behind him.

"Now, Agent Parker, back to our conversation," the woman said.

"I didn't kill anyone. I'm innocent." She put her hands on the table, palms up, the universal sign of submission and forthrightness.

The woman looked down at Sabrina's hands and then in the direction of the closed door. "I have reviewed the entire case, and the evidence they have against you. As of this moment, the evidence is not in your favor. However, I'm finding holes in Agent Couer's assessment of the situation."

Sabrina wasn't entirely sure what the woman meant, so she remained silent.

"There's not a lot of information I can give you at this time. However, if you help me in my investigation, it will not go unnoticed."

She implied she would get Sabrina a deal without directly offering anything. When interrogating, Sabrina used the same method to elicit trust from her suspects.

She couldn't get sucked into this woman's charade.

"And what is it that you would like me to do?" Sabrina asked, curious.

Agent Anderson looked back at the door, almost as though she expected it to open again at any second. If anything, it appeared as if she were more nervous than Sabrina was. "About the meeting in Seattle. We want you there. Along with Agent Couer."

"What? Why?" Did they want to publicly broadcast her shame for the rest of the Bureau? No. She wasn't going to be their whipping boy.

"I know you're gun-shy after what happened. But believe me when I say it's in your best interest to help me out." The woman reached over and gave Sabrina's hand a reassuring squeeze.

The simple action surprised her. The interrogation room was currently being filmed. Was the woman trying to tell her something that she couldn't say on camera? Or was she stringing her along?

"Trevor said he worked for the CIA. You don't think he's really involved with the illegal gun trade, do you?"

"Oh, he and his family are very involved," Agent Anderson said. "We believe he may be using it to increase his income. It's fairly common for those behind the curtain to participate in unsanctioned deals like this."

Sabrina couldn't help but feel even more deflated. The man she had fallen in love with couldn't be a criminal. He wasn't the man the Bureau made him out to be.

If they went to Seattle, she risked being made an even a bigger fool in the Bureau, and yet she would get to see

Trevor at least one more time. And she could prove that she had been right about distrusting him.

For all she knew, he wouldn't even be there and instead it would be a team of his people. It would be smart of him to call off the entire deal now that he knew that he and his family were under investigation by the Bureau.

A part of her also wanted to save him. If she went there, she could try to alert him to the danger.

She was already damned by the Bureau's standards, and probably out of a job now that she was under arrest. Even though she was innocent, she would be lucky if she didn't go to prison.

A chill ran down her spine as she thought about being stuck in a federal prison with inmates she had sent there. The situation wouldn't end well—but from the beginning of her investigation, the only thing that had gone well was the night she spent in the mountains with Trevor making love.

If only she could go back in time…to a time and place where things weren't so complicated.

Chapter 16

The gun sat heavy in Trevor's hands. Though the assault rifle weighed only a few pounds, it felt as though it was imbued with the weight of everyone who depended on him.

Zoey was sitting in the corner office, out of sight from where their operation would take place. Even if he couldn't get out, perhaps she would.

Though they had planned everything to the last detail, it didn't mean that it would go off without a hitch. Things had a way of going haywire any time guns were involved. He would be lucky if he made it out alive.

Chad was sitting above him in the skywalk, and as Trevor looked up, his brother gave him a thumbs-up. In a matter of seconds, and with a rearrangement of fabric, Chad disappeared into the darkness, perfectly camouflaged. For all intents and purposes, Trevor appeared to be alone.

In the quiet of the industrial warehouse, the buzz of the fluorescent lights sounded like a swarm of bees just waiting to descend.

Between the FBI and a swarm of bees, under normal circumstances, he would take bees.

He hated that this was where they were now—playing a game of corrupt politics and misguided leadership.

Though it appeared he was standing alone in the center of the industrial building, he could feel people watching him. No doubt, by now they likely had agents set up around the building monitoring him with some hidden tech. They likely had microphones and video cameras installed in the building as soon as they heard of their plan—if they were smart, they had every inch of this place streaming live at some central command center.

His phone pinged. It was time. Everything was in place.

The metal industrial garage door clicked as someone slid it open. In front of him was Gus, the man they had hired to help flush out Mike. Gus had been working for them over the last decade, always available at a moment's notice. They paid him well, but this time he wasn't sure if they were paying the man enough to deal with what was about to happen.

This time, Gus had brought three men and a woman with him. Gus was wearing a tailored linen suit, and his gray hair was slicked back with pomade. He reminded Trevor of a Miami drug lord. The men and women standing guard around Gus all wore black, and each had a pair of Ray-Ban sunglasses perched on their head—and they looked terribly out of place in Seattle's underbelly.

He gave the man a stiff nod. "Did Ahmal send you?"

"Does Ahmal send just anyone?" Gus said, looking at him like he was a stranger he didn't trust.

He played his role well.

"You have what I asked for?" Gus asked, motioning toward the big rig that was parked by the far wall of the warehouse.

"You have our money?" Trevor asked, lowering the assault rifle in his hand and leaning on it as if it were nothing more than a walking stick.

Gus looked toward the gun at Trevor's side. "Is that one of our M16s?"

Trevor took a step forward, moving to hand the man the gun. The woman stepped between them, as though she was really there to guard the man his family had planted.

Perfect.

"Have your woman stand down," he said, glaring at her.

"Marie," Gus said, sounding tired.

The woman stepped back, but her hand had moved to the gun strapped to her side.

Hopefully, Gus had told her that this mission was nothing more than a farce. He didn't want to have to worry about drawing any unnecessary friendly fire— he had enough to worry about when it came to the FBI and what they did or didn't know. One wrong move, one misplaced statement, and all hell could rain down.

He handed Gus the gun, keeping one eye on the woman to make sure she didn't make a mistake. Gus was smart, but just like them, he probably wanted to make this seem as real as possible—which may have meant that he had left his team in the dark.

"There are a thousand more of these inside that truck." He motioned behind him. "Did you wire us the money?"

"I only work in cash. I find it comforting," Gus said, motioning for one of his guards.

As the guard stepped forward, Trevor noticed the black briefcase in his hand. The briefcase was leather and adorned with brass, perfectly antiquated. It was almost comical, and far from the kind of thing most people would've expected, but Trevor had seen a lot of eccentricity in his travels.

In fact, one of the warlords they had been investigating in Africa brought a capuchin monkey to all their arms deals. In the end, STEALTH had planted a recording device in the monkey's collar. Because of a pet monkey, a dangerous man had been brought to justice and found guilty of war crimes.

"Half a million?" Trevor asked, reaching in his pocket and taking out the keys to the truck.

"In unmarked bills," Gus said. "Show us the guns."

Trevor walked toward the truck. Each step felt like it was in slow motion, as though he were walking toward his execution.

If this was how he went down… No, he couldn't give it any thought.

Trish, and the last look on her face—the look of terror, pain and the realization that death was upon her—came to the front of his mind and a wave of nausea threatened to take him to his knees. Somehow he kept walking.

The end of the truck was open, exposing the crates. Stepping up, Gus followed him and he reached inside the open crate nearest them. The guns had been chipped, even though this wasn't that kind of deal. Everything reminded him of the last time. He'd promised himself he would never be in this kind of situation again, and as he moved toward the crate his body stopped. It was as though he was glued to the floor of the truck, and no matter how badly he wanted to step forward and look inside that crate, his body wouldn't allow it.

"You like?" Trevor asked, trying to ignore the way his body defied him.

"They are all identical?" Gus asked.

Trevor nodded. They stepped out of the truck and Gus's men closed the back end.

The guard handed Gus the briefcase.

"Do we have a deal?" Trevor asked.

Gus handed him the briefcase and Trevor handed him the keys to the big rig. Every door in the warehouse flew open. There was the percussion of a flash bang, and Trevor hit the ground.

"Get down on the ground!" a man ordered. "Hands above your head!"

The FBI agents rushed into the building, running through the smoke of the blast. Trevor watched as Mike ran toward him, his gun raised. Sabrina was nowhere in sight.

Was she in danger? He had been assured by his people at the CIA that they had spoken to the folks at the Bureau and cleared everything up. But had there been more mistakes? Had the FBI screwed up again? Or had he been set up?

Mike glanced around, making sure that he was covered by the smoke and no one was close as he stopped beside Trevor. "Stand up, jackass," he ordered.

Trevor moved to his feet as he reached for his gun.

"Oh, please do… I've been looking forward to killing you." Mike's finger tightened on the trigger of the gun that was pointed straight at Trevor's chest.

"Mike, stop! Don't shoot!" he yelled, hoping that he could alert the FBI agents around him before this thing went all kinds of sideways and they ended up in a total firefight.

A shot rang out, rising above the melee of sounds around them of men and women shouting. Everything stopped.

Instinctively, Trevor pulled his gun as he did a mental check of his body. Nothing hurt, but adrenaline had a funny way of masking pain and he couldn't risk looking down to check himself for bullet holes.

Sabrina and another female agent stepped through the smoke behind Mike, each with their weapon raised. Trevor dropped his weapon and lifted his hands. Mike lowered his arms and there was a look of shock on his face.

"What in the hell?" Mike said, turning toward the women.

Blood seeped from his back, glossy and wet against the black fabric of his suit jacket.

"Get on the ground!" the other agent with Sabrina ordered.

"But—" Mike started.

"I said, get on the ground!" the woman repeated.

Instead of following orders, Mike raised the gun, pointing it straight at Sabrina. As he moved, Trevor lunged toward the man. He couldn't hurt her. Not Sabrina. Not this time.

There was the crunching sound of bones breaking as Mike's body hit the ground beneath him.

Grabbing the gun in Mike's hand, he flipped it out of his grip and threw it to the side.

He pulled the man's arms behind his bleeding back. "Mike Couer, you are under arrest for the murder of Owen and Earl Cussler, tampering with evidence, corruption, and impeding a federal investigation. Anything you say can and will be used against you in a court of law."

The agent beside Sabrina stepped beside them and Mirandized him.

Watching Sabrina stand over Mike with her gun drawn was a thing of beauty. This time, evil didn't win.

Chapter 17

The private jet was full of Trevor's family, friends and a few of the agents from the case; yet as Sabrina sat there beside Trevor, it was as if they were all alone. This wasn't how she had expected things to go. Nothing could have prepared her for the things that Rowena had told her on their way to Seattle. She had described her plan to take down of one of the most corrupt officials in the Pacific Northwest, and explained how Sabrina could help.

Mike had been transported to Seattle's Harborview Medical Center and would remain under surveillance until he was completely out of the woods from his gunshot wound. Admittedly, it had felt good to shoot the man who had threatened to take Trevor down.

She reached over and took Trevor's hand.

He looked at her. "You okay?"

Though it had only been a day, it felt as though months had passed, thanks to all the statements she'd been required to give and all the legal paperwork that needed to be completed. Rowena had been diligent in making sure that everything was filed and completed in a way that would leave Sabrina free and clear and able to jump right back into her position at the FBI when she was ready.

For the time being, she wasn't sure what she wanted to do. She definitely needed a break from things to assess her future.

"Babe? Do you need anything?" Trevor asked, pulling her from her thoughts.

"Oh no, I'm okay." Her voice sounded tired. She wasn't sure he was ready to give her what she needed now.

"It's going to be okay," he said, giving her a kiss on the forehead.

Undoubtedly, the Martins would want to leave Montana now that their quiet retirement had been upended... a situation that she herself had a role in creating. If only she had seen Mike for the man he had truly been when they were together.

As it turned out, their relationship had not only been terrible, it had been a sham from the very beginning. Mike had been using her to learn about his enemies all while sending her into this and other investigations half-cocked with spotty information—in the end, no doubt hoping to humiliate her. If only she'd realized what he was doing, smearing her name and thereby delegitimizing anything she might say about him or his dealings. She felt so used...and so angry.

But Mike would pay for his full-blown assault on

her character. And she would happily take the stand should she need to.

Trevor's phone buzzed. Opening up his email, he smiled.

"What is it?" she asked.

"Ballistics came in on your gun and Mike's." He moved the screen so she could see the message. "The slug they pulled from Earl was fired from Mike's gun... not the one they found at the shack, or yours."

Rowena leaned forward from the seat behind them and tapped her on the shoulder. "It looks like we just got a little more good news."

"What do you mean?" Trevor asked.

"In addition to your ballistics, the Evidence Response Team found the hunting cabin Sabrina told me you had been looking for." Rowena showed her a photo on her phone of a graying log cabin almost completely shrouded within a thicket of barberry. "About five hundred yards from the cabin, the ERT located a shallow mass grave. It appears to contain the remains of three men—one older, who we believe may have been the father—and two women. Right now, we can't confirm or deny their identities, but it appears that they are the rest of the Cusslers. My team is looking for the other family that was reportedly in the area, but so far they haven't found anything to indicate their whereabouts."

"Do you know what happened to the Cusslers? How they died?" Sabrina asked.

"It looks like it was execution style—but one had taken a shot to the kidney shortly before the time of death. They are guessing the guy was shot in the back—probably running. There was some level of healing, which means he may have been held for a day or two before he was executed." Rowena's lips puckered.

"How long had they been dead?" Sabrina asked, thinking back to the blood she had first found behind the shanty.

"They'd been down for a few days to a week at least."

"They are going to pull DNA and confirm identities as well as run any lead they recover through ballistics," Rowena continued. "I'd bet dollars to doughnuts that they were fired from Agent Couer's gun."

"How is the man I shot... Agent Heath?" Sabrina asked.

"It looks like he took a hit up there on that mountain, as Mike said. And while Agent Heath may have been acting on Agent Couer's orders, he also may have had a role in setting you up. We believe it was their plan to pick a time and place when there were no other witnesses—but then things went haywire."

"We got lucky."

"Not entirely. We have reason to believe he retrieved the gun from the Cussler shack and planted it in your things at your house at the Martins'. Needless to say, whether or not you were the one who pulled the trigger, it was a job well done." Rowena winked at her. "He is going to be thoroughly questioned, but I have a feeling he, too, will be spending quite a while in prison."

Sabrina smiled. She'd had a soft spot for Agent Heath, but if he had anything to do with trying to take her down, she'd be fine never hearing the man's name again. "Rowena, thanks for everything. I would have gone down for this if you hadn't started digging. I appreciate it."

The woman gave a humble nod. "It's my job. And if

someone tried to do this kind of thing to me, I would expect my fellow agents to see it to the end as well. Besides, we women of the Bureau have to stick together."

She wasn't kidding.

Rowena started to sit back in her seat but stopped. "Oh, and hey, I got word that there is going to be an open seat at the Missoula office…you wouldn't be interested in being the special agent in charge, would you?" Rowena said, cracking an elusive smile.

Trevor looked over at her and gave her a proud, approving grin.

What she really wanted to do was stay with him. On the other hand, her job was her life. Though her office would only be a short drive away, long hours and the stress that came with her job would inevitably drive a wedge between them. She was cut from the FBI cloth, and no matter what happened in her life, she didn't want to lose who she was.

"I'd love to take the job…you know, *if* it were to come my way," she said.

Rowena winked and sat back, taking her phone out and clicking on email. "I'll see what I can do for you."

Sabrina turned to Trevor.

"Way to go," Trevor said, but some of the light in his eyes had seemed to fade as he too must have realized what her job would do to their relationship.

"Thank you," she said, lowering her head so she could whisper to him alone. "But the truth is… I don't know if it's going to work."

"Why not?" He frowned.

She had always been told that a woman should never say *I love you* first, but she'd never been very good at being told what to do.

"Trevor, here's the deal… I love you. I know that what we had…it was probably just a forced proximity thing that was kind of convenient, but—"

"Our relationship was not *convenient*," he said, interrupting her. "I'm not the kind of guy who takes a woman to bed just for the hell of it."

"Oh yeah?" she asked, giving him a playful look. "Then you do it just for the jollies?"

He smirked. "No. I took you to bed because the second I saw you standing outside the shack that first day, I knew you were something—*someone*—special." He lifted their entwined hands and gave her fingers a soft kiss. "I loved you before we even met… I know it sounds crazy, but it was like we were made for each other…as if cosmic forces brought us together. I mean, think of the odds that were stacked against us ever even meeting, and then there we were at the same time and the same place, fighting the same side of a battle that we didn't even know we were fighting." His face flushed. "I sound ridiculous."

"No, you're cute when you're flustered," she said, happiness racing through her. "I didn't know you had it in you."

"Hey now," he said with a laugh. "If you're going to tease me, I don't have to keep going."

"No," she said, motioning for him to continue. "I like seeing you act the way I feel."

"Wait…" he started. "You didn't forget we had a bet riding on all this, did you? Turns out I was completely right about you being the target."

"Oh, yeah," she said, staring at him as they whisked through the clouds. The heat in her cheeks rose as she remembered the stakes. "Who do you think you are,

Mr. Martin? Do you think you can really use a bet to get me back into bed?"

"First, I'm the man who is going to love you for the rest of our lives. And second, I would never make you do anything you didn't want to do."

"Well, we did strike a deal," she teased, giving him an impish look.

"That's what I like to hear. I can't wait to get home," he said, laughing. "By the way, what was the favor you were going to ask for if you won?"

When they made the bet, she hadn't had a clue. Everything between them had been so distorted that she hadn't even really believed that they would get to the bottom of their investigation in time for her to save her job, let alone see who won the bet. Yet here and now, she knew exactly what she should have wished for.

"Are you sure you want to hear it?"

Trevor nodded.

"If I'd won, I'd have asked you to marry me." She gazed into his eyes, half expecting him to choke and shirk away, but instead he leaned in closer so their foreheads touched. "You're right, it's like we are meant to be together. When I look at you, I see a father to my children, a husband, a friend. When we are close all I want to do is move even closer. And when I was arrested, all I wanted was to know that you were safe and taken care of." She paused. "I know my asking you isn't conventional, but I can't stand the thought of losing you. Will you?"

"Baby, nothing about us has been conventional. I'd hate for us to start now." He smiled a smile larger than any she had seen. "I'd marry you right now if we could. So, yes. Absolutely." He reached up and took her chin between his thumb and forefinger. "I love you, Sabrina Parker. And I always will."

"And I you, Trevor Martin."

He leaned in to kiss her, but she stopped him. "And one more thing," she said with a grin.

"What?" he asked, his eyes heavy with lust.

"I'm keeping Cap'n Crunch around in case this thing goes south."

"Anything for you."

She giggled as their lips met. He tasted of promises, the savories of a life filled with adventure, and the sweetness of forever.

* * * * *

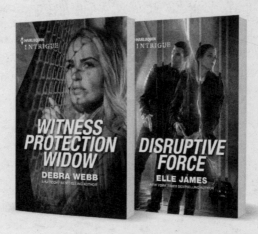

Prologue

The tears leaked out of Kay Duvall's eyes, even as she tried to focus on what she had to do. *Had* to do to bring Ben home safe.

She fumbled with her ID and punched in the code that would open the side door, usually only used for a guard taking a smoke break. It would be easy for the men behind her to escape from this side of the prison.

It went against everything she was supposed to do. Everything she considered right and good.

A quiet sob escaped her lips. They had her son. How could she not help them escape? Nothing mattered beyond her son's life.

"Would you stop already?" one of the prisoners muttered. He'd made her give him her gun, which he now jabbed into her back. "Crying isn't going to change anything. So just shut up."

She didn't care so much about her own life or if she'd be fired. She didn't care what happened to her as long as they let her son go. So she swallowed down the sobs and blinked out as many tears as she could, hoping to stem the tide of them.

She got the door open and slid out first—because the man holding the gun pushed it into her back until she moved forward.

They came through the door behind her, dressed in the clothes she'd stolen from the locker room and Lost and Found. Anything warm she could get her hands on to help them escape into the frigid February night.

Help them escape. Help three dangerous men escape prison. When she was supposed to keep them inside.

It didn't matter anymore. She just wanted them gone. If they were gone, they'd let her baby go. They had to let her baby go.

Kay forced her legs to move, one foot in front of the other, toward the gate she could unlock without setting off any alarms. She unlocked it, steadier this time if only because she kept thinking that once they were gone, she could get in contact with Ben.

She flung open the gate and gestured them out into the parking lot. "Stay out of the safety lights and no one should bug you."

"You better hope not," one of the men growled.

"The minute you sound that alarm, your kid is dead. You got it?" This one was the ringleader. The one who'd been in for murder. Who else would he kill out there in the world?

Guilt pooled in Kay's belly, but she had to ignore it. She had to live with it. Whatever guilt she felt would be survivable. Living without her son wouldn't be. Besides, she had to believe they'd be caught. They'd do something else terrible and be caught.

As long as her son was alive, she didn't care.

Don't miss
Hunting a Killer *by Nicole Helm,*
available February 2021 wherever
Harlequin Intrigue books and ebooks are sold.

Harlequin.com

HIEXP0121

Love Harlequin romance?

DISCOVER.

Be the first to find out about promotions,
news and exclusive content!

Facebook.com/HarlequinBooks

Twitter.com/HarlequinBooks

Instagram.com/HarlequinBooks

Pinterest.com/HarlequinBooks

YouTube.com/HarlequinBooks

ReaderService.com

EXPLORE.

Sign up for the Harlequin e-newsletter and
download a free book from any series at
TryHarlequin.com

CONNECT.

Join our Harlequin community to
share your thoughts and connect
with other romance readers!
Facebook.com/groups/HarlequinConnection

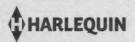

Get 4 FREE REWARDS!

We'll send you 2 FREE Books plus 2 FREE Mystery Gifts.

Harlequin Intrigue books are action-packed stories that will keep you on the edge of your seat. Solve the crime and deliver justice at all costs.

FREE
Value Over
$20

YES! Please send me 2 FREE Harlequin Intrigue novels and my 2 FREE gifts (gifts are worth about $10 retail). After receiving them, if I don't wish to receive any more books, I can return the shipping statement marked "cancel." If I don't cancel, I will receive 6 brand-new novels every month and be billed just $4.99 each for the regular-print edition or $5.99 each for the larger-print edition in the U.S., or $5.74 each for the regular-print edition or $6.49 each for the larger-print edition in Canada. That's a savings of at least 12% off the cover price! Shipping and handling is just 50¢ per book in the U.S. and $1.25 per book in Canada.* I understand that accepting the 2 free books and gifts places me under no obligation to buy anything. I can always return a shipment and cancel at any time. The free books and gifts are mine to keep no matter what I decide.

Choose one: ☐ **Harlequin Intrigue Regular-Print**
(182/382 HDN GNXC)

☐ **Harlequin Intrigue Larger-Print**
(199/399 HDN GNXC)

Name (please print)

Address   Apt. #

City   State/Province   Zip/Postal Code

Email: Please check this box ☐ if you would like to receive newsletters and promotional emails from Harlequin Enterprises ULC and its affiliates. You can unsubscribe anytime.

Mail to the **Reader Service:**
IN U.S.A.: P.O. Box 1341, Buffalo, NY 14240-8531
IN CANADA: P.O. Box 603, Fort Erie, Ontario L2A 5X3

Want to try 2 free books from another series! Call 1-800-873-8635 or visit www.ReaderService.com.
